ALSO BY MARY PAULINE LOWRY

Wildfire

THE

LETTERS

Mary Pauline Lowry

SIMON & SCHUSTER

NEW YORK   LONDON   TORONTO   SYDNEY   NEW DELHI

Simon & Schuster
1230 Avenue of the Americas
New York, NY 10020

First Simon & Schuster hardcover edition April 2020

SIMON & SCHUSTER and colophon are registered trademarks of Simon & Schuster, Inc.

For information about special discounts for bulk purchases, please contact Simon & Schuster Special Sales at 1-866-506-1949 or business@simonandschuster.com.

The Simon & Schuster Speakers Bureau can bring authors to your live event. For more information or to book an event, contact the Simon & Schuster Speakers Bureau at 1-866-248-3049 or visit our website at www.simonspeakers.com.

Interior design by Davina Mock-Maniscalco

Manufactured in the United States of America

10   9   8   7   6   5   4   3   2   1

Library of Congress Cataloging-in-Publication Data

Names: Lowry, Mary Pauline, author.
Title: The Roxy letters / Mary Pauline Lowry.
Description: First Simon & Schuster edition. | New York : Simon & Schuster, 2020.
Identifiers: LCCN 2019028995 | ISBN 9781982121433 (hardcover) | ISBN 9781982121457 (ebook)
Subjects: GSAFD: Epistolary fiction.
Classification: LCC PS3612.O9285 R69 2020 | DDC 813/.6--dc23
LC record available at https://lccn.loc.gov/2019028995

ISBN 978-1-9821-2143-3
ISBN 978-1-9821-2145-7 (ebook)

To Venus, the Goddess of Love.
I'll transcribe for you anytime.

And to my agent, Allison Hunter,
and my editors, Christine Pride and Carina Guiterman,
whose hard work, brilliance, and belief in this book made magic happen.

There's nothing more powerful than true friendship.
—Amanda Yates Garcia, the Oracle of Los Angeles

PROLOGUE

Re: Ground Rules

Dear Everett,

Perhaps I've invited you to move into my spare bedroom against my better judgment. But while living with an ex-boyfriend is never a good idea, I really need the money. Last week Roscoe—that irascible little wiener dog—ate not one, but two pairs of my underwear (and my fancy thongs, at that)! The resulting $600 emergency room vet bill, combined with my barely-over-minimum-wage employment and sizable mortgage, has made a housemate a financial necessity.

When you called to report you were getting kicked out of your highly desirable backyard shack (a.k.a. the Bat Cave) because your landlady's daughter called dibs, the perfect timing of our crises was like a sign from Venus. While normally I would have reservations about the possibility of a successful platonic roommate situation between former lovers, it's been years since we broke up and we've been getting along great since reuniting as friends. So I have high hopes we can both handle this mutually beneficial (and temporary!) living arrangement.

But in order to set us up for the best possible success, I've taken it upon myself to establish some ground rules, which are as follows:

You Will Not:

1a. Try to hook up with me. (While I respect that you sometimes get melancholy for our time together as a couple, I need you to respect that hooking up with an ex is akin to a Fleetwood Mac reunion—comforting, but lacking the original energy and magic. We haven't been a couple in four years, and this band isn't getting back together!)

2a. Bring Brie or any other cheeses into my house. (As you know, I'm trying to dedicate myself to a vegan lifestyle, and dairy is my weakness.)

3a. Eat my food. (One of the few perks of being a deli maid at Whole Foods is my ability to liberate certain vegan-friendly leftover items from the deli. Unless I specifically offer, do not partake.)

4a. Wear those turquoise jogger pants. (I don't care if pants with elastic ankles are "on trend." They look ridiculous!)

5a. Bring a woman into my house. (While I, on some level, hope you will move on from our relationship and find love elsewhere, I still have boundaries.)

You Will:

1b. Help with the furballs. (I'm already giving you a friends-and-family discount on the rent. Given that generosity, I would hope that on occasion you would be willing to take Roscoe for a walk, give him his insulin shot, and scoop Charlize

Theron's litter box. And the furballs are clearly thrilled you are moving in—when you came by to unload your stuff this morning, Roscoe's happy dance warmed my heart!)

2b. Keep your loom in your bedroom. (I love your weavings—your surrealist reimaginings of old-school, heavy-metal-band logos are my favs. But there just isn't room in the living room for the clutter of a loom!)

3b. Leave the house if I ever have a man over. (I've got my eye on this scrumptious little snack and a half, Patrick, who works in the Beer Alley of Whole Foods. And it's only a matter of time before I drum up the nerve to ask him out!)

4b. Keep your monologues about government conspiracies, chem-trails, and the likelihood that cell phones are (a) being monitored and (b) cause brain cancer, to an absolute minimum.

5b. Get a job. (I understand that while a resident of the Bat Cave, you often housesat for your landlady in exchange for free rent and a nightly dinner cooked by her personal chef. And sure, selling your weavings and doing a little dog walking on the side makes you some cash. But certainly it's now time for you to re-enter the world of gainful employment. I know too well the challenges of finding work in this town, which is overrun with hipsters happy to slave away at low-wage coffee shop jobs to support their band life. But I believe in you! You can do it! Or you can leave!)

And most important:

6b. PAY YOUR RENT ON TIME. (I'd like your prorated June rent as soon as possible!)

While I was reluctant to have you move in with me, the truth is it's surely better than renting the spare bedroom to some rando, which would upset the furballs. However, I am committed to keeping up my boundaries! I will not let your presence disrupt my state of "flow." Strong communication will be essential to the success of our new platonic-roommate situation. Therefore, if I have any further issues to address with you in the weeks and months to come, I won't hesitate to leave another note, right here on the kitchen table.

Your friend (without benefits),
Roxy

P.S. I should warn you about the tweakers in the yellow house next door. The darling old lady who owned it died six months ago and her awful son, Captain Tweaker, moved in. I'm almost positive he and his minions regularly cook meth in that rotting van parked on the curb. At least once a week they party loudly until dawn and chuck beer cans into my backyard. I try my best to ignore them and would advise you to do the same!

CHAPTER ONE

June 21, 2012

Dear Everett,

After what happened last night, I am now officially adding a new ground rule to the list. It's one I failed to include previously as it should be intuitive.

Ground Rule 6a: YOU WILL NOT come into my bedroom if the door is closed.

I was already in a funk last night that it was summer solstice and I had not gathered with an interesting coven of female friends to celebrate the longest day of the year with a series of elaborate rites. Rather, I'd been moping around in my room, trying to find solace in the poetry of Alice Notley and a pint of vegan ice cream, and wondering why it is I spend so much time home alone. I've drifted apart from my college pals who, in my defense, have let themselves fall into lives of bourgeois pleasures and office drudgery. If I was painting and drawing, or making love to some hottie, it would be fine. But usually after my shift at the Whole Foods deli, I just head home to hang out with the furballs.

Nor can I seem to muster the energy to blast myself out of this funk. I can't help but compare myself to Annie. I helped her get her job at the deli only six months ago, and already she has an interview for a position as assistant to Topher Doyle, the quirky CEO of Whole Foods. Don't get confused by his C-suite acronym—Topher Doyle is not the Chief Executive Officer; he's the Chief Ecosystem Officer, which is more like a CEO Lite in charge of supporting both the environment of this beautiful planet, the corporate culture of the company, and its "give back" initiatives. (While in theory, I want my friends to excel in life, in practice I don't want Annie to leave me behind! And I can't help but juxtapose Annie's motivation and ambition with my current lack thereof. When I graduated from the University of Texas over five years ago, I thought in short order I would launch an impressive career as a visual artist. But after two years as a gopher at an uninspired gallery on the East Side, during which I almost starved to death, I took a "temporary" job as a deli maid. Three years later, I'm still there!)

After marinating for a time in my lost dreams, I decided to take comfort in some self-pleasure. I had just taken off my pajamas, settled into bed with my purple merman vibrator, and opened my MacBook to read one of my favorite stories on literotica.com—written by the extremely prolific and rather kinky author Silky Raven—when you barged into my room WITHOUT KNOCKING. As my platonic roommate, I do NOT want you to see me naked, much less naked and masturbating!!! You scared the living crap out of me and more than ruined the mood. Thus I risked the insomnia-provoking blue light of my laptop without the narcoleptic effect of an orgasm to counter it.

Furthermore, you know I am terrified of spiders and yet not only did you come parading into my bedroom without invitation or warning, you did so shirtless, baring that sloppily rendered, yet very frightening stick-and-poke tattoo of a black widow. You tell me you cannot take back the past, or any decisions you made on that naval vessel sailing through hostile waters, but you can certainly put on a damn shirt! (Aha! Ground rule #7b: YOU WILL wear a shirt around the house!)

After I dove under the covers, you plunked yourself down on the edge of my bed, as if nothing had happened, and proceeded to tell me about how you signed up two new dogs for your fledgling dog-walking enterprise, a gigantic Rottweiler named Cuddles and a tiny Chihuahua named Biggie. Everett!!!! Boundaries, please! The episode clearly did not seem out of the ordinary to you, hence the need for me to explain in writing why your behavior was unacceptable!

When I invited you to live with me I was taking into consideration not only our romantic history, but also the abuse you suffered as a child, and the PTSD you incurred during your military service—during which you avoided the horrors of war, but not of toxic masculinity. I've had to reconsider this decision. First, the invitation was ultimately driven by my financial straits, and yet your prorated rent is a week late. Second, the fact that you've already been bringing home Brie wheels and encouraging me to eat them is a source of considerable frustration. (You know Brie gives me an acne beard!) Clearly you are trying to wreak havoc on my normally decent skin to the point where no other man will date me and I will be forced to get back together with you as a last resort. You have not declared your romantic intentions, but I could see them plainly in your desire to remain in the room with me and the purple merman! Everett, I need you to understand that when we finally reached the shore of our breakup after the tumultuous passage of our relationship, in my soul I burned the ship of our love to the ground once and for all. (As a former navy man, I hope this metaphor resonates with you without triggering your PTSD—it does pain me to compare myself to the cruel Hernán Cortés so rightly depicted as evil and syphilitic in much of the work of The Three Great Muralists.)

When I sat down to pen this letter, I had resolved to ask you to move out, but as I write, Roscoe is gazing up at me imploringly. That capricious little miniature dachshund loves you so much! (And you have been walking Roscoe every single day AND scooping Charlize Theron's litter box—a gold star for ground rule #1b!) I can hardly bear to consider the furball moping that will follow your permanent exit from my house. While your presence here threatens to be a gigantic cockblock, ironically the fact that you sometimes administer Roscoe's 8 p.m. insulin shot might actually allow me to someday go on a date with Patrick. So for now, my longtime friend, consider yourself on final warning.

Your **EX**-girlfriend,
Roxy

P.S. When are you going to return my backpack you borrowed? (This pilfering warrants a new rule #7a. YOU WILL NOT borrow my stuff. Hands off!)

June 24, 2012

Dear Everett,

It was one year ago today that Brant Bitterbrush abandoned me with hardly an explanation. He had promised lifelong fealty, he had sworn himself to be my soul mate, and then he was gone. Little did I know then that Brant Bitterbrush had an even worse betrayal in store for me, one that triggered my current state of artistic paralysis. Is it any wonder that my workday today, on this anniversary of my broken heart, was a total fiasco and may result in my termination?

My day was emotionally harrowing on so many levels! It all started when I was riding my bike to work. As I headed down Sixth Street, in the distance I could see the Waterloo Video sign had been taken down and replaced! As you know, I cried when Waterloo Video closed a few months ago. Sure, these days we can download any movie we want in an instant. But what a cheap and sterile replacement for wandering the grubby aisles of Waterloo Video, where the disgruntled staff members wrote loving recommendations (or warnings) on Post-its adhered to each video. When Brant Bitterbrush and I were still a couple, every time we wanted to rent a video we would spend a good hour in Waterloo, passing especially hilariously reviewed video boxes to each other. The last time Brant and I were there together—just over a year ago—I considered renting the Coen brothers' film "The Ladykillers." I picked up the box and the note read: "Put this down and go wash your hands immediately—you are holding a piece of shit."

Just as my love for Brant Bitterbrush was not enough to keep us together, my appreciation for Waterloo Video, a true cultural institution, was not enough to keep the store open. Until today, I held great hope an establishment worthy of the location's storied history would take its place. Perhaps a tiny brewpub or vintage clothing store would move in.

Even a funky greeting card stand would not have raised my ire. So long as a local store took over the space. As you know, that intersection of Sixth Street and Lamar Boulevard has always been a bastion of quirky local culture and business—BookPeople, Whole Foods (which, though now well on its way to becoming an international behemoth, was, not so very long ago, just a single tiny health-food store), Waterloo Ice House, Waterloo Records. The intersection was a haven of everything truly and uniquely Austin.

So as I peddled by on my twenty-four-inch cruiser on my way to work—sweating in this boiling heat (whose only blessing is to keep every Californian on the planet from moving to this city, which was so recently a Shangri-la)—I almost biked into the street when the new sign hanging over those once hallowed doors came into full view: COMING SOON: LULULEMON. Yes, it's true. A Lululemon store—destined to sell overpriced workout gear to trophy wives whose sole job is to attend Pure Barre and keep it tight—will open in the space formerly occupied so well by Waterloo Video. Is this glorious town we live in selling its quirky, beautiful soul to the highest corporate bidder? It seems so.

That store's arrival is a symbol of the sort of change that will price us all out of this town. Sure, I had the good luck to inherit $35,000 from my grandma and the good sense to use it as a down payment on my little house. But I can practically hear my property taxes growing as I write. And what about the artists and musicians and deli maids I hold dear—where else would they go? If you look at a map of Texas, it's clear there is no other livable option.

Dizzied by grief at this unexpected development—and perhaps a little addled by the 105-degree heat—I arrived at Whole Foods. Instead of eight hours behind the fogged glass of the deli case, per usual, I'd agreed to cover Annie's shift on samples while she had her interview with Whole Foods CEO Lite Topher Doyle. But first, I had to take a quick stroll down Beer Alley—a morning ritual during which I try to spot the scrumptious Patrick—but alas there was no sighting of my crush. I hurried to the deli to prep for my shift.

I put on my apron and unwrapped and microwaved some gag-inducing frozen tuna burger. Jason and Nelson came by to comment on how disgusting it looked and offer me sympathy about having to work samples for a whole shift. (Aside from Annie, they are probably my favorite coworkers in the deli. Jason is a passionate spray-paint-graffiti artist. Nelson surely has interests of his own, but I always just think of him as Jason's sidekick.) They helped me haul a sample table out to Bakery, where I set out my tray of morally repulsive morsels. Is there anything more humiliating than handing out microscopic snacks to strangers? I hate standing behind a bunch of wasteful mini-sample cups, smiling and offering a nibble to every passerby as if I'm some sort of culinary streetwalker. But it was for dear Annie so there I lurked, right around the corner from the three-foot-tall burbling chocolate fountain and beside a giant display of boxed crumb cake.

Dirty Steve came by right away to check on me. "Are you keeping a smile on your face, Poxy Roxy?" he asked. (Right after I started working at the deli, I contracted adult chickenpox. That's when Steve made up that hideous moniker! He's never let it go.)

I gestured at the display of crumb cake. "If I was handing out crumb cake, at least I could cheer myself by snacking on the samples."

"I always put vegans like you and Annie on meat samples. It cuts down on 'unexplained product loss.'" Dirty Steve seemed to take great pleasure in making air quotes.

"Touché," I replied, as Dirty Steve lumbered off to harass some of his other employees.

Everett, for three hours I was the poster child of Sample Grrrls—grinning, nodding, offering tiny freebies, mostly to ritzy women who circle the store eyeing one another, convinced they must stay vigilant or miss a crucial fashion trend. These hideous trophy wives treated me as if I was an extension of their help—invisible only as long as I did not displease them. I was entertained when two cops came in for their usual lunch and every deli maid with a warrant out for his arrest (i.e., Jason and Nelson) ran out the back door to hide in the alley. I was also cheered by the occasional broke musician cruising the sample stand multiple times with the overt casualness of the seasoned "sample abuser." I could at least offer them a human wink and receive a grateful nod in return. Like me, they probably suffer as wage slaves at underpaid and unfulfilling jobs. Like me, life has trampled their artistic dreams. Like me, perhaps they are platonically shacked up with an ex to keep a roof over their heads.

Then this guy sort of just appeared in front of me. He had a fit bod, tousled, indie-rocker hair, and totally cute dimples that I could see even under his Clive Owen stubble. He wore jeans (not skinny, thank Goddess) and a tight black T-shirt. The outline of the state of Texas was tattooed on his forearm. He was the kind of good-looking that told me he'd probably never had to bother to learn how to be good in bed. Definitely a musician. "Yeah! Crumb cake," he said. By the way he smiled at me, I might have been the crumb cake. But somehow it wasn't cheesy or icky. It was nice. (Everett, perhaps you don't want to hear about my moment of connection with a stranger. But until you pay up, too bad!)

"Sorry," I said. "Microwaved frozen tuna."

"Ugh," he replied. He gestured at the crumb cake display to my right. "False advertising. Why aren't you in the freezer aisle?"

"I'm guessing management is trying to avoid another employee frostbite lawsuit," I said. "Want to try my tuna burger?" Even as I spoke, I knew it sounded lewd.

"Hard to resist," he said with the hint of a smile. "But I'm a vegetarian." As he turned away, a leggy supermodel-type approached. She had Bettie Page bangs and wore a tailored rockabilly dress with peep-toe pumps.

"Texas! There you are!" she said, taking his arm. (Texas? I wondered if he had siblings named Arizona and Oklahoma.) They walked off, a perfect couple, which only served to remind me that I live with you, my ex-boyfriend, who doesn't pay rent on time. It also reminded me that the only "man" I've been with in I-won't-say-how-long is the purple merman. To make matters worse, several of the rich women shoppers were rather snippy about whether or not the tuna burger contained any guar gum as a stabilizer. I wanted to yell, "Have you seen living tuna? They are glorious creatures of the sea. Eating them is the problem, not a little guar gum." But like a dutiful employee, I held my tongue.

Preoccupied as I was this morning with thoughts of Brant Bitterbrush and the anniversary of my heartbreak, I had forgotten to eat breakfast and was moving into a rather hangry mood. If you had been there, Everett, I'm sure you would have pushed some Brie on me, but as you were not, I let my mood descend. Then she approached. She must have been a little older than I am, maybe thirty, her long red hair in a perky ponytail, and a diamond ring the size of a cherry tomato on her finger. In the grocery basket slung so casually over her forearm I spotted two bottles of DUCKIE & LAMBIE MOISTURIZER!!! Today of all days! The sight of those bottles—a symbol of Brant Bitterbrush's ultimate betrayal—was like a punch to my gut.

"Don't buy those," I said, pointing at the offending bottles.

"Why not?" the redhead asked. "It makes my skin so smooth." She popped a chunk of reheated frozen tuna burger between her bleached teeth, chewed, and said, "Mmmm. Crumb cake!" (To endure the nightly pounding she surely receives from her rich, sagging husband, she must have become completely ungrounded from her physical body and is thus unable to distinguish cake from seafood!) I looked her up and down and realized that her trim figure was decked out from head to toe in the offending brand whose name my hand shakes to write—Lululemon!

The wave of outrage at what she and her brethren are doing to my hometown overwhelmed me (and, with the distance of eight hours, I can now admit it—perhaps some of my fury was misplaced). I wish my retort had been clever or even condescendingly kind. But what came out of my mouth was: "You. Dumb. Bitch."

"Wait, what?" she said.

"You. Dumb. Bitch." I enunciated that second time.

The conflict snapped her right back into her body. She dropped her shopping basket, came racing around the sample table, and shoved me with all the power of her sculpted frame. I staggered backward. I'm proud to say I kept my footing—I can't say the same for the crumb cake display, which came crashing down around me. The cacophony of a hundred boxes of crumb cake hitting the tile caused every customer from Bakery to Hot Bar to turn and stare.

"So that happened," the redhead said, before sashaying off toward the exit. But at the sliding doors near the checkout lines she paused and turned to wave at me, flashing a smile that was more conspiratorial than triumphant. I found myself raising my own hand to wave in return. Then she slipped through the doors and was gone. What a baffling woman! While I initially took her for a West Austin pedigree, perhaps she is trailer trash or a military brat cursed with good looks and recently realized aspirations of wealth through marriage.

It was then I heard Dirty Steve's voice. He must have seen the whole thing as he headed out, probably for an early lunch of surf and turf at The Yellow Rose strip club. "Poxy Roxy!" he thundered. "I told you to keep a smile on your face, not incite an assault! Be in my office at ten tomorrow!"

Given that tomorrow's meeting could very well result in termination of my employment, I'm now more worried than ever about money.

All this to say, Everett: it's the 24th of June and you've been living in my house for almost two weeks, so by any measure your rent is WAY.

PAST. DUE. I understand you are underemployed right now. In this town, aren't we all? (I speak only for those of us with a shred of integrity, artistic or otherwise—the "new Austin" tech assholes are making billions as I write.) But I let you move into my spare bedroom on the condition that you would pay rent each month. The time has come for you to follow through on that promise.

Your frustrated landlady,
Roxy

P.S. I'm leaving this note on the kitchen counter so that you'll be sure to see it when you sit down to eat my purloined yucca fries and tofu nuggets (in clear violation of #3a! Do rules mean nothing to you?).

June 25, 2012

Dear Everett,

I made it to work early today, so I've ducked into the coffee shop of BookPeople to sip an iced matcha latte with almond milk and let the air-conditioning cool me down from the sweltering heat as I prepare myself for possibly being fired. I'm also going to take this time to write to you about an indignity that just happened to me, an indignity caused by your failure to fork over your prorated June rent. I need that money to pay down my credit card a bit. And if I don't make a payment in the next few days, my interest rate will skyrocket. I've begun to doubt you will hand over the cash in time. So as a last resort, I decided to hit up my parents. I'd planned to call them after my shift today, but as usual, my mother had her weird mom ESP turned on.

I was riding my bike to work and had just passed by that hideous new artisanal water shop—certain to sell $6 asparagus-essence water—that's going in on the corner where the Pronto Mart used to be, when my cell phone rang. Since you refuse to get a cell, you've never experienced this inconvenience yourself. I answered it while pedaling and put it on speaker. A precarious move, but I pulled it off with grace. And then I could hear my parents' voices, in unison, on speakerphone, which is annoying. Either they talk over each other, or to each other, or else one of them leaves the room without telling me and I don't know who's on the phone. Sometimes I'll start telling a story meant mainly for my mom, but she's wandered off to start a load of laundry or something.

"Hello, darling," my mother said. "We are just calling to see if you are going to be able to come to Peru with us." Have I informed you, Everett, that in late September my parents are planning on visiting my brother for a month at his Peace Corps outpost in Peru? "I think we are going to stay at an eco-lodge," she continued. "No internet, no cell service. Just long hikes and majestic mountains. But we need to know if you're coming so we can get our plane tickets and book rooms. We'll cover lodging if you'll pay for your own plane ticket. There are some great deals on tickets right now for fall."

If there's one thing my parents love it's a deal! When we all go to the movies together, my mom still tries to get me the kids' rate by joking that I'm under twelve. Often the person behind the ticket counter is so embarrassed for me that they just give her the discount.

"I don't think I can swing a ticket," I said, "or the time off work. Roscoe's vet bill was a real financial hit."

"Paying for you to go on a gap year and then to the Plan II Honors College at UT was a financial hit, too," I heard my father mutter. "But no one's reimbursing me for it." My dad is usually a dear, but ever since he retired from his dentistry practice last year he's been bored, and thus crabby.

I took a deep breath and tried to brace myself to ask them for money. But I couldn't even bring myself to make a direct plea for funds, so I went with the hint-dropping approach. "I'm so broke I even let Everett move in with me to help with the mortgage," I said.

"How are you ever going to find a new boyfriend if Everett is living with you?" my mom asked. An astute question, and one I've been wondering myself.

"Well, I have to do what I have do, Mom. I'm also working a ton to try to pay off the vet bill," I went on. "Really long shifts." I hated myself for pushing so hard for a parental cash injection, but what choice did I have?

"Roxy, what is your plan?" my mother said in her tough-love voice, which always infuriates me. "You're never going to get ahead in life working long hours at minimum wage. It's past time you decided on some next steps."

"I don't have a plan!" I was almost yelling. "That's the problem! Do you have any idea what it's like to feel so stuck?" Suddenly I felt completely overwhelmed by the whole conversation, and by the fact that I'm broke, have a crap job, and haven't made any progress on my painting or drawing.

"I know it can be hard for artists," my mother said, her tone turning sympathetic. She always knows when she's pushed me too far and needs to change her tack. "When you were a girl, all I had to do to keep you busy was buy you a bucket of sidewalk chalk. You'd stay out until dark. Even when the sidewalk was scorching, you'd draw and draw and draw. I couldn't stop you." She paused. "Have you done any drawing or painting lately?"

I was desperate to change the subject before it veered any closer to the fact that I haven't made any art whatsoever in six months. "Please, please, ask me about anything else."

"How are Yolanda, Rose, Kate, and Barclay? Have you seen them lately?"

"Not in a while," I said lamely. The truth is, I haven't seen my college besties in ages. They all seem to have moved on from our previous sisterly solidarity to the boring land of real adulthood and office-casual wardrobes—a place I doubt I'd like to visit, much less live! "What have y'all been up to?"

"Well, last night I went to one of those girls-only parties at Suzanne's," my mom said. "Maybe you could do that for extra money until you figure out your next move."

Just then I pedaled out in front of a douche in a black BMW. He slammed on the brakes and honked at me vigorously. I regretted that, having one hand on the handlebar of my bike and the other wrapped around my iPhone, I could not shoot him the finger. "Fuck you!" I mouthed. I remember only too well when an old VW van was status symbol enough for the average Austinite.

"Roxy?" my mother said.

"Yeah, sorry, I'm listening. Have parties for extra money?"

"It was like a Tupperware party, but instead of Tupperware they were selling really naughty lingerie. I bought the cutest little—"

"TMI! TMI!" I interrupted before she could describe an image I would never be able to forget.

"It's called a NaughtyWear party. Get it? Tupperware. Naughty-Wear? It's quite clever. You'd be great at it, and you could earn extra money." She paused dramatically. "But for now, I'll send you five hundred dollars."

"Thank you," I said, both relieved and totally ashamed to be twenty-eight years old and still hitting up my parents for cash. (And also a little disappointed she hadn't agreed to send me more money.) "And I'm really sorry about Peru."

"It's okay. Derek will be disappointed, but he'll understand. Anyway, I have to run to tennis, but really, next time Suzanne has a Naughty-Wear party you have to come. You can't mope around forever."

I know it's childish to wish I lived in a society that valued my skills as an artist when I haven't even made art in ages. But I can't help comparing myself to my parents. By the time my dad was my age he already had a thriving dental practice, and my mom had married him so she never had to worry about making money for herself again. I just wish I'd been born fascinated with some subject—like rotten teeth and sagging gums!—that would allow me to make a good living. But as it is, all my skills and interests are leading me down a road of obscurity and financial ruin. And the despair from my call with my parents will surely be compounded by my meeting with Dirty Steve, which starts in fifteen minutes. At best, he'll yell at me. At worst (and more likely), I'll be fired! Wish me luck.

Frustrated, nervous, and a little ashamed,
Roxy

June 26, 2012

Dear Everett,

I've been waiting to tell you about my meeting with Dirty Steve but you never seem to be home. (Where are you, anyway? I mean, you can't have that many dog-walking gigs. Do you have a girlfriend and you just aren't telling me?) Since you REFUSE TO GET A CELL PHONE, I can't even text you about my meeting. So instead of waiting and waiting, I'm going to write it all down for you while the glory is still fresh in my mind. I made my way to Dirty Steve's tiny windowless office, where I found him with his feet up on his messy desk. His gel-spiked hair gleamed under the fluorescent lights. I had barely sat down before he started rambling.

"You don't know about my life," he said. "It's so stressful. My advice to all young men is to never, ever fuck a girl too good. You do that, you can't get 'em to leave you alone. It's killing me." He paused enigmatically, as if hoping I would press him for details or reveal that I myself am actually, despite appearances to the contrary, a young man and one in need of sexual guidance. "Anyway, we need to talk about what happened yesterday," he finally said.

I made my face blank and stony—the Hindu goddess Durga meets PJ Harvey after a rough night. I never should have sworn at a customer! If he fired me, I'd be totally fucked. I need this stupid job. I need the benefits and the crappy pay. Without them, no way will I be able to make my mortgage. But no matter what happened, I promised myself I would not let Dirty Steve see me cry. "I made a mistake," I said. "I should have been more polite. But that woman was seriously unhinged."

He held up a hand to silence me. "I'm going to have to suspend you," he said. "I would say effective immediately, but Groken and Numnuts called in sick. Sick from sucking each other's dicks." The last part he said

almost as an aside to himself, and one that seemed to cheer him. One of
the highlights of Dirty Steve's sad life is raining politically incorrect and
wildly offensive abuse down on his employees. (As much as I mostly hate
Dirty Steve, I respect him for being a sort of one-man holdout against corporate culture. Since he started as a bag boy at the original Whole Foods
location in the early nineties, he and his ways have essentially been grand-
fathered in. He's worked here so long no one has the heart/balls combo
necessary to fire him.) "Also, Larry isn't coming back."

"Wasn't he supposed to be done with PharmaTrial last week?" I
asked, worried.

"He called and told me he has some kind of permanent kidney damage from whatever drugs they tested on him. Now he's on dialysis or
something."

"Fuck," I said, saddened another good one had fallen prey to the
PharmaTrial lore. Everett, you were the one who first told me about
poor Robert Rodriguez and how he went—broke and unknown—into a
month-long drug trial for the big, bad pharmaceutical company Pharma-
Trial. During his stint as a Big Pharma guinea pig, he wrote the screenplay for "El Mariachi" and came out with the $7,000 he needed to film
it on a low budget in Mexico. You were always so enamored by the story,
and you aren't the only one. Every local Austin artist who goes into
PharmaTrial convinces himself he's going to be Robert Rodriguez #2.
It's sad to me that it's one of Austin's most enduring and widespread fantasy myths—it's a dangerous one! As much as I want you to get a job
and a substantial income stream, I hope you won't succumb to this stupid myth. Hopefully by opening my home to you in your time of need
I've prevented you from doing something so desperate!

"Your sadness for your coworker's idiocy doesn't change the fact that
you're suspended," Dirty Steve said.

I stood up. "Well, I quit." I held my head high like Nefertiti or Patti
Smith—a regal queen unaffected by the petty decisions of common men.

"Seriously?"

I savored Dirty Steve's surprise for an all-too-fleeting moment. "I have a mortgage and two pets," I said. "Of course I'm not quitting." I tried to maintain my sense of nobility when Dirty Steve held up his hand for a high five.

"Good talk," he said.

"How long will I be suspended?"

"A week?"

"Are you asking me?"

"No. I'm telling you. Seven days off, no pay. After you finish this shift." He paused. Something about his face looked sort of unsettled and indecisive.

"Damn," I said. "Okay."

I turned to go, my mind already churning about the lost income. I was at the door when Dirty Steve called out, "Wait a sec! Look, my June resolution is to lie less. You're fired. But I really need you to work this one last shift, okay? It'll beef up your final paycheck. I know you need the money."

"Fired?"

"I was going to tell you at the end of your shift, you know, so you'd stick around for it."

I groaned in outrage and stormed out, but in a way that indicated I'd stay. He was right—I desperately need the money.

So I mustered my pride and went down to assume my position behind the deli counter. Luckily, Annie was there to listen to my outrage, looking gorgeous and statuesque in gold hoop earrings, her natural Afro in two big puffs.

I hope you meet her soon, Everett—she's been a stalwart friend since we met during our volunteer shift at Austin Pets Alive! over three years ago. And actually, I have a confession to make: I met Annie only a short time after our breakup, and, amicable as it was, I still felt compelled to process some of the things that annoyed me about you, which is how I ended up telling her about your tempoary bout of erectile dysfunction brought on by your anxiety that hackers would film us having sex if I left my cell phone on the nightstand. I'm sorry, Everett. I know I swore to you I would never tell another living soul, but disclosing harrowing secrets about past relationships is one of the critical ways girls bond.

"This might be the kick in the ass you need to find something better," Annie said. She paused. "I have to tell you something." She gestured at the ceiling, toward the fifth floor of Whole Foods where all the corporate offices are housed. "I got the job as Topher Doyle's assistant."

"Holy Jupiter!" I exclaimed. "Congratulations! When do you start?"

She looked at me sadly. "I hate to say it. But this is my last day in the deli."

"Really?" I said, and I couldn't keep the melancholy out of my voice. "I mean, I'm happy for you, but really?"

"Really," she said. "But look, I'm going to use my new position to really push a strong animal-rights agenda. Whole Foods tries to be conscious about animal treatment, but I think if I have Topher Doyle's ear I can really make some serious changes that will improve the quality of life for millions of farm animals. If I play my cards right, I could convince him Whole Foods should only sell eggs from free-range chickens. And not fake free range. I'm talking chickens with room to roam. And if I could convince him to make a multimillion-dollar tax-deductible donation to PETA every year, they could expand their federal legislative agenda."

She went on and on, talking animatedly through her goals, waving her arms to emphasize her most important points. That's Annie for you. Energetic, passionate, a badass to the core. She hasn't even started her new job and already she has a plan for how she'll use it to begin an animal-rights revolution. "Great, I'm fired for covering your shift. You're moving to the fifth floor to save the world," I said. I was sulking a little. I couldn't help it.

"You weren't exactly fired for covering my shift. And you've got to be more proactive," Annie said. "Work the system from the inside out. I can't change the fact that a wacky white guy is the Chief Ecosystem Officer of this company or that I'm basically moving from deli counter maid to secretary. But I'm going to be the secretary who gets animals treated better all over this barbaric country." She looked straight at me with those stern, cacao-nib brown eyes. "Stop complaining. Stop being so wishy-washy. You want the power? Take it."

"Well, I hope you'll use your newfound power to find out some deep background on Duckie & Lambie Moisturizer. If animals are being tortured in the making of that product I want to know!" I said.

Right then the two cops who always buy lunch at the deli came through the front door. Jason and Nelson, who had been chopping potatoes, dropped their knives and hustled toward the kitchen exit. Jason has a warrant for an unpaid fine he got the time he was caught spray-painting a mural in an alley off East Fifth Street. I think Nelson's warrant is for something less sexy. Maybe unpaid traffic tickets? "They never arrest anyone here," I called to their fleeing backs.

The officers came straight up to the deli counter, but instead of ordering their usual meat-centric sandwiches, one said, "We're looking for Steve Latwats."

Annie shot me a look that said: "You want the power? Take it." Or maybe it was: "This cop is hot" (which he was), but I took it as the former.

"Let me ask where he is. Be right back," I trilled, and tried to walk as calmly as I could to Dirty Steve's office. I slipped inside without knocking, closing the door behind me.

"What is it, Poxy Roxy?"

"What did you do?"

"What did I do? What kind of nonsense question is that? Get back to work."

"What. Did. You. Do?"

"You aren't going post-firing psycho on me, are you? Tell me you aren't going to kill me."

"Two cops are here asking about you. They're probably here to arrest you, man."

"Oh, shit."

"And I'm asking you why."

"Nunya."

"I could be your ticket out of here without handcuffs. But I want to know why."

"Nunya business."

"Okay, fine. I'll send them right in." I turned toward the door.

"Wait, wait. Fine," Dirty Steve said. "That stripper I've been seeing? I fucked her too good. Big mistake. She showed up at my house during a coke binge wanting more. I said no, and I didn't want to see her anymore, either. She freaked out and attacked me. I pushed her, but only to get her out of my house."

I believed him. Jealousy and a desire for control are the harbingers of the domestic-violence perpetrator, but when it comes to women, Dirty Steve seems to vacillate only between horniness and disinterest.

"If she filed a complaint against me, those cops probably have a warrant," Dirty Steve continued. As he spoke, he became increasingly frantic. "Oh man, oh man, oh man, I can't let them put cuffs on me at work. I'm the boss! And I didn't do anything!" He started pacing around his small office, mumbling under his breath about how he'd never survive the clink.

I saw an opportunity to seize. "I'll distract the cops long enough for you to get out of here," I said. "You can go down to the police station and turn yourself in, see if you can get this cleared up instead of being arrested here in front of everyone. If—"

"If I don't fire you."

"Exactly."

"I have to fire you."

"And you'll be handcuffed in front of all your employees and hundreds of customers. Maybe we can go apply for unemployment together."

"Fine. Fucking fine. You win. But I have to do something to show the other deli wingdings I'm not soft. Two weeks' suspension without pay."

"With pay."

"One week without pay, one week of sick leave. But you tell everyone both weeks are unpaid."

"Deal. When you leave, go out the front."

I hurried back to the deli counter where the cops were waiting for me. "Steve is training a new stocker. I'll take you to him." I felt Annie's eyes proudly on me as I escorted the cops through the store to the doors next to Dairy that lead to the stockroom. I took the cops wandering through the stockroom as I yelled, "Steve! Dirty Steve!" Finally I gave the officers an "aw shucks" look and said I couldn't imagine where he'd gone. When I made my way back to the deli counter, Annie asked me if I was still employed.

"You want the power? Take it," I said.

She gave me a high five. "I laughed my ass off to see Dirty Steve hightailing it out the front door. That was amazing," she said. It was only then I could actually feel happy about Annie's good news.

"Why don't you come over tonight and we can celebrate? We could watch that documentary about factory farming and bologna production? So fucking disgusting." As you know, Annie and I love to bond over our shared veganism. We watched every food documentary at Waterloo Video and are now, out of necessity, moving on to Netflix.

"I can't tonight," she said. "I've gotta prep for my first animal-rights meeting with Topher Doyle, which he doesn't yet know he's going to be having with me soon." She gave me her sassiest, get-shit-done grin.

Just as Annie walked away, who should appear at the deli but that snack and a half, Patrick. I almost knocked Nelson over to ensure I was the one to take Patrick's order. Everett, I could barely scoop up the revolting chicken salad he ordered, distracted as I was by his adorable nubby dreads, those bright hazel eyes, and that skin the color of an iced soy milk latte (Yum! He's so fine, I can't bring myself to care that he eats meat). He wore Vans, baggy shorts, and a The Kills T-shirt over his ripped little skater body. Casually, he mentioned that after work he was going to the skate park. Everett, before you judge, remember, a lot of guys in their early thirties still skate. There's nothing wrong with keeping it real. I actually admire Patrick's refusal to conform to societal expectations that we give up our passions as we age. It's inspiring, really.

When I "weighed" the chicken salad, I barely let the box touch the scale. Patrick clearly noted the heft of the box and the very low price. "Thanks, Roxy," he said. He leaned in toward the deli counter and lowered his voice. "You're always hooking me up. Hopefully someday I can repay the favor." He gave me a wink I felt deep in my lady bits. He could thank me by nibbling my sweet-and-sour peach, I tell you what. That would be a worthy way to finally break my post–Brant Bitterbrush man-fast.

It's been a roller coaster of a day! I was fired, found out Annie has started her meteoric rise, then heroically salvaged my job, and finally successfully flirted with Patrick! It's a lot to take in. Luckily, thanks to the power of Annie's pep talk and the support of my favorite planetary deity, I'm still employed. But I'm out a week's pay. So, dear Everett, you need to give me the rent you owe me by Wednesday or I'm advertising your room on Craigslist.

Ultimatumly, your newly empowered ex-girlfriend,
Roxy

P.S. And start thinking about your July rent, too. It's due in five days!

June 29, 2012

Dear Everett,

I've been wanting to thank you for bringing me fried avocado tacos from Torchy's the other night. It was great to catch up, eat something that wasn't liberated from the Whole Foods deli, and just spend some time together. I have to admit it's nice sometimes to have another human soul in the house. Being suspended from work while living alone would get depressing. And thanks for helping me clean my old, broken Vespa. If I can sell that thing I can make up most of the money I'm going to lose from my unpaid leave and maybe put a dent in my credit card. But where have you been since? You are both mostly unemployed and rarely home—a mysterious combination that begs questions as to your whereabouts and activities. Because you haven't been around, I'm forced to put pen to paper to communicate with you yet again so that I can tell you about today's triumph!

Annie called last night just as I was getting ready to give Roscoe a bath. "Look," she said. "I've been thinking. It's really time for you to make moves, too. Have you by any chance drawn anything new lately?"

"You sound like my mother."

"But you have some old drawings, right, from before you let that dum-dum ex-boyfriend derail you from making art?"

"What is this about?"

"Well, there's this contest. It's based out of Chicago, but people from all over the country can enter. It's called the Bucknether Art Competition. It's really prestigious and it pays out like thirty grand. And it's for social justice, so I thought you could use those drawings I saw once with—"

"—the duck and the lamb suffering horribly in a factory farm and alternately living a happy, bucolic life?" It was part of the series that ended up in the ill-fated hands of Brant Bitterbrush. Perhaps the factory-farm part was a metaphor for the drama and suffering of our relationship.

"Yes, they're really good, Rox." I was touched—I could tell she wasn't just saying it. Annie never blows smoke.

"But I hate to submit old stuff. It feels so stale."

"Well, let's go back to earlier in this conversation when I asked you if you have new stuff."

"Fine, but what if they find out my work has been used to market and sell— Oh, never mind. I don't want to talk about it again."

"How about if you don't do it you owe me the entry fee, which otherwise I'll pay. It's not a handout, it's a bet."

Annie knows my inner fifth grader can never resist a bet or a dare. "Fine."

"The entry has to be postmarked by tomorrow," Annie said. Before I could protest, she added, "So if you can't handle that, stop by my desk tomorrow with fifty dollars. I only accept cash."

ARGH! The joys and challenges of having such a friend.

So I did it, Everett! I didn't fuss over it for months like I would've if I'd had due warning. I just pulled together my best drawings and off they went. Done. It's not making new work, but it's something. Since Brant stole my artwork for a terrible purpose, I've been completely artistically blocked. But if I win this contest, or even place, it'll give me the kick in the pants to draw again. The top ten finalists will be announced in early September and the winner in October. Winning would give me the money to rent a studio, and even work less, and then I'll draw and draw. I remember how I used to hurry home from the deli to sit down at my big kitchen table and work on a new drawing or painting. It all felt so effortless then, and it all feels so impossible now. I wonder if I'll ever have that feeling again, that ink will always be flowing from my pen and it doesn't matter what anyone thinks about my creations as long as I'm creating them.

Hopefully,
Roxy

P.S. I appreciate the June rent. I really do. Now get ready to pay up for July!

P.P.S. Of course it would be pathetic to add a ground rule called "#8b, YOU WILL hang out with me at home more often," so I'm not even considering that. But I just wanted to reiterate that it was great to chill with you the other night. ARGH! What is going on? As soon as I penned those words the very ink with which they were written smelled pathetic.

P.P.P.S. Thanks so much for picking up the tweakers' beer cans from the backyard. I really appreciate it! But don't think that lets you off the hook for the rent!

July 3, 2012

Dear Everett,

The last couple of days have been—thanks to you—an utter bummer. I enjoyed our Jim Jarmusch movie marathon (though I fear you intentionally sat rather close to me on the couch, creating a borderline snuggling situation), but as a result I contracted your terrible summer cold and thus will probably have to miss the Willie Nelson Fourth of July Picnic tomorrow. It's a rather painful irony that I've actually been sick during what was meant to be festive paid sick leave. And as much as it can annoy me when you are here (particularly when you leave your dishes in the sink), your trip to visit pals in San Antonio during this time of my illness is rather irritating as well.

It would have been especially nice if you'd been here yesterday to help with Charlize Theron. She was acting weird, panting and meowing in this plaintive voice, so I finally took her to see the vet, Dr. Tristeza. Only he was out sick, too—this hideous summer cold is going around—and the receptionist said I should have called first. People and pets packed the waiting room so tightly the air conditioner couldn't put a dent in the body heat. I thought there was no one to see Charlize. I could feel myself sort of panicking, and then getting mad out of fear, and that always stresses Charlize out.

I was standing at the reception desk when out of the corner of my eye I saw a huge brown blur running in my direction. I turned to see it was a mastiff, let off his leash and making a beeline toward me!!! Charlize, surely terrified it was her last second on earth, propelled herself up onto a big waiting room cabinet. Without thinking, I leapt up onto a chair to grab her, only to remember I was wearing a short skirt with a thong. That's when I sneezed and lost my footing. I'd gotten ahold of Charlize, and as I fell I kind of pulled her off the cabinet.

Like a cat, I landed on my feet. So did Charlize, but on top of the mastiff.

Holy hell broke loose, with every cat, dog, and rabbit going as berserk as their particular restraints and health issues allowed. Only the mastiff stayed calm. I swear, I'd totally misread him. Charlize leapt back up onto the cabinet. I wanted to climb up and get her, but of course my stupid skirt/thong situation prohibited it. So I just kept calling, "Charlize! Charlize Theron!" in a manner I hoped would coax her down. The mastiff's owner—who had finally grabbed the dog by its collar—kind of laughed, and that's when I saw the tattoo of Texas on his forearm and recognized him as the guy who came by the tuna burger sample table hoping for crumb cake. (As much as I protest the fact that five hundred idiots from California move to Austin every day, it's still literally impossible for me to go anywhere in Central Austin without running into at least three people I know or—in this case—barely know. In that way, it's still an excruciatingly small town.) Texas is cute and a vegetarian, but I remembered only too well his six-foot-tall rockabilly glamazon girlfriend and how they'd sashayed off together, laughing smugly at their happiness.

"This chaos is because of your savage dog," I said. The mastiff looked up at me, so calm it was clear he had the soul of a Buddha.

"He's pretty dangerous," Texas said. He was wearing another tight black T-shirt, like he's sure we all want to see his nice pecs. "Normally I wouldn't offer to rescue anyone's cat from a tree, but it seems your movements might be limited by the trappings of the patriarchy . . ." He gestured toward my skirt, and sort of trailed off as if aware he'd overstepped his bounds.

"Did you just say 'patriarchy'?" I snarled, and for a second I thought I'd lose my shit, but with the waiting room full of pets and their owners watching us, I kept it together.

"May I?" Texas asked, gesturing up at Charlize.

I nodded, hoping Charlize would scratch him, but my sweet pussy betrayed me, allowing him to scoop her from the top of the cabinet. She even purred.

"I've always wanted to hold Charlize Theron in my arms," he said after he'd climbed down from the chair.

"I've always wanted to meet a man who would crack that oh-so-original joke," I replied.

"The vet tech can see you now," the receptionist said. I suspect she was desperate to get me out of the waiting room.

Texas handed me Charlize. "It's been a joy stroking your—"

"Don't you dare say it," I said.

"I wouldn't think of calling Charlize Theron a pu . . . rrrrfect kitten," he said.

"Ugh," I said. "A pun is worse than a pussy."

"I'll say," he agreed.

While I wanted to get the last word in, right then I was overcome by a sneeze storm. With Charlize in my arms, I was hard-pressed to contain my sneeze juice, which Texas gracefully sidestepped. I could practically feel his suppressed laughter as I sneezed through the dog gate to the exam room.

I blame you, Everett, for my lack of a final retort, as you are the virus monkey who brought this cold to our house. Thanks to you, my natural wit was buried under an avalanche of disgusting sneezes. I'm not sure yet what you can do to repay me on your return from San Antonio, but it will likely involve a pint of vegan gelato and a (purely platonic!) foot rub.

Snottily,
Roxy

P.S. Charlize Theron has a respiratory infection and needs to be force-fed a horse pill every morning. So perhaps your efforts to get back in my good graces could start there. The happy news is the vet tech expects a full—if not speedy—recovery.

P.P.S. PATRICK JUST TEXTED ME! He noticed I haven't been at work lately and got my number from Nelson! He just wanted to know if I'm okay! If I wasn't a walking sneeze, I'd ask him what he's up to for the Fourth. I'm beyond thrilled he's thinking of me!

July 5, 2012

Dear Everett,

Thank you for the rent—only five days late!—and for loaning me your copy of the brand-new Dear Sugar book to keep me occupied until this head cold recedes! (You're the only man I've ever met who loves Cheryl Strayed's compassionate and inspiring advice as much as I do!) Today as I lay on the couch, reading and sipping beer to ease my sore throat, Dear Sugar's exhortation that "the best thing you can possibly do with your life is to tackle the motherfucking shit out of it" reminded me that the thing I most want to tackle (to the ground) is the new Lululemon. As Dear Sugar encouraged me (and all her readers) to get "unstuck," I began to ponder my lack of direction and general sense of malaise. Perhaps the answer lies in my righteous anger! Perhaps my Great Work just might be to rid the intersection of Sixth Street and Lamar Boulevard of that corporate-as-fuck Lululemon and return it to a local business in tune with the funky nature of Austin!

That's when I remembered today was the grand opening of the Lululemon! As I felt the symptoms of my cold finally lift, I decided to follow Dear Sugar's advice. I would get off the couch! I would get unstuck like a motherfucker and go survey my enemy—so I pedaled down to the Lululemon, locked up my bike, and went inside. I was going to try on a pair of those stupid tights, a recon mission. (To sabotage a place, first you must know it well.) So I picked out a pair of capri tights and headed to the dressing rooms. Once I had them on, I turned around to look in the mirror and my breath caught in my throat at the sight before me. My ass has never looked so incredible.

I was like: "Damn, girl."

A voice trilled through the dressing room curtain: "Do you need anything? Another size?"

"I need fresh eyes to admire this ass of a vixen," I said, pulling the curtain aside with a flourish.

For a split second, my mind struggled to connect the familiar face of the saleswoman with the trauma I had so recently endured. But within a moment I knew she was the redhead who'd caused all the recent drama in my life. I'd like to chalk up running into her in such a way to the trickster interventions of a certain goddess (Hecate), but Lululemon and Whole Foods sit catty-cornered from each other and I'm sure all the Lulu employees saunter across the street to Whole Foods for their lunch breaks.

"What's up, Crumb Cake?" I said. Her face registered recognition as well. But it was hard to read what else was in her expression. Curiosity? Excitement? Disdain?

"My *name* is Artemis."

"Well, Artemis, I guess it's my turn to assault you at work."

She rolled her eyes and said in the fakest voice imaginable, "Those are so flattering on you. A perfect fit." She paused for a moment, and then spoke in a normal voice. "That's the thing about this place. You want to hate it because of its pseudofeminist messaging and ridiculous prices, but the clothes look so damn good. Those are actually great on you."

"I was just thinking the same thing!" I said, before I remembered she was supposed to be my enemy. I couldn't help but picture how she'd paused at the exit of Whole Foods to give me that conspiratorial wave, as if somehow we were both in on some great cosmic joke. "Why do you even work here?"

"I started at the Lulu in Barton Creek Mall about a month ago. But this new store is a better location."

"No, I mean, why do you work at a Lululemon at all?"

"I get to tell women they look beautiful all day, which in this society is revolutionary in and of itself. And I get a crazy discount on clothes for one of my alter egos."

"Alter egos?" I asked. I glanced at her bare left hand—the cherry-tomato-sized diamond had left the scene.

She saw my gaze. "Oh, I'm actually not married," she said.

Now I was really intrigued. "Then why were you wearing that gargantuan engagement ring?" I asked. "Please explain."

She leaned in, lowering her voice. "I wear a fake ring and full Lulu when I go to Whole Foods so I can be my trophy wife alter ego! As a trophy wife, it's so much easier to get hot guys that work there to bang me in the parking lot. Okay, I admit it—I've only been sleeping with two cashiers *lately*. But I swear every male Whole Foods employee is hot for trophy wife."

Everett, I've been crushing on Patrick in Beer Alley for MONTHS and haven't gotten past idle coworker chitchat. Meanwhile, all this Queen has to do is stop in for a green juice and she's consummating the deed before she leaves the premises. Clearly I'd misjudged her. "Really?" I said.

"Yeah. I'm pretty sure 'trophy wife' is a top-five fetish for underemployed artist types."

"What are the other four?"

"Debutantes and cheerleaders—I count those as one type since there's so much overlap. Lead singers of all-girl punk rock bands. If the guys are white, then black girls with natural hair—I can't pull off that one. And fixed-gear bike-riding girls with lots of memorial tats to their dead daddies—of course."

"Of course," I murmured. I was too impressed to say anything else.

"That last one's not my strong suit either. May I ask—did you get fired? I mean, after the crumb cake incident?"

"Nah, two weeks' suspension. I mean, my boss fired me, but then I blackmailed him." I didn't want to admit to myself that I hoped she was impressed.

"I did you a favor. You're destined for greater things than that job."

I studied her. I had the bizarre, delightful, and slightly intoxicating sense she could really see me. "I hope you're right about that."

"Oh, girl, I am. You'll see."

"One thing: Why did you say 'Mmmm, crumb cake' when you ate that piece of tuna burger?"

"When I'm trolling Whole Foods as my trophy wife alter ego, I go totally in character. You think a rich housewife so desperate for a hot lay that she'd fuck a Whole Foods cashier in the parking lot could stand her life if she was actually sensorily grounded in her body?"

"Wow," I said. I was stunned we'd had the exact same thought—it was as if we'd experienced some kind of intense (if limited) mind-meld.

Artemis glanced at her watch. "My shift's almost over. I have to head out to go teach my aerial dance class."

An aerial dance class sounds exciting! It made me realize I haven't had the mojo to actually try anything new in months. I suddenly imagined Artemis as a gateway to adventure, to a wellspring of energy I haven't been able to tap into of late. "Well, it was nice to meet you," I said.

"It went better this time, didn't it?" She winked at me, and then she was gone.

I changed out of the tights and biked off slowly, thinking about the strange encounter. When I got home, I found a pair of Lululemon shorts stuffed in the bottom of my backpack. And while I would give myself a gold star for stealing something out of that shit den, I didn't take them. I wouldn't be caught dead in public in them either (less because of brand disloyalty and more because the shorts don't have the sculpting power of the tights), but I'm wearing them around the house right now because they remind me of my new Great Work.

And I can't seem to get Artemis out of my mind. Her sassiness, her alter ego, the fact that she has no trouble quenching her libidinous urges with real live guys rather than a purple merman. I have a feeling she has much to teach me. It's ironic the first woman I've wanted to befriend in ages works at a store I'm beginning to feel it's my destiny to vanquish. But perhaps she could help me somehow in my quest to drive that stupid fucking store from that revered location. I'm sort of kicking myself I didn't ask for her number!

Everett, the more I think about it, the more I feel sure—I need Artemis (a.k.a. the Artist Formerly Known as Crumb Cake) to be my friend.

Exhilaratedly yours,
Roxy

CHAPTER TWO

July 6, 2012

Dear Everett,

Those fucking tweakers kept me up all night! They were on their patio, talking and blasting music—which I'm guessing you didn't hear since you sleep like a darted elephant. I went outside at 2 a.m. and told them to shut the fuck up, which was met with a volley of "Ooooh! We are in troubles!" from the tweaker minions, and a resounding, "You shut up, cunt!" from Captain Tweaker.

Afterward, I lay in bed wide awake with rage and did not sleep until dawn. This morning when I finally dragged myself from bed, you had already left the house without picking up the beer cans the tweakers lobbed into our backyard. Several tweakers were still partying on the patio, but Captain Tweaker was loudly leaning a ladder against the roof of his house. Once he was on the roof, he disappeared out of sight, so I ducked into your bedroom to see if I could see him better from your window. That's when I noticed you'd left behind my backpack that you borrowed.

I liberated it and inside I found—along with spare change, receipts for ThunderCloud Subs, and the other usual detritus that follows you everywhere—a box of blue medical gloves and a fifteen-minute lab timer.

Everett! Why didn't you tell me you are in school? I imagine you putting on your gloves and timing how fast it takes you to draw blood from your patient. Or maybe you are studying to be a vet tech? You are so good with the furballs. Their love for you is the reason you still have a roof over your head, and it makes cosmic sense that the benefits your love of animals brings to your life would expand to include a steady job. Or perhaps you are in school to be a vet acupuncturist and you have fifteen minutes to needle each animal? I cannot wait to grill you about this, but since you once again aren't home (I swear we hang out less now than before you moved in!), I'm taking my pen to paper as I sip my morning coffee.

"Who? What? When? Where? Why?" I demand. Tell me everything.

But wait—perhaps you haven't shared your return to school because you fear failure. You worry if I know of your aspirations and am rooting for you, it will become a sort of pressure that will inevitably create a block preventing you from doing your best work. You've told me about your brief stint at community college, how your mother's high hopes and your abusive stepfather's disdain percolated in your sub-conscious until you could not pull it together to drag yourself to class, much less complete your assignments. And when you received your grades, that row of Fs proved to you what you had always suspected about yourself.

Don't worry, Everett. I will never let you know how proud I am of you. I will root for you silently and with all the love a friend, former lover, and landlady can provide. I will not let on that I understand how hard you are working to improve yourself, your situation, your income, your life!

But in my heart I know you are striving to overcome the abuse you have suffered, as well as the low self-esteem that arrived in its wake. And I will eagerly await the day you come home with a certificate or di-ploma from whatever trade school or technical program you are cur-rently attending. Then together we will celebrate your victory over the deep darkness of the unconscious mind, that writhing octopus that seeks to wrap you in its tentacles and drag you down to the watery darkness. Until then, Everett, I am deeply and sympathetically,

Your friend,
Roxy

P.S. After I found the backpack, I again peered out your bedroom window to see that all the tweakers had gone inside, leaving their idiotic leader, Captain Tweaker, alone on the roof, likely taping a brick of meth to the inside of his chimney. As the chimney did indeed block his view of both my house and his side yard, I ran outside and through the gate. I swiftly pulled his ladder from the roof and laid it on the ground before darting back inside. I then enjoyed my second cup of coffee while peeking out the blinds to watch him wailing, grinding his rotten teeth, and shaking his fist at the sky until his brethren emerged to once again raise the ladder so he could climb down. I also called 311 and reported that the meth heads next door are always cooking in that decaying van permanently parked in front of their house.

P.P.S. Two hours have gone by and still no sign of the cops. In the worldview of the popos, white tweakers are clearly immune to the arm of the law.

P.P.P.S. For a moment I slipped and left this letter for you on the kitchen table, but then remembered I must hide it—along with my new knowledge of your current schooling and ambitions—from you. I am therefore going to secret it away in the last place you'd ever look—my period underwear drawer.

July 8, 2012

Dear Everett,

Since my new Dear Sugar–inspired philosophy is to "tackle the motherfucking shit" out of Lululemon, I decided I need to study my enemy with care. And so, since I'm still suspended from work and have nothing better to do, I rode my bike over to the corner of Sixth and Lamar to survey that crap store I am so eager to vanquish.

Okay, okay, you always see through me. I was also just really curious about that girl goddess Artemis, huntress of men. It's rare for me to meet a woman so intriguing. I cannot help it if I want to befriend her.

I cruised the store, fingering workout tops and tights as if I were a Silk Road trader, until I glimpsed Artemis's red ponytail. She came right toward me and said, in a delightfully fake voice that implied I was in on her joke, "May I help you today, miss? Perhaps you'd like to try our new Chase Me Onesie? It's only $118."

"I was thinking the Lost in Pace skirt at $125 would be more my style," I said. I managed to suppress my giggle, but a little snort escaped my nose.

"The fact that you'll look adorable in it will help you suffer through hot yoga and another day in the life of materialism that grips you like a vice," Artemis said. "It's what I tell all our regulars." Everett, that grrrl has been reading my mail!

"Since I'm still suspended from work, I've got more time than I know what to do with. So let me know if you'd ever wanna grab a coffee or a drink or whatever," I said.

I tried to sound casual, Everett, but I wasn't breathing. You know when you asked me out the first time? And later you told me it was like your heart had stopped because you were so hopeful? I felt like that, but in a platonic friend sort of a way. Artemis just shrugged and said, "Maybe."

But she did give me her cell number—her last name is Starla, Artemis Starla—and I left the store on cloud nineteen!

Floatingly,
Roxy

P.S. While I am leaving this letter on the kitchen table for you, I hope you come home tonight at a decent-enough hour for me to recount this story to you again in person!

July 10, 2012

Dear Everett,

I've been meaning to get this off my (very sexy) chest for a while. While I am happy enough to have you living here—as long as you pay me rent—it's important for you to know once and for all that I will not be getting back together with you. So please stop making jokes about how great it will be when we finally realize we are meant for each other. And while I enjoy an occasional "You look pretty," I feel the number of compliments you have been giving me recently exceeds that of a normal landlady/room-renter relationship.

It's true that I am eager to break the man-fast that has followed in the wake of my being unceremoniously dumped by Brant Bitterbrush, and have been enjoying your company immensely, but I do not think it's a good idea for you and I to hook up again. The reason is not, as you claim, a difference in education or class, or that you don't have a traditional career (or any career at all). Nor is it because you have an unlikely (and anachronistic) passion for heavy metal, or even because when we were dating and I tried to take you out for drinks with my college pals Yolanda, Rose, Kate, and Barclay, you always clammed up completely, morphing into what they perceived as a total dud. It's more that as a couple we lack the kind of sexual chemistry we would need to sustain us through the vagaries of this world.

Therefore, please take this letter as a heartening reminder that we are now platonic friends, and keep alive the hope that you will find someone who is a better match for you than I.

Officially,
Roxy

P.S. I texted Artemis Starla and she has not texted me back!

July 11, 2012

Dear Everett,

Now that I know you are off bettering yourself, I hardly notice when you aren't home. Also, though your rent is almost two weeks late, I am choosing to hold my tongue, pregnant as I am with the knowledge of your efforts to improve your situation. So this letter, already full of secrets I must keep from you, is destined not for the kitchen table, but for a dark corner of my period underwear drawer, which tells no tales.

It's 8 p.m. and I'm having a much-needed mug of chilled red wine, purchased with my Whole Foods employee discount. Today was a weird one. I was back at work for the first time after my suspension and a little nervous Dirty Steve would be mad at me for the tiny but righteous blackmailing episode. However, he seemed to be taking it in stride (though when I tried to grill him about his brush with the law, he gave me a "talk to the hand" gesture).

I've barely seen Annie since she moved up to her new job on the fifth floor, where she acts as a griffin guarding the priceless treasure of Whole Foods—its wacky C-suite exec and environmental warrior Topher Doyle. But today she came down on her break and stopped at the deli counter to see me.

"What'cha doing down here with the pleebs?" I asked.

"Buying kombucha. Lavender for me because I need to chill the fuck out. Pomegranate for Topher Doyle because he says it's a Greek symbol of eternal life and abundance. I do think he's actually trying to both live forever AND become the most influential corporate environmentalist on earth."

I used to brew kombucha faithfully, but since I landed in this slump I haven't bothered. "At least Dirty Steve isn't shooting for immortality."

"I like it when you see your glass as half full. Will you come up on your lunch break to check out my new digs?"

I told her I'd be elbow deep in a batch of kung pao tofu but she refused to accept such a bullshit excuse.

"Okay, fine," I said. "I can't because I'm too jealous you've escaped the confines of the deli case. If I see your admin desk I might swoon with envy."

She told me to quit whining and meet her at the elevators at 1:05 p.m.

I'd been acting like I was pretending to be jealous. But the truth is I am actually jealous. I've been standing behind that deli counter for three years with nary a move except that of keeping myself from being fired last week. (The fact that I consider that a move, dear Everett, shows just how stagnant my life has become.) Annie was my deli pal, sure, yet after only six months she rocketed herself upstairs to the nerve center of a health-food empire.

And so it was that I walked to the elevator at our meeting time, feeling a little sorry for myself. Annie was standing there waiting for me, looking happy and excited. She used her badge to gain us access to the fifth floor. The elevator doors opened and it was like a golden heavenly light shone on us. I was so disoriented by its glow it took me a while to realize it was a combination of sunlight coming through the floor-to-ceiling windows and some new age, high-tech lighting system Topher Doyle likely sprung for to prevent himself and the rest of the upper echelon of the company from being exposed to the draining effects of fluorescents. "It's crazy that when we were born, Whole Foods was still a tiny local chain with just a handful of stores," I mused. "It was small when we were small."

"I know. And now that we're grown, it's a corporate behemoth."

"Is it terrible that I think of it as our corporate behemoth?" I asked. And by "our" I meant not just me and Annie, but every other Austin slacker raised on the notion that true success means working a "cool" low-wage job—at a record store, coffee shop, or yes, at the one accept-able corporate giant Whole Foods—that barely supports one's artistic endeavors (or what the alchemists referred to as one's Great Work).

"Let me give you a tour," Annie said. First she took me to the Help Desk room, where a row of staggeringly attractive, tattooed men and women sat wearing headsets, cheerfully talking Whole Foods employees from around the country down from the hysteria of their minor tech di-sasters. They all smiled and waved at us, gesturing that they were too absorbed in their glorious duties supporting the empire to chat with us. I noticed that two of the men were super-hot identical twins.

Annie then took me to her desk, which sat just to the right of a closed door made of gleaming walnut. A nameplate beside the door read:

TOPHER DOYLE
CHIEF ECOSYSTEM OFFICER, WHOLE FOODS

(This nameplate was made from recycled six-pack rings plucked from the Gulf Coast and thus saved the lives of one to six baby seals.)

Just then, a guy with chunky glasses and an artfully arranged mop of hair approached. "I was hoping I could—"

Annie cut him off. "Topher Doyle is working quietly now. Feel free to email me a request to speak to him via Outlook."

The guy nodded and slunk away sheepishly.

"Oh my Goddess, you're like the personal guardian of Topher Doyle's uninterrupted mental focus," I said, a little awed by her proxim-ity to power.

"No one gets to Topher Doyle without my permission," Annie re-plied. On our way out, I spotted an open door to a big office with a giant drafting table. A man stood in front of a chalkboard easel. In deep red chalk, he drew a giant bunch of strawberries. It was just a sign for the produce section of the store announcing a sale, but it was so lovely that I stopped to stare, a wistful feeling coming over me at that unexpected beauty.

I lingered in the doorway, envious of the ease with which he created this chalk drawing, which—though bordering on the sublime—was destined to be erased in days to make way for the next store sale. It's funny that when I was a kid sidewalk chalk was my favorite medium, but now, maybe because it's so ephemeral, I would never think of using it. (Perhaps I lack the acceptance of the transitory nature of material life possessed by Tibetan monks who labor so hard over their beautiful sand mandalas only to dismantle them once they are complete.)

"Roxy!" Annie said, snapping me out of my chalk drawing reverie. I hurried after her. At the elevator, she gave me a hug.

"Thanks for coming to check out my new desk."

"It's like you've ascended," I said. "And now I'm headed back down to the underworld."

"A bout of self-pity a day keeps positive action away."

"You did not just say that," I replied, which was my only retort because she was exactly right. Just then the elevator dinged, ready to lower me back down to the hellscape of the deli. "Sorry for being a brat."

"I love you, brattiness and all," Annie said, just as the doors closed between us.

A melancholy mood enveloped me for the rest of my shift. I'm not such a baby that I'm not happy for Annie. It's just that no matter if she comes up with excuses to come see me in the store, it won't be the same. I've lost my deli pal, and serving food to sensitivity–ridden hippies, local scrubs, and yuppie moms isn't the same without her by my side.

I must have looked sad, too, because even Dirty Steve noticed. "Cheer up, you dirty freak," he said.

"Don't you have a stripper to assault or something?" I replied.

"Too soon," he said. "Way too soon."

My mood cheered considerably a few hours later when I finally got a text from Artemis! She asked if I wanted to meet up for coffee later this week!

Intrigued by a potential new friend,
Roxy

P.S. It's a relief to know I won't be giving you this letter, because as close as we are, I'd still feel embarrassed to reveal to you the depths of my petty jealousies and tendency to wallow.

July 13, 2012

Dear Everett,

I was hoping you'd be here when I got home tonight. I just had the most amazing outing with Artemis Starla and I want to tell you all about it. Before I left the house, I was so nervous and excited that I tried on three outfits, finally settling on a sundress and sandals. (What else did I think I could wear in this heat, really?) We had decided to meet at Spider House for coffee. Thank Goddess that Spider House is still going strong, despite the fact that Starbucks stores have spread through the city faster than an STD in a retirement home. Inside its dark interior, Missy Elliott blasted through the speakers while students hunkered in booths, drank espresso milkshakes, and pretended to study when really they were alternately flirting and reading snarky articles on "Jezebel."

I'd only been standing at the counter for a minute when Artemis breezed in, looking incredible in some sort of space-age silver minidress with white platform sandals. When she spotted me, her face lit up like a neon Lone Star sign. "Roxy!" she cried, in a way that made me feel amazing.

"Cute dress!" I said.

"Thanks, love. It's actually supposed to be part of a sexy space cadet Halloween costume. But I like it for summer."

We ordered iced lattes. Artemis insisted on paying, then glanced around the loud, dark room. "Should we sweat it out on the patio?" she asked. We grabbed our iced lattes and made our way outside, where we settled in at a slightly wobbly, brightly colored aluminum table.

From the moment we sat down, her phone kept buzzing—dick pic after dick pic rolling in via text—and she seemed totally unfazed. At the arrival of one photograph, she held up the phone for my inspection and said casually, "Must be photoshopped."

"Where do you meet these guys? On dating apps?"

"Never!" she said. "Those things are for people who don't know how to live." I wanted to grill her on this philosophy, but as we were only drinking coffee I didn't have the nerve.

"Then where?"

"Around town."

"Do you always pretend you are a trophy wife?"

"Only at Whole Foods," she said. "My avatars are location specific. What about you? Seeing anyone?"

"Well, there is this one guy at work." I felt sick with dread. "Any chance you've fucked Patrick from Beer Alley?"

"Nope. Cashiers only. I don't know why, but as far as Whole Foods employees go, they're my thing."

"Thank Goddess." Relief washed over me. I may have my charms, but I'm no competition for Artemis.

"So you and Patrick?" She made a lewd finger gesture.

"No. I mean, not yet."

"Then who's the lucky guy that's been keeping you satisfied?"

"Well . . . it's been a while."

"A while?"

When I confessed it's been a year since I saw ANY ACTION WHATSOEVER, she spat out a mouthful of latte, then composed herself enough to demand to know my emotional block.

"It's not so much emotional as physical," I said.

"Sexual dysfunction? Chronic yeast infections? VD? Bladder infections? Pelvic floor disorder? Girl, I have a host of referrals for hippy doctors who can fix it all."

"No, no. Nothing like that." I paused and considered telling her everything about Brant Bitterbrush. But I didn't want to delve into my maudlin heartbreak on my first friend date with Artemis, so I kept it simple, Everett. I blamed you. "I have a big old ex-boyfriend covered in stick-and-poke tattoos living in my spare bedroom."

Everett, she put her hands over her ears and let out a bloodcurdling scream that caused a passing barista to drop a mug, which shattered, spraying hot coffee all over the patio stones.

Then she removed her hands from her ears and said, "Homeboy is completely messing with your mojo. HE. HAS. TO. GO!"

Of course I explained everything to her about your social anxiety, your history of being unjustly fired from multiple jobs for talking to customers about conspiracy theories, your passion for weaving (a worthy but unlucrative art form), and the fact that you are secretly studying long hours at some vet tech vocational program or pet acupuncturist school in order to better yourself and your opportunities. (I thought I would be able to give you this letter, but now that I've mentioned your cloak-and-dagger undertaking, this missive is also destined for my period underwear drawer.) But she remained adamant that you HAVE to move out of my house. I finally changed the subject by telling her about my selfish sense of devastation at Annie's move to the fifth floor.

"She sounds like a boss," Artemis said.

"Well, she's actually the boss's admin assistant."

Artemis shrugged. "Still, she's making moves."

At that I felt the old familiar sadness that I am making no moves whatsoever.

Now that I'm safely at home, drinking chilled merlot from a coffee mug with the furballs and contemplating Artemis's operatic response to my admission that you are living with me, I realize that she is right—inviting an ex-boyfriend into my home has surely created a block, an impediment that keeps good, new things from flowing into my life. But still, I'm going to give you six months to finish your schooling and get back on your feet. I know all you are struggling to overcome. I admire—and even envy—your gumption. I feel like having the proper support could make all the difference for you.

Committedly, your friend and platonic pillar,
Roxy

July 15, 2012

Everett!

Why aren't you here this morning? It's 8:05 a.m. and those tweakers from next door are still up! They haven't slept and, as a result, neither have I! A couple of them are on the back patio right now, vaping and laughing. I mean, get a real cigarette, you creeps! Those guys are tanking my property value. I can feel it dropping with every batch of meth they cook in that damn van.

I have called 311 again and registered yet another complaint with the police, though of course the officer that answered my call didn't seem very enthused. He's likely just been assigned desk duty for some infraction and has lost the will to determinedly root out neighborhood drug crime.

ACK! I think Captain Tweaker just saw me peeking out at him through the blinds. Now if the police show up those meth heads will definitely suspect I made the report. What if they try to retaliate by poisoning the furballs? This is so stressful.

Anxiously,
Roxy

July 17, 2012

Dear Everett,

Congratulations! I'm overjoyed you got your line cook job back at Kerbey Lane Cafe! I ask you in advance to NOT bring me home any queso. Melted cheese is my Achilles' heel and wreaks equal havoc on my skin and my moral compass as a vegan.

Like you, I am making progress in changing my situation in life, thanks to the encouragement of a friend! Artemis and I have been texting and she gave me a "homework" assignment: find Patrick at work and actually talk to him! It seemed like a reasonable first step to busting out of my man-fast.

So, during my first break today, I headed over to Beer Alley. I found Patrick crouched down to stock a low shelf full of Guinness, his baggy shorts sagging to reveal the most adorable coin slot. "Hey," I said.

"Hey, Roxy," he said.

Artemis told me I should ask Patrick for a beer recommendation. She said it would make him feel smart and knowledgeable, and thus horny. I'm not sure I totally followed her logic, but I tried to follow her advice. "I'm looking for a new beer to try," I said. I was so nervous I reached out and touched a random six-pack. "I loved this one. Could you recommend another one like it?"

He made a confused face. "It's pretty hot outside for a chocolate stout. That's really more of a winter beer."

"Exactly! I'm looking for a beer like this winter beer," I stammered. "You know, one that's like that good, but summery, right?" Oh my Venus, I was totally mangling this attempt at flirtation! I could feel my face flush a merciless red.

"Yeah, it's scorching out there," he said. "Makes me want to swim at Barton Springs."

"Yeah, but I heard the fecal count in the water is actually really high after last week's rain." Why? Why did I say something so disgusting!!!! I could have mentioned my days lifeguarding at the Springs, or said something about having a new bikini. Why, oh why, did I instead say the word "fecal"? (But it's true. The more developed Austin becomes, the more nastiness is washed into beautiful Barton Springs when it rains, making the normally crystalline waters unswimmable for a time. And besides, Barton Springs has very complicated memories for me, given it's where Brant Bitterbrush and I fell in love.)

"Ugh," he said.

I tried to rescue the conversation by bringing up beer again. I escaped with a six-pack of something unpronounceable with a hint of orange, even though I hate orange-flavored beer. When it comes to love, or even cheap sex or basic coquetry, I seem to be hopeless. Venus! Oh, Venus! Goddess of Beauty, Love, and Friendship. Why have you forsaken me?

Discouragedly,
Roxy

NEST LIFE
Getting Started with Orgasmic Meditation

In orgasmic meditation (a.k.a. OM), a stroker strokes a woman's clitoris very lightly for 15 minutes within a very ritualized situation involving:

- A timer
- Gloves
- Lube
- A nest (i.e., blankets and pillows)

Orgasmic meditation is an innovative "Zen" tantric practice wherein both the stroker and the strokee focus intently on the sensation of the point of contact between finger and clitoris—much as the point of Vipassana meditation is to focus on the sensation of the breath passing over the upper lip as it enters and exits the nose.

At OM meet-ups, attendees take turns OMing and share tips, as well as their emotional journey with orgasmic meditation. OM meet-ups can be informal and involve only a stroker and strokee—perhaps at one practitioner's home—or they might involve a small or large group of people.

Our largest OM event took place at a ballroom at the San Francisco Convention Center and included 630 participants—315 strokers and 315 strokees in one room. Now that was a lot of orgasmic energy (and a lot of nests)!

To find an OM meet-up near you, go to:
www.nestlife.com

July 19, 2012

Dear Everett,

I was taking out the recycling today and when I dumped it into the blue bin, a flyer fell out and fluttered to the ground. When I picked it up, the words "orgasmic meditation" caught my eye and of course I immediately read the whole thing. Everett!? What in the world have you gotten yourself into?

When I found a box of medical gloves and a timer in my backpack that you borrowed, I thought you were IN SCHOOL studying to be a vet tech so that you could use your talents with animals to pay your rent on time and perhaps someday even get your own apartment. Of course it never occurred to me you've been spending your days fingerbanging strangers as a form of pseudomeditation. I'm rarely shocked, but damn it: I have to say I'm shocked. And concerned that you've fallen into the clutches of some crazy sex cult. Are you really stroking strange women's clits? It's hard to imagine. But I'm going to try . . . Now that I think of it, I'm sure that if you ARE going door-to-door rubbing clitorises, it serves as an effective distraction—if you're focusing with every ounce of your being on the point of contact between your gloved, lubed finger and some rando's clit, you are certainly not considering the actual situation of your life.

I've gone online to www.nestlife.com and watched one of your cult leader Nina Sylvester's YouTube videos. I admit: she is dynamic and attractive (That glowing skin! That mane of silky, dark hair!), and if I dare say it, even convincing. She claims orgasms are the cure for modern women's spiritual hunger, that partnered "orgasmic meditation" is a panacea. I can see how you might have fallen sway to her powers. But I beseech you to pull yourself back to reality. I mean, group fingerbanging as a pseudo-spiritual practice? Ugh! That might have been how the Manson family got started.

The bottom line is that a group founded on words such as "stroker," "strokee," and the oh-so-odious noun "nest," a group whose main tools involve a timer, lube, surgical gloves, and said "nest" is a group to be avoided like the syph (which you would probably contract from your fellow members anyway!).

I grieve you have fallen prey to the vision of Nina Sylvester, Nest Life's founder. You have been bewitched by this beautiful siren and, like Odysseus, have been lured off course. I implore you, throw away your gloves and timer before you forget to engage normally with both women and the world!

Hang on a minute. I seriously need a drink.

———————

Okay, I'm back.

It's true that I have blended and consumed a margarita to try to clear the swirling fog of curiosity and confusion about Nest Life (and maybe more than a little pique at you for keeping your new activity from me, and at myself for giving you credit for self-improvement where no credit was due!). I have just sipped my way through several more Nest Life videos and interviews with Nina. (The only video of her I haven't watched is her TED Talk, which is too long to tackle just now as I have to clip Roscoe's nails before bed—a distressing task for both of us!), but I can say that her vision of a world in which all men know how to nurture female sexual energy and apply proper pressure to a clit is laudable.

GAH! What's happening to me!? Everett, come home. Let's talk this through. I know I cannot trust you to clear the fog of deception Nina's lovely and articulate face has brought down around me over the past half hour, but just your human presence at this time of confusion would be a comfort.

OMingly . . . wait, no . . . skeptically?

Your morally discombobulated ex-girlfriend,
Roxy

P.S. Let me say it again: FOR WEEKS I THOUGHT YOU WERE NEVER HOME BECAUSE YOU WERE IN SCHOOL! I hid my (false) knowledge from you to protect you from a sense of pressure and expectation! But I will hide my truths, half-baked assumptions, and letters from you no longer! This one's going on the kitchen counter!

July 21, 2012

Dear Everett,

I've been in a swirl of emotion since you told me you've decided to move out because:

1. A room for rent has become available in the OM house. (Who knew such a place existed! Are the cupboards stocked with lube, gloves, and fifteen-minute timers?)

2. You claim to dislike my "judgmental attitude" toward your new sex cult.

You made your announcement hurriedly and then rushed off while my mouth was still agape with shock. It was uncomfortable, to say the least. While I had imagined I'd celebrate the day you announced your impending departure, the news felt unexpected and disconcerting.

Perhaps I should consider this chain of events fortuitous, thank Venus, and let you leave. But while I worry about you falling even more under the influence of Nina Sylvester, her followers, and their questionable sexual practices and beliefs, I also must admit that some part of me fears abandonment, if only by my underemployed ex-boyfriend.

Everett, I can't retract any "judgmental" statements I may have made about your new sex cult, but if in truth it's my complaints about your presence here that have driven you to decide to leave, I want you to know you are more than welcome to stay.

Sincerely,
Roxy

July 22, 2012

Dear Everett,

O woeful, woeful, woeful day! Yesterday after you declared that you are indeed moving out soon and left (to go . . . where? To the OM house to check out your new room, which is certainly dripping with hazmat? To an OM meeting to forget about our argument and lose yourself in clit "stroking"?), I tried to distract myself with that mindless stuffer, Facebook. What I saw was so unexpected and awful that it's sent me into a total tailspin.

You know months ago I heard through the Austin rumor mill that Brant Bitterbrush and Cold Connie Caldwell got married. I had accepted that fact (though I did go on a social media fast to avoid any photographic evidence of their happiness together). But today when I got on Facebook for the first time in ages I saw on Brant Bitterbrush's mother's page a photo (knife through my heart!) of Connie and Brant Bitterbrush's newborn IDENTICAL TRIPLETS! The horror! The horror!

They are Brant's spitting image. My heart has broken all over again. (While part of me is outraged no mutual acquaintance told me of Cold Connie's pregnancy, part of me is glad to have found out in the privacy of my own home!)

For the last hour I've been on a sad journey down memory lane—all the way back to when I was nineteen and Brant Bitterbrush and I worked together as lifeguards at Barton Springs for a seemingly endless summer just after I returned to Austin after my gap year travels. Back in those days, when Brant and I tried to pretend we weren't falling in love, Connie Caldwell was just an uptight, annoying coworker famous among us for pulling out her calculator at restaurants so she could calculate what everyone at the table owed down to the penny. A total dud, she once said to me—and I quote—"I don't like women." (I can't believe that on not one, but two separate occasions, Brant got together with Connie after he and I broke up! But I jump ahead in my melancholy tale.)

I can still replay the memory of our first magical night together—I see it in my mind like a film in HD. Brant and I climbed up onto the Barton Springs office roof, still warm from the sun. The glow of the full moon caused the water below us to sparkle, creating the perfect conditions for a romantic first tryst. And yes, Venus was out in the night sky. It was practically written in the stars that Brant and I would fuck for the first time on that fateful night, under her light.

From then on Brant and I were tangled together like puppies. But our love was eventually marred by his overindulgence in alcohol and meat products—we bickered about the little things, like his Sunday morning bacon-frying fests and my tendency to be "slightly messy." But the real problem was that Brant wanted to have children. Not someday, but soon, like before we were even thirty, which seemed absolutely insane. ("Twenty-seven is as old as Kurt Cobain ever got," he'd say. To which I'd reply: "That's no reason to have a baby!") But he swore he wanted to be a young dad. Also, he'd developed an apathy toward me that spoke of a great discontent—when I came over he'd often turn on the television instead of listening to me recount the details of my day. (Everett, you know I can tolerate almost anything except (1) the idea of procreating, and (2) being ignored.) Of course, once I broke up with Brant he realized I was the sun his world revolved around, but it was too late. We tried to remain friends, but anytime we saw each other we both wept. I remember how sad I was to find myself single on my half birthday when I was twenty-three. (I felt so old to be alone, which makes me chuckle darkly now.)

Once I was totally over Brant (so I thought!), you and I had our voyage of love, which shipwrecked a year later, leaving us both—miraculously—somehow fairly unscathed, though on new shores. After that were three years of being a swinging-single wild child. (Not on an Artemis scale, but back then I definitely had game—though I have to ask myself: Where has it gone? I believe it was crushed by abject heartbreak. But I get ahead of myself again.) Then . . . Screw Venus for making me run into Brant at that coffee shop—I never would have gotten back together with him if he hadn't been there. He was, of course, fresh out of a relationship with Cold Connie Caldwell. (Back then I felt as cheered by news of their breakup as when I heard Katie Holmes filed for divorce from Tom Cruise.) The chemistry between us was (still) electric. As we sipped our coffees and caught up, it was clear that we felt the fiery rekindling of our love. Brant had (seemingly) outgrown his tendency toward emotional withdrawal, and his former angst at being a poor community college student was replaced with pride at his job as a paramedic and his side business as a barefoot running coach.

Since Brant and I already knew each other so completely, we fell fast and hard back into being a couple, except this time there was all the magic and none of the drama. Within a few weeks we were spending every night together, and planning our life. We got a miniature dachshund puppy together (Roscoe!). Brant told me that he thought being the father of a fur baby would be enough for him. He'd decided he didn't need the hassle of parenting human children. We'd get married, maybe get another puppy, all was right in our world. I felt happy and whole for the first time, maybe ever. I was drawing like crazy and developed two characters named Duckie and Lambie. Brant asked if he could "collaborate" with me by making Duckie and Lambie out of some FIMO I had lying around. I said of course. The two little colorful clay figures he created were charmingly imperfect, a symbol of our love. Though I never said it to him (as some things are both too beautiful and cheesy to be expressed in words), I always thought of him as Duckie and myself as Lambie.

But then after only three months of bliss, Brant became moody and distant. At night, he'd often forfeit sex for the numbing blue light of television. (You know I love curling up on the couch to watch a movie as much as the next person, but Brant was doing some high-schooler-on-summer-break level binging.) I tried everything from dragging him out for drinks, to a honey jar love spell. Sometimes I even just watched hours of television with him, since that's what he seemed to want to do. One night we were watching a Hallmark movie—this is embarrassing but will tell you what kind of state we were in—and when the pregnant teen girl gave birth to her baby, I looked over and saw that Brant was crying. "Shit," I said, trying to make light, "maybe we better get another wiener dog puppy, prontito."

"I miss my old life," he said. And I shuddered to think he might mean his old life with Cold Connie Caldwell. But when I pressed him for details, he clammed right up. The next day I was working the deli counter when I received an earth-shattering text:

I CAN'T BE WITH YOU ANYMORE. I WANT TO BREAK UP.

I had barely begun to process that one, when another arrived on its heels:

I'M GETTING BACK TOGETHER WITH CONNIE.

That was it. That ghosting motherfucker didn't answer another text or phone call from me. Ever. I left him long messages, I sent him a torrent of emails, but received nothing in reply.

My grief was profound and visceral. I threw up violently for days and took, weeping, to my bed. I considered beating on his door in the night or lying in wait for him outside the ambulance bay at his work, but my pride stopped me. But pride or no, I did need to get back my shit— I'd left half my scant wardrobe at his place.

Since I had a key to his duplex, I went there to gather my things one day when I knew he'd be at work on the ambulance. He had intuited I'd come and had left me a note—that's how well he knew me— that said:

Don't worry, Roxy. You'll find your way.

P.S. Do you mind if I keep Duckie & Lambie as, like, my thing?

How had I been in love with such a heartless, patronizing fuck?

In a blind fury, I wrote across the bottom of his note: You can have Duckie & Lambie and I hope you shove them up your ass!!!!

I packed my stuff in a hurry, but before I left, I pulled out strands of my long platinum hair and tucked them in his bed, his T-shirts, the zippers of his jeans, everywhere, so that dark-haired Cold Connie Caldwell would certainly find them. In the face of my great heartbreak, it was a pitiful rejoinder. But my innate sense of dignity prevented me from a Carrie Underwood "Before He Cheats" sort of attack. And of course the thought of Cold Connie Caldwell spotting one of my platinum strands dangling from Brant's zipper provided more satisfaction than taking a baseball bat to his Honda Civic ever could. Still, it was a lonely, broken-hearted satisfaction.

I was devastated. I saw all men as betrayers. But then you called me and we went out for smoothies and vegan hot dogs at JuiceLand, and I was reassured that not every man I've loved is a heartless flake. That was so healing, Everett, and I'm still grateful for the ways you've helped me.

Then came another heartbreaking twist in this sordid tale: the day I was walking through the Whole Body section of Whole Foods and saw a giant display for Duckie & Lambie moisturizer. On every bottle there was a photo of the brightly colored clay Duckie and Lambie that Brant had made. When I read the label I saw that the moisturizer contains DUCK FAT and LAMB'S MILK as the key ingredients. "What the fuck!" I yelled so loudly the Whole Body manager hustled me over to the bulk bins.

You know what a disaster I was after that. Finding out that Brant Bitterbrush used MY DUCKIE AND LAMBIE to create a moisturizer laden with animal products gave me instant and profound artist's block that I have still not been able to shake. I considered suing him for taking my original characters and using them to make a fortune off the suffering of animals—I planned to donate the proceeds to an animal shelter—but the lawyer I consulted said that since I'd given him written rights, I had no legal leg to stand on. Now that Annie's on the fifth floor, I've asked her to look into the company and see what she can find out.

It sucks to think that Brant ghosted me so heartlessly and yet now has the family of his dreams, while I am lovelorn and lonely. Since he left me, I haven't so much as been on a date. And the most horrible thing is, though Brant Bitterbrush has crushed my heart and my artistic drive, I miss him still.

I'm an emotional hot mess, Everett. And this is going to sound pitiful, but I really hope you don't move out right now.

Forlornly,
Roxy

CHAPTER THREE

Dear Everett,

When I came home from work three days ago Roscoe ran to me as usual, but instead of barking and wagging joyfully, he gazed up at me with sad, wet, devastated eyes. I wandered to what I now and perhaps will forever think of as "Everett's room." You'd stripped your sheets and put them in the washing machine, a move that to me seemed more dramatic than thoughtful. Even your loom and your Motörhead posters were gone. That's when I knew you had really moved out—you've left me to go live in an OM house.

I still haven't heard a word from you.

Today I was thinking about the night of my disastrous five-year high school reunion. (If comedy is tragedy plus time, then a five-year high school reunion is the equivalent of a joke told way too soon.) I never actually had a boyfriend in high school, as I was too weird and artsy to attract the attention of most Austin High School guys, but by five years out I had a great degree, was drawing and painting furiously, and felt good enough about myself to want to return in triumph with you on my arm. But by the time we left the reunion, I was furious at you. You'll recall your total social collapse at that event where, instead of chatting

with my fellow members of the class of 2002 while looking at me adoringly, you'd sulked at a table alone, binge eating chips and queso. But
then in the car on the way home, you told me you had a surprise for me.
We stopped at Magnolia Cafe for takeout love veggies and then hiked
down to the Hike and Bike Trail. In the dark we walked to the middle of
the MoPac Pedestrian Bridge spanning Town Lake and you showed me
how to climb over the rail and leap down three feet to the ledge jutting
from the pylon holding up the bridge. It was like having a silent, moonlit
private patio over the water all to ourselves. We sat down next to each
other, our backs against the pylon. "Does it matter if you were popular
in high school?" you asked me. "Or if you are 'successful' in life if you
can enjoy this?" And I knew then I was having more fun, and feeling
more understood, than anyone at that bullshit reunion.

So yes, I'd thought I would feel light and unburdened at your departure. But instead is it any wonder I am weepy and estranged (and also
rather angry you have left me living vulnerable and alone next to a drug
den)? Is it any wonder that I am still writing these letters to you, my
beautifully flawed friend who has always understood me, and has always
known the thing to say and do to make me feel better?

Owner of a Lonely Heart,
Roxy

P.S. Everett, while I would never actually admit this to you, I've started
wondering, "Why did I break up with Everett in the first place?" True,
due to your tight right psoas muscle, you are often unable to hold down
a low-wage job; and you are prone to nonsensical and boring monologues
about government conspiracies, but you're amazing with animals and
were actually decent in bed—and that was before all the OM practice
you've had since our breakup. Perhaps I should reconsider my hard
stance against revisiting a romantic relationship with you.

P.P.S. I just texted Artemis to float the idea by her and she said: "Getting back together with an ex-boyfriend is like eating your own vomit." I'm not sure I understand either the simile or her vehemence on the matter. Instead of being sympathetic that you've moved out, she's exuberant— but her excitement isn't contagious.

July 27, 2012

Dear Everett,

This morning I read over the past few letters I've written to you and I could see I have been cycling through the early stages of grief—shock, denial, pain, anger, depression, reflection, and loneliness.

So to try to shift my energy toward the "upward turn" stage of grief, I'm focusing today on the positive side of your move. To that end I did some quick banishing work to rid the house of bad energy, which involved sageing every room, then scrubbing everything down with a mixture of vinegar, salt, hot water, and rosemary. So far in my life I have only ever dabbled in witchcraft, a DIY sort of spirituality that is empowering to women, grounding, and requires no intermediary between the seeker and the spiritual world. I hope to one day (soon!) get it together to become a more regular practitioner.

I then went online to check out dating websites. Seeing all those headshots of smiling men reasonably close to my own age made me feel as if I was in a candy shop looking at a brightly colored wall of bins— they were delicious for my eyes to devour, but also gave me a sort of bellyache of the lower chakras. But my root chakra lit up like a lustrous ruby when I saw Patrick from Beer Alley's face smiling out at me! I don't have a profile so I couldn't message him. But it did assure me that he is single and looking for love, or at least some hot sex.

Stupidly, it made me wish you were here so I could tell you about it. We could have a good, old-fashioned argument about online dating versus meeting people in real life, or about Nest Life, or astrology, or whether or not "Girls" could be a more brilliant show if it would incorporate young women from a wider variety of cultural and socioeconomic backgrounds. But of course you are off in your Palace of OM, which I imagine as a falling-down old Victorian off of Manchaca Road that—despite the surgical gloves—would light up under a black light like a hazmat Christmas tree.

Perhaps the sageing and witch scrubbing have cleaned a film of denial from my eyes but, for whatever reason, the reality is finally sinking in—my love life and artistic endeavors are totally stagnant, my current pool of friends alarmingly small. At some point, changes will have to be made.

With great lethargy and sadness,
Roxy

P.S. I should call my old college pals Kate, Rosa, Yolanda, and Barclay at some point. Sure we grew apart as they settled into lives of office work and mediocrity, but they are extremely nice and sometimes make even stories about copier malfunctions amusing.

July 30, 2012

Dear Everett,

I'm eager to report I finally have something to write about other than my moping and sense of solitude at your departure. But how I wish it were a tale without a calamitous end! It all started yesterday when Artemis came into Whole Foods shortly after I started my shift. I was completely thrilled to see her—though we've been texting a bit, we haven't met up since our coffee at Spider House. Artemis asked if I wanted to go to Emo's with her after work. There was some band she wanted to see that started at 11 p.m. (Since you moved out I've mostly been working the 3 p.m. to 11 p.m. shift, and I have to RACE home on my thirty-minute break to give Roscoe his 8 p.m. insulin shot. Thanks for that!) When I told her I had to close and wouldn't have time to go home again and change, she said she'd bring me fresh clothes.

"But I'll be all deli greasy," I said.

"What size shoes do you wear?"

"An eleven," I said sheepishly.

While most people would exclaim over my gunboats, she didn't even raise an eyebrow. Such poker-faced acceptance is hard to find in this world. She peered over the deli counter at my pink Chuck Taylors. "I'll bring you a dress to match those," she said.

"There's no way I can squeeze my sexy haunches into anything you own," I said.

"Don't worry about it," she replied, and because I was so sick of staying home alone and moping, I didn't. Having just left her job at Trophy Wife's Overpriced Closet, Artemis was of course in her full Lululemon getup with her fake cherry-tomato diamond ring on her finger. She gazed over toward the cashiers.

"I'm really liking the looks of Register Number Ten," she said as she sailed off.

"His name is James and he has a girlfriend," I called out after her. This in no way slowed her down.

A little while later, Dirty Steve came out of his office to harass the deli maids. "Poxy Roxy, you look practically homeless," he said.

"Well, my outfit's cuter than a prison uniform," I said. "Right, Steve?"

"You're funny," Steve said. Then—in an uncharacteristic gesture of humility and friendship—Dirty Steve offered me a free California tuna roll from the deli case! Of course I normally do NOT eat tuna, but it seemed to indicate that Steve secretly, truly appreciated the help I provided in his escape from the police, so I graciously accepted his peace offering. Also, as you know, before I embraced my vegan lifestyle I was known to down dragon rolls like they were popcorn.

Despite witty repartee and friendly gestures from my high-class boss, the deli is just not the same with Annie upstairs working to save the quality of life of animals far and wide. That girl. I don't know how she does it. I mean, I adore animals and would love to help their well-being on a larger scale, but it's all I can do to take care of the furballs and stay (nearly) committed to a vegan diet. Is that sort of apathy a sign of depression?

I fear it may be. It's probably the reason I'm still stuck behind the deli counter with Jason and Nelson watching wealthy hippy women sporting "lovin' head" (i.e., a mess of tangled hair at the base of their necks that's a sure sign they've just gotten some lovin') contentedly push their grocery carts past the deli counter, as if still floating in a cloud of postcoital hormones. It makes me wonder—have they just been OMed? And if so, was it with you, Everett? Ugh. You can see how these sorts of thoughts would make for a very long shift.

On the plus side, Jason did tell us a funny story about almost being arrested while spray painting a mural on a train paused on the tracks over Lamar Boulevard last night. Together we complained about the Austin Police Department's obsession with vandalism. It's true I am getting to know Jason and Nelson a little better now that Annie and I aren't a constant band of two. I've also bonded with Nelson over how much we think children look like creepy little mini-humans. We've pinky sworn to never procreate.

Artemis appeared at 10:45 p.m. carrying a bag from Goodwill and wearing goddess sandals and a slinky black dress, her red hair in wild, shining curls. "You look amazing!" I said. I felt a tangled mix of envy and awe.

Of course, Dirty Steve appeared behind me just then. "Poxy," he said, "you could definitely get some tips from your pal here on how to dress."

The thing about Dirty Steve that really gets me is how sometimes his meanness is completely spot-on. But Artemis snapped back, "You look like you could use some help your own self. I think the Fashion Police have been arresting men for wearing white sneakers since 2003."

I chortled, but clearly Dirty Steve chose to see her cutting retort as some sort of flirtation, because he told me I could take off ten minutes early in a transparent attempt to try to impress Artemis with his "power."

Artemis and I made our way to the less frequented and thus relatively clean bathroom toward the back of the store, where Artemis whipped out a whole case of beauty supplies like some sort of makeover fairy. There was a battery-powered curling iron—like something out of a sci-fi movie written by a woman—some dry shampoo, and more makeup than you'd find backstage at "RuPaul's Drag Race."

"May I?" she asked.

"Have your way with me," I said.

Twenty minutes later I was transformed. No kidding, that girl knows about smoke and mirrors. "What do you have in the bag?" I asked.

"I went to the Gucci Goodwill in Tarrytown." She pulled out an off-the-shoulder gray dress and silver cowgirl booties in a size eleven, both of which were totally rock and roll and actually flattering. "What are you, a fairy godmother?" I asked. "I'm going to give you money for this."

"You can pay for my cover. And our first round of drinks."

When I was all dressed, Artemis said, "I got you one more thing." She pulled out a little box from Crystal Works and I opened it to find a gorgeous labradorite pendant on a silver chain.

"Holy Venus, Goddess of Friendship! It's so pretty. Labradorite, for—"

Artemis and I spoke the words at the same time: "Magic and protection."

"Thank you!" I said as I put it on. I was overwhelmed. The necklace was perfect, but the gesture was grand enough to be disconcerting. "Are you in love with me?"

"It'll help you get your groove back," she said.

"Who says I need to get my groove back?"

She raised her eyebrows. "When we met you were handing out samples of tuna burger."

"Shuuuuut uuuuuupppp!"

When we walked out to the parking lot, Artemis unlocked a black BMW with the click of a key fob. I climbed into the passenger side. The car smelled like new leather seats. "Damn," I said. "Where'd you get this? I mean, I know nothing about cars and even I can tell this is insanely nice."

"I hope it's nice enough to appease the Parking Gods," Artemis joked, and sure enough, we found a spot a half block from the club. Walking through the darkness with her, I realized it had been ages since I left the house to do something fun. Annie is amazing, but she hasn't been partying since she got her new job. And when you were living with me, dear Everett, we just watched TV together and ate vegan junk food, or I stayed home alone and drank and wrote you missives about things you were doing that annoyed me. It's all too easy to justify staying in when I make barely double minimum wage, am financially crushed by vet bills, and hardly have the funds for nightlife. Thoughts of my financial woes made me wonder how the hell Artemis could afford a BMW.

"But seriously, where'd you get that car?" I asked as we stood in the short line to get into Emo's. "Do you have—?"

"A trust fund? A sugar daddy? A boyfriend who robs banks? Yes, yes, and yes!" Artemis said as we arrived at the bouncer. I was happy to see it was Logan Ray Jones working the door. Logan is another one of those Austin guys who sees "keeping it real" as the ultimate success. His social media feed is like: "I'm working at Antone's Record Shop all afternoon. Come see me," along with a photo of Coltrane on vinyl. He and I slung thunder sauce together at ThunderCloud Subs years ago, so he waved me and Artemis in without charging either of us a cover. I may be broke but, in my own way, I've got this town wired.

Artemis and I stepped into the dark, dirty, graffitied world of Emo's. She dragged me through the crowd to the bar, which was three deep. "Since you're buying, I'll go hold us a place up front. You are going to love this band," Artemis said, and disappeared. When I finally made it to the bar myself, I caught the bartender's eye. But when I raised my hand to order he turned away. The next time he looked my way he stepped toward me, but then I felt someone slide in next to me and the bartender turned to him instead.

"My man," the bartender said. "What can I get you?"

"A club soda with lime," said the interloper.

Indignant, I turned to stare him down. "Excuse me! I've been waiting—" But I trailed off when I found myself face-to-face with Texas—the hottie from the vet's office. If he was surprised to see me, he didn't let on.

"Vet Girl! How's Charlize Theron?" he asked.

"Reluctant to let me shove a giant horse pill down her throat every morning, but otherwise recovering nicely. You shouldn't cut a lady at the bar." Everett, you know I'm as devoted as anyone to bringing down the kyriarchy, but I'm still not going to excuse a total lack of manners.

"I usually wouldn't but I'm late for work."

"Work." I rolled my eyes. "So that's what you call hanging out in a bar with a fresh drink?"

"Exactly." He grabbed his glass and slipped off the stool and into the crowd.

I finally ordered and before the bartender could set the two G&Ts down in front of me I heard a guitar strumming and the high-energy tapping of drums that sounded like happiness. I made my way through the crowd to Artemis, who eagerly took her drink and sucked away at her straw like a hummingbird at a flower. The band—four guys who called themselves FAIL BETTER!—played a dialed-up, rocking cover of Wilco's "Heavy Metal Drummer." The singer must have sewn himself into his pants with dental floss. "His name is Arsen Alton," Artemis said. "He's so fucking sexy."

When Arsen Alton sang "She fell in love with the drummer/She fell in love with the drummer," it of course reminded me to check out the drummer. And that's when I saw Texas WAS the drummer. He crooned into his mic, earnestly singing backup. I couldn't help but notice that, in addition to his nice pecs, he had great forearms, a ski-slope nose, and really lovely white teeth. Humph.

Artemis bumped my hip with hers to remind me to dance and so I did. The next time Texas sang "She fell in love with the drummer," he met my eye and winked, which caused Artemis to nudge me in the ribs and then head to the bar for another round. The next song was a Kiss cover—played all light and hipster-y like a Death Cab for Cutie number or something—which made me worry everyone in the band was way up their own asses. But on the whole, the set was actually fun, mostly original songs and all really danceable and upbeat.

Alas, two drinks in, instead of being ready to take my dance moves to the next level, I had started to feel a little queasy. Through the next two songs, I barely swayed on my feet, moved as much by a mounting nausea as by the beat of the drums. A light-headed sweatiness had come over me. I figured it was from the gin and the crowd and having worked all day and not really having eaten anything since that tuna sushi. When the band stopped to take a break, I told Artemis I needed to sit down, so we made our way through the crowd out to the back patio. I plunked down on one of the old picnic tables. "I feel really weird," I said. A deep nausea rolled through me, but then all of a sudden Texas sat down next to me. It was like he'd appeared out of nowhere, I swear.

"Great show," Artemis said.

I swallowed over and over as saliva filled my mouth; a mustache of sweat beaded my upper lip.

"Thanks," Texas said.

"How do you guys know each other?" Artemis asked, gesturing from me to Texas and back again, clearly eager to hear our meet-cute. I swallowed hard. "I'm not sick," I told myself. "I'm at the club. Everything is good. I got this." Meanwhile, my stomach felt like a bag full of wiener-dog puppies were wrestling around in it.

"We've never officially met," Texas said.

"I'm Roxy," I said.

"And I'm—"

"Texas," I said.

"We keep running into each other around town," Texas said. He looked me in the eye. "And every time, something really unexpected happens." I felt a jolt of electricity tingling through my body.

Suddenly the rockabilly supermodel I'd seen with Texas at Whole Foods appeared in front of us. "There you are!" she said. I looked up at her long mane of hair, styled in perfect waves. "I've been looking for you everywhere." She was clearly not pleased, but trying to rein in her annoyance. "Have you been hiding again?"

"Hide from you? Never," Texas said with a smile.

It was then that the most horrifying thing you could imagine happened—I leaned forward and threw up. Vomit splashed everywhere, including onto the rockabilly girl's nude, patent leather heels.

"Oh God!" the flawless beauty shrieked, jumping backward out of the spray.

I heaved again, so hard it made my stomach muscles cramp. Instead of recoiling, Texas took my elbow, but even the awareness of his hand on my skin didn't stop the next heave and splash. Artemis sat down on the other side of me, patting my back. "I got you, honey," she said. "I got you."

All of a sudden it came to me like a bolt of truth lightning and I yelled: "Dirty Steve! You bastard," and heaved again.

As soon as it seemed the heaving had subsided, Artemis said, "All clear for a minute?" I wiped my mouth, nodding.

Artemis helped me to my feet and hustled me out through the club. Another wave came over me but I fought it down until we were past Logan Ray Jones and on the sidewalk, where I threw up again ferociously.

"Get it, girl!" Logan yelled.

Immediately the wave of nausea was replaced by a great wave of euphoria that one only feels after a serious bout of puking has passed. "That's it for now," I said.

"Let's get you home, then," Artemis said.

Texas stepped outside, hurrying toward us. "Are you okay?"

"I'm fine," I yelled, a little wildly.

"I got her," Artemis said. "We're parked right there." She pointed toward her car.

"Parking angels. I'm not drunk, by the way," I said with all the haughtiness I could muster. One of Texas's eyebrows shot up. It might have been cute if I'd been in a better state.

"We're fine," Artemis insisted. She put her arm around me and we tottered off toward her car.

On the drive back to my house she had to pull over so I could lean out the car and puke until I was staring at a barf puddle. "Pull forward," I said, and Artemis rolled the car forward just a little so I had a fresh patch of pavement to look at as I barfed some more.

When we pulled up in front of my house, she said, "I'm going in with you."

Roscoe exploded into joyful yapping to see us. That's one thing about having pets—you never walk into your house and feel unloved or ignored.

"What an adorable wiener dog!" Artemis exclaimed.

I staggered into my bedroom, kicking off my new boots and peeling off my dress. "I'm sorry to ruin our fun night," I said, as I pulled back the covers and crawled into bed.

"You only had a couple drinks," she said from the doorway. "Do you have a stomach bug?"

"I think my boss Dirty Steve gave me some expired sushi as revenge for blackmailing him."

"That fucker," Artemis said, plopping down on the edge of my bed.

"I should have known better. Free sushi is never a bargain." That made her laugh. "What a dick," I heard myself saying, and I wasn't talking about Dirty Steve anymore. "I mean, that girl. She was about twenty-two and a giraffe."

"Probably his sister," Artemis said without missing a beat.

"Ha! In rom-coms it's always, like, his niece, right? But that was no-body's niece." My own voice sounded ominous.

"Don't worry about it. Drummers are always scrubs," she said. She lay down on top of the covers, her head on the pillow next to mine, her eyes on the ceiling. It was nice and reminded me of all the times back in college when Yolanda, Rose, Kate, and Barclay and I had stayed up late talking. "They're too afraid to take a front seat in life. Always hiding back there, looking sexy, unable to pay their bills."

"He definitely looks broke."

"Definitely."

"At least I got her shoes pretty good," I said. We both started giggling uncontrollably.

"That you did." We laughed a little more and then things quieted.

"Can I ask you a question?" I said.

"Shoot."

"When was the last time you had a real boyfriend, like, not just a hot guy to bang?"

Artemis laughed but there was no lightness to it. "I'm a little much for one guy to handle." She paused. "Sometimes I think no one would want to handle me for very long." Her face looked so sad.

"Of course they would. You have serious man trap!"

"Man trap? What kind of Roxy-ism is that?"

"It means guys like you. Like, a lot."

"But I don't trap them. The thing is, when it comes to me and guys . . ." She paused. I waited for what she was going to reveal, not daring to breathe. But then her face changed, as if she'd made a decision not to wallow, and she sat up. "I'm catch and release, baby," she joked as she leaned over and tugged the bedspread up under my chin. "Well, I'm gonna head out." She stood up and walked to the doorway.

"No way. We're lucky we didn't get pulled over on the way home— you had like six drinks. You can stay in Everett's old room," I said. "There are fresh sheets."

"I can drive."

"Don't be an idiot. I'm in no shape to go bail you out of jail."

"Okay," she said.

"I keep spare new toothbrushes in the cabinet."

"Of course you do."

"Artemis?"

"Yes."

"Thanks for the necklace."

"Sure thing. You deserve it."

I can't explain it, but when I heard the water running in the bathroom, it made me happy. There's truly something to having another human soul in the house.

Feeling both humiliated and well friended,

Roxy

P.S. As my spiral notebook fills with letters to you, letters I know I will never give you, I have to consider this as a bizarre new anti-phase to our friendship. And though you have "abandoned" me for a household of sexually venturesome OMers, it's refreshing to know I am capable of finding friendship and support elsewhere.

July 31, 2012

Dear Everett,

I feel so much better today—though considerably weakened, I am no longer sick. The vomiting that laid waste to my dignity was definitely food poisoning and not a virus. This morning I texted Annie and during her lunch break she came by to visit. As soon as I opened the door she said, "Oh man, you look terrible." In contrast, she looked fabulous, with big gold hoops and her hair in braids. She bustled in with her bag full of vegan broth, natural ginger ale, and gluten-free crackers. A moment later I was alternately sipping broth and telling her the whole story of what happened at Emo's.

"Dirty Steve is just wrong!" Annie said. "Do you want me to tell Topher Doyle he poisoned you with expired sushi?"

"I don't know," I said. "I don't think that's necessarily the best use of your proximity to power. Also, Artemis told me she thinks I should never rat out Dirty Steve, that I can just totally get revenge on him myself."

"The girl just sounds off," Annie said. "I mean, the things you've told me about her make her sound like some kind of sex-addicted mental patient. I'm not sure she should be a go-to person for life advice."

"Well, I think she's right about not involving Topher Doyle. It's like going to a Daddy-type authority figure for help with something I can figure out myself. If we want to tear down the patriarchy, we have to start by resisting the urge to ask Daddy figures to step in and solve our problems."

"Now you're feeling better!" Annie said. "Oh, and I have some good news for you. I looked into Duckie & Lambie Moisturizer, and it's totally aboveboard on animal treatment. They're sourcing everything from some small family farm. And they're only in Austin stores, so it's a real mom-and-pop operation."

"Great," I said lamely. But somehow it did not make me feel better. "Do you think you could convince Topher Doyle to stop stocking their products in Whole Foods stores anyway?"

"What happened to not turning to patriarchal figures to solve your problems?"

"Did you find out whose farm it is? Is it Cold Connie Caldwell's family farm?" I asked. "And how much is that company making? Could you find that out too?"

"Look, I'm sorry your ex was a dickhead. Really sorry. And I'm sad he stole your artwork and is using it to a hideous end. But I love you enough to cut you off from an ex-boyfriend shame spiral," she said. "So I'm gonna talk about myself now." She then told me about a crush she's developed on the two identical twins—Jeff and Joe Castro—who work at the Whole Foods IT help desk. She says she wants to ask one of them out, but isn't sure how to decide which one, since she can't tell them apart. It was so good to see her and hear about her fifth-floor antics, and the broth really made me feel better. I also appreciated that she looked into the moisturizing company that shall not be named. She's a real friend. When she left to go back to work I made her promise not to be a stranger.

Poisoned by my lack of self-discipline as a vegan,
Roxy

August 1, 2012

Dear Everett,

Yesterday after Annie left I lolled around the house alternately reading Tom Robbins, masturbating to Silky Raven, and wishing you hadn't moved out so you could bring me glasses of water and saltines. Then I spent a considerable (perhaps embarrassing) amount of time trying to find out more about Texas, FAIL BETTER!'s drummer. The band's website revealed that his full name is Texas Johnson, which I have to admit is pretty cute. So cute it's only a millimeter to the left of annoying. I found an "Austin Chronicle" profile of the band from last year, but it mostly talked about Arsen Alton, the skinny jean–clad front man who isn't my type.

I figured maybe I could find out more about Texas via some deeper cybersleuthing, but a thorough Google search of "Texas Johnson" turned up nothing at all. I had no luck with a Whitepages search either. His lack of a Google-able job or residence means that Artemis must be right—he is a total scrub, likely unemployed, maybe even couch surfing. I'm disappointed that in the twenty-first century, when privacy has allegedly ceased to exist, I am unable to dig up more info on a guy that I absolutely do not have a crush on.

Artemis texted me demanding I meet her out for a late afternoon beer. (I insisted we meet at Spider House again so she could drink IPAs while I imbibed a chamomile tea—my innards are still not up for alcohol!) There she cheered me up tremendously. She told me that my clash with Dirty Steve is more of a long-term war than a single skirmish. I won a round by keeping my job. He won a round by poisoning me. But the war isn't over and I need not be discouraged but rather should keep my eyes peeled for opportunities to strike out at him again. (Looking back on it now, this reasoning seems less sound than it did at the time, but it really did cheer me up, which is perhaps all that matters.)

I then confessed that I'd spent enough time cyberstalking Texas to give myself a mild case of blue-light poisoning and that I was still mortified about the vomiting incident. Artemis insisted I didn't need to worry about what some drummer thinks about me as:

1. I don't even know Texas; and

2. Because he's

    a. cute, and

    b. a drummer,
        he's probably a buster/scrub who relies on women to
        support him and thinks a date is meeting at Tacodeli
        for breakfast tacos, which the woman pays for.

She also pointed out that my yelling "Dirty Steve!" as I was projectile vomiting onto the nude pumps of Texas's model-looking girlfriend (or niece?) was a sort of Dadaist feminist manifesto that was brilliant, hilarious, and surreal; and that Artemis (and likely the lanky girlfriend) will remember for all time.

That got me laughing—sort of in horror at myself—but still, I'll take it.

She also said—commanded, really—that I need to go ahead and ask out Patrick from Beer Alley. We discussed a strategy as well as first-date ideas and, as nervous as it makes me, I think she's right! It's time to bust myself out of this celibate rut! But sitting in the coffee shop for hours with a new friend also reminded me that nothing—not even a hot date with a sexy skater—can replace girlfriends. I sometimes wonder if straight women fed up with men shouldn't just live in a big house together, going to private bedrooms for merman time and reconvening for spirit-raising socializing. See, Everett! Your guru Nina Sylvester isn't the only one who can envision a different kind of sexual utopia/dystopia.

I'm headed in to work tomorrow and Patrick better watch himself. Dirty Steve better watch himself, too, but in a defensive rather than a sexual way! (Though Artemis did warn me not to escalate the battle immediately but rather to lay low in the manner of a strategic student of "The Art of War.") I asked her if I should envision myself as Durga, a goddess with countless arms, each hand holding a different weapon, and thus prepared for any type of battle—be it one of vengeance or romance. Artemis looked bewildered, but said sure.

Empoweredly,
Roxy

August 2, 2012

Dear Everett,

I woke up this morning thrilled and trepidatious to know today is the day I would finally ask Patrick out. I put on my labradorite necklace from Artemis and as I dolled myself up with some of Durga's weapons—a little concealer, blush, and mascara—I thought of Artemis's advice that my invitation should be casual. "Nothing is more likely to scare off a slacker Austin guy than the threat of a REAL DATE!" she explained. "Invite him over for a home-cooked meal and he's one hundred percent sure to stand you up. Ask him to meet you for a cheap beer in a dive bar and he's ninety-eight percent likely to show." (In lieu of biking, I drove with the air-conditioning cranked. I feared that if I pedaled into work in this heat, by the time I arrived I'd have sweated off all the makeup.)

When Dirty Steve smirked at me and asked me how my night at Emo's went, I said, "Fantastic! I saw one of the greatest live shows of my life." (The ability to conceal and reveal information as needed is another one of Durga's weapons!) The quiver of disappointment in his face told me that he had indeed purposefully food poisoned me. I wanted to confront him right then, but I need this stupid job—not only does it cover my mortgage and provide benefits, it also offers me "free" groceries. And as they say: revenge is a dish best served cold (an expression with which Dirty Steve is clearly familiar because that past-its-prime sushi came straight out of the refrigerator case).

During a lull between customers, Nelson relayed to me that Jason was arrested last night for spray-painting "Stop Gentrifying East Austin" on stop signs on Holly Street.

"That's insane!" I said. First, we natives of Austin cannot expect to stand by silently while everything we love about this city is destroyed. Second, what the fuck, cops? They seem to think it's fine for white tweakers to cook meth night and day in a van on the south side. Law enforcement cannot be bothered to rouse themselves for such calls, chalking it up to the norm of a "hippy neighborhood." Meanwhile, free speech by a young man of color in the form of perceived "vandalism" is an arrestable offense. My outrage about the whole issue was enervating.

It's strange to say, but I felt generally energized and buoyed up, and not just by indignation at Jason's arrest. In some way my disastrous puking, followed by the excellent pep talk from Artemis, has popped me out of my melancholy surrounding your egress and has imbued me with a carpe diem sort of feeling, not in a clichéd, modern-day mistranslated "Seize the Day" sort of way, but rather in the original sense that Horace intended in his great work "Odes" (23 BC). The literal translation of the phrase would be "pluck the day [as it is ripe]." It was time to use my newfound energy to pluck that tasty snack and a half, Patrick, right off the Beer Alley vine! On my break I went to the bathroom and put on a little more blush—to channel that rosy-cheeked goddess Venus—and then headed to the other side of the store. Sure enough, when I sailed through the sliding glass doors into the refrigerated Beer Alley, lined on both sides with every domestic and exotic beer imaginable (and all of them overpriced), there was Patrick stocking shelves.

"Hey, Patrick," I said. "Any chance you have any Pliny the Elder?" Jason and Nelson often wax poetic about how Pliny the Elder is a beer both delicious and difficult to obtain. Apparently Pliny shipments arrive every first and third Thursday, and the beer is sold out by Friday noon.

"You like Pliny?" Patrick asked. His eyes lit up and I could feel them run the length of my body, as if taking the (physical) measure of a woman with such exquisite taste buds. (Luckily I'd removed my dirty deli maid apron before heading over to Beer Alley.)

"Delicious," I said, afraid if I started throwing in words like "hoppy" or "chocolatey" I would miss the mark since I've never actually tried Pliny myself.

"I've got a special stash. What time do you get off? I'm going to the skate park after work. Maybe you could come watch me skate while you drink a Pliny?"

All praise to Venus, Goddess of Love, I didn't even need to ask him out! I just had to radiate a seductive energy and HE asked ME out. Artemis is a genius. But then the lameness of his offer began to sink in. Being from Austin, Patrick's proposition should not have confused me. But still it took me aback for a moment. I am twenty-eight years old and Patrick is a couple years older, and yet this technically grown man had just invited me to drink beer while I watch him skateboard? Artemis had warned me, but this date seemed considerably lamer even than meeting for a beer in a dive bar, which would at least be air-conditioned. I mentally wished I had a headset in my ear being manned by Artemis who could guide my response.

"What do you think?" Patrick said.

"I might have this thing," I said.

"That's cool."

"Let me check. Can I tell you, like, right before I get off?"

"Sure."

I ran outside and called Artemis, who picked up on the first ring. I described the situation to her.

"He's hot, right?" she asked.

"YES!" I said.

"So duh! Do it!"

"But I'm almost thirty."

"So what if he's a man-child? You think those cashiers I hook up with are going to take me to the opera?"

"Good point."

"Go tell him yes, and then sit on the edge of that skate park and get yourself a buzz, girl."

On the way back to Beer Alley I realized perhaps having to consult with a friend as to whether or not I should accept the skate park invitation was almost as childish as the invitation itself.

Patrick looked surprised to see me appear again so soon.

"I'm in," I said.

When he smiled I could see his teeth were straight and a glorious white, and I wondered for a split second if he had parents who had paid thousands in orthodontic fees when he was a child and how they felt about his current occupation and hobbies. But I pushed the thought out of my mind. In Austin, isn't everyone in my tribe well educated and underemployed? And doesn't it mean something to stay true to our passions and fundamental sense of integrity rather than sell out to bullshit societal expectations?

The skate park is just three blocks away from Whole Foods, tucked back behind Ninth and Lamar. Since Patrick got off work an hour before I did, I walked over to meet him there. I arrived, glazed in sweat, to find Patrick sitting under a tree with a backpack and his skateboard. He told me he was stoked I had come, then he popped the top off a Pliny wrapped in a brown paper bag.

"For you," he said, and handed it to me.

"Thanks," I said, and took a swig. It actually was delicious.

As I sipped, I surveyed the surroundings. Dozens of skaters whizzed around the concrete bowls. Teenage girls sat around the edge of the park in clumps, giggling, pushing each other on the shoulder, reapplying lip gloss or fiddling with their hair.

"There are more grown men skating than I thought there'd be."

"It can be hard to stick with it sometimes. But I'm here almost every day," Patrick beamed.

I felt my eyes grow wide and took a second slug of Pliny to avoid responding.

"I've got another one in my backpack with an opener," Patrick said. "Help yourself."

Then he turned and dropped down into the bowl on his skateboard with a sort of casual, magnificent, animal grace rarely seen in an urban environment. I wanted to judge him—for his job in Beer Alley, for his hobby of whizzing around and around a concrete bowl in the ground on a little board with wheels on it. But as I drank the Pliny in the sun-dappled shade, a breeze blowing through my hair, I realized I truly respected his dedication to a simple lifestyle, a Zen pursuit of the physical, an utter lack of status-seeking (perhaps even a pride in that lack of status-seeking?)

As I started in on my second bottle of Pliny, a teenage girl near me pulled out a makeup mirror and reapplied her eyeliner. Why, I wondered, in the twenty-first century, were there no women or girls skating? I literally did not spy a single one. Everett, thanks to Title IX, we've made tremendous progress in team sports, but this skate park remained utterly devoid of female participants. I tried to remember what I was up to when I was nine or ten, the age Patrick likely had been when he got his first skateboard. Had I been watching television? Playing with my pink convertible Barbie car? Holed up in a corner reading a book in an effort to find the intellectual stimulation my public school education lacked, while simultaneously trying to deny the existence of my physical body, which would soon betray me utterly by going through puberty and growing cumbersome boobs and an ass I perceived as oversized?

By the time I was halfway through my second bottle of Pliny I approached the teenage girls with a friendly swagger. "Mind if I join y'all?" I asked.

They shrugged. I sat.

"How come y'all don't skate?" I said, in a way that was very casual. I started to feel a bit like an immersion journalist. Like Joan Didion in Haight-Ashbury in 1967, plunged into the youth culture.

Again, the girls shrugged.

"It doesn't have to be just for guys, you know," I said in a way that was more inspiring than didactic.

A blond girl with corkscrew curls looked skeptical. "But you don't skate," she said. "I mean, you're too old." Ouch! It reminded me of the part in Joan Didion's essay "Slouching Toward Bethlehem" when a bunch of dropout kids in the Haight told Didion that at thirty-two, she could perhaps aspire to being "an old hippy." Did she take it personally? Hell no. Instead she used it as witty fuel for her scathing exposé.

I realized it then. These girls needed a role model, an inspiration. Someone who wouldn't tell them girls could skate, too, but would rather show them. Patrick popped up over the rim and said, "Hey, glad you made some friends."

"Actually, I was just going to show them that skating doesn't have to be a pillar of the kyriarchy," I said.

"The what?"

"The kyriarchy," I said. "You know, a set of connecting social systems built around domination, oppression, and submission. Sexism, racism, classism—all the 'isms' combine to make up the kyriarchy."

He still looked confused.

"Never mind. Just give me your board."

"What?"

"Give me your board. Just for a minute." Doubtfully, he held the skateboard out to me. Even buzzed on Pliny, I knew better than to try to skate the bowl. Instead I put the board down and stood on it with one foot, pushing myself along with the other. I put both feet on the board and suddenly I was flying along. It was exhilarating, magical, so much easier than it looked. I couldn't believe I had missed out on this glory all my life. The wind caused my hair to stream behind me. I was goddess-like, an inspiration even to myself—the alternative sports role model I'd never had. "See!" I yelled so that the teenage girls could hear me. "Sisters are doing it for themselves!"

Just as I sailed out from under the shade of the giant tree and into the blinding light of the August sun, the board shot out from under me. The top half of my body fell in slow motion, arms akimbo as if trying to find some nonexistent purchase, while the bottom half of my body moved at the speed of a gunshot, my legs flying into the air as if I was a cartoon man who'd just slipped on a banana peel. I landed on my tailbone with the most insane sensation of my entire spine cracking, vertebra by vertebra. I'm embarrassed to say it, Everett, but I started to cry.

Patrick rushed over, asking, "Are you okay?"

No, I wasn't okay. It took Patrick and two of the teenage girls to get me to my feet. Patrick had skated to work, but one of the girls volunteered to drop us off at the emergency room. "I'm not ready for this crazy-ass shit to end" were her exact words. I rode in front and the blond girl drove. Patrick was crammed in the backseat with three other teenage sylphs, which I worry he was actually enjoying.

"Y'all are lifesavers!" he said, when they dropped us off at the door of the ER.

Diagnosis: bruised tailbone. Treatment: sit on a donut pillow for the next six weeks. (It hurt so badly I was very slightly disappointed nothing was broken.)

When I came out with the donut pillow, Patrick and I both started laughing. He insisted on paying for an Uber to Ken's Donuts on Guadalupe, so I could sit on my donut pillow while eating an actual donut. In the Uber we were giggling and talking really easily, as if my fall from the skateboard hadn't just practically cracked my tailbone, but had also broken open the awkwardness between us.

Once we settled into a table with our donuts I said, "Maybe there's a reason no one learns to skate when they are in their late twenties."

He laughed.

"I'm sorry if I wrecked your street cred," I said.

"At the skate park where you busted your ass? Or here at Ken's Donuts where I'm being seen with a woman sitting on a donut pillow?"

"Shut uuuuppppp!" I said. Flirting made the pain recede a little. He leaned forward and kissed me, lightly, on the lips. I had a bite of donut in my mouth so I couldn't really advance the kiss, but it was still nice and (pun intended) very sweet.

Since I am out of practice at sex and have a bruised ass, I decided that in lieu of trying to further our sexual relationship, I'd better call it a day. Patrick had his skateboard, so I insisted on ordering my own Uber to take me back to my car, which was still in the Whole Foods parking lot.

As I placed my donut pillow in the backseat and climbed inside, Patrick said, "I had fun with you today." And then he smiled his orthodontically perfect smile, and closed the car door.

As soon as I got home I ran to my room and whipped out the merman. It took me a bit to get settled on the donut pillow, but after that it didn't take a minute at all.

Pluck the day, Everett, for it is ripe,
Roxy

CHAPTER FOUR

August 4, 2012

Dear Everett,

I woke up yesterday in a panic thinking about the inevitable ER bills I'm going to receive, and with an insane pain in my tailbone to boot.

My mortgage was due last week and I paid it in full myself. But now my bank account is down to almost zero and I'm still paying down the vet bills from when Roscoe got into my dirty laundry hamper and ate the crotches out of my underwear. I can't help thinking about you holed up in some disgusting OM den while I'm here alone trying to keep myself afloat financially. I've been considering putting a "Room for Rent" flyer up on the bulletin board at work, but as you know, this house is small and the thought of sharing it with someone I hardly know seems daunting to me and potentially traumatizing to the furballs. Perhaps the pain in my tailbone makes the possibility seem even bleaker than it really is.

So I broke down and called my parents.

They put me on speakerphone, of course, and I told them about my fall, leaving out Pliny the Elder and even Patrick.

"Tell me again what you were doing at a skate park?" my mother asked.

"I told you, mentoring at-risk teenage girls. They were clearly desperate for guidance."

"But you don't even know how to skate," my father said, bewildered.

"A recent Harvard medical study showed that sixty-two percent of personal bankruptcies result from medical expenses," I said, bringing us back to the point. "I am responsible. I have health insurance through my job, but the deductible is two grand."

"Just mail us the medical bills when they come in," my father said with his usual droll calm. "We'll pay them." Since he's a retired dentist, he understands the way that medical expenses can crush a person.

"Thanks, Daddy," I said, almost gagging at the sound of my own self-infantilization.

When I was younger, hitting my parents up for money didn't sting. But now that I'm in my late twenties, working almost full-time and still unable to pay my medical and vet bills, it feels humiliating! It's so freaking hard to be a grown-up! I'm almost thirty and still can't seem to manage on my own. It makes me question my own Austin slacker ethos, which emphasizes "cool" employment over actual financial stability. But what well-paid job am I even qualified for?

Today Annie met me outside the store on my break so I could show her my donut pillow. "Artemis is going to make so much fun of me," I said.

"When do I get to meet the famous Artemis?" Annie asked, her voice dripping with envy that I have a new friend.

"Um, at some point," I mumbled. Annie and Artemis will HATE each other, so I'm not in a hurry to introduce them. Annie is mono-focused on career advancement in the name of animal rights, while Artemis is obsessed with her own brand of artifice and sexuality. If they ever met, each would find the other's interests incomprehensible. And I'm sure they would be vying for status as my best friend, making it impossible for them to spend time together without a landscape of iciness and resentment.

"I don't need to meet her to know she's a questionable influence," Annie said.

To change the subject, I asked Annie for advice on Patrick. She said I should wait for Patrick to call me, or for us to naturally run into each other at work. "He's a man-child," she said, "and man-children balk if they feel pursued."

"I'm not going to pursue him," I said, though I'd been planning on cruising Beer Alley on my next break. Annie took me to hang out for a bit on the fifth floor. She's finally asked out one of the IT help desk identical twins. The only problem is she doesn't know if it was Jeff or Joe. We cruised by the IT desk and she waved breezily at both twins, who are smoking hot individually, but next to each other are smoking hot squared.

Not only is Annie's love life perking up, she's already convinced Topher Doyle that Whole Foods should only source lobster from ethical "growers" who require two cubic feet of aquarium tank space per lobster. She's also made him agree to give 10 percent of local store proceeds one day a month to Austin Pets Alive!, everyone's favorite no-kill shelter. She's been at her new job for only six weeks and already she's making a real difference in the lives of countless animals. (One thing she hasn't done is rid the store of the moisturizer everybody loves to hate—Duckie & Lambie.) Though I feigned happiness for her, she could of course sense I was moping internally. (I wonder what percentage of female "joy" at the success of our friends is actually false performance, little bouts of emotional labor that barely cover our own feelings of inadequacy and jealousy?)

"What about you? Could you try a little watercolor or something?" Annie asked. "Now that Everett's out of the house, you've got no distractions."

"Ugh," I said. "It's hard to explain how paralyzing it is to have had my art stolen from me and used for a purpose anathema to my beliefs. And to support the ex–love of my life and his new brood!"

Annie looked at me like she wanted to stab me AND Brant Bitter-brush. "How about something nonartistic, then? I've read it's good to do something else creative if you are feeling a little blocked. Cook a colorful stew or whatever."

"I'm not cooking a fucking stew."

"But what would you LOVE to do, just for fun, to get you out of this rut?"

There is something I've been thinking about ever since I read Dear Sugar's advice on how to get "unstuck," but I was reluctant to tell anyone, even Annie, because it sounded so crazy. "I do have this one idea. This one thing I feel passionate about," I said. "But maybe it's totally ridiculous."

"Well, what is it?" Annie demanded.

I took a deep breath, a little worried that if I said it out loud, somehow I would have to follow through on it. And how would that change my life? It's impossible to say. "I want to tackle the Lululemon at Sixth and Lamar to the motherfucking ground."

"What does that even mean?" Annie asked.

"It means, I want to force it to close down, to move the fuck out of that location."

"How?"

"I don't know. Organize a protest. A store boycott. Whatever."

"YES!" Annie yelped. "And you could make all the signs yourself. So you're taking social action and making art. Or at least making something."

I had expected Annie to say the idea was a clear no-go. Her enthusiasm caused me to backpedal. "I wasn't serious."

"Maybe you should be."

"I'll think about it. But for now I've got to get back to the deli."

Annie walked me to the elevator, and when the doors dinged, she gave me a kiss on the cheek. As I entered and the doors began to close, she yelled, "Don't pursue the man-child!"

Back in the store I felt a pull to Beer Alley, but instead muttered to myself, "Man-child, man-child," as I headed back to the deli. I stuffed my donut pillow in my locker and got back to work, all the while scanning the store for signs of Patrick headed toward the deli. Surely he would get hungry and come over on his break? I know how he loves our revolting chicken salad.

But it was Artemis I spotted headed my way. As she pretended to order large amounts of food from the deli and I pretended to package it for her, I whispered a quick account of the skate park incident. "So did you . . . ?" she asked, using her signature lewd finger gesture.

"I mean, we kissed in Ken's Donuts."

She rolled her eyes. "Have I taught you nothing?"

I shrugged and then explained Annie's theory about man-children.

"You're not planning to ask him to marry you!" Artemis said. "You just want to break your dry spell."

True. It's confusing how convincing she and Annie both can be in the moment. I tried to bring my own philosophical convictions to the situation but felt overwhelmingly that if I could just hang out with Patrick—man-child or not—it would cheer me up and perhaps even alleviate the pain in my tailbone.

"Next time you have a break, saunter over there to Beer Alley and say hello. And after work, meet me over at Deep Eddy Cabaret for a beer," Artemis said. "Oh, and bring your friend Annie. I'm dying to meet her."

There's no way I'm putting those two in the same room. "I'll meet you at six thirty," I said.

When I arrived at Deep Eddy, Willie Nelson was playing on the jukebox as usual, his voice soothing, every word he crooned a reminder to everyone in the bar that we are not alone in this world—we all have Willie to guide us. Artemis was already there, settled in at a table under an old Shiner Bock ad. As I sat down, my phone dinged. Though, as you know, I loathe technology and only have a smartphone for bare bones social reasons and in case of pet emergencies, I could not resist checking the email. It was from the Bucknether Art Competition! I'm a quarterfinalist! And in only three weeks they should announce the finalists! I was so excited I blurted out the news to Artemis.

She leapt up and gave me the hugest hug. "Oh my God, I'm so fucking excited for you!" she said. Then she looked flustered. "I'll be right back." She ducked out the front door. Everett, it was weird—she just left me—but I was getting sort of used to Artemis's unpredictable nature. It was part of her charm. I went up to the bar and ordered a Lone Star, which I was halfway through when Artemis burst back through the door waving a bottle of champagne. She popped the cork and yelled, "Congratulations!"

"You can't bring that in here," Lulah the bartender said. You probably know Lulah? She's a tough lady in her fifties, the type who doesn't put up with any shit. I held my breath.

"Lulah, I'm toasting my friend," Artemis said. "Have a glass on me."

And sure enough, Lulah set out three more pint glasses and Artemis poured her a half pint of champagne and then brought the bottle and the other glasses over to me. That's when I saw the label on the bottle. Dom Pérignon Brut Rosé 1998. "Shit, Artemis, where'd you get that?"

"At the liquor store just down Lake Austin Boulevard," she said, gesturing in that direction. She poured us each some champagne, then took a swig off the bottle. "Delicious," she said approvingly. "What was that Tom Robbins line about champagne? 'I'm drinking stars, I'm drinking stars!'"

I took a tentative sip. It tasted incredible. "How much did that bottle cost? Did you pay for it?"

"Of course I paid for it. It was like three hundred bucks."

"Artemis!" I said, shocked. Her love language is clearly extravagant gift giving. Shit, maybe she really does have a trust fund or a sugar daddy.

"My girl can't drink swill the night she finds out she won the Bellwether Award."

"Bucknether. And I'm only a quarterfinalist."

"So far!" she said. "You did it. You motherfucking went for something. And it's paying off. If that isn't worth celebrating—" She drank again out of the bottle. "So, world conqueror, what's up next for you?"

For a moment, I wasn't sure if I should press the issue of the champagne. I mean, did she fucking steal it? Or did she really spend $300 on it? I'm not even sure which would make me feel weirder. But she seemed really happy for me (and not like she was doing emotional labor pretending to be happy, but who knows?). So instead of pushing the champagne issue, I let myself be carried along on the wave of her enthusiasm. "Well, I have been thinking about this one project."

"Spill," she demanded.

"This champagne is so good."

"You're coy as a virgin on prom night."

"I don't know," I said. "I thought my whole idea was just me being aggro and contrary, but I told Annie and she was all for it, which surprised me."

"Well, what the hell is it?" Artemis asked.

So I told her about my ridiculous idea to protest Lululemon.

"Genius!" Artemis said.

"But you WORK there," I said in mock objection. The champagne and Artemis's gusto had combined to make me giddy.

"So what? It's a stupid fucking soulless store. I know the clothes are crazy flattering (and more durable than the hype implies), but I still think you should make it your mission to TAKE. THAT. STORE. DOWN. You're always complaining about how it's a symbol of the death of the spirit of your hometown."

I feel strangely as if Annie and Artemis, rather than being my friends, are my divorced lesbian mothers who have never before agreed on anything in their lives and now are agreeing on this one bizarre, ludicrous idea. "Men love protesters," Artemis added.

"That's not the point!" I yelled. Artemis is so sex-crazed it sometimes seems to be a form of mania.

"I think you should do it. I really do. It might be just the thing to blast you out of this all-around rut you seem to be in." She pulled up a calendar on her phone. "Let's set a date. You need plenty of time to make a shit ton of protest signs, organize your strategy, get the word out via social media, blah blah blah."

"But we need to ensure the date is auspicious. Can you find a lunar calendar?"

Artemis navigated to a lunar calendar faster than a blink.

"I think a full moon would be just the thing—large gatherings are always more energized and successful during a full moon," I continued. "But we also have to do it on a weekend, so people can come."

"September thirtieth? It's a full moon and a Sunday."

"Perfection!" I said. September 30 it is.

While at the time I was high on Dom Pérignon, now that I am sober, I still have the tingling feeling I get when something really wild is about to happen. It's always a sign from Venus, my favorite planetary deity. But what is she trying to tell me?

Tinglingly,
Roxy

August 5, 2012

Dear Everett,

Today Artemis took me to Spider House for a double cappuccino with extra foam—and an espresso milkshake. I noticed when she ordered she told them her name was Larimar. (When I asked her about it she admitted she has a different "handle" for every coffee shop and bar in town. That girl's quirks are endless and fascinating.) Then when I was so hopped up on caffeine that all I wanted to do was BUY STUFF! and SPEND MONEY! she took me to Asel Art Supply, where I promptly bought $200 worth of sign-making supplies and put them on a credit card. By the time I made it through checkout, I had to pee desperately, so I went in the Asel bathroom, leaving my purse with Artemis.

She helped me load the sign-making stuff in my car and then hurried off. I was driving home when my phone dinged. I didn't look at it until the red light. But when I did, my heart lurched with excitement. It was a text from Patrick: SURE. WHAT'S YOUR ADDRESS?

My eyes scrolled up to read the text right above it. That's when I realized Artemis had texted him the following from my phone while I was in the bathroom:

HEY QT! WANT TO COME OVER TONIGHT AT 8? I'M MAKING SOME BOYCOTT SIGNS. YOU COULD HELP ME PAINT. DRINKS ON ME. WEAR SOMETHING SEXY.

I could kill that girl. I haven't shaved my legs in a week, my couch is covered in dog hair, I have no booze in the house, and it's already 6:30 p.m. Argh!

6:45 p.m.: I've vacuumed both sofas and the floor.

7:15 p.m.: I ran to the liquor store but became trapped in a vicious hell of indecision. What kind of alcohol do you buy for a hip yet immature thirtysomething skateboarder who works in an aisle of exotic beer?

I finally decided on Bulleit Bourbon and an ironic six-pack of Tecate in a can with lime. But then I realized they only had lime in a plastic lime-shaped squeeze bottle and not real lime, so I had to put the Tecate back. Finally I decided on an Oakland IPA microbrew. I don't know why the bottle has a cute drawing of artichokes on it. Hopefully Patrick will like artichoke-flavored beer?

7:30 p.m.: I've showered and shaved my armpits and legs, but despite societal pressures, I've left my power triangle wild and ungroomed. I was wavering on my commitment to this wild thatch of hair until I recently read Mario Vargas Llosa's "In Praise of the Stepmother." In the novel, Rigoberto is always delighting at having his wife's full pubis up his nose. I found it very inspiring in a manner utterly lacking in twenty-first-century American literature and film. The mention of pubis is absent in early twenty-first-century literature, while in film women are always pressuring one another to wax or go full Brazilian in the manner of prepubescent girls. Luckily for me, I'm sure the bush will make a comeback. It's great to be on the forefront of a fashion trend for once. Oops! It's 7:52 p.m. Where is my hairbrush?

8:03 p.m. Humph. He's not here yet. Will have a quick shot of bourbon to boost morale. This rushing around makes me feel ridiculous and slightly incompetent, in the manner of feminist anti-hero Bridget Jones.

8:13 p.m. Sign materials are out. I'm making a boycott sign whether Patrick shows up or not.

8:27 p.m. Doorbell ringing! Roscoe ecstatic! I think he's here!

Hurray!!!
Roxy

August 6, 2012

Dear Everett,

Patrick arrived last night without mentioning he was twenty-seven minutes late. But he pet Roscoe right away and seemed really happy about it. It's hard enough to date without wondering whether or not a man will fit in well with the furballs. And some guys can be such dicks about Roscoe's miniature stature. Patrick engaged in some gentle wrestling with Roscoe—one of his hands versus the little guy—then I put Roscoe outside, latching the dog door behind him, and poured drinks for us. I explained my hatred for Lululemon and my ideas for the protest, which will take place on Sunday, September 30. Patrick was very enthusiastic and we ranted together about the general downward trajectory of Austin.

"I feel like the city is, like, turning on us, man," Patrick said, "so that we can't even afford to live here anymore."

I did not want to tell him that I haven't drawn or painted in over six months—Venus gifted me with the insight that carrying on about Brant Bitterbrush, moisturizer, and betrayal would not be aphrodisiacal. So I boldly began to outline words on a sign. The first one read:

HONK IF YOU LOVE YOUR BODY

I gave Patrick very detailed instructions on exactly how the words should be filled in with paint. My next sign read: NO $100 TIGHTS, WE WANT OUR RIGHTS—TO BUY LOCAL. With Patrick's encouragement and the beer and bourbon lowering my inhibitions, I drew curvy girls, dollar signs, and symbols of the Austin we want to live in on our two signs. It felt glorious to put pen to paper. I found that drawing something totally low stakes (i.e., boycott signs that will not bear my signature but will rather be carried in the streets "by the people") was rather liberating. As Patrick and I passed each other markers and paints, electric sparks of sexual tension jumped between us. I have to admit, Everett, that while I have missed you at times, it was a relief to know you would not be barreling through the front door. Thus I would have no need to explain to Patrick who you are and how you fit into my life.

We got so drunk that I'm not sure who kissed who first, but he fucked me on the floor of the living room. (We had to pause the proceedings for me to find the donut pillow and properly position it beneath my bruised coccyx.) He was on top and I didn't come, but I told myself it was because my tailbone hurt a little. It was still hot, especially because of that totally ripped little skater body of his.

We went for Round Two in my bedroom, doggy-style, and I was SURE he'd give me the reach around, but he didn't so I rubbed my own clit. However, I've been using the merman so regularly that non-battery-powered stimulation was slow going and Patrick came before I could. (There's a movement among witchy women to use sex toys made out of crystals such as rose quartz and amethyst, thus avoiding the overstimulation trap of the battery-powered sex toy, and while I have no inherent urge to rub myself off on a rock, I'm starting to see their point.) Then Patrick passed out immediately, snoring in a way that would have been cute had I not been so hot and bothered.

I knew I'd never sleep if I didn't get off, so I pulled out the merman—its buzz didn't even stir Patrick, that's how out he was. It was simultaneously fantastic to finally have an adorable man in my bed, and mildly depressing to STILL be revving up the merman in order to orgasm. But when I came, I shuddered so hard it woke Patrick. He panicked, grabbing a pillow and shoving the corner of it between my teeth. When I yanked out the pillow I yelled, "What are you doing?"

"I was trying to keep you from biting your own tongue while you were seizing," he yelled back, clearly in a panic.

"That wasn't a seizure! I was having an orgasm," I said. We eventually laughed it off awkwardly and then we both went to sleep.

I was hoping Patrick would get me off in the morning, but as soon as he woke up he said he was late to meet his roommate (??) and hurried out with nothing but a quick kiss.

Now I feel rather dreamy at having lost my post–Brant Bitterbrush born-again-virginity and hope Patrick and I can have another go at doing the do—a go that will surely involve a little more attention paid to my clitoris.

Dreamily,
Roxy

August 7, 2012

Dear Everett,

Yesterday before my shift started I texted Annie to meet me out back near where I like to have my kombucha break (because frequent work breaks aren't just for smokers anymore!). I told her about my sign-painting night with Patrick. But she was more excited about the fact that I was doing some sort of art than she was about my sex life.

So I texted Artemis to meet me for a drink after work. For the rest of my shift I kept cruising Beer Alley on my breaks, but there was no sign of Patrick.

When I left Whole Foods, I rode my bike home to give Roscoe his insulin shot, then down to the Mean-Eyed Cat. It was so muggy I was covered in sweat by the time I got there, and the bar was so jam-packed that we decided to go to Deep Eddy Cabaret instead. (How clearly I remember the time when I could always find a table at any bar in town. Oh, the pain of enduring the overcrowding of a city that was once perfection!) I think the stress made my tailbone hurt and I'd left my donut pillow at home, so I stood up at the bar as I told Artemis the whole story.

"Oh no! Not another lazy Austin buster who thinks sleeping with a woman is just about looking good and thrusting!" she cried.

"But what about when you hook up with cashiers in the parking lot?" I asked. "Do they pay attention to your clit?"

"Parking lot sex is down and dirty. It's fast and furious. But you were having sex in your house IN. A. BED! He needs to be paying homage to the princess AND her pea."

When I recounted the merman seizure incident she laughed so hard she snorted, but then quickly adopted a serious expression. "But really, you gotta lay off that battery-powered shit. Get to work, girl. Manual labor." She waggled her pointer finger at me. "You rely on the vibrator, you become its slave."

She might have a point.

Manually,
Roxy

August 10, 2012

Dear Everett,

In a decisive move, I boxed up the purple merman and put him on a shelf in the garage, then practiced masturbating to literotica.com with only manual stimulation. After forty-five minutes of enjoyable yet ultimately frustrating reading and self-pleasuring, I gave up. I had not realized that during my last celibate year the merman had overstimulated my clitoris to a prohibitive degree. I am now on a mission to recalibrate. Also, I now realize that Patrick cannot be blamed for my failure to orgasm, as currently orgasm via nonbattery-powered means seems to be impossible.

It's been four days since Patrick and I did the do and he's only texted me once! I texted him back immediately, but received no further reply.

Discouragedly,
Roxy

August 12, 2012

Dear Everett,

It's been almost a week since my date with Patrick and I still haven't even seen him in person—he texted me again yesterday but the missive seemed decidedly lacking in energy and enthusiasm. I had a feeling I would see him today, so I spent extra time getting ready for work and thus made myself late, so I drove instead of riding my bike. I ended up sitting in traffic on Lamar Boulevard for almost half an hour. Oh, my aching tailbone! When I was a kid, it would have taken five minutes to drive the two miles north from my house to Sixth and Lamar. But today I would have made better time on my cruiser! I walked into work ten minutes late, at which point Dirty Steve yelled: "Poxy Roxy! How can you manage to be late for work when you don't even have to get here until three p.m.?"

"I was alternately painting protest signs and trying to dial 'O' on the pink telephone," I said.

"Yeah, right," he responded, but he seemed pleased at the repartee.

It was actually true—between the feverish sign painting and the feverish yet ultimately futile attempts at masturbation, I'd lost track of time. I feel frustrated yet determined at this post-merman orgasmic desert I'm in. But I'm sure the Princess and her Pea will overcome!

On the bright side: my creative juices seem to be flowing on the Lululemon protest-sign-painting project, perhaps not IN SPITE of the fact that it's not "real art" but because of it. The stakes are low and so my energy is high! This morning's sign read: HONK IF THEY DON'T SELL YOUR SIZE HERE. (Lululemon's "EXTRA LARGE" is a size twelve, which is infuriating given that the average American woman IS a size twelve.) I now have three completed signs. It's slow going, but the Temple of Venus wasn't built in a day.

As soon as I was behind the deli counter I started obsessing about when and if Patrick would stop by to say hi. Part of me wants an immediate redux of the other night, while part of me wants to hold off until I've successfully double-clicked the mouse. I finally broke down on my break and cruised Beer Alley. There he was, stocking the shelves with another IPA with a label featuring a pile of artichokes.

"Hey," I said. "When did artichoke-flavored beer get to be all the rage anyway?"

"Hey, Roxy! You're hilarious," he said. "Artichoke beer!" He laughed. "Hey, what are you up to tomorrow night?"

What was I supposed to say? That I'd be engaging in a ménage à moi in hopes of relearning my Goddess-given ability to climax without the aid of a purple plastic merman? "No plans."

"Want to meet at the Redbox at the H-E-B on East Riverside? We could rent a movie and go back to my place?"

"Um," I said, feeling a little put off by the lameness of the proposal. I am almost thirty years old, and while I don't expect to be taken to see Arcade Fire at an "Austin City Limits" taping or anything, a meet-up at the Redbox in a grocery store parking lot locally famous for drug deals seemed to show a considerable lack of effort on his part.

"I'll bring the beer," he said, gesturing around him. "Artichoke!" he said, and chuckled again. What was so funny?

"Um, no way am I meeting you at the Redbox. Why don't you pick the movie and I'll meet you at your place?" I said.

"All right," he said. He sounded like I'd hurt his feelings, but I'm not repentant. The East Riverside H-E-B parking lot is sketchy as fuck.

"Text me your address," I said. Is it too much to hope that a guy I've been on two sort-of-dates with (and screwed twice on the second sort-of-date) would ask me out for a beer and a slice before our next round of sex? Everett, when did men get so damn lazy? I mean, when you and I got together you were broke as fuck, but you at least sprung for the dollar movie at the theater and snuck in some candy and beer for us.

I sent Artemis and Annie an emergency group text to see if they could meet me for a beer after work. I was surprised they BOTH said yes. Now I'm off to rendezvous with them at the Horseshoe Lounge. The moment has come for them to meet! It can be avoided no longer! Wish me luck.

Later:

I arrived at the Horseshoe Lounge to find Annie and Artemis sitting at the bar. Annie was explaining her job in a self-conscious, stiff voice. Oh no! My worst fears were coming true. My best friend and my new best friend were NOT going to like each other. With three of us it would have been awkward to stay at the bar, so we all sat down at a table, me on my donut pillow to cushion my poor tailbone.

"What do you do, Artemis?" Annie said, in the formal voice of a re-luctant stepparent questioning her new kid's unruliest friends about their favorite subjects in school.

"I'm a strategic team sales partner and educator," Artemis said, in a fake chipper voice.

Annie looked perplexed.

"Artemis works at Lululemon," I explained.

Annie is earnest. Annie works hard to change the world. Annie doesn't really do stupid sarcasm about bullshit corporations. I braced myself for fireworks.

"Do you like it?" Annie asked.

"I get to tell women they look great all day. Women always look beautiful, and most of them—even rich yuppies—don't hear it enough. So yeah, I kind of like it."

Annie nodded and smiled. And I felt a pang of disappointment that Annie and Artemis weren't fighting over me. Could it be possible they were going to LIKE each other?

"Goddess, this donut pillow is a pain," I said, adjusting it beneath my booty.

"What did you think was gonna happen when you started getting drunk at a skate park?" Annie said.

Artemis totally cracked up, and Annie looked pleased. I felt both left out that they were getting along so well, and a little miffed they were making fun of me. Artemis asked Annie if she was dating anyone, and Annie launched into her dilemma about the hottie identical IT twins, which Artemis lapped up. After we finished hashing out Annie's lust squared, I told them about Patrick's "date" proposal.

"Oh. My. God!" Annie shouted. I do love it when she drinks. Her diet is so organic and pure that she's hammered after two beers. "What have things come to when men get their feelings tragically hurt when called out for being horrible scrubs? It makes no sense."

"Exactly!" Artemis yelled, tipsy herself. "The only trick is to out buster them. Expect less than the smidge they are willing to give and move on to the next one. It leaves them gagging for more."

Annie and I looked at each other—perplexed—but then simultaneously began drumming the table and yelling in approval.

When it quieted I said, "Hey, random question: Why is talk of ubiquitously popular artichoke beer hilarious?"

"Artichoke?" Artemis said.

"You know, on the label. All the beers these days have artichokes on the label."

"Those are hops!" Annie howled. "Did you tell the guy who works in Beer Alley you like 'artichoke beer'?" She and Artemis laughed so hard that when Annie fell off her chair, Artemis tried to help her up and ended up falling down on top of her. Harumph! If the sight of them, and the unexpected sense that I am now in a cool grrrl gang, had not been so pleasing, I would have been quite offended by their ridicule. How am I supposed to keep up with every food and alcohol trend in the world or know what a hop looks like, for Venus's sake?

Artichokedly,
Roxy

P.S. Late-night update: Success!!! Pure unadulterated success! I have managed to get myself off in a completely merman-free manner, using only my pointer finger, a tiny bit of coconut oil, and one very sexy story on literotica.com. I am ready for my date! Redbox! Bring it!

August 14, 2012

Dear Everett,

In the end, I convinced Patrick to come to my house. That way I didn't have to give Roscoe his insulin shot early. (If you were here, Everett, and had not bailed on me in lieu of constant fingerbanging of sexually "open" women, I would not have this dilemma and could go on a romantic date to the H-E-B parking lot like other decidedly classy, almost-thirty-year-old women.) Patrick arrived with a movie from the Redbox. The American version of "The Girl with the Dragon Tattoo." I couldn't argue with his feminist choice. But I admitted that picturing him at the Redbox gave me a bout of melancholy about Waterloo Video being shut down. "What about your protest?" he asked.

"I have three signs," I said. "I need to make twenty and I've got like six weeks to do it."

"Maybe after the movie we could make a couple more together," he said. Then he told me all about how he's getting into organizing shows. Rhymcfest—some bff of Kanye West's—is coming to town in a few weeks and Patrick is putting on the whole event. Apparently event organizing is one of his true passions.

As soon as we started the movie I remembered it has an icky abusive sexual scenario as the horrid obstacle that the girl with the dragon tattoo must overcome in order to achieve her full power. This put a bit of a damper on the mood for everyone until I suggested we swap out the movie for my pre-release copy of *Pitch Perfect* that one of the IT twins burned for Annie. Patrick was initially reluctant—as any heterosexual man would be—to watch a movie about an all-female collegiate a capella group, but soon realized that sexy college youth shimmying and cavorting and cracking jokes serves as much better foreplay fodder than a young woman's rape by her legal guardian. We started "Pitch

Perfect" and next thing I knew we were grinding our hips together to an a capella cover of Rihanna's "Please Don't Stop the Music."

I dragged him to my bedroom. After we'd stripped off our clothes, I angled myself crossways to him so I was on my back with my legs over his hips. That way he'd have easy access to my clit as we consummated the act. But he made no moves to finger my pearl. So I finally grabbed his hand and put his finger right on the sweet spot. He rubbed for a minute but then seemed to lose interest. At that point I closed my eyes and started rubbing my clit myself. But his thrusting messed up my timing and I was getting kind of annoyed at that point anyway. I finally gave up and decided to just enjoy the warmth of a cute boy pumping into me in my cozy bed. As soon as he came he rolled over and started snoring like crazy—we are talking full-blown bump and roll here!

I didn't even have it in me to give myself a "seizure." But I'll be proud to tell Annie that I did get up, put on some pajamas, and go to the living room, where I painted two more signs—KEEP YOUR PSEUDO-FEMINISM OUT OF MY YOGA TIGHTS and CORPORATIZATION IS A LOSS FOR THE NATION—before I finally climbed into bed for good and went to sleep.

This morning Patrick did stay for one of my famous vegan bulletproof coffees and joked it would make him unstoppable all day. If only he could have an unstoppable tongue or pointer finger! He did give me a very sweet kiss and also patted Roscoe before heading off to Beer Alley. I went straight back to bed for a self-tickling session that put my mood right. Am I destined to spend life satisfying myself sexually while reading the complete works of Silky Raven on literotica.com? To distract myself from this morbid thought, perhaps I'll try to paint one more sign before I head in to the deli.

Industriously,
Roxy

CHAPTER FIVE

August 16, 2012

Dear Everett,

I was so ashamed by Dirty Steve's comparison between myself and his mother's dog that yesterday I pretended to myself that the near-freezing air of Beer Alley—in the manner of a poorly thought-out "high concept" sci-fi film—actually incubates a rare disease that causes those infected to instantly develop a full acne beard. I have always had strong visualization abilities and this technique actually kept me from going near Beer Alley for my entire shift.

Last night Annie and Artemis and I decided to meet at The Highball for a beer. Let it be known that when I was a kid, the shopping center where The Highball and the hipster burger-and-a-beer-with-your-movie Alamo Drafthouse Cinema are located was nothing but a near-empty strip mall housing a cruddy grocery store and a low-budget weight-lifting gym. While I am often resistant to change and growth in this city I love, even I had to admit that The Highball and the Alamo Drafthouse were improvements. While once I would not have deigned to frequent said shopping center, I now adore going to The Highball for ironic karaoke or bowling, or just a cocktail in a Rat Pack–like setting. And the Alamo Drafthouse is the best movie theater in the world. (I mean, who

August 15, 2012

Dear Everett,

In theory, I am grateful that six months of the year this town is as hot as the face of the sun because I sometimes think that is the ONLY thing that keeps everyone in the United States of America from moving here. But I must say, in reality, the heat is starting to wear me down. Yesterday I arrived at work dripping sweat, but my damp clothes instantly turned to near ice in the cold blast of the store's air-conditioning. I spent my entire shift scanning the store to see if Patrick would make his way over from Beer Alley to say hi to me. I admit it cut into my natural productivity. Finally Dirty Steve snuck up behind me and said, "What are you doing, Poxy? If you have time to lean, you've got time to clean." Grrr! Dirty Steve is the worst. I suspect he knows he will one day look back on his time as the coke-snorting manager of the Whole Foods deli as his glory days and the knowledge angers and frightens him. He bested me with that rotten sushi, but don't think I've let it go!

I finally gave up on my resolve to be aloof and went over to Beer Alley on my break. I wove my way through clouds of breeders with whining little children trailing after their shopping carts (Goddess, I'm glad I don't have kids!), but Patrick wasn't in Beer Alley. He must have been on *his* break. In a fit of conviction that he had made his way to the deli to see me at the same time I'd gone to Beer Alley to see him, I raced back over to the deli counter but he was nowhere in sight. "You look like my mom's dim-witted golden retriever when it's chasing a ball back and forth across the living room," Dirty Steve shouted at me over the counter. "What are you doing, anyway?" I was so embarrassed I just went back to work right away, missing most of my break. But Patrick never came by at all.

Sheepishly,
Roxy

DOESN'T like to get drunk at a "Grease" sing-along?) But growth and change should have limits and decency.

When I drove up to where The Highball and the Alamo Drafthouse were just last week, I found a giant hole in the ground with a crane towering over it! I pulled over and texted Annie and Artemis, who agreed to meet me down the block at Maudie's Tex-Mex for margaritas. I grilled the bartender there who said that the new construction will involve high-rise condos, chain restaurants and shops, and a parking garage. "But don't worry," she said. "They'll put The Highball and the Alamo Drafthouse back in there too."

"They will be buried under a looming tower of new-build tackiness, and inaccessible due to gridlocked traffic!" I shouted.

Annie and Artemis had arrived by then and maneuvered the subject away from the horrors of corporatization, allowing the bartender to gratefully slink away. The new topic was what the hell we were going to do about said corporatization. Annie whipped out a notebook and helped me outline a plan of action for the Lululemon protest that involves social media marketing, a sign-painting schedule, and drafting of chants. It was quite invigorating.

Artemis confessed that while she's excited about the protest, she's growing to love her role at Lululemon as a guerrilla body-image counselor. "Today this twenty-two-year-old hard body in a size four was in the dressing room sobbing. When I asked what was wrong she said, 'I feel fat.' I said, 'Good thing feelings aren't facts. You need to wake up to what is a fact: you are young, hot as hell, and wasting it crying in a dressing room.'"

"So what happened?" Annie asked.

"She bought the tights and a top to match and strutted out of the store happy as a clam. If it weren't for the other fact that I'm helping plot the overthrow of the store via peaceful protest, I'd say I deserve a raise."

Then, with absolutely no transition, Artemis said her toilet had gotten stopped up with a tampon she'd accidentally flushed the day before. After extracting it, the plumber told her to stop flushing "bloody white mice."

"EW!" I laughed in horror. "What a creep."

It's not that I don't love hearing about Artemis's plumbing, but as soon as there was a natural lull in conversation, I brought up Patrick. After hearing another tale of his laziness in bed, even Artemis wanted me to chill out on pursuing him further. ("He probably doesn't even know that only eighteen percent of women can orgasm through vaginal penetration only," she yelled. "Jesus, this is why 'Cosmo' should be required reading for guys.") She and Annie seemed to have eerily mind-melded and they gave me the exact same advice: "Do not reach out to Patrick."

Annie said: "I am about to drop some heteronormative, sexist-as-shit nonsense on you. And you need to listen to it. WOMEN WERE MADE TO RECEIVE. YOU ARE A VESSEL. PATRICK SHOULD BE GIVING TO YOU IN THE FORM OF TEXTS, PHONE CALLS, DATE REQUESTS, ETCETERA."

"At this point he should be giving to you in the form of buying your motherfucking dinner!" Artemis shouted. She was getting drunk and seemed slightly wound up. "Or at least a rip-roaring orgasm!"

We could all cheer to that. Buoyed up by their cohesive philosophy and support, I vowed to stay away from Beer Alley for another day.

Decisively,
Roxy

August 18, 2012

Dear Everett,

I thought about calling you tonight as I no longer feel safe in my own home. (Though given you don't own a cell phone, I would have had to call the landline of the OM house, and the thought of some clit-crazed creepo answering caused me to lose my nerve.)

When I rode into the driveway on my bike today after work, Captain Tweaker's side patio was full of—you guessed it—tweakers. There were several crushed beer cans on my side of the fence, and when I entered the house and Roscoe ran up to me, I saw that he was LIMPING! As you know, he comes in and out of the backyard all day via the doggy door in the kitchen. Infuriated that these meth heads had thrown a bottle or some such detritus at my furbaby, I stormed over to the fence separating our patios, forgetting my natural caution. "Don't you dare throw beer cans at my dog!" I yelled.

"What are you talking about, you crazy lady?" Captain Tweaker asked. He was chomping on a mouthful of white gum and smoking a cigarette.

"We didn't hurt your dog," one tweaker said. He was a grown man, but hardly taller than a girl gymnast. He, too, had a giant wad of gum in his mouth. "I love dogs."

In my outrage, I'd left the door cracked behind me and Roscoe trotted outside. I was sure he'd growl at the tweakers, but instead he limped toward them. The tiny tweaker reached his hand over the fence and Roscoe—as if to prove the tiny tweaker's point about being a dog lover—jumped up to sniff his scabby hand. The tiny tweaker grabbed his paw. "Don't you hurt him!" I yelled. The tweaker gingerly pulled a little white paint cap from between two pads in Roscoe's front paw. "I think he was limping because of this," he said, holding up the paint cap helpfully. I've been leaving sign-painting supplies all over the living room and Roscoe must have stepped on a stray paint cap. Poor thing! I felt terrible, which served to make me somehow even madder at the tweakers.

Captain Tweaker grabbed a box of Nicorette off the table and extracted another piece of gum, which he shoved in his mouth to join the giant wad already there. He took a furious pull off his cigarette. I was dealing with seriously crazy people.

"Well," I said, "you can keep your litter on your side of the fence."

"You can keep your stinky cunt on your side of the fence and stop accusing us of crimes we didn't commit," Captain Tweaker said in a fake Irish accent that—though nonsensical—had the other tweakers busting up.

A large cardboard box sitting at the edge of the patio spilled out dozens of boxes of Nicorette, which the tweakers must have lifted off a truck or something.

"Nicorette is for after you've QUIT smoking," I yelled. The tweakers laughed heartily and gave off a chorus of "Ooooh" and "Burn" as I turned around and stormed back inside, only to realize Roscoe was still out there pressing himself against the chain-link fence in order to be as close as possible to the tiny tweaker. I opened the door and yelled, "Roscoe! Get in here." He came, but reluctantly, with a glance over his shoulder at the tweakers that seemed to say, "Isn't my mom a drag?"

All in all, it was an utterly humiliating experience. I've been watching out my window periodically as a total of seven cars have "stopped by" the tweakers' house for a quick visit. I want those drug dealers out of here!

With all the righteous indignation of the unjustly neighbored,
Roxy

P.S. I have decided I will be a doormat no longer. My home is my sanctuary and I will defend it!!!! It may take time for me to figure out how to oust the tweakers, but oust them I will. In the meantime, I will turn my vengeful energy toward a shorter-term goal—finally brainstorming revenge on Dirty Steve for intentionally food poisoning me. Perhaps I will pull a tarot card for guidance.

Ahaha! I have drawn the Four of Wands, and with that glorious card comes a brilliant idea for revenge. The Four of Wands is a card of home and hearth. A card that says it's a good day to stay home, drink a glass or two of cold merlot, and bake a motherfucking pan of laxative brownies for my boss! Take that, Dirty Steve.

August 19, 2012

Dear Everett,

Today I casually presented a ziplock bag with a couple of brownies to Dirty Steve. "They're not full of weed, are they?" he asked. "You freaking hippy."

"Weed-free," I said. "I swear on the Goddess Venus."

"I shouldn't eat this," Dirty Steve said, as he tucked in to the first brownie. "I have serious FP." FP is Dirty Steve's own acronym. It stands for "Fat Potential." And it's true. Dirty Steve has the sort of build that could quickly slide from burly to obese.

I was experiencing a heady mix of anticipation and anxiety thinking about Steve eating the brownies, so I considered going to see Patrick as a distraction, but I reminded myself I am a vessel, meant to receive. So instead of going to Beer Alley on my thirty-minute break, I walked across the street to Waterloo Records. (Waterloo Video may be closed, but I thank Venus that Waterloo Records is still going strong, due to a combination of in-store performances by popular bands and the fact that, in addition to selling CDs, they now also sell a wide variety of novelty knickknack crap such as "Handerpants—Underpants for Your Hands!")

I was surprised to spot a giant new poster in the window of Waterloo Records: FAIL BETTER! splashed across the top in big black letters, over a photo of Texas and his bandmates standing in the middle of Main Street in Marfa, Texas. "Hipster bullshit," I grumbled to myself. "Marfa hasn't been actually cool since 2007. Marfa is dead." I couldn't help but notice that Texas looked pretty freaking hot in the poster, showing off his nice physique in a tight black T-shirt and jeans. In the corner of the poster was a smaller sign, announcing FAIL BETTER! would be doing an in-store performance on Friday, September 21.

I went inside the store and found FAIL BETTER!'s new record and then sat in the listening booth for ten minutes so I could hear the first couple songs before I had to go back to work. The music was upbeat and danceable, but an edge of melancholy crept in sometimes, the sadness tingeing the joyful sounds, as if the band was saying: "Yes, today we are enjoying life. But we know that someday all we know and love will wither and die." And then of course with the music came the happy memory of shaking my ass with Artemis at Emo's (before the vomit drama), and it moved me more than I wanted it to, such that I was loathe to pull the noise-canceling headphones from my ears and head back to work. I have to confess that on my way out I bought the CD.

As I walked back across the street, I felt a little sick with worry, anticipation, and even dread. When I was at home last night—enraged by the tweakers—the ex-lax brownies had seemed like a delightful and just idea, but now I was concerned I might have been momentarily possessed by the spirit of a mildly psychopathic frat boy who thinks of himself as merely mischievous. Also, after listening to the sweet sounds of FAIL BETTER! the prank seemed lacking in vision and originality. If I was to defeat my true foe, Captain Tweaker, I'd have to rise to higher heights.

Just before I headed back into the store, my phone rang. It was Yolanda. She said it's been too long since she, Kate, Rosa, Barclay, and I all got together. She misses us. She knew it wouldn't be the same once we graduated college, but we've grown too far apart. I didn't think it prudent to mention I don't see her and the other girls much because they've become such a firm part of the square community. And then she dropped the bomb. She's getting married on New Year's Eve and wants me to be a bridesmaid. After I gushed the usual obligatory congratulations, I asked the critical follow-up question: "What sort of monstrosity will I be required to wear?"

"Anything you want. I love you, Kate, Rosa, Barclay, and my sisters too much to force you to wear big green bridesmaid dresses."

I struggled for some other reason to object. Just as I settled on the idea that bridesmaids are supposed to be mute and beautiful, a row of silent eye candy for the wedding attendees to objectify, Yolanda jumped in.

"I know you hate being in a situation where you can't talk," she said, "so I wanted to know if you'd like to give a reading, too. A little poetry, a quote about love, you pick. Okay?"

I felt myself tear up. Yolanda knows me so well. Why haven't I made an effort to keep up with her and my other girls? It's not as if my dance card is full. I told her I'd be honored. When we hung up I wiped my eyes and headed back into Whole Foods.

The rest of my shift, I found myself keeping a watchful eye on Dirty Steve but I saw no signs of gastric distress. In fact, he was as surly and abusive as ever. "Hey, Señor Slowpoke!" he yelled at Jason. "Hurry up with that coleslaw."

"That's a microaggression and—at even a less progressive company—a fireable offense!" I thundered.

"Shut up, Poxy Roxy," Dirty Steve said. "Why don't you go make a batch of meatballs?" Dirty Steve knows that, as a vegan, I detest the squish of ground meat between my fingers. I suddenly felt certain that a case of ex-lax two-step WAS fitting retribution.

I went outside to join Jason and Nelson on their smoke break (as usual, they offered me a cigarette and as usual, I countered that I was fine with my kombucha). I ended up complaining about Dirty Steve, and finally confessed about the brownies. Jason smiled and put his hand on my arm when he said, "Gracias, guapa. Just what that pendejo deserves." It's rare for Jason to dip into Spanglish and it seemed like a little intimacy-reward for the risk I had taken.

It made me all the more furious Dirty Steve had called him such an awful nickname. I hate "Poxy Roxy," but what Steve called Jason was so much worse. "You know, Annie told me if we ever wanted, she could complain to Topher Doyle about Dirty Steve. You know, tell him what the deal is."

For a moment we contemplated the possibility in silence.

"I don't hate Dirty Steve," Jason said with a shrug. "I mean, I'm glad he's about to have the Texas two-step, but I don't hate him."

"If some corporate lackey replaces him it'll be so much harder to slack off and steal food," Nelson said. "Also, that asshole gives this place character."

I had to admit the truth of his statement. Whole Foods, once a local hippy grocery store, is now turning into the McDonald's of health-food chains. You can buy kung pao tofu in a Whole Foods deli in Boulder, Colorado, or Austin, Texas, or Manhattan and it'll taste the same. In a way, Dirty Steve is a throwback to a time when the store, and this town itself, was a little less clean scrubbed, and not yet on commodified offer to the world. Dirty Steve doesn't represent a part of the old Austin that I love, per se, but it's a part that I'll be a little nostalgic for once it's gone completely.

"You're right. Fuck that guy," I said. "We won't rat him out to Corporate, 'cause we can handle him ourselves."

Nelson pulled out a little pipe and we all took a hit. As I breathed in, I imagined myself as an empty vessel, receiving the gift of the smoke. When I handed the pipe to Jason, our hands touched and I felt a proverbial spark. He has a girlfriend and it was nothing, really, but enough to keep me from even thinking about a walk down Beer Alley. Lucky for me, because the last thing I need right now is a rare disease that gives me an acne beard.

Contemplatively,
Roxy

August 20, 2012

Dear Everett,

I was off work today so I asked Artemis if she wanted to go with Roscoe and me down to the Hike and Bike Trail for a walk. She gave me her address—somewhere off Old Enfield Road. I figured she'd live in some crappy old apartment complex, one of the ones that's destined for the demo crew in the next few years. But when I pulled up to the address, I saw it was a nouveau mid-century-modern town house. (Sugar daddy jokes aside—where does she get her money?) I was going to park and knock, but Artemis was already trotting down the sidewalk. She climbed into the passenger seat.

"Hey," I said. "Is this your parents' house?"

"They're in the deep freeze in the garage," she said, and laughed.

"That's horrible!" I said, but I laughed too.

"It's actually just a rental. I don't even have a garage," she said.

Traffic down to the Hike and Bike Trail was hideous, the skyline full of cranes. I counted seven, each one building another towering upscale downtown condo that will soon be packed full of douchebags arriving from San Francisco and LA. Those D-bags may be in search of authenticity or the real America, but they will each contribute to diluting the essence and soul of this town that means everything to me. Oh how I wish I could do one tiny something to preserve this place that I love! When I moaned about it to Artemis, she said she was glad I was transforming my ire into action by making my Lululemon protest signs. I have to agree.

By the time I found a parking place near the trail I was about to get in a mood, but it only took ten minutes walking along the lake with Artemis and Roscoe before my spirits lifted. The trees were gorgeous and the sunlight threw sparkles across the water, where rowers skimmed the surface and stand-up paddleboarders made their way lazily along. Even though it was totally relaxing, I kept thinking about what Artemis had said about her parents being in the deep freeze. "Where do your parents live, anyway?" I asked very casually.

"Don't worry. I didn't murder them," she said. "They're divorced. My dad lives in Manhattan, so I go visit him sometimes. My mom, she's here. I don't see her as much as I should. But she's all right. She's a worrier."

"Totally," I said. "I get it. My mom too."

"What does your mom worry about?"

I had the sense Artemis was trying to steer the subject away from her family. "Lately I think she worries about me because I've been doing this dead-end job for so long and I'm not making art and I don't even have a boyfriend. I think parents want one positive talking point about their kid that they can say to their friends to show their kid isn't a total fuckup. Like, 'Brenda's doing great; she works for the Wicked World Bank.' Or, 'Suzie was able to catch a man and she's breeding like crazy.' Or, 'Derek is great; he's saving the world in the Peace Corps' (which my brother actually is). But right now my mom doesn't really have a talking point for me, so it makes her worried that something is really wrong with me." I was going to ask Artemis more about her mom, but just then, we got interrupted by a quick stop-and-chat with Esmeralda Limon, who I went to high school with, and then another one with Ms. Woodall, my elementary school art teacher. I also waved at a few regulars I see down there a lot.

"You know everyone," Artemis said.

"That's the great thing about the Hike and Bike Trail," I said. "You get sun and socializing. Sure, this town may be changing, but the Hike and Bike Trail is always glorious." I didn't know how to explain that all that smiling and waving and exercise and endorphin-releasing is that much better because it happens on the edge of the water, which, like the Temperance card in the tarot deck, brings a sense of balance and healing.

By then we'd done a full loop around the lake and had made it almost back to the car. Roscoe looked up at me imploringly, dying for a swim. But I was worried if I let him off his leash, he wouldn't behave. Artemis encouraged me to let him wade a bit, so I did. I was in such a good mood that the crazy traffic on the way back to Artemis's house didn't put me out of sorts. I was going to invite myself in to see her place, but when we pulled up she looked at her watch. "Shit! I'm gonna be late for my aerial yoga class! Thank you for a fun afternoon!" She kissed me on the cheek and jumped out, running lightly up the walk, and then—like the woman of mystery she is—she slipped into her house and was gone.

Curiously,
Roxy

August 23, 2012

Dear Everett,

I have calmed down considerably since the Nicorette incident. All was quiet in Tweakerville this morning, so I was able to sneak Roscoe and his patchy fur out of the house without jeering or ridicule. After I dropped him off at the groomers—who showered him with adoration and love—I went to Caffé Medici to drink a delicious latte and reread "Bridget Jones's Diary" while I waited. As always, it was delightful to be so deeply offended by the portrayal of a woman as an anti-intellectual bing-bong head always in need of rescue by a man. I have to admit I did laugh until I snorted, more than once. I then drove to a little lingerie boutique next door to Crystal Works and bought a pair of faux-leather (a.k.a. pleather), pink python-print panties so that—just in case Patrick and I ever hook up again—I'll have sexy undergarments. When I picked Roscoe up he seemed quite proud of his new haircut. Indeed, I fear all the attention he has received of late may be going to his head.

Later at work, I saw Patrick headed my way. "I am a vessel, meant to receive," I said to myself over and over. Like Roscoe, Patrick had a new buzz cut and looked incredibly cute, but I feigned nonchalance as he asked me what I've been up to.

"Just the usual," I said, because I couldn't very well tell him I've been dosing my boss with ex-lax and cutting tweaker Nicorette out of my dog's fur. "You?"

"I've been working really hard getting ready for Rhymefest," he said. "But I could use a break. Want to hang out tonight?"

"I'm kind of busy, but yeah. Sure," I said.

When he asked if my place was cool, I said sure again, partly because it would be good for the tweakers to see a guy at my house and know I am not a vulnerable single female, partly because I don't like

August 21, 2012

Dear Everett,

WHAT A DAY! It's been a roller coaster of enemies turned (sort of) allies, and other enemies turned worse enemies. First I went into work to find Dirty Steve standing in front of my apron hook, arms crossed over his chest. "You gave me diarrhea from HELL," he said.

"What are you talking about?"

"Those brownies."

"Baked goods are not generally known to cause gastric distress."

"They do if you load them up with ex-lax."

I feigned ignorance and outrage.

"Don't lie," Dirty Steve said. "After I got the shits, I gave the last brownie to my brother. The motherfucking jig is up."

"Well, that's what you get for PURPOSEFULLY GIVING ME FOOD POISONING," I said.

"What are you talking about?"

"The free sushi!?"

"I offered you sushi I was gonna throw out. You're the one who decided to eat it. I'm not gonna POISON you on purpose. What am I, a fucking psycho?"

Dirty Steve lies a lot, but he does so terribly. It was clear he was telling the truth. I felt a horrid wave of guilt, which of course made me want to justify myself. "I thought you were trying to get retribution on me for blackmailing you into not firing me."

"I was GRATEFUL to you for helping me out. I didn't blame you for trying to keep your job in the process. Jesus."

"So now are we square?" I asked.

"What the fuck does that mean?"

"Like, are you going to seek revenge on me?"

"Of course not, you nutbag. Quit tilting at windmills and go make some tuna salad."

Humph! Perhaps I do sometimes jump to conclusions. I wonder if Dirty Steve has actually read "Don Quixote"?

I spent the rest of the afternoon burdened by remorse, and then soon learned how the Universe would punish me! After work I walked through the front door and Roscoe charged up to me. At first I couldn't figure out WHAT HAD HAPPENED to my baby. He had white devil horns sticking off his head and big white clumps hanging from his fur ALL OVER HIS BODY. I leaned down and touched one. It stuck to my fingers. After that it only took me a minute to realize he had giant chewed up wads of Nicorette smashed into his fur. Roscoe must have gone into the yard through the dog door when I was gone, and that's when the tweakers got him. They must have chewed themselves nearly to a Nicorette heart attack to get that much gum.

My hands shaking with consternation, I considered calling 911, but—always prudent—I decided that I would be taken more seriously at the nonemergency 311 number. When the desk jockey cop answered, I told him about the state Roscoe was in and how I expected an immediate arrest of every member of Tweakerville living next door to me. But even my near-hysteria could not break through the cop's apathy.

"Some guy put gum on your dog? Sorry, lady, but we've got bigger fish to fry."

When I hung up after our fruitless convo, I let out a cry that was half yowl of frustration, half battle cry. It was clear—I would have to take matters into my own hands. "Tweakers!" I yelled. "This means WAR!"

However, I knew that before I could deal with the tweakers, I had to get their saliva-filled Nicorette off my innocent furball. I immediately called the dog groomers, but as it was 8 p.m., every groomer in town was closed. So I got Roscoe into the kitchen, put on dish gloves, gave

him his insulin shot, and spent THREE HOURS cutting Nicorette out of his hair. While I was disgusted and angry, Roscoe seemed pleased at the attention. Charlize Theron, who usually keeps to herself, came out to watch for much of it, as if worried and a little intrigued.

I can barely write this as my hands are quivering from working the scissors. I now have a brown grocery bag full of chewed-up Nicorette and dog fur that makes me rage gag every time I look at it. While normally I am a devout Venus girl, I am preparing an offering to Mars, the planetary deity that governs combat. The offering consists of tobacco, cayenne pepper, some polished red aventurine, and a sliced mango doused in chili powder. I am going to need all of the energy of will and creativity of aggression that the fourth planet from the sun can offer in order to accomplish my aims of taking those tweakers down!

Rattled and angry,
Roxy

leaving the furballs alone, and partly because I was afraid if I saw Patrick's bachelor-guy squalor I wouldn't want to hook up with him. "I am a vessel, meant to receive," I thought again and then I realized something: there's no way I can MAKE Patrick bring me flowers or buy me dinner through the sheer force of my will. But I could Tom Sawyer him into giving me some more free labor.

"So you can come over, but only if you promise to paint another sign," I said in a manner I hoped was flirtatious.

He actually looked pleased to be challenged to live up to his heteronormative biological imperative of giving to a woman. "Sure," he said, promising to come over at 9 p.m. The time annoyed me, as it guaranteed there would be small opportunity for him to even spring for a pizza, but I let it go.

So now I have two hours to madly clean up the house, change the sheets, vacuum the couch, and sweep the remaining bits of dog fur off the kitchen floor, then attend to making myself look (casually) sexy and don my pink pleather python panties before Patrick arrives.

Baby steps to receiving,
Roxy

P.S. The tweakers are on the patio, but I have my blinds shut and am ignoring them for now. I am confident that soon enough Mars will gift me with a plan of retribution!

August 24, 2012

Dear Everett,

The date was not all a girl could dream of. Perhaps the best part was listening to FAIL BETTER! as I cleaned up the house. Their album is so cheering and even I have to admit the drums give the band its true sound, its beating heart. I put on a little makeup and my labradorite necklace. I felt fierce, ready to slay in the manner of Venus . . . or Beyoncé. Patrick showed up—only fifteen minutes late. He did bring beer, probably bought with his employee discount—and we each drank a couple while talking about how we were going to paint signs. I told him the story of the tweakers and he valiantly offered to protect me from them whenever needed. (I told myself: "I am a vessel, receiving protection!") Then we fell on each other in a frenzy of lust.

I gave Patrick what was—if I do say so myself—a rather spectacular blowjob. I thought we would then continue the fun, but he immediately sat up, buckled his pants, stretched, and said, "That was amazing. What a great date!" Then he looked sheepish and stared off into the distance—or at the corner of the room as if it was the distance—before he finally spoke again. "But, you know, you probably won't even hear from me for a couple of weeks, because I'll be so busy with Rhymefest."

The words were like a slap across my face that left me speechless. Not only was he not going to get me off, he wasn't even going to see my new pink pleather python panties! Within a few minutes he'd said good-bye and left the premises.

I immediately called Artemis and told her what had happened. "When Annie said you are a vessel, meant to receive, that's not what she intended," she said. Then she started laughing hysterically.

"I hate you," I said. "Seriously. You are dead to me."

"I'm coming over to help you paint signs," she said. She paused. "I'm starving all of a sudden. You hungry?"

I realized I was ravenous. "I was so busy shaving my legs, trimming my giant power triangle, and vacuuming up dog hair, I forgot to eat dinner."

"I'll bring over a pizza," she said. "Don't worry, I'll get half vegan."

And she did. We hung out, delighting in the gooey slices, and she told me all about some guy who farted during her aerial yoga class, and I laughed until beer came out of my nose. I drew signs that she painted under my careful direction until like two in the morning. And it was so fun.

Well friendedly,
Roxy

CHAPTER SIX

August 26, 2012

Dear Everett,

Stupid, worthless day! Disaster! Disappointment! Drudgery! Heartbreak! Pathos! Oh, how I hate pathos! (Also, while I'm whining and on a side note: It's now late August and it's hotter than fucking ever. The forecasted high for today is 105. Every time I step outside, it's like I'm being boiled alive in my own sweat.)

Today at work, we were all prepping to open the store, chopping and slicing and sautéing like crazy, when Dirty Steve stormed in dramatically. "Nelson's grandma kicked it and he's going home for a couple of weeks to help his parents sell her house. Imagine asking Nelson for help with real estate! He's dumb as a dildo! Anyway, we're gonna be short-staffed for a while. I'll need everyone pulling doubles."

We all groaned but not very enthusiastically, as we all like Nelson. (And I owe him, because he sometimes covers shifts for me, like last June when Roscoe ate the crotches out of my dirty panties and I had to rush that naughty wiener dog to the emergency vet for a panty-ectomy.)

My phone dinged and I saw it was an email with the list of ten finalists for the Bucknether Art Competition. My name wasn't on the list. Oh, Everett, you can imagine my devastation and disappointment!

I needed a moment, I really did. So I went out back behind the dumpster. Jason was there smoking a cigarette.

"Want one?" he asked.

I was actually tempted—I could let the nicotine soothe me, while looking haughty and glamorous in the manner of a 1940s film star. "Nah," I finally said. "It's too late to start now." For a while we stood in a companionable silence as he puffed away and I sipped my kombucha. "Hey, if you talk to Nelson, will you tell him I'm sorry about his grandma?"

"His grandma has been dead for like ten years," Jason said.

"What?"

"Nelson got accepted to a three-week PharmaTrial study. They're testing some acne medicine on him. So maybe his skin will clear up AND they are going to pay him like five thousand dollars."

"Fuck me."

"Yeah. You know how Robert Rodriguez went into PharmaTrial for a month and wrote 'El Mariachi' and came out with enough money to film it low budget in Mexico?"

"Yeah," I said.

"Nelson is convinced he's gonna do the same thing, but with a TV pilot about stoner deli maids."

"Oh," I said. I wondered if Nelson was even literate, but there are some questions that don't need to be asked.

As if reading my mind, Jason said, "I went to school with him, yo. Homeboy wouldn't know a three-act structure if one bit him in the ass."

For some reason that made me feel really sad. Like sadder than I was when I thought Nelson's grandma had just died. And I started to cry.

"It's okay," Jason said. "I mean, maybe he can learn."

"It's not that," I said, wiping at my tears. But I wasn't sure how to explain—it was that I wanted to be an artist and here I was slinging tofu. And Nelson wanted to be a screenwriter but I knew he never really would be, not in the way he was hoping. And maybe I'd never be a real artist either. Everything just seemed really pointless and sad. And maybe I should accept that deli maid was as good as I could do, as good as I'd ever be. And then I cried harder, so hard Jason started looking worried.

"Hey, hey," he said, and then he was hugging me, like, really sweetly, and he kissed my cheek and then we were kissing for real. The door opened and I turned and it was this deli maid, Groken, that we don't hang with really because he's a sulky goth who believes friendliness is anathema to his moral code. He disappeared and the door slammed behind him—like the sight of us had driven him back inside.

"You have a girlfriend, right?" To my credit, I'd just remembered.

"Shit," Jason said. "Yeah. She's pregnant, too. I'm sorry. I never know how to comfort girls." He meant it nicely. He really did.

"Congratulations," I said. "On the baby, I mean. You did okay. Just don't do that again." And then I wiped my eyes and hurried back into the store.

The rest of my shift I forced myself to pretend I was fine, but I'm not fine, Everett. I'm a failure in love and I'm a failure in art. And this letter is staying in my spiral notebook with all the other ones I've written to you lately, because I don't want you or anyone else feeling sorry for me.

Morosely, your failed ex-girlfriend,
Roxy

August 27, 2012

Dear Everett,

Annie wanted to cheer me up after my disappointing news about the Bucknether Art Competition, so last night she came over and we watched that new Netflix documentary about bologna production. We screamed in disgust through the whole thing. It was seriously like watching a Stephen King movie—only so much more horrifying because it's real. It was also weirdly fun to be totally grossed out while curled up on the couch with Annie. The documentary mentioned how bologna is so full of acidic preservatives that it's been used in a series of vandalism incidents. Basically sometimes vandals will put slices of bologna all over cars and the acid from the preservatives burns off a layer of paint. It really is great to have a friend who thinks this sort of thing is as fascinating as I do.

Before she left, Annie hugged me and told me how proud she is that I entered the Bucknether Art Competition. I cried a little.

"I think you should make a gratitude list," she said.

"You really are a bossy woman," I said.

"It's easier to make a gratitude list than it is to be combative."

"Okay fine. I'm grateful you are my friend. I'm hella grateful for the furballs and that I have no human children. And I'm really grateful I own my own house." It actually did make me feel better.

If Annie and I wouldn't drive each other crazy, I'd ask her to move into my spare bedroom.

Cozily,
Roxy

August 29, 2012

Dear Everett,

Meth heads have been coming in and out of the house next door all week. I was on my patio last night having a beer when a bunch of them came out on their patio. I haven't seen them face-to-face since the Nicorette incident. "Want some gum?" Captain Tweaker yelled at me. I stormed inside, knowing I cannot engage until Mars gifts me with a strategy. But I couldn't help but think that whole batch of meth heads and their meth-cooking van and their rotten meth mouth teeth are SERIOUSLY grosser than bologna.

That's when Mars struck me with a truly brilliant idea. I don't want to diffuse the potency/energy of the scheme by writing about it before I execute it, so for now I'm off to work.

With plans for vengeance,
Roxy

August 30, 2012

Dear Everett,

Yesterday was insane. Thanks to that goth fucker Groken, word spread like wildfire through the store that I kissed Jason. All the cashiers kept glancing at me and the guys over in Bakery were looking my way and talking to each other behind their hands all afternoon, like middle school girls.

Patrick must have heard because he came round to the deli today asking for his usual chicken salad. He was very flirty, asking me what I've been up to and all that. He did not mention being oh-so-busy with Rhymefest. This should have been infuriating—why couldn't he just pay attention to me because we like each other and not because he's heard a rumor I kissed a coworker? But I was actually glad to see him. He looked more ripped and adorable than ever. However, when he asked if we could hang out, I held my ground and told him I'm very, very busy.

"Could you make some time for me later?" he asked, his eyes big, hazel, imploring, and luscious.

"I have a supersecret and important mission to go on after work," I said. "You can join me IF you are up for helping me AND you don't mind breaking the law."

This seemed to further ignite his newfound interest in me, and he agreed to meet me in the parking lot after work. As soon as I finished my shift I bought fifteen packages of preservative-free vegan bologna. Patrick let me put my cruiser in the back of his car, and on the way to Albertsons I told him my plan. He agreed the idea was genius. At Albertsons I bought two packages of regular grosser-than-gross bologna.

In my house I found dark beanie hats for both of us, and we hung out while we waited for the lights in all the houses on my street to go off. Blessedly, the tweakers seemed to be having a very quiet night. I could tell Patrick wanted to kiss me, but when he sat on the couch I sat in the beige chair that (as you know) is out of arm's reach. I stayed friendly yet distant, and gave off an unattainable vibe, enjoying the new power dynamic and Patrick's obvious lust for me. (Take that, Rhymefest!)

Once all was dark on the street we snuck out and put slices of non-toxic, preservative-free vegan bologna all over my car. It gave us the giggles to crouch down like cat burglars, sticking slices of bologna to the paint. When my car was covered with the pink discs, we ran together across the street, and covered the across-the-street neighbor's Acura in vegan bologna as well. We then hit seven more cars on my block. It was as if Patrick and I had been transformed into an outlaw couple, destined to become legends through our explosive chemistry and fearless daring. The meth van was the only vehicle we covered in slices of real-live, acidic, preservative-filled bologna. (This tactic would create the impression of a large-scale vandalism attack and would divert suspicion from me without doing actual damage to anyone's property—except for Captain Tweaker's meth van, of course.)

Patrick and I hurried back into my house and as soon as the door closed behind us, we burst out laughing. Roscoe danced at our feet, charmed by the magic between us. Even Charlize Theron peeked out shyly at us from behind her scratching post. Patrick leaned in to kiss me. I let him, and it was delicious. I felt myself melting into him, succumbing. But then I could hear his voice in my head saying, "You probably won't even hear from me for a couple weeks because I'll be so busy with Rhymefest," and I pulled away.

"Thanks for your help," I said.

"Sure thing."

I opened the front door. "See you at work."

"Okay," he said, looking so disappointed that I wanted to throw myself on him. "Keep me posted?"

"Sure," I said. "Come see me at the deli anytime."

With great force of will, I closed the door behind him, then collapsed on the couch, Roscoe licking my face as if to congratulate me on my resolve.

This morning one of my neighbors called the cops to report the bologna. Of course the popos—who regularly ignore my complaints about the meth cooking and drug dealing next door—hurried out by 8 a.m., as they love to make arrests for petty vandalism. The meth heads were still asleep. I came out to "see what was going on" and acted shocked and appalled about the bologna dotting my car.

The cops asked if they could interview me and I anonymously suggested they take a look inside the bologna-covered van while they were at it to see if they happened to find a meth lab. Apparently, some of my other neighbors had made the same suggestion. I watched triumphantly from my window as the cops hauled the whole lot of those meth head assholes out of Tweakerville in handcuffs. Captain Tweaker emerged looking enraged and defiant, and while I wanted to wave as haughtily as a British royal, I maintained self-control. There was no need to spoil my perfect crime by gloating.

The police are still swarming the meth van, collecting evidence of all the cooking that's been going on in there. The bologna has started dropping off the van, and sure enough, it's now marvelously polka-dotted.

Crime fightingly,
Roxy

August 31, 2012

Dear Everett,

I'm familiar with the age-old sexual axiom ATTRACTION + OBSTACLE = DESIRE. Yet I still forget about it sometimes—I'm shocked to see once again how true it is. Patrick was totally happy to blow me off until he began to sense I am no longer available to him. Now he seems positively desperate to spend time with me. He came by the deli today asking me what I'm up to for the long weekend.

Though he looked amazing, I felt a little high on my newfound power. So I told him that on Labor Day my parents are having a few neighbors over for burgers and Lone Star and maybe some boring talk about their HOA rules or whatever. (While it's not a glamorous destination, I feel more empowered being honest than I would telling a lie about a more fashionable yet fabricated event.)

"They live in that sexy swingers old folks' community?" he asked.

"Where did you hear it was like that?"

"My friend Nathan's grandpa went there. He was getting dementia or something. So Nathan's parents paid extra for the grandpa's house to have high-tech sensors and everything so they could see how many hours the grandpa was sleeping, if he turned the stove off, all that stuff. Super expensive. Anyway, the techno-bed registered that a couple nights a week THREE people were sleeping in Grandpa's bed."

"Good Goddess!" I said.

"That's what Nathan's parents said when they found out they were paying a fortune for Grandpa's threesomes. But Nathan's grandpa, he's never been happier. He's had, like, a major rebound in his cognitive skills 'n shit."

"Wow," I said. "Talk about sexual healing."

"Let's get down tonight," Patrick said, with a little Marvin Gaye dance step that was really irresistible. He does have moves. "So take me."

"Take you where?"

"To see your folks. To their boring barbecue in Sun City. I've always wanted to check it out."

Inside I was freaking out. He wants to meet my parents? But I played it cool. "That's weird. But okay," I said with a shrug.

"Righteous," Patrick said. He was beaming.

This makes me supremely nervous, as I haven't introduced anyone to my parents since Brant Bitterbrush. I don't want them to think it's a big deal! Maybe I'll warn them Patrick is just a friend. Though I'm sure my mom will run with it anyway. But what the hell? Besides, maybe it will give her a positive talking point about me when she and her friends start comparing their grown children's achievements. I can just hear her now: "Well, Roxy brought a new beau to our house on Labor Day." Oh Goddess, that actually makes me cringe! Maybe this is a terrible idea!

As an aside, I must write a note to self to remember that anytime I feel a man losing interest, I must feign having lost EVEN MORE interest.

Ruminatively,
Roxy

September 3, 2012 LABOR DAY!!!!!!

Dear Everett,

I have to apologize to you. While I often tell myself you were a terrible boyfriend—always broke, riddled with social anxiety, etc.—at least you never stood me up. I had just gotten dressed in what I hoped was appropriate attire for a senior living community Labor Day barbecue. (Unfortunately, my wardrobe consists primarily of work and club clothes. I feared if I went with club clothes I would perhaps cause spikes in blood pressure through the male and lesbian populations of Sun City. Yet if I went in my normal deli attire my mother would criticize my appearance in front of Patrick.) I finally settled on my labradorite necklace from Artemis (of course!) with a sundress and sandals (no cleavage, flow-y skirt) that I hoped would be alluring to Patrick, but NOT TOO alluring to my parents' cohorts. I was in the bathroom curling my hair when Patrick texted.

I'M SORRY I CAN'T MAKE IT TODAY. I FORGOT I PROMISED MY FRIEND SAL I WOULD GO TO A BURLESQUE SHOW AT THE 29TH STREET BALLROOM.

Of course I made the horrid mistake of telling my mom and dad I'd be bringing a "new friend" and they've surely trumpeted the news to all of their Sun City friends and neighbors. So now, off I go, alone, unshielded, battling my shame. Why, oh why, is this town full of a hexed combination of beautiful, brilliant women and slouchy, immature, yet-still-attractive man-children?????? I could strangle Patrick. I really could.

Angrily,
Roxy

September 4, 2012

Dear Everett,

Sun City was a greater horror show than I ever could have imagined. The only saving grace was that Patrick stood me up. Thank Goddess he stood me up!!!!! (This makes me believe more strongly than ever in the "Good News, Bad News, Who Knows?" Chinese parable.)

I sat on my donut pillow as I drove out to Georgetown on I-35, which was choked with holiday traffic. I pulled up in front of my parents' house to park but the driveway, the lawn, and both sides of the street were jammed with golf carts so that I had to park around the corner.

As I approached the house on the sidewalk—my donut pillow tucked discreetly under my arm—I could see through my parents' front window. The house was jammed with people. I opened the door to find The Rolling Stones blasting and everyone talking and laughing and eating hors d'oeuvres.

"Roxy! So great to see— Where's your date?" my mother said, making a beeline for me and speaking in her most booming voice.

"Got called into work at the last minute," I said.

"Oh, honey. Stood up again!"

I noticed my mother was wearing a leather miniskirt and, even worse, was somehow pulling it off. "You look great!" I said tentatively. She did look tan and dewy.

"It's all the tennis I've been playing," she said. "I'm trying to get in shape for our trip to Peru! Oh, how we wish you would come with us."

"You made it!" my father called, opening his arms wide for a hug. I stepped into them. My dad does give the greatest hugs.

"How are you?" I asked. "How's retirement?"

"I'm so bored I could gouge out my eyes," he said. "I mean, it's perfection."

"Oh, Dad. I just know you are going to find your post-retirement calling."

"Her date didn't come," my mother informed him in her loudest stage whisper.

"How about something to eat?" my father said, whisking me out of range of my mom. At least two dozen senior citizens packed the house—the place was really lively and happening with everyone drinking beer and margaritas. The snacks were disgustingly meat-centric, of course, but the guests scarfed them down as if they were scrumptious.

My mother rang a Tibetan bell—where and why she had acquired such a thing I will never know—and the room quieted. "Gather round! Take a seat!" she called gaily. "It's time for the main event."

Main event? What was going on? I was confused and had the deeply intuitive sense that something mortifying was about to occur.

The now-tipsy guests settled in on the giant sectional couch and chairs. The room was so crowded that the under-seventy set remained standing. A perky-looking senior with a dyed black bob that might have been a wig took the floor. She set a little mini-suitcase on the coffee table. "Now we all know that by the time we hit retirement age, we can lose a bit of our drive. But that's not to say we can't get it back!" Oh Goddess, I was both mortified and coming to understand that being stood up for this event was perhaps one of the best things that's happened to me in months.

She popped open the case and, to my absolute horror, I saw it was chock-full of a carefully organized row of dildos and vibrators. The guests gasped and giggled with the sort of group titillation that might erupt from a classroom of third graders who've heard the word "booby."

"With today's technology, there's nothing stopping each and every one of us from being a SEXY SENIOR!" The saleslady pumped the air with her fist and several women around the room let out little whoops of encouragement. "Now we all know the pharmaceutical industry has created a miracle cure for men that allows them to stay sexy and active at any age. But after menopause, we women can be, shall we say, a little less JUICY than before. But now there's a cure." She pulled a giant squirt tube of lube out of the suitcase. "This SENIORLICIOUS LU-BRICATOR will make you feel like a teenager. Take my word for it," she said with a lascivious wink that made all the men giggle. She popped the cap on the lube and held it out to Barry Lewis, a once silver fox now sagging toward eighty. He reached out his hand and she squirted a bit of lube onto his fingers. He rubbed them together.

"Slippery!" he said, and everyone laughed raucously.

"Taste it!" she cried.

Barry made a show of licking his fingers, as if he was a 1977 Mick Jagger going after a Jerry Hall–flavored ice-cream cone. "Tastes like butterscotch!" he shouted. The room erupted in laughter.

"We carry a delicious black licorice flavor as well," the saleswoman said.

My mother had tricked me! She was going to let me bring a date to this? Horror at the thought of all these seniors lubing up and grinding their bits together sent me into a sort of panic—I had to get out of there! I muttered something to my father about remembering I'd left the stove on. "I agree this is a little much," he whispered. "I think your mother wanted you to come because she was thinking maybe you could sell this junk yourself." He grimaced sympathetically. "If you slip out the back, I'll tell her later."

The betrayal! By my own mother! "Thank you," I mouthed, and made a break for it, donut pillow still under my arm. On the ride home I felt hot with horror and mortification at what I'd witnessed, coupled with the excruciating knowledge that every single member of Sun City probably has a more exciting sex life than I do.

I'd done full hair and makeup, and sensed that Venus, Goddess of Beauty, wouldn't want me to waste it all on going straight home. I was a

little wilted from the heat, but still, cuter than usual. I'd text Patrick to
see if he wanted company at the burlesque show. At a stoplight I looked
for my phone but realized I'd left it at home. Perhaps I could just surprise him! He'd be excited to see me and introduce me to his friend Sal.
And watching a rollicking burlesque show together—the stage full of
women of all shapes and sizes delighting in their own brand of beauty—
might prove titillating for both of us. Then afterward we could go back
to my house for some hot sex, and I'd prove to myself that those Sun
City seniors have got NOTHING on me.

Once I parked around the corner from the 29th Street Ballroom, I
made an executive decision to leave my donut pillow in the car, tailbone
pain be damned. A bouncer at the entrance demanded ten bucks. I
handed it over, thinking it a small price to pay for some afternoon delight. Tinsel hung over the dim, crowded room, giving everything a festive air. I felt my spirits lift.

Onstage, a troupe of three girls shimmied and high kicked and
stripped down to pasties. One of them was full-figured, one twig thin,
and the third perfectly proportioned with hair dyed a hipster jet black.
The dancers were categorically terrible—all their synchronized dance
moves were out of time, and their clothing removal was awkward at
best—but they looked like they were having so much fun that I cheered
rowdily as they pranced off the stage at the end of their number. As I
scanned the room for Patrick, the spotlight dimmed. In the darkness
two men carried a giant claw-foot bathtub onto the stage. A large emcee
in a suit announced the next dancer.

"Let's all give a big round of applause to Sin Sation!" he cried.

I was expecting another pleasingly amateur local girl, but the spotlight illuminated the back of a woman with milky-white skin and long
red hair who wore an exact replica of the outfit Marilyn Monroe donned
in her iconic "Diamonds Are a Girl's Best Friend" number. Dean Martin's
"I'm Forever Blowing Bubbles" began to play and an offstage bubble ma-

chine pumped a stream of bubbles in the direction of the bathtub. The woman turned around. Everett, you can imagine my surprise that this sex vixen was none other than my new best friend Artemis!

How many alter egos does that girl have?

As she began to dance, I stood transfixed. She bumped and ground, yanking off first one elbow-length glove, then pretending the other was stuck so that the audience laughed as she "struggled" to remove it. She ripped off her dress in one smooth motion and danced in tiny underwear and pasties, throwing in a mix of shimmies and shakes that even had me feeling funny. At the end of the number, she climbed into the bathtub and pretended to blow pretty bubbles in the air!

I hurried toward the front of the stage, clapping and whooping. After bowing gracefully, Artemis (a.k.a. Sin Sation) sashayed off into the wings. Where was Patrick? I scanned the crowd, and at a table off to the side I spotted the gorgeous black-haired burlesque dancer with the great figure snuggled up with her boyfriend. I felt a stab of jealousy. She'd certainly never spent an afternoon at a senior sex toy party. Ugh. She and her boyfriend began to kiss passionately, and as he turned his head to avoid bumping noses with her I could see his profile. He looked just like . . . PATRICK!!!! I moved in more closely. It was Patrick! I stormed over to him, tapping him on the shoulder. He looked up at me, but before his face could even register surprise, I yelled, "WHAT THE FUCK?"

Totally nonplussed, the raven-haired goddess turned to Patrick and said, almost as if she was bored, "Do you know her?"

"It's not like we're exclusive," he said. I wasn't sure if he was talking to her or me.

"You stood me up for Sun City for this?" I yelled.

"You were going with HER to an old folks' home?" the evil siren laughed. "That's rich." I started feeling foolish, and before either of them could say anything else, I stomped off. Without my phone I couldn't text Artemis, and the bouncers wouldn't let anyone backstage (where I'm guessing the burlesque girls were still in various stages of undress), so I waited outside in front of the 29th Street Ballroom for a while, hoping I could spot her. Then I started worrying Patrick and the girl would come out together, so I just gave up and left.

When I arrived home, the furballs went crazy to see me, but for once it didn't feel like anywhere near enough. I normally would have cried, but the combined memory of that butterscotch lube and Patrick kissing the sexy burlesque girl literally dried up even my tear ducts. I am destined to spend my naturally juicy years with one dog, one cat, and— now that I'm on strike from the overpowering merman—my own pointer finger.

Self-pityingly,
Roxy

P.S. Everett, why am I complaining to you about my loneliness and celibacy? You are fingerbanging multiple women daily in a meditation designed to raise female sexual energy. There is no way you could possibly relate to my current plight.

CHAPTER SEVEN

September 5, 2012

Dear Everett,

Last night, alone, still feeling jilted and in despair, I decided to watch the TED Talk of Nest Life founder and self-proclaimed sexual visionary Nina Sylvester. That woman may be a cult leader and nut, but she is certainly an eloquent, attractive, and convincing one. There she is owning the stage with her silky hair and power-lady sheath dress that would have made Gayle King proud, describing the first time she convinced a guy to stroke her clit to a fifteen-minute timer. Somehow this seminal stroker intuited he should begin the session by telling her that her vagina looked like a rose in bloom, which caused her to have a spiritual experience. "I wept," she said.

At that point I was like "Ack! Bitch, please. This isn't 'The Color Purple.' I don't want to hear you weeping about your damn labia. Celie earned it. You haven't earned shit."

Then Nina described how the guy went on to lube up his finger and slowly stroke her clit. She said he did it with a touch no firmer than one you would use to stroke the "tender skin of a ball sack." Gross! Clearly she'd thought through that description and used it like a hundred thousand times. She was really pleased with herself and I was really not on board. But then she said: "Nothing much happened at first. I was just envisioning past and imaginary erotic scenarios, trying to get myself in the mood. I wasn't really there."

Everett, that's when I perked up. I've read so much literotica.com that sometimes when I have sex I just play those stories through my head instead of really being present with what's actually happening.

This is where things took a turn.

Nina honed in on what was going on in her mind during that seminal fingerbang. "I was replaying a sexual fantasy I have where I'm The Bachelorette and any guy I give the rose to has to do whatever I want. I was a thousand miles away."

The audience was laughing hard and I was too. Then she went in for the kill.

"But suddenly that story, that fantasy dropped away completely," she said. "I was absolutely and completely in my body. I was present for what was happening to me. I was completely open to each and every sensation. And for the first time ever in my adult life I was totally tuned in to the wavelength of another human being. I was no longer lonely and isolated and ravenous for connection. For once I knew that I was exactly where I needed to be."

I felt my eyes well up.

I want that connection.

After a year of celibacy followed by some fun (but certainly NOT clit-centric sex) with Patrick, I want to feel what it's supposed to feel like to be sexually connected to another human being. I had that connection with Brant Bitterbrush. As much as I resent him for leaving me, and for making a killing off Duckie & Lambie at the expense of actual ducks and lambs, I also miss our incredible sexual chemistry. Will I ever have that with anyone else again? (No offense, Everett. While our sex life was certainly more than passable, I think we both know we didn't have Chemistry with a capital C.)

Nina Sylvester claims partnered female orgasm is essential to creating human connection. She talks about being with another person as both of you meditate on the same (very intense) point of contact—the finger meets the clitoris!—and how it creates a healing link between you.

After a brief fling with Patrick, I'm back to being connected only to a merman. It's true, last night I relapsed. ARGH! It seems like too much to bear.

You probably remember how, at the end of the TED Talk, Nina says, "I never imagined that having someone intently rub my clitoris for fifteen minutes on a regular basis would so profoundly change my life. So I encourage you to give it a try. What do you have to lose? Loneliness? Sexual frustration? A profound sense of isolation? What do you have to gain? Peace. Connection. An orgasm so intense it will shatter your limitations, heal your soul, and touch that place deep inside that's always been unreachable." Despite Nina's horrid and unintended pun, I hear what she's saying.

Everett, I've made my decision. I'm going to swallow my pride, call you, and ask you if you can refer me to a good Nest Life meeting. I hope you will be able to keep your gloating to a minimum.

Intrigued and a little sheepish,
Roxy

September 9, 2012

Dear Everett,

Thank you for sharing the address and time of an Everett-approved OM meeting. There was no need for you to get huffy in confirming you would not be in attendance at the next few meetings of that particular group. I now must inquire (at least rhetorically) what a girl is supposed to wear to lose her OM cherry. I have looked online at the Nest Life website and I see they do sell OM legwarmers ($29.95) so a grrrl can keep cozy and still expose her vagina to a room full of strangers. However, that seems like fashion for the advanced OMer (and a way for Nina Sylvester to turn an extra buck), and also impractical in a town as hot and muggy as this one. I hate to rely on the same flowery sundress I wore to Sun City, yet it seems more dignified somehow to lift up one's skirt than to try to peel off a pair of skinny jeans in front of an audience. Also, underwear selection will be of utmost importance. I assume there is a trendy type of panties for OMers—just as all the women at barre class wear Lululemon tights and open-backed "Flashdance"-style shirts, or everyone at the skate park wears baggy cargo shorts. I'm imagining lacy, black, classic panties. A thong seems unsanitary.

Oh, wait! I can wear my pink pleather python panties! Perhaps I'll set a fashion trend for vegan OMers!

I can't believe I'm really doing this.

Oh, shit. I need to leave in ten minutes and I still have to feed the furballs and put on a little makeup.

Uh-oh. I just sniffed my armpits and it seems like OM nerves have given me anxiety B.O. Now I need to shower, too! Shit!

Hurriedly,
Roxy

September 10, 2012

Dear Everett,

Yesterday I arrived at the cute blue craftsman-style two-story off Duval Street. I sat in my car listening to my FAIL BETTER! CD for two whole songs. It's become a soothing habit to play their sweet sounds before any major occasion, but it didn't have its usual calming effect. I still could hear blood pounding in my ears, so I reached over and rifled through my glove compartment until I found an old expired bottle of Klonopin. I took one.

A woman named Beatrice answered the door wearing an adorable flowered baby doll dress with Mary Jane shoes, looking so cute and normal that it was disarming. I thought maybe OMing wasn't as weird and fringe as I'd made it out to be. (And I was glad I'd chosen well in the outfit department.) She welcomed me into her living room, where about eight people were hanging out—it looked like an almost even mix of men and women, and no one seemed repulsive or crazed.

Beatrice chatted me up rather enthusiastically, asking me how long I'd been OMing. I told her I'd never OMed before. "Oh, I'm jealous! I'd give anything to go back to my first time; I mean, especially knowing what I know now. It will CHANGE. YOUR. LIFE," she exclaimed, with such excitement I didn't know if I should be convinced or worried. "It's literally transformed me—I mean, I was lonely and seeking, and now I just feel happy!"

For a moment I pondered that some variation of that same monologue was likely being recited at that exact same moment in various church basement AA meetings, Mormon potlucks, and Buddhist meditation meet-ups. It fascinates me what we fragile humans find and cling to and convince ourselves is our salvation. I felt a sudden sense of waffling. Sure, Patrick wasn't great in bed, but now that I'd gotten over the hurdle of sleeping with someone who wasn't Brant Bitterbrush, couldn't I find someone who wasn't totally lazy in the sack and ask him to rub my clit for fifteen minutes or so? Did I really need to be in a room with this group of friendly zealots?

But before I could make a break for it, Beatrice clapped her hands lightly and called for everyone to gather in a circle. Some people sat in chairs, some on the floor, and for a horrified moment I thought I might be called on to lie on the ground in the center of the gathering and pull up my skirt. But no, this seemed to be some sort of intimacy building warm-up exercise. We all went around the circle and introduced ourselves, and then Beatrice said, "Now, let's share what we're most afraid of."

Shit! Shit! Shit! I had not signed up for some sort of group therapy session. I regretted not asking Artemis and Annie their opinions about whether or not I should attend an OM meeting. But I hadn't done so because (while Artemis was a wild card) I knew—more or less—what Annie would say, which was "Are you fucking crazy? Don't do that." Advice I would have felt compelled to heed and thus I wouldn't be here, forced to confess my deepest fears to a roomful of strangers.

As we went around the circle, I did appreciate the opportunity to check out each person closely without seeming like I had a staring problem. There was Lisa, a sultry thirtysomething who was scared of dying alone; Kevin, a muscular thespian who was scared of never having his artistic talent recognized ("You stole my fear!" I wanted to shout); Sharon, a striking woman with hair dyed so platinum blond it looked like it might be possible to break the strands like matchsticks, who was afraid of never finding true love; Samantha, who in her early forties would have been pretty if she hadn't paid to have her face shot full of Botox and fillers ("Let me guess," I wanted to say, "you are afraid of aging and losing your sexual power!"), who said she was scared she and her daughter would never get along. An Australian guy named Mike who was in his mid-fifties and wore coke-bottle glasses confessed his fear that he wouldn't get a green card. Beatrice said she had to "second the emotion" of Kevin's fear of never receiving recognition as an artist. Then everyone giggled, making it impossible for me to "third that emotion."

I felt a great, unexpected anger well up in me. I did not want to be able to relate to these people at all. I wanted my fears to be special and absolutely unique. As I was up next and the very last to share my deepest fear, everyone in the group stared at me expectantly. The room went totally silent, and when I spoke it was like a dam broke open inside me, and I flooded the room with angry words.

"Lots of the very best artists are never recognized for their work," I said. "Henry Darger was a hospital custodian. When he was alive no one knew he was writing 'The Story of the Vivian Girls.' It was fifteen thousand pages long, with an additional several hundred painted illustrations. Or take James Hampton, another janitor. He spent fourteen years building a 'gilded' throne for Jesus's Second Coming. Sure, 'The Throne of the Third Heaven of the Nations Millennium General Assembly' is in the Smithsonian now." (As a side note, I sometimes think Ignatius J. Reilly was right to call the Smithsonian "that grab bag of our nation's refuse," an interesting argument in the case of "The Throne," which was constructed entirely of trash.) "But in James Hampton's lifetime? No one knew he was even building The Throne. And that lack of recognition isn't my fear. It's a PETTY FEAR," I said, staring hard first at Kevin and then at Beatrice. "The fear of not being recognized is a petty fear because the artistic work done in anonymity is often the bravest and most worthy work." I was crying by that point. I don't know what had gotten into me. "No. My fear is that I won't fucking do the work at all."

I was sobbing, and Beatrice—who I'd just been really nasty to—kindly handed me a box of Kleenex. The rest of the group looked at me, nodding sympathetically, and finally Beatrice said, "Amazing work, Roxy."

The other OMers kept nodding. A few looked at me with deep sympathy, and a couple muttered, "Glad you're here."

I should have left then; I really should have. But the vibe of acceptance was so strong, it kept me stuck to my spot on the floor. The furballs are great company, but they are immune to my artistic angst and philosophies. And those numbnut OMers may or may not have understood the point I was trying to make, but I could see that, regardless, they listened without judgment.

"Okay," Beatrice said. "I think it's time. Who's driving?"

Several of the OMers raised their hands. "Driving?" I asked. Was this OM-speak for the first males to glove up? What were they talking about?

"We're going to the OM Convention at the Hyatt," Beatrice said.

"Convention?" Alarm bells rang in my head. "That sounds next level. I'm new. I'm not going to a convention."

Beatrice chimed in, "But Nina will be there!"

"Nina Sylvester?" I asked. Now I was interested.

"Imagine seeing Nina in person," Beatrice cooed. "It'll be revelatory."

"A rare appearance," Kevin agreed. He looked right at me. "You're so lucky."

"But I don't think—" I stammered.

Samantha, the Botox lady, chimed in, "I'm not sure Roxy is ready for the convention." She spoke in an annoying, motherly tone that made it clear why she has a rebellious daughter.

"Roxy's a natural," Kevin said. "I mean, we all saw her ability to be so incredibly emotionally open." All the OMers paused and stared at me, nodding slowly in agreement and approval.

The force of their acceptance overwhelmed my better judgment. "What the hell," I said. "I'll go."

In retrospect, I clearly should have made a break for it, but the

"Greatest Fear" exercise had succeeded in stripping me of my natural defensiveness and sense of self. And I hate saying no to a challenge. So I moved with the amorphous blob of OMers outside and, still sniffling, climbed into the backseat of a blue minivan driven by the Australian. Kevin sat next to me. I was suspicious of him as an OMer—he was so fantastically handsome it was hard to imagine him being concerned with perfecting his clit-rubbing technique. Perhaps he had some sort of erectile dysfunction? Or OMing provided him with access to women he perceived as "sexually loose"? Regardless, I started thinking I wouldn't mind being OMed by him. As the old nerdy Australian drove us downtown, I asked Kevin what plays he's been in recently. "I'm between plays right now, so mostly doing commercials," he said with faux humbleness. "And a couple of J.Crew catalog shoots."

"What do you think about Lululemon? Would you ever do a shoot with them?" I asked suspiciously.

"I don't have anything against them. Why do you ask?"

"No reason, never mind," I said. Kevin then proceeded to gently ask me about my art, but I told him I wasn't interested in talking about it with him right then. "Your share was really brave," he said. "It's orgasmic to be so open. It usually takes newbies a while to get to that point."

For a second I thought about hollering for the old Australian guy to turn the van around and take me back to my car, but I abruptly felt indescribably weary and also very, very mellow. Looking back on it, the Klonopin must have kicked in, so it was easier to just sit there in the backseat of the van as it rolled along the highway than fight the current and make a fuss. Everett, I should have known then that complacency is the enemy. But I was too sad and lonely and disappointed in myself and my life, too stripped by my outburst of grief and anger, too sedated by head meds to go against the group tide. Perhaps I was also just really freaking curious to see Nina Sylvester in person.

At the Hyatt, the Australian parked the minivan and we made our way to the hotel lobby, where someone slapped wristbands on all of us. We wandered down a hallway and then stood together in front of the doors of an enormous ballroom/convention room. I felt a kinship with this particular group of weirdos—I had, after all, known them, albeit briefly, in the outside world. I'd been assuming all along I'd be partnered to OM with Kevin, but when I turned to him to confirm he said, "Beatrice is my OM partner for this session." He glanced at his watch. "But I'll meet you for the two o'clock sesh if you want?"

"Sure," I mumbled. I turned to search out a partner and found myself face-to-face with the old Australian guy with the scraggly beard and inch-thick glasses.

"I see you are looking for a partner," he said. "I'd be honored."

Before I could protest, a large group pushed open the doors of the ballroom and we floated in with them. The scene before me was bizarre and surreal. Every bit of furniture had been removed from the vast, cavernous room. On the carpeted floor, hundreds of brightly colored yoga mats had been laid out—red, purple, yellow, orange—each with a large round purple pillow with a silky cover set upon it. For a moment I felt like I'd wandered into nothing more than a meditation or yoga convention. But the giant space seemed overly crowded with people—all of whom were trying not to step on the yoga mats and pillows—and a quiet, anticipatory energy filled the room.

My panic and apprehension still lurked within me, but they had been dulled by the Klonopin. If I hadn't been on drugs, I'm sure I would have totally fucking bolted. (And now I remember why I quit taking Klonopin—it soothes my natural alarm systems, which are there for a reason! As such, Klonopin is not my fucking friend!) I felt a surge of gratitude that I was in a dress and thus would be spared the indignity of really disrobing. I was wearing the pink pleather python panties. At home they'd seemed edgy and cool, but now I was regretting the choice. "I'm looking forward to this," the Australian guy said, and I wished I could remember his name. "I've heard a large group OM can be really powerful."

Just when I thought again about making a run for it, an incredibly hot guy took to the stage to a smattering of hand clapping. "Ten years ago," he said into the microphone, "I was lost. My life lacked joy, connection, and meaning. But then I met Nina Sylvester, and she told me about another way to live." Nina! He was going to introduce Nina! He continued, "Over the last decade, I've spent more time with my finger on a woman's clit than most people have spent watching movies, television, and social media combined. I've become a relationship coach and I have done studies on the female orgasm and the profound effects it has on women, as well as on their partners. This has allowed me to develop new ways of helping people relate to each other. And I owe it all to Nest Life founder Nina Sylvester. Can we have a big round of applause for Nina?"

The applause was thunderous as Nina Sylvester herself took the stage. She wore a fitted, sleeveless green dress that accentuated her lithe body. "Women, take to your nests," she boomed, with such a commanding voice and presence I couldn't help but obey.

Things got even weirder when all around me, women shimmied out of their pants and sat down on their "nests." We are talking hundreds of women disrobing from the waist down, creating an eerie rustling of fabric, as hundreds of men stood around and tried to act like they weren't watching. A woman nearby me hopped around awkwardly on one foot as she tried to peel off a pair of leggings. I stood there reluctantly as all the women sat down on the pillows (a.k.a. nests) and the men knelt on the ends of the yoga mats near their feet. Without yet removing my panties, I crouched down so as not to draw attention to myself.

"This is going to be an incredible experience for all of us," Nina continued. "I want to express gratitude to our door counters. Thanks to them, we know that at 672 participants, this will be the largest OM in the history of the world!" Whoa! I was going from zero to the Guinness Book of World Records—I was helping to break a sex cult record! Everyone in the room applauded enthusiastically, and I felt a momentary surge of enthusiasm courtesy of Nina. "Men, don your gloves." The Australian pulled on latex medical gloves. Next to me, Beatrice had lain back on her nest with her knees flung apart, her head thrown back as if in anticipation of abandon. Kevin knelt down in front of her.

Wait, what was I doing here? The energy of seconds ago morphed just as quickly into confusion as I surveyed panties scattered on the floor all around me. What individual choices had I made that had resulted in me being in a room with 336 women naked from the waist down? I could not quite call to mind the string of events that had led me to be dropping my own pink pleather python panties to the floor of a hotel ballroom. I lay back on the nest, butterflied open my legs, and squeezed my eyes shut. I suddenly understood the ostrich that sticks its head in the sand as I hoped madly that closing my eyelids to the crowded ballroom would cause it to cease to exist. "Get ready, get set, OM!" Nina said as a loud and sonorous bell rang to signal the start of the fifteen-minute OMing period.

The Australian's lubed finger touched my clit, lightly, ever so lightly. It certainly felt as though he knew what he was doing. I relaxed into the sensation, trying—as Nina had exhorted in the videos I'd watched—to focus all my attention on that point of contact between his finger and my clit. Just as it was starting to work, all around me women began moaning and sighing. It made it hard to focus. A few nests over a woman started warbling and clucking like a perturbed chicken. A couple rows in front of me another woman commenced squawking as well, as if the barnyard noises were somehow contagious. In contrast, all the men worked with silent, focused intensity. The woman next to me screamed and I looked over to see if she was all right, but it was clear when I saw Beatrice's face that the screams were of ecstasy. That, Everett, is when I saw you, two rows down and staring right at me! There is not enough Klonopin in the world to take the edge off having your ex-boyfriend watch you get fingerbanged by some old Australian while the ex-boyfriend himself fingerbangs some other woman, all in a hotel convention ballroom full of . . . Well, I don't have to tell you. You were there.

That's when I jumped up, crammed on my sandals, and ran from the room, weaving between nests as I went, all of those pink and purple and brown vaginas staring at me, hundreds of vaginas (THREE HUN-DRED AND THIRTY-SIX, to be exact). I ran on and on through the endless wave of nests, as if in some nightmare Freud himself would not have dared analyze.

I burst through the double doors. They swung open, releasing the sounds of hundreds of women receiving sexual pleasure—many of them apparently sound exhibitionists and many more (inexplicably!) intent on imitating the racket of farm animals. With the doors still wide open, I ran straight into the sculpted chest of a man wearing a black T-shirt. I stepped back and almost fainted. It was none other than Texas, the hot drummer from FAIL BETTER! He first looked beyond me to the inside of the ballroom where he saw hundreds of OMers hard at their medita-tive work. The doors slammed shut behind me as our eyes met, both of us in a kind of traumatized shock. "Vet girl," he said.

"Texas," I said.

"What are you— What are you doing here?"

"What are YOU doing here?" Deflecting was clearly the only way to muddle through this surprise encounter.

"I'm here for work."

Was he waiting tables at the hotel's restaurant? Or—oh Goddess!—was he working a catering gig for the OM convention? "Oh, well, I'm just headed out." I gestured wildly down the hall toward the hotel en-trance.

He glanced down, his attention caught at floor level. "Your under-wear seems to be hanging from your shoe," he said. I looked down with horror to see my pink pleather python panties snagged on my sandal.

"They could be anyone's," I stammered.

"Apparently," he said dryly, with a glance at the ballroom doors. He took in the sign by the door that read: ORGASMIC MEDITATION, LARGE GROUP SESSION 1 P.M. "I've been meditating for years, but apparently I haven't been doing it right." He gave me a sly smile.

"It's not too late to start," I said. "But I wouldn't recommend it." I bent down and pulled the panties from my shoe, wadding them up in my hand. Just then, the ballroom doors swung open again. The sounds that hit us, the sight of that veritable sea of vaginas, curdled my blood. Out stepped the old Australian, his eyes magnified to the size of silver dollars behind his glasses. He still wore a blue medical glove on one hand, the fingers shiny with lube. A half erection strained at his pants. "There you are!" he said. "Are you okay? I know it's been an emotional day for you. But you were just loosening up!" My curdled blood drained out of me. I was submerged in a vat of shame, so scorching and foul I felt as if it was steaming my skin off.

Texas and I looked at each other. His eyes were inscrutable. Was he amused? Embarrassed for me? Horrified?

"I've got to go," I told Texas. The Australian I ignored completely. I fled, squeezing my panties tightly in my fist as I ran down the hallway. The burnt-orange carpet covered in gold swirls stretched out in front of me like a hideous psychedelic trip that would not end.

Outside I frantically tried to pull up an app on my phone to call a driver, but my fingers shook so badly they fumbled at the screen. That's when you came out of the hotel doors. Everett, you were so kind in talking me off the ledge and driving me home.

I wish I could have explained to you then that my crying in the car the entire ride was about a lot more than the OM Convention, or being

OMed by an old guy, or even running smack into Texas. It was also about Patrick, and Brant Bitterbrush, and the fact that I don't draw anymore, and that I'm underemployed, and lonely. You kept telling me you were sorry. But it wasn't your fault. My life isn't your fault at all.

I can't tell you how much it meant to me that you fed the furballs, and gave Roscoe his insulin shot, and Charlize Theron her pill while I took a hot shower, put on my most conservative pajamas, and got into bed. But I'll tell you now—it was nice to have your help again. And as you sat there in the chair in the corner of my bedroom until I fell asleep, it felt like you were a hapless angel sent to watch over me, or a kind old friend eager to make amends.

Traumatized but also weirdly grateful,
Roxy

September 11, 2012

Dear Everett,

When I woke up yesterday morning, I got your note that you'd already given Roscoe and Charlize Theron their meds. Sad to find myself alone in the house again, the reality of my situation descended. The thought of going into work and possibly having to see Patrick was more than I could stand, so I called in sick.

"Let me guess," Dirty Steve said, "you are sick from dropping molly at some fire dancer performance?"

"I'm not sick. I went to an orgasmic meditation session where 336 men fingered 336 women in a hotel ballroom and it was so shameful and horrifying that now I can't get out of bed."

"I thought I'd heard every excuse in existence," Dirty Steve mused. "That is disgusting." He sounded impressed. I said I'd be in tomorrow and he said not if he fired me first.

I lay in bed all day, staring at the ceiling in a state of depressed isolation. At nightfall, I finally gathered my resolve and sent Annie and Artemis an SOS. They both immediately agreed to come over and bring alcohol.

Artemis arrived first with a six-pack and a splurge bottle of High West bourbon. "You look like shit," she said.

"What's up, Sin Sation?"

"WHAT? How do you know about that?" she asked.

"How many alter egos do you have?"

"Girl, I lose track." Just then Annie knocked on the door. Once we'd settled in with drinks, I gave them a blow-by-blow of my spiral of humiliation.

"Epic!" Artemis said. "First you barf on the FAIL BETTER! drummer's girlfriend's shoes, and then you bust out of a doorway leading to seven hundred people masturbating each other with panties dangling from your shoe. Shit, girl. He's gonna be intrigued."

"She's right," Annie concurred. "You are most definitely on his mind."

Artemis launched into her theory that the crazier and weirder and more eccentric a woman seems, the more a man worth his salt will want to get with her. She was talking so fast her words seemed to bump into one another, as if each was a reckless driver who couldn't obey the speed limit.

"Who said Texas is worth his salt? You are the one who told me all drummers are busters," I added. Then Annie began a rousing condemnation of guys in Austin who think just having a pulse and a dick that gets hard should suffice and that no further effort or courtship is required on their part.

Artemis countered in an increasingly slurred voice that a pulse and a hard dick were perfect offerings, really, because who wanted to deal with a man who would hang around? It was a fantastic night overall, and for a bit I even forgot my sorrows and humiliation.

But now today I am hungover and cannot call in sick again for fear I will lose my job. And I hope I don't have to face Patrick. I don't want to think about him rising to the occasion of a skillful coupling with that sexy burlesque girl. Oh why, oh why did I let myself think getting my honey where I make my money was a good idea!???

Melancholily,
Roxy

September 12, 2012

Dear Everett,

Well, as I anticipated, yesterday work was a living hell. Nelson is still gone to PharmaTrial so we were short-staffed. (I console myself with the thought that at least I have not hit the rock bottom of selling my body to Big Pharma.) Customers stood three deep at the deli counter all afternoon and were thus grumpy once they were finally able to place their orders. I kept my eyes peeled for any sign of Patrick. For hours there was nothing, but then at about 4 p.m. I spotted him standing in line at a register with the raven-haired burlesque grrrl who must have come in to eat a late lunch with him on his break. When he and I were doing our "dance" of flirtation, he never once asked me to have lunch!!!!!! A lunch date seems so casual yet intimate that it must be a sign of a seriously burgeoning relationship. I feel humiliated and alone and somehow convinced the burlesque goddess has already taught Patrick how to lavish (non-weird, non-masturbation cult) attention on her lady bits.

On my break I walked over to Waterloo Records just to get out of Whole Foods. I was again greeted by the giant FAIL BETTER! poster in the Waterloo window announcing their upcoming in-store performance. Texas looked down on me like the billboard eyes of Dr. T. J. Eckleberg in "The Great Gatsby." Seeing his cute face and ripped physique in that tight black T-shirt brought back the horrible memories of what I now think of as "the Great OM Debacle of 2012." Though in real life, run-ins with Texas have brought only profound embarrassment, strangely his band's music still gives me comfort. I even ducked into the listening booth for ten minutes of the soothing sounds of his drumming.

Though I was momentarily calmed by the sounds of FAIL BET-TER!, I now feel I am destined to be alone with the furballs, and that any attempts I make to form a romantic bond with another human will be met with failure and disappointment.

Sadly,
Roxy

P.S. Perhaps to make myself feel even worse, I texted Artemis to ask if she would please participate in the Lululemon protest. NO WAY! she texted back. I'D BE FIRED SO FAST. I LOVE YOU, BUT I LOVE HAVING A JOB AS A GUERRILLA BODY IMAGE COUNSELOR MORE.

I HATE TO ADMIT IT, BUT THAT MAKES ME FEEL BETRAYED, I countered.

I HATE TO ADMIT IT, BUT YOUR SELFISHNESS KNOWS NO BOUNDS, she said.

I'm not sure if either or both or neither of us was kidding.

P.P.S. The one bright spot of my day—before work I saw a cleaning crew hauling dirty couches and other crap out of Tweakerville. It looks like I've successfully ousted Captain Tweaker and his brethren from my life forever!

September 15, 2012

Dear Everett,

I will admit that when you told me last night that you're "seeing" a woman who lives at the OM house, it felt like a punch to the gut. (And of course she has a totally sexy, mysterious name—Nadia! A name that all the world will forever associate with a perfect 10!) I always secretly comforted myself with the idea that you wanted to be with me. It made me feel like I was alone by choice. I never even admitted it to myself, but I liked having you on standby as my fallback option. And now you perhaps love another. (Though I have to wonder—what does it mean to be "seeing" someone in a house where everyone fingerbangs everyone else? Do you still glove up when you hook up with her? Are you now "exclusive" as OMers? Or do you still partner swap for timed sessions?)

Now that I know you have a girlfriend, I have to ponder the fact that I haven't given you a single letter I've written to you in months, certainly not since before you moved out. Writing to you just served in the end to make me (falsely) feel you would always be available to me as a back-up boyfriend. But I cannot lay down my pen. And whether or not you are my boyfriend, you will always be the person whose listening ear got me marginally back on my feet after my heart was crushed by Brant Bitterbrush. You are the person I find it easiest in the world to talk to and so talk to you I will, if only in a one-sided way you will never hear. I will continue to write out my truths to you, starting with this one: I am a failure with men.

If the thought of munching on a vagina didn't make me feel unbearably squeamish I would convert to lesbianism on the spot. Regrettable (and even prudish) though it may be, even in my fantasies all I want is dick. My recent failed attempt at romance with Patrick makes me miss Brant Bitterbrush and our relationship all the more, which for so long was delightful and happy, frolicking and passionate. How long will I yearn for the days when we slept tangled together? How long will anger and shame at his double crossing vex me? Sometimes I think the only way to truly exorcise him from my spirit would be to get Duckie & Lambie kicked out of Whole Foods. But is it truly my path to obsess about revenge in every corner of my life? Also, Annie says if I don't stop pestering her about it she will no longer be my friend. "Putting your energy into doing something bad to a new father of triplets—even if he deserves it—is not going to make for a happier life for you," she says every time I bring up the fact that she should be using her sway with Topher Doyle to evict Duckie & Lambie from the aisles of Whole Body.

Artemis came over for coffee yesterday and I confessed all to her as we painted two signs. She dumped quite a bit of bourbon into her coffee and I got the impression she may have had a few swigs off the bottle on the way to my house. (Sometimes I think I should worry about Artemis, but she's so much fun it's impossible to do so with any seriousness.)

"You, my friend, have a case of one-itis," she said. "Hand me the gold paint."

"One-itis?" I rooted through the paint tubes until I found Solid Gold Tacky, which I passed her way.

"It's where you are obsessed with ONE GUY."

"That's not entirely true. For a while I was obsessed with Patrick."

"But over the past year, you've spent most of your time thinking about—"

"Brant Bitterbrush. No question."

"There is only one cure for one-itis," she said seriously, as if she was a doctor doling out a difficult medical treatment. She squeezed too much gold paint onto a scrap of cardboard. Go figure—that girl does absolutely everything to excess.

"And?"

"It's to go out and fuck twelve guys. Then come back and tell me you are still pining for Brant Bitterbrush. 'Cause ya won't be. And that Duckie & Lambie shit? Forget about it. Thinking about revenge is just giving that guy more of your lifeblood." As she spoke she waved her hands in the air and then dragged her fingers through her hair, like a mad sage desperate to impart her wisdom to me.

I looked over at Artemis's sign. I'd carefully outlined the words: BUY LOCAL. DON'T BUY A (LULU)LEMON, but she was doing a sloppy job filling in the paint. "Careful with that," I said. "And forget it. I slept with Patrick and that just made me feel worse. It was like another scoop of heartbreak on the banana split of my Brant Bitterbrush sorrow."

"But he was lousy in bed!" Artemis roared. "You don't just need sexual healing, you need clitoral healing, too!" I must have told her at some point about Patrick's Marvin Gaye dance moves. "At least that cock-block Everett has moved out and moved on!" Artemis's philosophies and theories are questionable, but her enthusiasm never fails to cheer me up. "Can you draw a pucker-faced lemon for me?" she asked, pushing her sign over to me.

Speaking of blocks: two months ago, if someone'd asked me to draw and paint a lemon, I wouldn't have been able to even attempt it, but now I set to work, knowing it was just a stupid sign and one someone else would probably be holding.

Artemis was so drunk by the time she was ready to go home that I ordered her a ride. While we were waiting, she started talking about how worried she is that the plumber who unstopped her toilet a while ago is going to come back and berate her for putting some spaghetti down her sink. (???) It didn't make a lot of sense, but I'm chalking it up to drunk talk. Mostly I think Artemis is talented and wild and fun, but sometimes I wonder about her.

Worriedly,
Roxy

September 17, 2012

Dear Everett,

Artemis's uplifting effect stuck with me for a couple of days, but had largely worn off by yesterday morning. As I sat outside having my morning coffee and moping slightly, I realized I have NOT been showing up for Yolanda in this, the run-up to her wedding. I've barely spoken to her since last month when she asked me to be a bridesmaid. I felt a twinge of guilt at being so focused on myself at a time when I should be showering attention on the soon-to-be-bride. As I was also rather lonely, I gave her a call. Even though she was at work, she picked up right away and asked if I'd meet her, Kate, Rose, and Barclay for a happy-hour drink at some yuppie bar on West Sixth. I reluctantly agreed and—to my surprise—the whole experience was delightful. Those girls are hilarious, and even their tales of motion-activated kitchen sink faucets and stultifying jobs are somehow chortle inducing. How have I let myself become so isolated? Seeing them made me realize something: I don't have to be as wild as Artemis, or as professionally savantish as Annie. I don't have to plan a wedding like Yo, or hold down a boring nine-to-five job like Yo, Kate, Rose, and Barclay. I can love them all and also kind of make my own way. Unfortunately, my way is currently characterized by professional and romantic doldrums. I am hoping if I pay further homage to Venus, Goddess of Friendship, things will really open up for me.

But for now, the grrrls and I have committed to meeting up at least once a month until Yolanda's wedding festivities ramp up in December, at which point I'll see them more often. The only question is, what shall I read at her wedding? There's a glorious passage from Denis Johnson's "Jesus' Son" about the love Fuckhead feels for a bartender with a heavy pour that might suffice!

With the energy of renewed friendships,
Roxy

P.S. Now I'm off to Crystal Works to gather items for a new Venus altar before I head in to work. It's unfortunate that such a parlor of crystals and sage should sit in the shadow of House Park Bar-B-Que, whose sign reads: NEED NO TEEF TO EAT MY BEEF. But that cannot be helped.

September 18, 2012

Dear Everett,

I went out and ran some errands today and when I arrived home I opened the door and, for the first time ever, Roscoe didn't run up to greet me. "Roscoe?" I called, hurrying through the house, but he wasn't there. Panic and adrenaline surged through my body. Where was my baby? I ran to the kitchen and peered through the window to see a man on his hands and knees in the backyard digging a hole.

It was Captain Tweaker!

And next to him on the ground lay Roscoe's very blingy dog collar. Fueled by a wave of wrath at this fresh, horrific knowledge that Captain Tweaker had murdered my Roscoe and was now burying him, I grabbed the giant bottle of olive oil off the counter by the neck and blasted out the back door.

I charged Captain Tweaker. He looked up at me from his hands and knees and his face registered surprise before I bashed him in the side of the head with the olive oil. The bottle broke, dousing us both in oil. I dropped to my knees and grabbed the trowel Captain Tweaker had been holding as he fell to the ground. I dug frantically to unbury my sweet Roscoe. But then my trowel hit glass with a clink. I dug more frantically and pulled out a mason jar full of jewelry and other items I couldn't quite make out due to the dirt clinging to the jar. I shook Captain Tweaker violently. "What did you do to my dog?" I screamed.

Captain Tweaker came to, slowly.

"Where is Roscoe?" I yelled.

"At the vet," he said. "My sister's with him at the vet."

"WHAT?" I yelled, shaking him. "What did you do to my dog???!!!"

Captain Tweaker sputtered out that he had arrived in my yard to find Roscoe choking on something. His sister (???) had hurried Roscoe to the vet. None of this made sense to me but I dragged him to his feet and toward my car. "Where?" I yelled. "Where are they?"

"At the emergency vet on Mary Lane," he said.

I've been to the emergency vet more than once so I knew the way. We climbed into my car—still dripping olive oil—and I drove at lightning speed. Captain Tweaker was rambling on but I couldn't process anything he said, I was so panicked. At the vet ER I jumped out of the car and ran in yelling, "Roscoe! Is my Roscoe okay?"

The receptionist said, "He's going to be fine. You can see him now. He's in Exam Room Eight."

I hurried through the dog gate and down the hall, bursting into the exam room, where Roscoe was happily playing with a woman who looked like an elementary school librarian. I fell to my knees, sobbing and hugging him. "What did you do to my dog?" I said to the woman accusingly.

"She saved his life," the vet said. He held out a masticated blob of my pink pleather python panties. "If she hadn't brought Roscoe in when she did, he would have died. These are much less breathable than the cotton panties he ate last time."

Roscoe licked my face happily, and I didn't understand anything. And in my relief I didn't care.

Once I had calmed down and paid the receptionist some exorbitant fee that once again maxed out the credit card I've been paying down, I took Roscoe out into the parking lot, Captain Tweaker and his librarian-looking sister on my heels.

"So what the fuck?" I said. "Give me one reason I shouldn't call the police right now."

"I've been sober since the day I got arrested," Captain Tweaker said.

"Why aren't you in jail?" I demanded.

"I'm a first-time offender. My friend Riff Raff—the little guy—it was his van and his operation. So I just pled to intent to distribute and got probation. Riff Raff and some of the others with priors are going away for years. But when I was living next door to you, I had some stuff that belonged to our mom." He gestured at his straitlaced sister. "And I knew if the other guys found it, they'd pawn it. And then my sister would literally kill me."

"I would," his sister said. "I literally would."

"So I buried it in your yard in that mason jar," Captain Tweaker explained.

"And I told him we needed to go dig it up," the sister said. "Where is it, anyway?"

"Shit, I left it in the yard," Captain Tweaker said.

The sister let out a groan of despair and anger I only too well recognized and smacked him on the arm.

"Hey!" Captain Tweaker protested, then turned back to me. "So we went together to your house to dig it up."

"I didn't trust him to do it by himself," the sister explained. "I was all for just knocking on your door and asking for your help."

"But I knew you'd never let us. So my sister waited in the car while I went into your backyard, and I saw your little dog was choking on something. And in AA and NA I'm learning that you have to do the right thing in the moment, as best you can. So I got off his collar and tried to get out whatever was stuck in his throat. I couldn't, so I grabbed the dog and took it to my sister's car. She wouldn't let me in the car until I had the mason jar, but said she'd drive the dog to the emergency vet."

"It sounds harsh, but I've been through a lot with him," the sister said.

"I get it," I said.

"So then you came home and found me." He rubbed his head ruefully.

"Can we come get our mom's things?" the sister asked, her eyes glistening. "She died eight months ago. That's when this one really went down the tubes." She gestured at her brother.

"Okay," I agreed, still trying to process the unexpected developments. Captain Tweaker saved Roscoe's life?

"Thank you," Captain Tweaker said, and in his eyes I saw something I thought I'd never see there—humanity and even gratitude. I thought he looked almost handsome, and then he smiled and his horrible, meth-rotten teeth totally ruined it.

Miffed and exhausted by the emotional roller coaster of the day,
Roxy

September 19, 2012

Dear Everett,

Venus is a crazy bitch and magic scares me. Let me explain.

I didn't have to go into work today until 2 p.m. so I did a Venus invocation this morning. First, I set up an altar on a box on the floor. I covered the box with an altar cloth and then put out things Venus likes: rose quartz, sweetgrass, jade, green candles, ylang-ylang essential oil, chocolate, rose kombucha, and a bouquet of roses. I called Venus in, burned sweetgrass and lit the candles, anointed myself with the oil, and then talked to her, telling her all about my nervousness about the Lululemon protest, which is less than two weeks away. I thanked her for every blessing in my life I could think of.

Then I told her about my shambles of a nonexistent love life and asked for her help and intervention in that arena. I asked for fortitude for times I see Patrick at work. I asked especially that she help me to 100 percent get over the ghost of Brant Bitterbrush. Then I closed things out by reading the traditional "Orphic Hymn to Venus."

Then, in Venus's honor, I made a batch of kombucha. I used to always have a batch of booch brewing, but I'd fallen off the fermentation wagon a few months ago. Luckily I still had a SCOBY (that's a Symbiotic Culture of Bacteria and Yeast to you, Everett!) chilling in vinegar. This time I decided to cast a spell over my booch. "I bless and consecrate you, oh creature of water, and cast out from you any malignancy so that you return to your state of purity, refreshing, cleansing, and blessing all who partake of you," I said. "You turn sugar into healing medicine. Anyone who drinks you will be strong and confident, and will attract good luck and success in love and work." I covered up the sweet tea and SCOBY with a cloth and stuck it under my sink to do its thing.

I was so cheered up and it was such a lovely day that I loaded Roscoe into the car and drove him down to the Hike and Bike Trail. I knew we'd have just enough time to walk the three-mile loop. Then I could drop Roscoe off at home and head to work. I parked by ZACH Theatre. After I got Roscoe on his leash I spotted a serious hottie doing pull-ups at the pull-up bars right at the trailhead. He was shirtless, with great tattoos and ripped abs, and he smiled at me! It made me feel as if Venus was saying, "Here's a little treat for you, Roxy, and there's more where that came from!"

Roscoe and I set out on the trail, both of us walking along jauntily. The sun shone brightly, filtering through the trees to create a magical sun-dappled effect on the gravel. It was boiling hot and I was sweating like a pig, but I wasn't fighting the heat in my mind like I sometimes do. I just accepted it and that made it easier to handle. We walked a couple of miles and when we made it to the sandy bank of the lake by the water fountain, Roscoe looked at me mournfully and whined to be let off the leash. I felt so guilty for leaving out chokeable pleather panties that I couldn't deny him his great wish of a swim on a hot day. So I unhooked his leash and he immediately dog paddled out into the middle of the lake!

"Roscoe! Roscoe!" I called, at first playfully, then with increasing anger, then panic. He wasn't coming back. He managed to keep his head above water, but wasn't budging. A glance at my watch revealed that I was going to be late for work if I didn't get Roscoe back to shore quickly. He whined and started to paddle more frantically with his short little legs, as if he'd realized he was out of his depth and was panicking, too. But he still wasn't really moving toward shore. With a sigh of frustration I took off my shoes, put my phone and wallet in them, and stuck them behind a rock. Then I took off my shirt and swam out into the dirty lake wearing only my shorts and sports bra. I hit a slimy clump of algae and let out a squeak of horror, but pushed forward with a determined breaststroke, all the while keeping my eyes on the prize of my very bad little dachshund.

I had girded myself so that when I hit the next algae patch I didn't even scream. Roscoe's pleading eyes seemed to be saying: "Why am I out here? Will you hurry up and help me already?"

When I made it to him he barked as if he'd never been so overjoyed to see anyone. I grabbed his collar and side stroked toward the shore, the dirty lake water sloshing up into my ears. My presence seemed to have given Roscoe renewed energy—he paddled hard and we made slow if unwieldy progress. My feet hit the muddy bank and Roscoe and I stepped onto dry land. The bottom half of my hair was drenched, and disgusting strands of lake algae hung from my arms and shoulders.

Passersby stared at me, most looking alarmed, though a couple of them chuckled. Roscoe shook himself of water and danced gratefully at my feet, then charged at a couple coming toward us with an impossibly wide baby stroller. He jumped up, putting his dirty wet paws on the husband's leg. "Roscoe!" I yelled, running toward the family. I was still barefoot and dripping and I grimaced at the pain of the gravel on my bare feet. Right before I reached Roscoe I looked up at the man he was jumping on. Our eyes met. BOOM! I was face-to-face with none other than Brant Bitterbrush!—who Roscoe clearly recognized even though he was only a six-week-old puppy when Brant left me. A puppy we had meant to raise together. I wiped some algae from my hair in an attempt to be more presentable, but it was a lost cause. Cold Connie Caldwell stood next to Brant. She was pushing a triple-wide stroller that held three chubby babies. She looked a little tired but also fairly svelte, as if she'd never been stretched out to ungodly proportions in order to birth three little Brant Bitterbrush look-alikes.

"Roxy!" Brant said.

Cold Connie Caldwell stared at me with the contemptuous eyes of a woman who has never found herself running barefoot, half-dressed, and covered in lake algae through a public space. Though she said nothing, one eyebrow shot up in arch disdain.

As Brant bent to pet Roscoe, I looked at the three little identical baby boys in matching sky-blue sailor suits. They looked so much like Brant it made me think if I had birthed them rather than Connie, they would look exactly the same. For the first time in my life, a pang of longing pierced my uterus. And then one of the babies began to wail. Like a line of Brant Bitterbrush dominoes, the second and then the third tot began to cry. Connie bent down to comfort them and also block them from my sight, as if feeling my mere gaze upon her progeny could cause them harm. "Oh, honeys," she cooed. "Did the Creature from the Black Lagoon scare you?"

In the wailing chaos Brant said, "Roscoe, buddy, so good to see you." Roscoe was jumping around like an orphan who's encountered his long-lost father.

"He swam out into the lake," I stammered.

"I see that," Brant said. His eyes scanned my soaking wet body, naked except for a sports bra, shorts, and copious amounts of lake algae. His eyes locked on mine. For a split second it felt like the old days. I remembered that night we made love for the very first time on the warm tar roof of the Barton Springs Pool office. I imagine he remembered it, too.

As if they could sense their father's wander down memory lane to a time before their existence, a time when their mother had been relegated to anal-and-annoying coworker, the babies wailed even louder. One of them spit up an alarming amount of white liquid all over his sailor suit.

"Hang on," Brant said. He bent down next to Connie and extracted the vomit-covered minion from his seat. Somehow he whipped off the baby's shirt and began to wipe him down with a wet wipe that had materialized from Goddess knows where. He laughed. "Bruno," he said. "He holds the family record for projectile barfing. Our own little poltergeist."

Connie chortled at Brant's terrible dad joke as she handed him a tiny spare shirt she extracted from a large ziplock bag full of infant clothes. (Where did they have that stashed? This breeder stuff seemed to require such organization!) She pulled the shirt over the baby's head, then took him from Brant and set him back in the stroller next to the other sprogs, who were now totally calm. "I guess, we'd better—" Brant said, gesturing at the triple-wide stroller.

"Yeah. We better get going," Cold Connie said with great hauteur, as if I was Gregor Samsa and she had better things to do with her time than spend it chatting with a dung beetle.

It would have been like me to say, "I'm glad you're enjoying your life of sloppy seconds." Or even: "WOW! I bet those adorable babies WRECKED your vagina." But instead of using my usual take-a-swing-with-the-olive-oil-bottle-now-ask-questions-later approach, I paused for a moment. And then in lieu of spitting out something mean on impulse, I ignored Cold Connie Caldwell completely. To Brant I just said, "Yeah. Sure. Of course. I have to go, too."

I turned and walked back toward my shoes and shirt, hunched over to hold tight to Roscoe's collar so he couldn't escape and make another beeline to Brant. As I walked, my mind raced to process all that had just happened. Brant had seemed so happy as a dad, so natural. And Connie, she'd laughed like crazy at his terrible joke. As annoyed as she was to run into me, as a mother she was clearly in her uptight element. Wet wipes, spare clothes—I bet she kept the whole operation running smoothly.

I realized it then. Brant had wanted so much to be a young dad. And not just a young dad of fur babies, but of real human babies. For my sake, and for the sake of our love, he'd tried to sublimate that wish. I had been too caught up in our romance to see it. I had been impractical. Dare I say it? I'd been selfish. Maybe he had bailed on me with no explanation, but hadn't he been honest about what he really wanted all along? And hadn't I basically ignored his wishes and instead worked to convince him he didn't need fatherhood in order to have a happy life?

As I fastened Roscoe's leash and sat down on a rock to pick gravel out of my feet and pull on my shoes, Connie and Brant passed me by. Brant gave me a lame wave and a final glance over his shoulder. I watched their retreating backs, the jumbo stroller rolling along smoothly in front of them. To my great surprise, I didn't feel heartbroken. I just felt wistful. If I was a different person—a person who longed for babies myself—that could have been me. But I'd been true to myself and refused to have kids. And in the end, Brant had been true to himself, too. I was oddly happy for him.

I mean, I'll always feel that in some way Brant Bitterbrush was my soul mate. And maybe if we'd met when we were fifty and his kids were grown we could have had decades together. But our timing just wasn't right. Not for this lifetime, anyway. It was time for me to stop thinking about what might have been. What might have been was done for the moment those three babies emerged from Cold Connie Caldwell's uptight vagina. And in reality, I had to admit it was probably done for long, long before that.

I was ghosted by Brant Bitterbrush, and as a result, Brant Bitterbrush had been haunting me for a whole year. But now I'd seen that Brant Bitterbrush was actually not a ghost at all. He's a real, living guy who made a choice to follow his dream. He could have stuck around and pressured me to have kids. But instead he moved on. And I promised myself that no matter how much it hurt, I would move on too.

I've walked around Town Lake at least fifty times since Brant left me and I've never seen him, but today I was finally ready and Venus knew it. Our run-in caused me to die a little bit—of embarrassment and a dash of envy—but like a snake, as I stood by the lakeshore I shed my skin of heartbreak and longing and became fresh and new. Like a phoenix, after burning up in the fires of humiliation, I rose from the ash. (I'm mixing metaphors, but after what happened to me today, who could blame me?)

But I couldn't think about Brant Bitterbrush or my rebirth anymore, because I had to race home, rinse off the algae, throw on some clothes, and hurry to work. I was an hour late and as I walked into the kitchen Dirty Steve said, "That's it! You're fired."

"Fair enough," I said. "An hour is really, really late."

"Are you developing the ability to own up to your mistakes, Poxy Roxy? I never thought I'd see the day. What were you doing, anyway?" he asked. I summed up the Hike and Bike Trail debacle for him. "The Creature from the Black Lagoon." He laughed. "That's a good one. Okay. One more chance. But only because your ridiculous antics entertain me. Next time the firing is going to be real."

So the day was strange and full of revelations. I'm still a bit confused regarding Venus—during my invocation this morning I asked her for help with my love life and instead got a very embarrassing run-in with my ex. Perhaps she is more fickle and brutal than I imagined. Or perhaps she's the wrong planetary deity for me altogether! (But what other planet could I work with? Jupiter would be the obvious choice—except that while Venus loves offerings of flowers and chocolates, Jupiter expects roast meat on his altar, which as a vegan, I can't in good conscience provide!) I'm choosing to believe Venus was just helping me clear my emotional deck. I know well enough by now that magic always comes with a bit of a surprise. But I have to wonder—if relationships are all about timing, then when will the timing be right for me? The stars have aligned for Brant Bitterbrush—and I can't help wondering when and if the stars will ever align for me. One thing I know for sure: Roscoe is an incorrigible and very badly behaved wiener dog.

Emotionally spent,
Roxy

P.S. In an unusual flash of insight, I realized the only thing that could get me to stop obsessing about my bizarre day and my longing for love would be doing something nice for someone else. So even though it's late, I called my dad and asked him if he would fix Captain Tweaker's teeth as a retirement side project. After I told him the whole story, and really talked up Captain Tweaker's epic recovery from addiction resulting from the tragic loss of his mother, my dad finally agreed. Before my parents' trip to Peru, my dad's going to try to do a couple marathon dental sessions with Captain Tweaker! Yippee! Hurray! I now have the glowing (and slightly unfamiliar) good feeling of having done something selfless for someone else!

September 21, 2012

Dear Everett,

I slept like a log last night and when I woke up this morning and went out onto the patio to drink my coffee, the air felt cool and fresh—a cold front had arrived in the night, and for the first time in five months, the heat of summer has finally broken! If that isn't a sign of Venus rewarding me for shedding my skin like a snake, I don't know what is! I'm ready for love, Venus! I'm open to whatever this day may bring!

Renewedly,

Roxy

CHAPTER EIGHT

September 22, 2012

Dear Everett,

I may be officially done with men permanently and forever. Yesterday was the day of FAIL BETTER!'s in-store performance at Waterloo Records. I had vowed not to go, and had to work anyway, but things were slow at the deli and Dirty Steve told me I could leave a little early. I thought it would do no harm to walk across the street and catch the tail end of the performance. While I told myself I had no desire to see Texas again, it felt silly to deny myself a chance to hear one of my favorite new bands play live. I took off my apron, put on a little lipstick and mascara in the bathroom, and headed across the street.

Waterloo Records was packed and I made sure to stand at the very back of the store, where I could watch the band but wouldn't be spotted by Texas. I only caught their last song: a new original called "Plea Deal" that the lead singer said Texas wrote himself. As soon as the band was done playing, I slipped into a listening booth with a CD to hide out until Texas and the other members of FAIL BETTER! had packed up their gear and exited the premises. I heard a knock on the glass and looked up. Texas was standing there with a piece of paper pressed against the glass that read: "Hey, Vet Girl!"

I pulled off my headphones and opened the door. "Hey," I said.

"Hey," he said back. "I saw you come in during our last song."

"It sounded good," I said. You could have cut the awkwardness with a cheesecake knife. "Hey, last time I ran into you—"

As if to spare us both from my explanation, Texas cut me off. "I was there getting some CLEs—you know, for work."

Whatever that meant. "I was just at a work training the other day, too," I said. "Getting some BFDs."

He laughed. "Those are probably more interesting." Another agonizing pause ensued, during which I'm sure both of us were remembering our horrid last encounter. I'd just decided to move to Alaska when he said, "We're all going to grab some pizza in a bit. Want to join?"

"I have to go give my dog Roscoe his insulin shot."

"Oh," he said. He looked disappointed. "Okay then."

"But I could meet you after," I said.

His face brightened. "We're going to The Parlor."

"I love The Parlor! It's my favorite anarchist pizza joint."

"So I'll see you there in a bit?" he asked.

I ran home, gave Roscoe his shot, rinsed off the deli slime, put on a little more makeup, and raced over to The Parlor. I walked in and it took my eyes a bit to adjust. As dark as it was outside, it was dimmer still in The Parlor, which was all concrete floors and blaring punk rock. I looked around for Texas and the FAIL BETTER! crew, but they weren't anywhere to be found.

I sat at the bar, lonely and starving, and drank a pint of beer.

"Hey, Roxy!" I turned around, hoping for Texas, but it was only Ken, who I've known since junior high. He's a history teacher now at Griffin School, a neighborhood private high school for artsy weirdos. "How's it going?"

"Been better. I just got stood up," I said.

"Then you better have a beer and some pizza with us." He gestured to a table full of misfit teachers.

So I did. They even had half a pizza with soy cheese. Every time the door opened I looked toward it to see if it was Texas. But it never was. Ken and the other Griffin School teachers told great stories about their students, though—one of whom showed up to school yesterday wearing only hot pants and duct tape on her nipples. "I didn't say a fucking word, just made sure I didn't look below her nose EVER," Ken said. "Eventually she got embarrassed and put on a sweater." We all laughed. Then Ken looked at me. "Hey wait, the guy that stood you up—did he say which Parlor he was gonna meet you at?"

"Which Parlor? This is the only one."

"Nope. They opened up a new one in Hyde Park, at Guadalupe and Forty-First Street, where the old Tae Kwon Do studio used to be," he said.

"Shit," I yelled, jumping up. "Great to see you, Ken. Nice to meet you, teachers!" I ran out into the parking lot and jumped into my car. Luckily it's only a five-minute drive from The Parlor on North Loop to the new one on Guadalupe. Outside I took a deep breath, finger combed my hair, and then stepped through the doors. I scanned the room and saw Texas staring at me as if he'd been watching the door. He stood up and walked over to me.

"Hey," he said.

"Hey," I said.

"I thought you weren't going to make it."

"I went to the other Parlor."

"There are two?" He looked somehow both panicked and relieved.

"Exactly," I said. "I was halfway through my second anger pint, sure you'd stood me up." I glanced toward his table, where the other guys from FAIL BETTER! were pretending they weren't checking me out.

"We ate all our pizza. Want me to order you another one?"

"Good Goddess!" I said. "That's horrible! What do you need to do? How can I help?"

"Our other friend Doug lives just around the corner. He's picking me up to take me to the hospital."

"Do you want me to take you?"

"No. You don't need to be dragged into this mess." He held his phone out to me. "Give me your number?" he asked.

"Of course," I said. My hands shook as I created a new contact in his cell phone—Vet Girl—and typed in my number. I handed it back to him. "Will you let me know how it goes?"

"Yes," he said. "I'll text you in the morning."

I stood outside with him as we waited for his friend Doug. The enchanted feeling of our date had evaporated with the phone call. Texas looked worried and sad. His friend Doug pulled up in just a couple minutes. "We can give you a ride back to The Parlor."

"No, it's okay. I'll walk. It's just a few blocks."

He leaned in and kissed me on the cheek. "I'll talk to you soon," he said. "It was so great to see you. I'm sorry I have to go." Then he climbed into the car and slammed the door. And then he was gone.

That was last night. And now it's 8 p.m. and I've heard NOTHING from him. Not one text. Not one word. Did he make up that elaborate ruse to get out of his date with me? It doesn't seem possible.

Hell hath no fury and all that, but I can't even be mad because maybe his friend actually died or something.

Deflatedly,
Roxy

"No. I stuffed my feelings at the other Parlor. Want a beer?"

"I don't drink," he said.

"Oh," I said.

"Maybe we should go to Dolce Vita and have a coffee or something."

"I love coffee," I said stupidly.

"Want to meet my friends first?"

We walked over to the table. "Hey, guys, this is Vet Girl," Texas said.

I laughed. "I'm Roxy."

"We know," Arsen Alton said. "Texas has been ripping out what's left of his hair worrying that you weren't going to show." Texas blushed an adorable bright red.

"He's got all his hair," I said. Texas turned around and tilted his head over so I could see a cute little bald spot in the back. "So some of your fur has been loved off," I said. "That's what makes you real."

"'The Velveteen Rabbit' is one of my top five favorite children's books," Texas said.

The FAIL BETTER! guys glared at Texas with a collective look that surely meant, "Shut the fuck up, man!" But I have no idea why. There's nothing wrong with having a working knowledge of a wide range of literature.

"I love it too," I said. We all chatted for a minute, and I tried to casually display my knowledge of FAIL BETTER!'s album without seeming like a groupie. It was a difficult balance to strike, but one I think I did well. Texas told them we were headed over to Dolce Vita for a coffee, and they shot one another knowing looks. I told them it was nice to meet them and Texas and I headed out the door.

"They definitely seemed tuned in to the fact that I'm a girl."

"I told them about you, is all."

"That other girl I always see you with. Is she your girlfriend?"

"Gazelle? She used to dance onstage with the band. She's just my friend."

"Women who look like that aren't anybody's friend."

"Are you being beautyist?"

"I'm just saying."

"Okay. I think maybe she wanted more. And I didn't. So we haven't been hanging out as much."

"Why didn't you want to date her?"

He paused. "I don't want to say anything bad about her. She's a nice woman. Our interests just weren't a total fit. She was so into hair and makeup and clothes. I just can't keep up with that stuff. What about you? Are you and that Australian guy an item?"

"That's just mean."

"It's not! Last time I saw you, it seemed like you were close." He shot one eyebrow up on his forehead in a teasingly Sherlock sort of way.

"Shut uuuuuppppp!" I said. "The road to that moment in time was winding and terrible. And it's one I will not be taking again."

"It did seem rather," he paused as if searching for a word that wouldn't offend, "adventurous." He took my hand and then we were walking along with our fingers clasped. Holding hands! When was the last time I'd held hands with someone? Every single ounce of attention in my body was on the places where our skin touched. It was literally one of the most erotic things that's ever happened to me, no offense to our past sexual relationship, Everett. A couple years ago I had a Spanish tutor. And the way we practiced Spanish was just by talking about our dating lives. And if one of us met someone the other would always say, "¿Hay chemica?" which means, "Is there chemistry?" And there hardly ever was, because good sexual chemistry between two people is rare. But as soon as I held hands with Texas, I knew for sure that we had it.

I asked about how he started playing for FAIL BETTER! and he said before he joined the band, he'd had an electric drum kit that he played all the time in his garage.

"An electric drum kit that doesn't make any noise?"

"I mean, I could hear noise in my headphones."

"You were a silent drummer!" I said.

"I was a silent drummer."

"That's so sad in a way."

He laughed. "It was kind of lonely."

"I'm glad you found a great band to play with."

"What about you? Do you have an art form?"

"I do," I said. For a moment I was on the verge of blathering about how blocked I was artistically and why. But then I felt this sudden waft of intuition and instead I said, "Right now my medium is protest signs."

"Protest signs? Yes! Social justice is my thing. I want to hear more." We were walking through the door of Dolce Vita then and we ordered cappuccinos and sat down at a little table. I took a sip. "Oh my Goddess, that's good," I said.

"I'll probably be up all night and I don't even care," Texas said.

I refrained (barely) from saying something lewd about what he could do all night while he was awake.

"Roxy, I want to hear all about your protest signs, but there's something I want to tell you first," he said. What could it be? He has AIDS. He has herpes. Both of those things I could work with. He's gay? He's bi? He's moving to South America? Right then his phone dinged, and dinged again. "I'm sorry. I have to see what this is." He looked at his phone and all the color drained from his face. He seemed suddenly older, and very sad, and a little afraid. "I'm sorry. I have to make a call."

"Whatever you need to do," I said.

He dialed. "Hello," he said, his brow furrowed in concern. He listened. "Oh God. Oh no. Yeah. I can go to the hospital. I'm at Dolce Vita, but I don't have my car. Okay. See you in a few. I'll be out front." He hung up and looked at me. "My friend Stuart, who I'm kind of responsible for in some ways, he tried to kill himself."

September 24, 2012

Dear Everett,

Still no word from Texas. I lunge for my phone every time I get a text—which confuses Roscoe, who barks excitedly as if it's some sort of sick game—but nothing! I'm trying to imagine what I did to cause Texas to ghost me. Maybe I am a man repellant? I am trying not to obsess on unanswerable questions, but rather to focus on improving myself and my life.

While I am now pretty freaking scared of magic, I still put a bar of fancy chocolate on my Venus altar last Friday. And I tasted my new batch of powerful, spellbound kombucha today. It's almost ready!

Artemis and Annie came over last night to help me with final preparations for the protest on Sunday—just six days away! Annie invited everyone we know on social media. We tweeted it and twatted it and emailed all our friends and coworkers (except for Artemis's coworkers) and now it's really happening. The signs are done. They are not perfect, but I'm glad I drew all the lettering and images and symbols myself and only let Patrick and Artemis fill in my work with paint. The signs may not be art, but they are the sum total of my creative output for the last year, and I am relatively happy with them. Annie told me she was proud of me. Artemis ranted about how we are going to topple corporate America like it's a statue of Saddam Hussein in April 2003. (This was slightly annoying since she's not even coming to the protest.) But then she veered off again, talking about that plumber who fixed her stopped up toilet last month. She said she's pretty sure he's draining her bank account. Annie asked a lot of practical questions about identity theft, calling the bank, Artemis canceling her credit cards, etc. But Artemis didn't seem interested in a solution. It was a little worrisome.

Then we all got progressively drunker and conversation veered toward my recent romantic mishaps. They both admitted that Texas did sound really nice right up until the ghosting, which made it even more loathsome and despicable.

Annie told us she's started seriously dating Jeff Castro in IT, though she's still desperately hot for his identical twin Joe, too. This caused trouble with Jeff the other day when she "accidentally" grabbed Joe around the waist in the kitchen. She swore she mistook Joe for Jeff, but for some reason this didn't assuage Jeff's consternation.

"Maybe you could just say, 'If there were two of me, wouldn't you want to be the meat in that sandwich?'" Artemis suggested.

Annie's love life may be full of tension, but she's rocking her job. Topher Doyle recently called her "my right-hand woman." Ever since their marketing campaign about how Whole Foods lobsters are now housed in ethical lobster condos, sales of lobster have risen 40 percent and overall store sales have risen, too. Annie is angling to have her title changed from "Assistant to Topher Doyle" to Whole Foods's first "Vice President of Animal Rights" (VP of AR), and she's framing it in terms of how great it will be for the company's worldwide image if they have a VP of AR. A fitting move for a woman whose mantra is: "You want the power? Take it."

Artemis confessed she's working on some secret art project, but she won't tell us anything about it. She did promise to let us see it when the time comes. She was very funny and mysterious about it, which has me curious, to say the least.

There is so much cultural hype about boyfriends and husbands, but I'm starting to think that having good girlfriends really is the greatest thing on earth. But now that my house is empty (except for the furballs), Sunday's Lululemon protest looms. This protest will be the first time in ages I will have ACTUALLY DONE SOMETHING I CARE ABOUT. I hope it's not a total failure, or else I may feel I'm "doomed to suck." I am really very nervous about it. It's one thing to complain interminably about the stupid Lululemon. It's another thing entirely to actually try to do something about it.

Best,
Roxy

September 26, 2012

Dear Everett,

Yesterday I went to Sun City to say goodbye to my mom and dad before they take off on their trip to visit my brother Derek in Peru. They found an amazing eco-lodge that has an organic spa and a natural hot springs heated by a nearby volcano, but does not have internet or cell service. As we gushed over the pictures of the swim-up bar and water slide, I felt a serious pang of FOMO that I wasn't able to swing the trip. But after Roscoe's most recent panty-eating episode, my financial situation is even worse than when my parents first started planning the vacation. With no housemate to help with the mortgage, I just don't have the money. My credit card is maxed out again from vet bills and my checking account is always slightly negative by the time I get paid.

My dad opened the door. He was grinning, jaunty like I haven't seen him since he retired, and listening to a novelty country song called "What Would Willie Do?" I finally got it out of him that for the past three days he's been doing twelve-hour marathon dental sessions on Captain Tweaker (who my dad calls by his real name, Franklin). It seems the work has reinvigorated my dad. "It's nice to feel useful again," he said.

"Roxy, it seems this charity project you've cooked up might have saved our marriage," my mother said.

"What?" my father said, feigning outrage.

"If you hadn't snapped out of your grumpy spell, I might have left you," she teased. My dad swatted her on the ass. I'm happy they've rekindled their spark, but ew!

"If you need us when we are gone, dear," my mom said, "you'll have to call the Peruvian consulate." She was wearing a white tennis skirt with hot-pink racing stripes down the side.

"I won't need you," I said. I felt a little jealous they were going to stay somewhere swanky without me, but I didn't want them to know and feel sorry for me. "I hope you have an amazing trip. Give Derek my love." I teared up when I hugged them as I was leaving. While deep down I wish I had a mom who understands me and has a great sense of style, I really do love my parents.

And now they are off to Peru without me.

Feeling slightly orphaned,
Roxy

P.S. The magical kombucha I brewed is ready! I am now dedicated to sipping the elixir daily to increase my strength and confidence, and to attract good luck and success in love and work!

September 28, 2012

Dear Everett,

Nelson is back from PharmaTrial and during our shift at the deli he was waxing poetic about how great it was. He especially seems to have loved having had all his choices taken away from him. "You eat when they say eat," he said. "You sleep when they say sleep. It's like a sort of weird nirvana where all the pressures of modern life have been removed." As he was talking I couldn't help but notice he has a serious eye twitch he didn't have before the drug trial. But his skin actually looks amazing—the experimental drug they were testing on his acne seems to have been quite effective.

"That sounds a lot like prison," Jason said. The further along his girlfriend gets in her pregnancy, the more testy he seems.

"It's in a voluntary prison where you can be truly free," Nelson said.

"What the fuck are you carrying on about, Dingle Dufus?" said Dirty Steve, who seems to have forgiven Nelson for lying about his grandma's death in order to get out of work. "PharmaTrial is a place where Big Pharma tests drugs on poor people. If you think that's freedom, you're even dumber than I thought." It felt unsettling to totally agree with Dirty Steve.

That's when Nelson pulled out a wad of screenplay pages. "I sent the screenplay I wrote while I was in PharmaTrial to a manager at Circle of Circles in LA. I'm pretty sure I'll hear back from them soon." I took the proffered screenplay from Nelson's hand and skimmed the first page. It was absolute jibberish that did not adhere to any common laws of grammar, syntax, or proper screenplay formatting. Poor Nelson! I hope the happy twilight of his delusions is never punctured by the harsh sunlight of reality.

On my break I decided to walk over and do a final recon of the sidewalk in front of Lululemon to mentally prepare for the protest the day after tomorrow, which of course meant I had to pass by Waterloo Records. Even though FAIL BETTER! has already done their in-store performance, that stupid poster still hangs huge in the Waterloo window. Texas looked down on me as if to say, "I never texted you like I said I would, and now I'm rubbing your face in it." It gave me a pang for sure, but I tried to focus on my mission of scouting my protest space.

The Lululemon sidewalk is pretty small, but there is a decent-sized parking lot adjacent to it that could give us a little more room to move. Also, right next door is an open area for people waiting to go into Amy's Ice Creams (a wonderful local business deserving of the location!). As I surveyed the area, I felt a fresh wave of outrage that Lululemon deigned to open a store in the building that previously housed the glorious Waterloo Video. They have replaced a veritable mecca of excellent video rentals and local quirk with a store dedicated to the idea that women should be svelte, athletic, and rich enough to buy overpriced tights while swallowing a shopping bag full of positive affirmations and feel-good quotes such as "Do one thing a day that scares you." (Actually, I'll take that slogan to heart! This protest scares me, and yet I'm ready to charge it like Durga!) Energized by my fury, I let out a Zena war cry, which caused several passersby—unfamiliar with my mission—to stare at me and then hurry past.

I now feel as ready as I'll ever be to drive the offending Lululemon from the hallowed intersection of Sixth and Lamar. I may not be able to topple the whole corporation, but I will boot that one store out of there! Sunday is the big day and I am ready! Let's see if our one-day protest can be enough to turn public sentiment against the store and wreck their bottom line!

Excitedly,
Roxy

CHAPTER NINE

October 1, 2012

Dear Everett,

Let it be known that the protest did not go entirely as planned! But then of course you already know that. However, it was such an epic and wrenching day, I must write it all down for posterity (or maybe just as a form of processing and therapy?).

I was so nervous and excited that the night before the protest I loaded all the signs into my car so I'd be ready to go in the morning. At one point I had thought about having protest attendees make and bring their own signs, but Annie said no way. You could perhaps expect a few people to show up at an anti-Lulu rally, but with all the other more substantial problems in the world it would be too much to ask for them to show up with a homemade sign. "Save that for some pro-choice or women's rights rally," she said. Part of me thinks she was right, and part of me thinks she was so sick of me complaining about not painting or drawing she was just trying to get me to do something even vaguely like art. As I loaded the signs into the car, I was full of apprehension. What if no one came? What if the signs were dumb? What if this whole endeavor was self-indulgent and all-around stupid? And again, what if no one came?

Artemis was still scheduled to work at Lulu during the protest. She said it might actually be to my advantage, as she could text me any insider info she gleaned regarding how protesters were being perceived, as well as any possible countermeasures being planned by the manager. "Fine," I'd said. I know it's stupid and irrational, but it hurt my feelings she was going to be working for the enemy on my big day.

I arrived five minutes early and parked my car in the Waterloo Records parking lot. Texas and his bandmates stared down at me from the FAIL BETTER! poster with eyes that said they'd learned how to both celebrate the world AND feel its underlying melancholy. Assholes. While Annie had sworn to me she would arrive right at 11 a.m., my phone dinged with a text from her saying she was running really late but would be showing up with a surprise. I climbed out and walked around the corner to Lululemon. There was absolutely no one there. My heart fell to my stomach. I waited for five minutes and then ten and then thirty, too shy to pull a sign from the back of my car and start protesting the corporate chain all by myself. Everett, when you walked around the corner it was a roller coaster! First relief at seeing a friendly face, and then when I saw Nadia on your arm, a tinge of jealousy. She's so beautiful, Everett! Her long hair tinted purple. I wish I could pull that off. I was nervous to meet her. But she was so sweet, throwing her arms around me in that giant—if surprising—hug. It was hard to imagine her getting regularly fingerbanged by her entire household of Goddess-only-knows-how-many OM house residents.

When we went to my car I was careful to pick out a really great sign for each of us. Mine read: I BRAKE FOR WOMEN OF ALL SHAPES AND SIZES and had a painted drawing of a curvy goddess I'd covered in gold glitter. Nadia's read: VENUS SAYS DON'T BUY SWEATSHOP CLOTHING with a painting of Venus rising out of Town Lake on a half shell. The sign you carried was one of my favorites: CORPORATE BIGOTS OUT OF DOWNTOWN AUSTIN with a 3-D paper sculpture of the Capitol building I'd made bursting out of it.

I was happy with the signs. But it suddenly seemed ridiculous to think that marching around in front of a Lululemon store would have any effect at all. It wouldn't change my hometown back to the way it used to be before it became traffick-y and overcrowded and full of corporate stores. For a moment I just wanted to toss the signs back into my car and drive home for some couch time with the furballs.

But when you told me you were here for me, that I could do this, I felt a little better. Everett, you always know what to say to me. I nodded, so grateful a tear spilled out and ran down my cheek. You put your hand out and Nadia puts hers on top, nodding for me to add my hand to the pile. Just as I did so, Nelson and Jason jogged up.

"We want in!" Jason yelled, and they scooted in to join us.

"We're gonna say, 'One, two, three, Buy Local,'" Nadia said. "One, two, three."

"BUY LOCAL!" we all yelled.

"Does Whole Foods count?" Nelson chuckled as we broke apart. I handed Nelson and Jason signs. Jason's read: HONK IF YOUR THIGHS TOUCH, which made him laugh.

As a motley group of five, we walked toward Lululemon.

"I thought you and Nelson were scheduled to work today," I said.

"We are," Jason said. "But we told Dirty Steve we were walking out to support you and your mad cause."

"I bet he loved that," I said.

"He said anyone who follows the cult of Poxy Roxy deserves to be covered in chickenpox boils."

"Ouch!"

We were now standing in front of Lululemon. I could see a couple of employees inside craning to see what we were doing, but I couldn't spot Artemis among them. I tentatively raised my sign up high and everyone else followed suit. We marched in a small circle. I started the chant timidly, but my voice grew stronger when you and the others joined in. "Hey,

hey, what do you say. Down with Lulu, all the way." After about five minutes of that I realized again how idiotic this whole endeavor was, how
stupid, and how much time and energy I had wasted painting these ridiculous signs, organizing this nonsense, and daydreaming to myself about
how I would wrest this previously fantastic spot from the clutches of a
lame corporate store selling tights sewn by children in the developing
world to tech trophy wives recently moved to Austin from California. But
I forced myself to soldier on. Next we chanted, "Sixth and Lamar is for
Local Stars," then "Lululemon is a full-blown lemon," which was a crowd
pleaser. A couple heading into Amy's Ice Creams stared at us. A car driving by honked at my sign and we all waved.

But other than that: nothing.

My big protest was in reality just me marching in a circle with four
friends.

This march would affect no change.

It was a Failure with a capital F.

Artemis cruised by the window of the store. I refrained from waving, not wanting to give her away as an informant. I put down my sign to
text her. TOTAL FLOP, I wrote. I'M GOING HOME.

HANG IN THERE, she texted back. MY EIGHT BALL TELLS ME THINGS
WILL PICK UP SOON.

Sure enough, ten minutes later, Kate, Rosa, Yolanda, and Barclay
showed up. Yolanda is trying out some eyelash extensions to see if she
likes them enough to wear them at her wedding, and though in theory I
object to eyelash extensions—what could be more horrifying and patriarchal than having women hot-glue appendages practically on their del-
icate eyeballs?—they looked amazing. "These signs are incredible!" Yo
said. I went with the girls to my car to grab more.

"These are glorious!" Barclay gushed. "You've always been so talented." Barclay, Kate, Rosa, and Yolanda are the best. I'm so glad we are
back on the road to seeing one another regularly. (Thank you, Venus!)

Barclay's sign read: KEEP AUSTIN LOCAL, YOCALS! Kate's sign read: HER LIPS ARE LIKE THE GALAXY'S EDGE with hot-pink lips that bled off into the Milky Way. "It's so bold, surrealist, and political," Kate said. Rosa's sign read: MY BIG SEXY THIGHS TOUCH. CAN YOUR CRAP TIGHTS HANDLE THAT?

Yolanda's sign had Betty White's face like a Warhol painting with the quote: "WHY DO SOME PEOPLE SAY 'GROW SOME BALLS?' BALLS ARE WEAK AND SENSITIVE. IF YOU WANT TO BE TOUGH, GROW A VAGINA. THOSE THINGS CAN TAKE A POUNDING." The sign was a little off topic and I'd had to write the words really small to fit them all on the piece of cardboard, but I thought it was still pretty impactful.

When my college crew of four joined our existing five, the protest started to feel legitimate. More cars honked in encouragement and everyone passing by stared. Several people stopped to ask what we were protesting and I handed out a flier I'd made outlining the reasons Lululemon—as a corporate store with a pseudofeminist agenda—did not belong at an intersection that symbolizes the real Austin of music, books, local businesses, quirkiness, etc. People walked away reading the fliers.

Progress was being made.

Next a few of your friends from Kerbey Lane Cafe showed up and I gave them signs, too. Then Lulah, the bartender from Deep Eddy, arrived with her husband and daughter in tow. Our chants were growing louder. It was getting to be a respectable protest. All of a sudden, I felt a tap on my shoulder.

I whirled around. Annie stood there with Whole Foods CEO Lite Topher Doyle at her side! "Surprise!" she said. "I brought a special guest."

I was so excited I hugged her and Topher Doyle, too. He seemed kerfuffled (but not entirely displeased) at the invasion of his personal space.

"This is quite a protest," he said. "Your signs are something else." I couldn't even manage to say thank you, I was so floored. All I could do was hand him a flier. He read it carefully, then said, "I've never really thought as much as I should have about how this intersection is a core location for local values and local businesses. But it makes total sense. I have to say I agree with the ethos of your protest."

"Thank you," I managed to say. "Would you like to carry a sign?"

"I'm not sure I'm ready to be the poster child for a battle against Lululemon. My PR director would have a stroke! But count me in as a supporter. I have to get back to my office now, where I'll be working to create an international anti-GMO coalition led, not by our nation, but by our company," he said with a wink.

As he and Annie turned to walk away, she looked over her shoulder and gave me a giant thumbs-up. "I'll be back," she mouthed.

"THANK YOU!" I mouthed back.

We all marched and marched and then a giant gaggle of about fifteen or twenty women came around the corner from the Waterloo Records parking lot. A couple of them were carrying huge speakers and another woman lugged two car batteries. I went over to one. "What are y'all doing?" I asked. Too late, I recognized her as the dark-haired burlesque goddess who'd been making out with Patrick. "Shit, it's you," I said.

"Roxy?"

"Yeah."

"I'm sorry—I didn't know when I got together with Patrick that you'd been hooking up. I didn't even know you existed. I shouldn't have been so rude. I'm Sal, by the way."

"So what are you doing here?"

"Artemis has a surprise for you," she said. "She told me to tell you to roll with it."

What choice did I have? I had no idea what they were up to. But the women expertly set to work hooking the big speakers up to the car batteries. By that time we had way more protesters than signs, and we filled the sidewalk all the way down the block. I'd spotted old pals from my ThunderCloud Subs days—including Logan Ray Jones, currently of Emo's bouncer fame—and a few of my Barton Springs lifeguard buddies, too. Chants of, "Hey hey, ho ho, Lululemon has got to go!" reverberated in the air. Traffic on Sixth Street was almost at a standstill as rubberneckers slowed to check out what we were up to.

The door to Lululemon burst open and Artemis stormed out decked from head to toe in Lululemon and wearing a full face of dramatic makeup. "You guys need to shut the fuck up and listen!" she yelled.

We all fell silent and turned to gape at this redheaded Erinyes who had burst into our midst. Had she gone insane? The burlesque girls moved quickly to stand behind Artemis in a triangle formation with their redheaded queen at its foremost tip. The speakers began blaring the opening of a pop hit it only took me a moment to place.

As the lyrics sounded, the women began to dance in unison.

Girls, we run this motha, yeah

The burlesque girls had clearly been practicing, because they were tearing some shit up. I'm not saying Beyoncé would have been proud, but she would have been something. The crowd cheered as the dancers stomped and shook and slid and shimmied; they high-kicked and did a military march. Then together, they yanked off their pants and skirts in one motion so that they were all dancing in shirts and gold underwear. Artemis must have rigged her Lulu outfit with stripper snaps for a quick removal. I looked around to see two women on the edges of the crowd filming with their iPhones. Horns blared. Protesters jumped and cheered. My heart swelled with emotion. I'd thought Artemis had forsaken my protest for her lame-o job, when in actuality she'd clearly spent weeks practicing her moves with the burlesque girls, working them over with her enthusiasm, manic energy, and choreographic talents until each and every one of them could finally hold their own. As the song ended with "Who run the world? Girls!" the dancers all ripped off their tops, revealing bare breasts ornamented with gold pasties. Across all of their stomachs the words LOCAL NOT LULU! had been written in black paint.

A cacophony of horns blared and the protesters went absolutely fucking nuts. I was crying and jumping up and down, yelling with joy, completely carried away. A burlesque girl pulled two cans of spray paint out of a backpack. Artemis grabbed them, tossing one to me. Instinctively I shook my can, and we both ripped the caps off.

"Come on," Artemis said as she stepped toward the glass front windows of the store. She gave me her hugest grin. With the crowd cheering us on, I didn't hesitate. I raised my can of spray paint and began to write: LULU OUT!

I could see Artemis spraying, KEEP AUSTIN WEIRD!

The act of spray-painting the windows of Lululemon in broad daylight with a crowd cheering me on was more liberating than anything that's ever happened to me in my life. It felt like a wonderful dream, as if Wonder Woman and a troop of fairies would fly out in a moment and crown me and Artemis Co-Queens of the Motherfucking World.

The police car must have pulled up without a siren. I didn't even realize at first who had grabbed me from behind. I just knew someone had both my arms pinned to my sides—I heard Artemis's voice screaming "ROOOXXXXYYYY!"—and in my panic I fought like holy hell, kicking and thrashing and screaming. By the time one of the cops came around into my field of vision I'd already managed to kick one, and I think I might have butted another in the nose with the back of my head. The protesters all around were shouting on my behalf. "Artemis!" I yelled. But when I looked around I didn't see her in the crowd. As the cops wrestled my hands behind my back and put handcuffs on me, I could hear someone screaming, inexplicably, "We are the ninety-nine percent!"

I scanned the line of protesters. I saw you and Nadia and Annie—who must have returned without Topher Doyle around the time the dance started. I saw my friends from college, and Jason and Nelson, and the burlesque girls. I saw my old pals from Barton Springs and Thunder-Cloud Subs. All of them yelling and shaking their signs and looking concerned on my behalf. So much support. So many people I love in this growing, changing town.

But where the hell was Artemis?

I kept scanning the crowd until the cops turned me around and walked me toward a police car. One of them pushed my head down so that I'd be forced to step into the back of the cruiser. The last thing I heard before the door slammed behind me was Annie yelling, "We'll get you out, Roxy!"

At the station the cops took my mug shot and fingerprinted me, then said I could make one phone call before they put me in the cell. Just when I decided I would call my parents, I remembered they were in Peru at their phone-free, internet-free eco-lodge. I started to panic. The police had taken my cell phone and I didn't have anyone else's phone number memorized. But Annie had yelled that she'd come for me, so I decided I'd just sit tight and hope she followed through. I mean, everyone I know had seen me be arrested. Surely at least one of them would try to help.

The officer walked me down to a holding cell. At the push of a button the doors opened. I stepped inside as all the women looked up at me. The cell doors clanked shut behind me. The holding cell was about what one might expect: concrete floors, bars, and three metal picnic table–style benches bolted to the floor—which was ironic as this place had nothing else even remotely picnic-y about it.

The women at the benches looked like life had knocked the

stuffing out of them. Several sat with their heads down on the table. One lady with dirty hair lay passed out on a bench. Everyone was surprisingly subdued, though one older woman let out an occasional moan and said, "My daughter-in-law is going to kill me!" Another woman wept quietly in the corner, her head in her hands. My heart was a turmoil of feelings as I paced the room. It had been so amazing to have so many people show up for my cause. But what a crazy and disastrous ending to it all! And how the fuck was I going to get out of jail? I would surely have to post bond, which would be impossible as I had exactly $52 in my bank account and some maxed-out credit cards.

I kept expecting the doors to open and the police to force Artemis into the cell, but long moments passed and she didn't appear. How had she escaped when I'd been snapped up before I even saw the police arrive?

Finally, I sat down next to a middle-aged woman with dark braided hair. I figured she would ask me what I was in for, but instead she said, "You got a panty liner?" Having just been stripped of all my belongings, I had to admit I did not. I hung my head in shame at being unable to help my fellow jailbird in her moment of feminine need.

And then I remembered—Roscoe needed his insulin shot! There was no one to give it to him.

I paced the cell for hours, sick with worry, imagining Roscoe lying in a diabetic doggy coma on the kitchen floor. This worry pushed out other worries of the consequences of this arrest spooling out ahead of me. When boots finally sounded in the hallway, I was relieved to hear the officer call my name.

When I stepped outside it was pitch-dark out—I'd been in jail for hours. You, Annie, and Nadia stood on the front steps of the Travis County Jail. You rushed forward to hug me. "Thank you so much for getting me out of there!" I said. "I love you so much!"

"We weren't going to leave you to rot in the county jail," Annie said.

"Roscoe! His insulin shot!" I said, almost hyperventilating with worry. That's when you told me you'd gone to my house and given it to him, which made me shaky with relief. (You've never given me back the key to my place, of course, which could have been annoying, but in this case was a lifesaver.) I'm so grateful for you. I should have said it right then. "How much was bail?" I asked.

There was a long pause.

"Three thousand dollars," Annie said.

"Oh, shit! Who paid it?"

"I put down twenty-five hundred dollars," Annie said.

"Nadia and I raised the other five hundred through donations from our Nest Life group," you said. "She sent out an emergency group text to all the OMers, and the donations came flooding in."

It was so sweet and kind that it literally felt like someone was stabbing me in the middle of the chest with an icepick. No offense, but all that time I thought you were a giant cockblocking mooch, when really you are the truest friend anyone could ever imagine. And Annie—well, she had surely wiped out her entire savings.

"How can I repay you?"

"Go to your hearings and we'll get the money back, you beautiful idiot," Annie said.

It was almost painful to have such amazing friends.

I was a little annoyed on Nadia's behalf, when you said to her, "It's probably her blood sugar. Roxy always gets like this when she's hungry." I mean, perhaps she is trying to forget our history and how well you know me?

I asked if anyone knew where Artemis was. Annie said no one had seen her since the protest. I was a little sad when you and Nadia said you were tired and were going to head home. Nadia's goodbye hug was so intense I could hardly breathe. It was nice of her to give me her cell phone number since you, Everett, do not have one. I feel silly I got so choked up when I told y'all to thank the OMers for their help. I am going to be sure and get their money back asap!

Annie drove us to Kerbey Lane for pancakes—I was starving!—and on the way I charged my phone, which had died in police custody while I was locked up. I had eight new messages and even more texts. But none were from Artemis. I texted her, asking if she was awake and if she wanted to come meet us. She didn't respond. And when I tried to call her, she didn't answer.

Over blueberry-gingerbread pancakes and giant glasses of hibiscus iced tea, Annie showed me news coverage of the protest on her phone. Someone had filmed Artemis and the burlesque girls' dance, and clips of it had run on the local evening news with black bars concealing their boobs. A perky blond announcer who spoke from behind a tan mask of base makeup and concealer said: "One protester has been jailed. What exactly the protest was about isn't clear. But even though we have no idea what they were trying to accomplish, those dancers definitely got our attention."

"They sure did, Cindy," said the lascivious, white dudebro announcer sitting next to her.

"Ugh," I groaned. "Did any of the stations mention that we were protesting the existence of a corporate store with a shady ethos on the corner of Sixth and Lamar—an intersection known as being an epicenter of local business and culture?"

Annie shook her head. "That didn't come through."

"Didn't they read my flier?"

"I'm guessing not."

"Fuck!" I said. "So what do people think the protest was about?"

Annie shrugged. "It's a little confusing. A crowd of protesters, signs with somewhat mixed messages."

"Mixed messages?" I said.

"The signs were genius. But some said, 'Honk if you love your body,' while others said: 'Her lips are the edge of a galaxy.'"

"Every woman's lips *are* the edge of a galaxy," I said a little hotly.

"There was also a stripping Lululemon employee backed by twenty members of a self-taught local burlesque troop dancing to Beyoncé. And spray-paint graffiti that says 'Lulu Out' and 'Keep Austin Weird.' It may have been somewhat perplexing for the uninformed layperson, is all I'm saying," Annie said.

"I would not have written 'Keep Austin Weird.' That was Artemis."

"'Keep Austin Weird' is an ad campaign encouraging people to support local businesses. So that one actually makes the most sense."

"Aaaargh!" I said, putting my head down on my arms. What a catastrophe!

"Cheer up," Annie said. "At least you put on a hell of a protest—whether people knew what it was about or not, no one will be forgetting it anytime soon."

After our midnight breakfast, Annie dropped me back off at the Waterloo Records parking lot. When I thanked her, she said, "Of course. You can be a real pain in the ass, but I adore you and I'd do anything for you. You're totally worth it."

She didn't drive away until I'd let myself into my car and started the engine. Then I pulled out of the Waterloo Records parking lot onto Sixth Street, driving slowly past the Lululemon. The sidewalk was empty; all the protesters long gone; the store closed; all traces of my protest signs vanished. They'd surely been chucked in a dumpster where they belonged. The protest was over. I had achieved nothing except depleting Annie's bank account and getting myself arrested and charged with vandalism and resisting arrest. At least you, dear Everett, had made sure Roscoe got his insulin shot.

At my front door, I found a note lying on the doormat, pinned down by a rock. The note read:

Roxy,

Artemis Starla is a figment of our collective yearning and imagination.

Watch out for the army of bloody white mice and the plumbers who shepherd them. The plumber has cleaned out my bank account. He's obsessed with me. I don't want it to happen to you.

As I read it a chill ran through me. It was written in Artemis's strange, loopy handwriting I recognized from the silly notes she would leave servers on the checks—which she always paid in cash. Was that so I wouldn't see her real name on her credit card?

Artemis had a different handle for every location and situation. It had been foolish for me to believe she had revealed her true identity to me the first time we met. And why had I ever believed Artemis Starla was a real name? It was so obviously an alias. But even more worrisome was the creepy talk about the plumber. It did not make any sense.

I shoved the note in my pocket and when I opened my front door, Roscoe went berserk to see me and even Charlize Theron came running to rub herself against my legs. I felt this immense wave of gratitude for them, and an even bigger wave of gratitude that I have no human children to feel disappointed in me for fucking up.

I tried again to call Artemis. No answer. It was too late and I was too tired to go to her house. So I washed my face and crawled into bed.

For once I let Roscoe and Charlize get in bed with me, their warmth and fur a great comfort as I fell into an exhausted and worried sleep. I woke up this morning at almost noon to my landline ringing. A robo-call from the Travis County Public Defender's Office telling me to come in for a 9 a.m. court appointment on Thursday the fourth.

I finally steeled myself to listen to all my voice mail messages. Most were from friends wondering if I was okay. But the final message was from Dirty Steve. "You are fired. For real—no taking it back ever, FIRED! You have lured half my staff into skipping out on their shifts. And now you AREN'T HERE FOR YOUR SHIFT. Don't come into work ever again! Don't call me! Don't show up here! YOU. ARE. FUCK-ING. FOREVER. FIRED!"

It seems I've lost my only source of income.

This is now my life.

Dreams crashing down,
Roxy

October 2, 2012

Dear Everett,

So yesterday I really started worrying about Artemis. I called and texted her first thing when I woke up, then went over to her place. Though I'd been there before, the day we walked around the lake, her town house was even nicer than I remembered. Why hadn't I angled harder to get an invite inside? She wasn't there, and neither was her car. I checked in with Annie, who still hadn't heard a peep out of her either. "Maybe she's shacked up with some guy?" Annie asked.

"She always texts me back!" I wailed.

"Maybe she lost her charger."

So I told Annie about the note, which even she admitted was alarming. "Maybe she was drunk?"

"When is she not drunk? But she never disappears, not for twenty-four hours. We've got to find out her real name," I said. "Then maybe we could find her."

"Do you know anyone else who knows her?"

I pondered. "No," I said. "I mean, she's never introduced me to any other friends. And I met her in the—" That's when it hit me. "The Lululemon! They are bound to know her real name in the Lululemon. To get a job there she must have shown an ID at some point."

"You just got arrested vandalizing that place. They aren't going to tell you anything."

"If there's one thing I've learned from hanging out with Artemis, it's the power of a disguise. People see what you want them to see."

Annie just shook her head. "They've probably got a restraining order against you by now."

"It doesn't count if I haven't been served. Meet me at Amy's Ice Creams at eleven," I said.

"I'm at work!"

"Take an early lunch break and walk over. This is important!" I said, and hung up.

Then I went to my garage and dug out the prop microphone and news camera from the Halloween that I was a news anchor and you, Everett, were my trusty videographer. My brunette news anchor wig was a little dusty, but nothing a good hard shake couldn't fix. And my navy blazer was in my closet, so I was good to go.

I arrived early at Amy's and bought a scoop of dairy-free mango ice cream for confidence and self-soothing. Annie arrived, looking intrigued despite her earlier resistance to the project. She was also clearly impressed by the thickness of my anchorwoman makeup.

"Are you even under there?" she asked.

When I gave her some of my ice cream AND told her that her only job was to silently hold the cardboard camera on her shoulder, she agreed she was in.

As we approached the Lululemon, I saw a cleaning guy scrubbing the last vestiges of graffiti from the window with a scraper and a bucket of soapy water. I felt a stab of guilt. Annie and I walked into the Lululemon and all of the employees immediately turned to look at us. It was so quiet you could seriously have heard a scrunchie drop.

"May I speak to the store manager?" I said to no one in particular, hoping I held the cardboard microphone with confidence.

"I'm just an educator," one of the women said before scurrying away as if afraid of being captured on film.

A moment later a smiling blonde in (you guessed it) flattering tights appeared from the back of the store. "I'm Louise, the store manager."

"I'm here from Channel Five hoping to interview the Lululemon employee who masterminded the flash mob at the protest."

"Zoe Panagopoulos doesn't work here anymore," the pert manager said with a smiling finality that could have only concealed a great anger.

(I would never have taken Artemis for a Zoe—to me, Zoe's will always be dark haired, blue eyed, and adorably twee. Thanks, Zooey Deschanel! But Panagopoulos! That made sense—the Greeks have always been bold!)

"Thank you!" I retorted. "By the way, you might want to look into potential long-term health impacts of the emotional labor of your job." And then I hurried out, Annie on my heels. We rushed down the sidewalk, out of sight of the Lululemon and toward Whole Foods.

"I cannot believe that worked," Annie said. "Now what?"

I told her my plan and Annie wished me luck, insisted I keep her posted, and hurried off to work while I drove home to further my investigation.

I went to the Whitepages online and searched for the last name Panagopoulos in Austin. Six listings came up. I started with the first one.

"Hello," a gruff man voice said.

"Do you have a relative named Zoe Panagopoulos?" I asked.

"When I was a kid we asked if the person we were calling had Prince Albert in a can," the man said and hung up.

The second number yielded a ruder response. But when I called the number for Demetria Panagopoulos, an elegant, older-sounding woman answered.

To my query she replied, "Who is this?"

"I'm Zoe's friend."

The woman sighed heavily, as if weighed down by some great grief. "Zoe," she finally said.

"You know her?"

"She's my daughter."

"I'm her friend and I can't get ahold of her. Do you know where she is?"

"I do."

"Well, where is she?" I tried not to sound impatient.

"Are you the girl that got arrested last night?"

"I did! Did she tell you?" Part of me wanted to explain it had been Artemis who encouraged me to spray-paint the glass windows of the Lululemon, that I'd been carried away by her charisma. But I didn't want to place blame on my friend. I was the one who had taken the spray paint can, after all. No one had made me do it. "But I've never been arrested before." I paused. "I'm just worried about Artem—I mean, Zoe."

"You sound like a nice girl," she said. "She always picks a nice girl to be her friend. It might be best for you if you just let her go her own way."

"I can't do that," I said. I didn't know how to explain to this posh woman how much better my life had gotten since the day Artemis shoved me into the crumb cake display. "She's done too much for me."

She sighed again. "You sound determined."

"I am," I said.

She paused for a long time—so long I wondered if she'd hung up and I'd missed the click. "Zoe's at the Shoal Creek mental hospital," she finally said.

"What?" I almost yelled. "Did you have her committed?"

"I drove her there, but she checked herself in. She's bipolar. She's having a severe manic episode. She knows it now."

For a moment I found myself reeling. But in an instant so many things made sense. The fact that Artemis had shoved me the first time we met. Her alter egos. Her insatiable sex drive. Her energy. Her wild talking spells. All her paranoid talk about the plumber. That creepy note. Now I really understood: Artemis (a.k.a. Zoe) wasn't just talented and creative and energetic and incredibly original. She was also mentally ill.

"Can I go see her?"

Again, there was a long, thoughtful pause. "Visiting hours are from four to seven."

"Is there anything I can take to her there?" I asked, unsure of the appropriate gift to bring. Certainly some things I might think to take—Bulleit Bourbon, man candy, fireworks—would be forbidden.

"I'm sure you'll think of something," she said. "She'll ask you for a curling iron, of course. But they aren't allowed."

So in two days I have to go to court, and in the meantime, I'm going to visit one of my very best friends in the mental hospital. I'm feeling overwhelmed and very, very sad.

Just,
Roxy

October 3, 2012

Dear Everett,

I was nervous as hell to go see Artemis. I thought about asking Annie to go with me, but decided this was something I needed to do alone. First I went to CVS and bought a box of no-heat spiral ringlet hair curlers, which I was sure Artemis would be thrilled about.

I was oddly comforted that Artemis was in a hospital in Central Austin and not out in some hideous, soulless location north of town and right off the MoPac Expressway. At least Shoal Creek hospital actually sits right on Shoal Creek, which has a nice walking path and lovely drooping oak trees, and from her window she can probably see the Tres Amigos patio and imagine having a margarita. At the front desk of the hospital I told the receptionist I was there to see Zoe Panagopoulos. The receptionist checked my ID, had me sign in, and gave me a visitor's badge, which I pinned on my go-to flowered sundress. I took the elevator to the fourth floor. When I told the nurse at the nurses' station I was visiting Zoe Panagopoulos (Had I ever really believed her name was Artemis Starla? It seems ridiculous to me now), she said, "Room 472. Just down that hall and to the right."

While I'd feared padded cells and a terrifying "One Flew Over the Cuckoo's Nest" vibe, the hallway seemed like a typical hospital—linoleum flooring and fluorescent lights. Paintings of sunsets and beaches hung from the walls in a failed attempt at cheer. At room 472, I knocked on the cracked door. "Come in," Artemis said. I steeled myself for the worst, then entered.

Artemis was sitting in a chair wearing pajamas. Her face was freshly scrubbed. I realized I'd rarely seen her before without a full face of makeup. It was as if all artifice, all glamour had been stripped away and what was left was a pretty but sad-looking girl, her usual crackle dulled by psych meds.

"Artemis!" I said. I could not bring myself to call her Zoe.

"Roxy," she said, her voice flat. She didn't stand up to give me a hug or even offer that I sit, so I just stood awkwardly.

"How's it going?" I finally asked.

"Well, since I'm in a fucking mental hospital, it's clearly not going all that well."

I didn't know what to say. "I brought you something."

"You did?"

I nodded.

I pulled out the box of curlers. "Your mom told me you can't have a curling iron in here."

She took the curlers and set them down on the table next to her chair without looking at them. "Cool," she said. I suspect her disinterest was feigned, because she couldn't help but pick the box up again. She opened it and pulled out a single ringlet curler, examining it and giving it a tug. "I've never used these before."

"They'll give you Shirley Temple hair. But sexier, you know, for a grown woman." I wished I didn't sound so stilted, but I was new to all this. "Want me to help you put them in?"

Artemis looked at me as if I'd offered to help her with a tampon. "Um, no thanks." So much for my fantasy of us bonding as I put curlers in her hair.

"I brought you this, too." I handed Artemis a little cardboard jewelry box, and when she opened it her face actually glowed— for a moment she looked like the Artemis I knew.

"For magic and protection," we said at the exact same time.

"It'll help you get your groove back," I said.

"Who says I need to get my groove back?" she deadpanned. A split second later we both laughed, and I had hope that Artemis would be okay, and that our friendship would somehow be okay, too. She held out the box and I took the labradorite necklace she had given me on the night we went to Emo's to see FAIL BETTER! and fastened it around her neck.

"I brought one more thing," I said. I pulled my Rider-Waite tarot deck out of my bag. "Tarot. Want to draw a card?"

Artemis shrugged. "Sure."

I shuffled the deck and set it down in front of her. "You can think of a question you want to ask and then pull a card and the card is a kind of answer."

"I know how tarot works," Artemis said, suddenly sullen as a teenager. "My question is: Why the fuck am I in this place, really?" she asked. She cut the deck and lifted a card. I held my breath as she turned it over.

It was The Devil card.

A naked man and woman stand below a scary devil. They each have a chain around their neck and the devil holds the chains. They seem to be being held against their will, but a closer look reveals the chains are so loose the man and woman could just take them off if they wanted.

The Devil is a card about addiction and feeling trapped. It's a card that can be about the wild side of sexuality, but it also reminds us that giving in to any kind of addictive pleasure can feel great in the moment, but wreak havoc and harm in the long term.

"The Devil?" Artemis said. "Fuck me. Who brings tarot cards to a mental hospital anyway?" She threw the card onto the pile, then shivered and rubbed her arms as if she had a sudden chill. She was right. What had I been thinking? I'd been sure she'd pull something cheerful like The Sun, or inspiring like The Queen of Wands. The tarot deck had clearly been an awful idea. "This place sucks," she continued. "All the young people in here are spoiled meth-smoking brats with no sense of style." The anger behind her words threw me.

"Artemis, why didn't you tell me you were sick?"

She rolled her eyes. "You wouldn't understand."

"Your name isn't really Artemis Starla, is it?"

"Of course not," she said. "What kind of fucking idiot would believe that was a real name?" The words echoed through my head. I felt like a sucker punched little kid who'd just found out that Santa, the Tooth Fairy, and the Easter Bunny were all a giant lie made up by adults to make kids believe the world is an enchanted place where incredible things can happen, when actually it's the opposite. I'd been in a funk for a long time, and it was meeting Artemis that helped blast me out of it. But our whole friendship had been based on a lie, and maybe all the progress I'd told myself I'd been making had been a lie, too.

I was used to Artemis being vibrant and full of energy. Always she had pushed me to be more, do more, live up to my potential. She'd had so many layers, so many secret projects. Always she surprised me—with her Sin Sation burlesque performance, where she had shone as a professional among amateurs; at the protest where, after telling me she would not show up for me she had shown up in spades, bringing an army of impeccably choreographed dancers with her. I knew her as larger than life, always positive, and now she was shriveled and mopey, and maybe even a little mean, slumped down in the vinyl chair.

"I guess just this kind of idiot," I said quietly. We sat there for a moment in awkward silence.

"You should go," Artemis said. "I don't want you here. You can't help me."

"It's okay. It's just me," I said. I understood. She didn't want me to see her like that, vulnerable and without her glamour magic. "I'm here for you."

"Here for me? You don't even fucking know me."

"I want to," I said.

"You couldn't understand me if you tried. I said get out of here!" Her voice was rising and there was real anger in her words. "Just leave!"

"Okay," I said. "Okay, I'll go. But I love you. Let me know if you need anything." .

"Just go," she said in a voice so controlled and firm that I did what she told me to do.

I didn't cry until the elevator doors closed in front of me. But when I started sobbing I couldn't stop, and I cried all the way home.

Now I'm home snuggling the furballs and I'm maybe down a best friend—I hate feeling powerless to help Artemis. And tomorrow I have to go to court. I am terrified. I tried to call Annie but then remembered she was at some PETA gala, so that's when I called Nadia's cell phone. She answered, and sounded legitimately happy to hear my voice. I guess living in an OM house where everyone is fingerbanging everyone else rids a woman of the sort of petty jealousies that would make her uncomfortable talking to her new boyfriend's ex-girlfriend? Anyway, she put you on the phone and I asked if I get thrown back in jail after the hearing would you and Nadia watch the furballs for me, and you said of course. I can't help but remember back to the time when one of my biggest problems was wanting to get you to move out of my house. I kind of miss those days.

Morosely,
Roxy

CHAPTER TEN

October 4, 2012

Dear Everett,

I am now drinking a cup of coffee and wearing my most conservative outfit—a pair of black slacks and my news anchor blazer (which didn't start out as a Halloween costume. My mom actually bought it for me once when she was hoping I'd interview for a graphic design firm job. I remember being enraged at her about the whole thing and now I can't even remember why).

The only positive aspect of having to go to court today is that it will guarantee Annie and the OMers will get back the money they put up for my bail. The last thing I want is to be some kind of mooch leech, sucking my friends (and their fellow sex cult members) financially dry. Otherwise, I'm just terrified I'm going to end up sentenced to serious jail time. While I've always considered myself to be relatively adaptive and resilient, I see now I am neither of those things.

And I know it sounds stupid, but I feel totally heartbroken that Artemis and I have maybe broken up. It's like the searing pain of a boyfriend breakup except without the knowledge that I am entering a sexual desert. (But I'm in the desert already, so it seems just as bad.) Artemis was right—I was an idiot. Not for failing to realize Artemis Starla wasn't her real name—though that seems obvious now—but for not realizing that she was mentally ill. I just thought she was a "wild and crazy" kind of crazy, not actually suffering from mania. (In retrospect, her belief the creepy plumber was trying to empty her bank accounts should have tipped me off.) The fact that she has a mental illness doesn't make me love her one iota less, but I am worried she will keep pushing me away.

At least I still have Annie, and you, dear Everett. I'm telling myself I'll be okay no matter what. But really I don't believe it. Especially now that I'm unemployed and perhaps headed for a stint of jail time. Part of me wishes my parents were here so I could ask them for advice, but part of me is relieved they aren't, as they'd probably insist on hiring me a lawyer, which I'd of course accept. Then I'd likely spend the rest of my life feeling both self-infantilized and guilty for my bad choices. But maybe guilt would be better than whatever I'll feel in a women's prison.

Terrified,
Roxy

October 5, 2012

Dear Everett,

Yesterday was a crazy-ass day. I swear I spend half my life being totally annoyed that Austin has overgrown itself and is bursting at the
seams, and the other half feeling like it's a tiny town where I cannot
leave the house without running into someone I know but would really
rather avoid.

I drove to the downtown courthouse and of course there was nowhere
to park, so I circled around for fifteen minutes worried I would be late,
but I finally found a meter. I practically ran into the courthouse, which
was grimy and smelled like pee. The front desk person told me to go up to
the courtroom on the fifth floor. It was crammed full of sad-looking,
desperate people (like me, but probably without upper-middle-class
parents) waiting to be called in front of the judge. I sat there for half an
hour, wishing I hadn't left my book in the car. I prayed to Venus to give
me strength to get through the proceedings and—since she governs
friendship and love—to even make the judge like me a little bit. He was
quite the silver fox, I have to say. When he finally called my name, I stood
up. "Present," I called, which made him frown.

"To the bench," he said.

I walked down the aisle and stood before him, trembling a little in
spite of myself.

"You are being charged with vandalism and resisting arrest," the
judge said. "Do you have an attorney?"

"No."

"Would you like the court to appoint you an attorney?"

Visions of some overworked, uncaring young stoner attorney unable
to find employment outside of the Travis County Public Defender's Office danced through my head. But as a deli maid, I don't have thousands

saved for a high-powered attorney. So what choice did I have? Also, I really, really, really want to be a freaking adult for once and take care of this myself, not hit my parents up for money and ask them to generally bail me out.

"Yes," I said. "Can I just say that I've never been in any trouble before? And that I only resisted arrest because the cops grabbed me from behind, so I didn't know they were cops?"

"That's something you can discuss with your attorney," the judge said. "You can meet with your PD at this address at two p.m.," he said, sliding a slip of paper across the desk at me.

"PD?" I asked.

"Public defender," the judge said. "And try to stay out of trouble on your way over there." He smiled. Was he flirting? I'd thought he was cute but now felt a little outraged at this clear abuse of power. I barely refrained from mouthing off to him.

I drove over to the Public Defender's Office, which was south of the river on Post Road. It looked like your typical craptastic government building. As I sat in the parking lot trying to gather the nerve to go inside, I contemplated the fact that the building was likely full of lawyers who had once had enough gumption to go to law school but whose energetic wagon must have lost a wheel along the way, leaving them stranded in this hellhole of poor people justly or unjustly charged with a wide array of unsavory crimes. I should have known the day that Artemis first assaulted me at Whole Foods that any friendship with her would likely end in this particular disaster—me sitting heartbroken in the parking lot of the Travis County Public Defender's Office.

"Venus," I said aloud, "please, please, please help me." And then I climbed out of the car and went inside.

The receptionist smiled at me and seemed really friendly and competent. "Your attorney, Sam Johnson, is great," she said.

"He is?" I asked nervously.

"The best," she gushed. "And he's a super nice guy. Very caring." She nattered on as she walked me to a small, windowless room. "If you wait here he'll be right with you," she said. I'd remembered to bring in "A Confederacy of Dunces" and was happy for the distraction. I was actually chuckling at Ignatius's antics with the weenie wagon when the door opened. I looked up. With his tattoo covered by a tailored blue suit and his arms full of file folders, it took me a split second to recognize the man in the doorway. Texas!

I felt out of my body, or as if I'd drifted into another, stranger reality.

"Vet Girl," Texas said.

"Texas." Not very witty dialogue on either of our parts, but I think we could both be excused due to the bombshell of a situation. "What are you doing here?"

"I . . . I guess I'm your attorney." He sat down across from me. I was used to listening to FAIL BETTER!'s album, used to seeing Texas gazing down at me from the giant FAIL BETTER! poster at Waterloo Video. But having him so close to me again made it hard for me to breathe. "I have to apologize." He paused as if deciding what tack to take. I held my breath, eager to hear what excuse he could possibly give for ghosting me. "Usually I review cases on my own before I meet with a client. But I had a stack of four land on my desk this morning and I haven't had time. I was going to—"

Disaster! Not only had I been assigned a completely shit attorney, but he was a completely shit attorney who was distractingly good-looking in a suit and who wouldn't even acknowledge he'd blown me off after our sort-of date.

"Why didn't you text me?"

He looked honestly surprised. "I texted you three times. And then you texted me back saying, 'Stop texting me.'"

"WHAT????"

Texas pulled out his phone, scrolled through his messages, and then held the phone out to me. Sure enough, there were three texts from him.

The first text said:

I HAD A GREAT TIME LAST NIGHT. I APOLOGIZE AGAIN FOR HAVING TO LEAVE SO ABRUPTLY. MY FRIEND IS GOING TO BE OKAY.

The second said:

WOULD YOU WANT TO GET TOGETHER AGAIN SOMETIME THIS WEEK?

The last one, which really broke my heart with the thought of what might have been, read:

IT'S A BEAUTIFUL DAY. WANT TO GO TO ZILKER PARK?

And then finally a response:

VET GIRL: STOP TEXTING ME.

"Oh my Goddess! I never sent that." I thought hard. Had I sent it drunk? Could someone have gotten ahold of my phone? "I didn't send it!" I felt my voice rising. Then I had an idea. I looked at the number the text had come from. "That's not my number," I said, relieved. "My number is 512-555-8792. That's 8793." The realization soaked into me slowly. "Which means I accidentally put my number into your phone wrong."

"Oh, shit," Texas said. "My feelings were really hurt."

"Mine too!"

We sat there for a moment as all this sunk in. Finally, Texas broke the silence.

"Let me see," he said, opening a file folder with my name on it. He scanned the documents inside while I sat there silently, boiling with relief that I hadn't been ghosted again and discomfort that my former crush was now my public defender. "Um . . . I think . . . Can you hang on just one moment?"

"I don't know what else I would do," I said, but I was concerned that Texas was more flustered than I was, given I was the one facing possible jail time.

He stood, picked up the folders, and hurried out of the room, clos-ing the door behind him. I sat and sat and sat in the stuffy room, wait-ing and waiting, when finally the door opened and another guy came in. He was shorter than Texas with a close-cropped head of dark curls.

"Roxy? I'm Mitch Turner."

"What happened to Texas?"

"I ask myself that all the time. I think when Ann Richards was gov-ernor in the 1990s, the right-wing Republican establishment realized they were going to have to really step it up—"

"No! Not the state of Texas! My lawyer. What happened to Texas, my lawyer?"

"You know Sam?"

"Oh my God, is no one in my entire life telling me the truth about their name?"

Mitch cocked his head and studied me. "So you know him?"

"Yes. But why are you calling him Sam?"

"Sam is his real name. Texas is the name he goes by when he plays out with his band."

"Oh. Why?"

"Why?" Mitch looked uncomfortable. "It's like his nickname. So his clients don't go see him when he plays, which could be really awkward."

"Oh," I said. "I see."

"He likes to keep work and music separate, you know?"

I suddenly, and for no explicable reason, felt my face burning red with a fierce, fiery, and uncontrollable blush.

"The thing is," Mitch continued, "there's been a mix-up and I'm ac-tually going to be your attorney."

"I knew I should have hired my own lawyer," I moaned.

"Again, I apologize," Mitch said. "This sort of thing is highly unusual for us." He kept talking but I couldn't even focus on what he was saying. I was so unnerved. Texas must have recused himself from my case. I couldn't help but feel the bitter irony that having Venus as a planetary deity was supposed to make people like me more, not run out of the room to get away from me. It didn't make sense, since we'd just cleared up the misunderstanding about him ghosting me.

"Would you mind if I take a minute and really read over your case?" Mitch asked.

"Go ahead," I said. I cracked open "A Confederacy of Dunces" again. As I read, I comforted myself with the idea that Ignatius J. Reilly's protests didn't ever go as planned either.

When Mitch finally looked up at me, I put the book down. "Okay. You are being charged with vandalism—a Class A misdemeanor. And resisting arrest, which is a felony. The entire incident was captured on video, which is on record. Let's watch it together, see what we're up against."

Mitch pulled out a laptop, logged into some PD evidence database and opened a video, which he began to play. It had been taken with an iPhone and showed the protesters marching in a circle and chanting. The presence of the burlesque girls made the protest in general look much sexier than your average anti-corporatization march. I spotted myself, carrying my sign, looking incredibly happy and kind of overwhelmed as I shouted, "Don't give me no overpriced tights; we just want our civil rights." (No wonder news stations were having a hard time pinpointing the point of the protest—at the time our chanting had seemed clever and passionate, but I realized it made no actual sense.) Then Artemis came busting through the door of the Lululemon yelling, "You guys need to shut the fuck up and listen!" She looked so fierce as the burlesque dancers moved into formation behind her.

"She was one of my two best friends," I said mournfully.

"Did she die?" he asked, alarmed.

"No. We broke up," I said.

By then Artemis and the burlesque girls were running the world with their sexy dance moves. As the song ended, the person holding the iPhone moved in for a closer shot of me taking the spray paint from Artemis's hand—my face was clear as day in the video—and then Artemis and I stepped forward together and started spray-painting the store windows.

Now the cops were on the scene. The popos grabbed me. Artemis screamed my name, ripped off her gold pasties one at a time, and threw them at the cops. As Artemis stormed toward me and the police, chest bare, an older, squat woman came out of the crowd, grabbed her, and yanked her back into the throng. The cops tried to follow them, but Artemis and the older woman seemed to disappear. By then I was kicking and fighting like hell, and once they had me in the police car, Mitch turned off the video.

"What's going to happen to that other girl?" I said, meaning Artemis.

Mitch looked at me. "Can I give you some advice?"

"You're my lawyer. Isn't that your job?"

"My advice: tend to your own butter churnin'."

"What does that mean? And I'm vegan, by the way. I don't churn butter."

"It means mind your own business. I'm pretty sure that will keep you plenty busy."

I had not expected my public defender to be a life coach, too. I was annoyed at being bossed around, but I could also kind of see his point.

"They grabbed me from behind—I didn't know they were cops," I said.

"So we could argue that in court," Mitch said. "And if it worked, you could get off on the resisting arrest charge. But no jury will let you off on the vandalism charge when there is a crystal-clear video. And if you ARE convicted of resisting arrest, with an unsympathetic judge or jury, you could get two years in prison."

I felt as if the air had been forcibly squeezed from my body. "Shit," I said.

"I rarely recommend my clients plead guilty to anything. But I think you should plead on the vandalism count in exchange for asking that the resisting arrest charge be dropped."

"What would that mean?"

"In Texas, vandalism and destruction of property could be charged as a Class B or Class A misdemeanor—or even a felony. But I think reasonably we could get a Class B misdemeanor. That would mean up to a five-thousand-dollar fine. And up to one hundred eighty days probation. But probably no jail time."

"Five thousand dollars!"

"But maybe little or no jail time."

"If I had an expensive lawyer, what would she say?"

"Probably the same thing," Mitch said.

"And if I plead guilty for a misdemeanor charge, what does that mean in the long run?"

"Depends. Let's see what I can get and then we can discuss what it would mean."

I sat there for what seemed like a long time. "What would you do? If you were me?"

"I'd try for the plea deal."

"Okay," I said.

"Now the assistant DA might not go for it. There's been a lot of vandalism downtown lately so it might be she'll want to make an example out of you. We'll have to see. I can go call her now?"

"Okay," I said. "I'll wait. But don't seal the deal until you tell me all the deets."

He smiled in a really nice way. "I wouldn't do that to you. Oh, wait." He paused and pulled out his own iPhone, opening an app. He held out the phone so I could see the app was called "My Girls: Period Tracker." Then he studied it for a moment.

"Sweet!"

"What?" I asked.

"The assistant DA is ovulating. This could be fortuitous."

"You track the assistant DA's menstrual cycle?" I asked, totally incredulous.

"I track the cycle of every lady judge, assistant DA, and admin in the Travis County court system," he said. "Makes my life hella easier."

"Oh my Venus!" I said.

"Well, to be honest, I only track the few lady judges who aren't post-menopausal. A judgeship is a powerful position, and one most women come to later in life."

"That just seems wrong."

"Using My Girls is a must," he said. "What? Hormones are powerful, are they not? I'm using all the tools and technologies at my disposal in my clients' best interests. In your best interest, that is."

"How do you know when these women have their periods?"

"A courthouse is a microcosm. It's not an antiseptic environment. And the clerks like me."

He winked as he left the room and I sat there for what felt like hours. And even though my fate was on the line, I couldn't help but wonder where in the building Texas (a.k.a. Sam) was and if he was thinking about me and, if so, what he was thinking. Probably he was hoping I wouldn't show up at a FAIL BETTER! show like a piece of criminal trash blown in off the streets to projectile vomit everywhere.

I realized this has been a pattern all my life—I worry about boy problems instead of my real problems. It's actually a fairly effective method for managing stress, but one I hope to someday outgrow.

Just when I finally decided that Mitch had forgotten all about me, he reentered the room. He punched his fist with his open palm. "Deferred adjudication on a Class A misdemeanor, baby!" he yelled.

"English, please!" I said.

"No jail time. A five-thousand-dollar fine. Three months' probation,

246 MARY PAULINE LOWRY

and once probation is completed the whole thing is dismissed. Wiped from your record. Nada. Nothing. As if it never happened."

"That part sounds good," I said. "But a five-thousand-dollar fine?"

"You have to pay it off by the time you finish probation."

"I'm unemployed," I said. "I can't get that kind of money together in three months."

"Well, you better get employed with the quickness. Employment is a term of your probation anyway."

"How do poor people do this?" I'd always struggled with underearning. But now I realized there was a difference between my version of being "broke" and being really, actually poor.

"Honestly? Lots of times it sinks them like a stone. But I promise you, this is your best option. You need to recognize that you are totally privileged. You have every advantage. If you work hard, it won't sink you. You can do this."

"Okay," I said, but my heart felt heavy. "I'll take it."

And now, while I'm relieved I'm not going to jail, I am very stressed out about being unemployed and owing the court $5,000. And I'm weirdly sad that Texas reappeared in my life only to disappear again.

Financially fucked, but otherwise still celibate,
Roxy

October 6, 2012

Dear Everett,

Last night I slept on it and I woke up today knowing what I had to do. I drove down to Whole Foods, Austin's skyline laid out before me. This city, with its limitless growth, should be full of job opportunities. But the University of Texas graduates 15,000 bright young minds a year, and all of them want to stay in Austin. So for every decent job there are hundreds of applicants. And what jobs am I qualified for, really? Our society is not designed to offer a regular salary to artists of the non–graphic design variety.

I parked in the Whole Foods parking lot and walked slowly toward the building. I could do this, I told myself. I could drink a giant bucket of shit and piss and blood and everything that's gross. I could eat my humble pie.

I slipped through the deli to Dirty Steve's office, gesturing at Jason and Nelson so they'd know not to swarm me. They understood right away what I was there for, giving me little lifts of their chins as if to say: we've been there too.

I stood outside Dirty Steve's office. I took a deep breath. I knocked.

"Come in, Dingle Dufus!" he yelled.

I stepped inside. He turned. "Poxy Roxy? What the fuck are you doing here? Didn't you get my message?"

"Look, I really need—"

"I don't care what you need. You're fired. That means you don't work here anymore."

"I really need my old job back. I can explain—"

"Oh no. Let me explain," he said, in a way that was so calm AND full of rage that I shut right up. "First you accuse me of poisoning you. Then in some kind of nutball 'retribution'"—he made exaggerated air quotes with both hands—"you dose me with ex-lax brownies. Who does that? Though I have to say I did enjoy testing that last brownie out on my brother. Thank God we have separate bathrooms. Anyway, you are late over and over despite multiple warnings that you need to arrive to work on time. You regularly steal copious amounts of deli food. I put up with ALLLLLLL that. But then you recruit half of my deli staff to bail on their shifts to go to a nonsensical protest of a ladies' exercise clothing store? Poxy, I worked an entire deli shift behind the counter practically BY. MY. SELF! And that I ain't having. THEN the very next day you are a no-call, no-show? Oh no. I've had it with you. So you can take your sad, mopey, pouty little face the fuck out of my office and go deal with the consequences of your actions elsewhere. YOU ARE PERMANENTLY FIRED FROM THIS DELI. Capeesh?"

"Sheesh. Capeesh," I said. And for the first time, I could actually see (most of) his point. "But by the way, the ex-lax brownies were dictated to me by my tarot deck, so—"

"Get the fuck out of my office!" he yelled. I think he must have been in the midst of a hideous coke hangover.

"Okay, okay," I said.

I hurried out, making a gesture at Nelson and Jason to convey I had been unsuccessful in my plea and would burst into tears if pressed to discuss it further.

I pulled myself together and drove home wracking my brain. What kind of job could I find that would pay me decent money, much less enough to cover my mortgage AND my fines? In this town, where the cost of living far exceeds average incomes—nothing. I was so up in my head I had to slam on my brakes at the last second to avoid running a red light. My parents would be home in three weeks. I could always hit them up for money—my usual move. But I'm really ashamed about all this and am going to try my damndest to make sure they never have to know about any of it. True, they've always been incredibly understanding, but:

1.   This mess is embarrassing.

2. If I give in to the urge to be rescued at this point, I may be stuck in this twilight postadolescence forever.

In summary: I want to figure out how to sort this mess out myself instead of going to them, hinting and wheedling that I need cash.

I could rent my house on Airbnb, but then I'd have to find somewhere to sleep and a place to board the furballs. I pulled into my house and ran inside, opening my laptop and looking to see how much houses in my neighborhood rent for. Seventy bucks a night for a small two-bedroom, one-bath seemed to be the going rate—not bad. But then I looked up furball care. To board both my animals it would cost $60 a night. So that was a no-go. Maybe the furballs and I could couch surf with a friend? But that would be a double mooch. I wanted to figure out how to take care of this on my own, like—Goddess help me—a Real Adult.

Then it came to me. The clouds parted. Light shone down from the heavens to illuminate my face.

PHARMATRIAL.

PharmaTrial was a low bottom—the lowest of the low, in fact—but goddamnit, it paid. Did I really want to be a guinea pig for Big Pharma? Hell no. Did I need to figure out how to make thousands of dollars in a few weeks without turning tricks? Hell yes.

I googled "PharmaTrial clinical-trials test subjects" and found the page listing upcoming trials and test subjects needed.

OBESITY TRIAL—SEEKING ADULTS AGE 34–60 WHO ARE AT LEAST 40 POUNDS OVERWEIGHT.

While I feel plump at times, realistically that was a no.

ACNE TRIAL—SEEKING ADULTS AGE 18–44 WITH SEVERE CYSTIC ACNE.

Perhaps if I ate enough Brie?

HAIR LOSS TRIAL—SEEKING MALES WITH BALDING PATTERNS AGE 22–55.

A definite no.

Fuck. I realized there was going to be nothing for me. And then I saw it.

SEEKING ADULTS 18–55 FOR MEDICATION STUDY.

No specifics on what they were testing but I was definitely an adult age 18–55. I called the number listed and an automated voice answered. I dialed in the "trial number" posted in the ad, and a woman's voice answered almost immediately. "I'm calling about the trial for adults age eighteen to fifty-five," I said.

"Great! We had that trial filled but two of our trial subjects backed out yesterday. The trial starts tomorrow. Could you come in today for an interview and blood testing?" she asked.

"What is the drug you are testing?"

"It's a pain medication. An opioid," she said. Which is absolutely perfect, Everett, because if there's anything I need right now more than I need money, it's a cure for pain.

"How much does the study pay?" I asked.

"It's a two-and-a-half-week live-in study and it pays seven thousand dollars," she said.

The words "seven thousand dollars" reverberated in my brain. "Can I come right now?"

She said I should come in at 4 p.m.

So now I'm headed to PharmaTrial to hopefully rent out my body to a pharmaceutical company to pay off court fees. I feel trashy and ashamed, yet slightly exhilarated by my ingenuity and resourcefulness.

Scrappily,
Roxy

P.S. Shit, shit, shit! If I get accepted to the study, what am I going to do with the furballs? I'll figure it out later. If I don't leave now I'm going to be late.

October 8, 2012

Dear Everett,

I'm in! I can hardly believe it. They wouldn't let me bring much with me into this place—they even made me leave my cell phone at home, and there's no internet access for drug-trial participants, either—so I'm glad I have my trusty spiral notebook. I need to write down everything before Nurse Ratchet comes around to give me my first daily dose of on-trial opioid, at which point I'll be too out of it to function.

First let me say it means a lot to know the pets are in safe hands with you! (It did feel strange to ask you and Nadia to housesit, which was basically requesting that you violate ground rule #5a.) And I've been thinking nonstop about that dachshund puppy mill bust you told me about—forty dachshund moms and their puppies all needing homes! I hope you and Nadia are able to move out of the OM house so you can adopt one of those puppies! Taking care of Roscoe should be a good trial run.

I left Annie a voice mail message about going into PharmaTrial when I knew she'd be in a work meeting—I didn't want her to talk me out of this! And I told my public defender Mitch, too. He said while it doesn't count as employment in the eyes of the court, it'll be a good way to pay off my fines, and I can start applying for jobs as soon as I'm out.

Yesterday morning after I arrived and was checked in, my roommate—a skater chick and self-proclaimed PharmaGrrrl named Cheryl—and I went to the cafeteria for breakfast. All the other trial participants straggled in as well. As soon as I sat down, a cafeteria worker slammed down a tray in front of me. "Enjoy," he said with fake brightness. The tray held the following vegan's nightmare:

1.   One little carton of whole milk

2. One "high-fat breakfast sandwich" consisting of an English
    muffin, cheese, an egg, butter, and a giant slice of ham

When I went in to apply for the study and got poked and prodded, the scientist guy asked if I had food restrictions. "At PharmaTrial, all clinical-trial participants have to eat the same thing to minimize variability of medication effects," he said. "So we can't allow participants with food restrictions."

"I eat everything," I said. I knew in that moment I would be selling not just my body to Big Pharma, but also my vegan values. But I glossed over it in my mind, figuring I could push meat around on my plate, eat the bread and veggies, make the best of it.

Now faced with a repulsively animal-product-heavy breakfast, I pulled the ham and egg out of the middle of the breakfast sandwich. As dairy is my weakness, I figured I could polish off the milk and English muffin with cheese and call it good. But before I could even nibble on the English muffin, my coordinator Melanie was at my side saying, "You have to eat everything on your tray."

"Seriously? I don't like ham," I said.

"Equivalent calorie consumption between clinical-trial participants is an integral part of minimizing variability," Melanie said in a voice that reminded me of the love child of Nurse Ratchet and an evil robot.

I put the ham and egg back on the English muffin and lifted it to my mouth. I literally gagged as I took my first bite, imagining the poor, factory-farmed pig that had lived a miserable life and then died a violent slaughterhouse death so that this high-fat breakfast sandwich could exist. "Thank you, piggy," I thought as I chewed. I forced down the high-fat bite with a swig of whole milk. Ugh.

"You don't like it?" the guy across from me asked. He had friendly eyes, a shaved head, and stainless steel loops in both ears.

"I'm a vegan," I whispered. "I haven't eaten pork in years."

"I was in here one time with this girl Ximena? She was, like, lactose intolerant or something, and man, you shoulda heard her burping. I never heard nothing like it before."

"Ximena?" another guy a few seats down with a neck tattoo of a crowing rooster said. "She's my girlfriend, man. She's the one that told me about this study."

"No way, bro," the guy across from me said, and laughed. "Small world."

They reached across the table to bump fists.

"A small world of poor, disenfranchised people whose only option for turning a quick buck is coming in here," I said. The two guys stared at me as if I'd started speaking in tongues. "Never mind."

The guy with the shaved head turned to Rooster Boy. "She's a vegan," he said, as if compelled to explain my outburst. "She ain't eaten pork in the longest and it's making her cranky."

I nodded. A fair assessment. All around us the coordinators circled, encouraging us to eat. I lifted up my high-fat breakfast sandwich and glumly took another bite.

"You can do it," Rooster Boy said.

"We believe in you," the guy with the shaved head said.

The fact that Rooster Boy (Tim) and Shaved Head Guy (Mario) were actually really nice helped a little, but choking down that breakfast sandwich was one of the most repulsive things I've ever done.

Afterward, we sat in a main lounge full of couches and recliners as the coordinators called us one by one back into a room like a doctor's office, gave us each a little cup of pills, and watched as we swallowed them. Then we all had to go back into the cafeteria and sit at the tables again. I brought a drawing pad and a pen, but almost no one else had anything with them to read or do. By the time I sat down, the drug was kicking in. I felt floaty and calm and then just incredibly sleepy. I lay my head down on the table, and even though it was a cold, hard cafeteria table, I was so doped up it felt sort of cozy and wonderful. I could get into this study, really. The food was hell, but getting stuffed full of opioids and napping was not going to be so bad.

SMACK!!!!! A noise like a gunshot sounded almost inside my head. I sat bolt upright. Beside me Melanie stood holding a ruler she must have slammed down on the table right next to my ear. "No sleeping," she said. "We are minimizing variability by having all patients remain awake during the day."

"You're fucking kidding me," I slurred.

"No, ma'am. I am not," she said.

"Don't calls me 'ma'am.' Ornly my mom calls me 'ma'am' when shc's mad. Nor you. You're nor my morm," I said.

So I had to sit there at the table for hours, too tired and drugged to read or draw or really even talk, all my energy going toward battling sleep, knowing that if I succumbed for even a moment I'd be awoken with the fiery crack of Melanie's ruler hitting the table inches from my skull. It. Was. Literally. Hell.

For lunch, I gagged down a hamburger and soggy fries. After lunch we each received another dose of the opioid and spent a long afternoon sitting at the cafeteria tables. I tried to draw all of us in Dante's sixth circle of hell but was so sleepy I couldn't focus on dragging my pen across the paper. There is something particularly horrible about being doped up and ready to blissfully nod off but then not be allowed to do so. Every little while a clinical-trial participant would give in to the narcoleptic effects of the drug and then the ruler would come slamming down, causing all of us to jump. Tim and Mario played Rock Paper Scissors for hours as it was the only game simple enough to follow when stoned stupid on painkillers. Luckily I was too fucked up to consider what the drug might be doing to my system, or what the food was doing to my vegan morals. For dinner, we ate steak fingers (gag!) and institutionalized green beans from a can.

Last night I lay in bed and cried with sadness and shame. "It's okay," my roommate said. "I've heard hardly anyone has to get rushed to the emergency room during opioid studies, so there's nothing to be afraid of. I cried through my whole first study, too, but that's because whatever drug they gave us made me have stabbing liver pains. You'd be surprised what you can get used to, though. By your second or third drug trial, none of this will seem so scary."

Hopefully the long-term side effects of the opioids will not be terrible. But I haven't pooped since I got here. The meat/opioid combo has caused my digestive system to go on strike. Only twenty minutes until Nurse Robo-Ratchet calls us for our high-fat breakfast and then loads us back up with opioids and refuses to let us nap.

I am a failed artist. Single. Unemployed. I have had a falling-out with one of my very best friends—the woman who brought light and joy back into my previously stagnant life. I have sold out my vegan values and my body to pay off court fines in an effort at "maturity" and "responsibility." Hopefully this is as low as this story will go.

Mired in a dark night of the soul,
Roxy

October 14, 2012

Dear Everett,

Last night Tim and Mario and I watched "Point Break" again. Mario argued that Keanu Reeves's stiff acting made the film, while I argued that it almost ruined it. Only Patrick Swayze (as Bodhi) carried the thing. You could give him the shittiest lines in the world—"I could never hold a knife to Tyler's throat. She was my woman. We shared time."—and he would turn them into gold. But we all agreed the last line of the film was dazzlingly bad. FBI agent Johnny Utah catches up to Bodhi at Bells Beach, Australia, as a storm rages and "waves of the century" form. Instead of arresting Bodhi and taking him to jail, where he would surely die from the unhealthy stifling of his testosterone-fueled longing for adrenaline and adventure, Johnny Utah lets Bodhi go out into the sixty-foot waves and fulfill his dream of surfing to his death, thereby paying the ultimate price for the ultimate rush. "Vaya con Dios," Johnny Utah says as he lets Bodhi go, in what could be the worst example of a Chinese Hawaiian English American speaking Spanish in the history of film.

In PharmaTrial we are the opposite of the "Point Break" adrenaline junkies. We aren't taking life-threatening risks that make us feel truly alive. Rather, we are being doped up with a drug that—though possibly life-threatening—makes us feel nothing but sleepy. (If it kills us, it will be years from now, and slowly.) If we die of anything here in Pharma-Trial, it will be boredom.

Sleepily,
Roxy

October 16, 2012

Dear Everett,

I can barely remember a time before this place. When I wake up, I rub the chunk of rose quartz I brought in with me as a way to honor Venus. It seems like a pitiful effort, but it's the only thing that ties me to my old life. Tim and Mario are my only friends. They call the world beyond PharmaTrial "the free." Tim says, "When I'm back out in the free, I'm gonna take my girl Ximena out to dinner at Pappadeaux."

Mario says, "Nah, man. Forget Pappadeaux. When I'm in the free, I'm gonna take my money and get me underglow for my Dodge Charger."

"But you gotta eat," Tim says.

"Mi mama is gonna make me some carnitas tacos," Mario says. "No offense, Roxy. I know you don't like eating meat."

"None taken," I say. I am too sleepy all the time to be offended by anything. I can't even call to mind what I would want to do once I am out in "the free." I remember caring about things, feeling bad that my protest failed, being sad about being here, thinking all was lost. But now all I care about is how much I want to sleep.

ZZZZZZ,
Roxy

CHAPTER ELEVEN

October 19, 2012

Dear Everett,

I am home! I am home! It feels so amazing to be sitting at my very own kitchen table! It was so great to be reunited with Roscoe and Charlize Theron. Thank you for taking such great care of them. I really cannot believe I checked myself into that hellhole thinking that was my only option!

You are probably wondering about the events that led to my texting Nadia earlier today to let y'all know I was coming home earlier than planned (and please forgive me for sending y'all packing back to the OM house a week ahead of schedule). This morning was business as usual at PharmaTrial. I woke up, showered in the prison-like showers, choked down my soul- and ethics-killing high-fat breakfast, got my dose of opioid, and sat at the cafeteria tables playing Rock Paper Scissors with Mario and Tim while trying not to nod off. I wasn't even sad anymore about being there. I was numb, complacent, all I cared about was not falling asleep because I've come to absolutely hate being woken up by the smack of the ruler on the cafeteria table.

Then a horrible shrieking sound erupted! A fire alarm! The coordinators looked—for the first time—a little panicked. They started yelling for us all to line up at the door, but for a few moments none of us could be bothered to move. Finally, Melanie slammed her ruler down on one of the tables. "Get the fuck up!" she yelled.

Startled by the crack in her professional facade and suddenly convinced this was not a pointless drill, we all lumbered to our feet and ambled like opioid zombies to the door. (Luckily, I had my trusty spiral notebook with me, on the very off chance I'd feel clear-headed enough to write, and I had the good sense to grab it.) We made our way toward the stairwell and trundled slowly down the stairs, as Melanie yelled, "Move! Move! Move!" We exited onto the first floor, which was full of greenish-gray smoke. Had there been a terrorist attack? Perhaps some rogue group of anti–Big Pharma activists had bombed the place. I knew I should be panicked, but all I could summon was a mild feeling of curiosity. As the alarm sounded with a piercing urgency, I lurched along with my fellow clinical trial participants toward the front exit. We walked with eyes squinched shut against the smoke, arms extended, like walking dead unable to fully feel our fear.

We burst through the front doors, all of us shielding our eyes from the light of the sun, which we hadn't seen in days. When my eyes finally adjusted, I spotted a woman with long blonde hair wearing giant sunglasses and a ridiculous neon-pink Lilly Pulitzer dress leaning against a minivan at the edge of the parking lot.

"Roxy!" the woman yelled.

Surprised, I stumbled toward the sound of my name. At fifteen feet away, I realized it was Artemis in a wig and disguise. The sun glinted off her labradorite necklace. "What are you doing here?" I asked, thoroughly confused.

"I'm here to bust you out of this place."

"Did you set a fire?"

"I lit a smoke bomb, big deal. Let's go."

Through the fog of the opioid, I remembered the number one rule of PharmaTrial: if you leave, you don't get your money. "No way," I said.

"If I stay in there another week, I get seven thousand dollars. I need it to pay my court fines and my mortgage."

As if from the heavens, I heard Annie's voice. "Topher Doyle loves your art," she said. "And now you've got a job interview for a badass job on the fifth floor. But we gotta go now."

Perhaps the drugs were making me hallucinate. I looked at Artemis. "Did you hear that?"

"Of course I heard it. Annie's hiding in the van. Are you coming or what?"

I looked over toward the building. Smoke still billowed out the front door. All of my fellow clinical-trial participants had adjusted to the sunlight and now seemed to be basking in its glow. Only Mario and Tim looked my way. I waved my hand at them. Tim, looking a little discombobulated, raised his hand in return. But then Mario lifted his fist above his head. "Vaya con Dios," he called.

"Vaya con Dios!" I yelled back.

Then I turned and pulled the handle of the automatic minivan door and climbed into the backseat. Artemis jumped behind the wheel and we peeled out of the parking lot. As soon as we were out of sight of the building, Annie popped up from the floor of the front seat and put on her seat belt.

"What are you doing?" I asked.

"You think I want to be caught on the PharmaTrial security cameras with this criminal?" Annie said, gesturing affectionately at Artemis.

"Good point," I said. "Could we please stop and get me a coffee? And then you can explain this to me. I'm so fucking sleepy."

Artemis pulled off her blonde wig. "Sure thing," she said.

At Caffé Medici, I ordered a quadruple latte AND a mocha, both with almond milk. At PharmaTrial they just served Folgers. By the time we all sat down at a little table, I'd guzzled the latte and started sipping on the mocha. Artemis said, "I'm sorry I was such an asshole when you came to visit me."

"It's okay."

"The worst thing about this fucking disease is that when I get really, really manic, I don't think straight. I don't treat people the way I want to treat them. And I'm sorry you got arrested. I should have dragged you out of there with me. But once my mom got ahold of me I didn't feel right fighting her off. I've put her through a lot."

"I saw the prosecution's video. The lady that grabbed you and dragged you into the crowd was your mom?" I said.

"I was so addled I invited her to see the dance performance."

"Wow," I said. "It's okay. At least you got that one cop pretty good with your nipple tassel. Thanks for quitting your job just to come to my protest. You were amazing."

"The dance was pretty good, right?"

"The best," I said.

"I stopped taking my meds," she said. "Right before I met you."

"What are you like when you're on them?"

"I'm on them now. And I'm still me," she said. "Just a little calmer. And a lot less deluded. But sometimes I miss the wild, electric, manic me. The me that fucks cashiers in parking lots."

"Makes sense."

"Next time I try to convince you to do something really illegal, say no, okay?"

"The cops have you on video but you didn't get charged with anything, did you?"

"Nope."

"Because your mom is insanely rich?"

"Yes."

"Which brings me to the illegal shit you just did at PharmaTrial. You know I could have walked out of there anytime, right? You could have just called me on the clinical-trial participant landline and talked me into leaving."

"Shit," Artemis said. "Seriously?"

"Yes, seriously. Anyway, what am I even supposed to call you now? Zoe?" I could hear the tinge of vexation in my voice.

"What do you want to call me?"

"To me, you'll always be Artemis, girl goddess, huntress of men." My voice softened.

"Call me Artemis, then. There's no need for the drama."

"I hate to interrupt, but we're on a tight schedule here," Annie said. "Topher Doyle loved your protest signs. I mean, he wouldn't shut up about them. And then our store artist, Joaquin, turned in his notice. He's going to the MFA program at The City College in New York. So I suggested you to Topher Doyle and he wants to interview you."

"Store artist?"

"It's like three hours a day of work. You draw asparagus on chalkboards in the store, stuff like that. And then the rest of the time you can do your own work in your office studio."

"No way."

"Way. Joaquin created his whole portfolio on the clock. Topher Doyle likes it as he feels like he's supporting a struggling artist. And it pays. Full benefits. A great salary. Everything. Like, you could pay off your court fines in no time."

"Does he know I got fired from the deli?"

"He doesn't give a shit about that. He said he likes your spunk."

"When would the interview be? I mean, if I decided to do it."

"In an hour."

"WHAT?" I said. "I'm still groggy as holy hell." The espresso was cutting through the fog, but only somewhat. "And look at me." I was wearing PharmaTrial pajamas and my hair was a mess.

"We need to do it now, before one of Topher Doyle's nieces pops up and says she wants the job."

"Roxy, come with me to the bathroom," Artemis said.

In the bathroom, Artemis pulled out an interview dress for me from her miracle backpack—a vintage-inspired Johnnie Boden number—and black Mary Jane pumps in a size eleven. She turned on her battery-powered curling iron, doused my hair in dry shampoo, and set to work doing my makeup. Once I was transformed, she poured some crushed Ritalin on the sink and handed me a rolled-up dollar bill. "Just this once," she said. I stared at the Ritalin. I'd taken it a few times before, and I knew it would blast right through the opioid fog. It would make me lively and vivacious for my interview. I took the dollar bill and bent over the sink.

But before I snorted, I remembered the last time Artemis had offered me something—i.e., a can of spray paint—I'd ended up in jail. I love Artemis, but I wanted to do this my way, not hers. I stood up and handed her the dollar bill.

"Come on," she said.

"No way. I'm seriously never taking your advice again."

"You shouldn't," she said. And we both started laughing.

"Are you gonna snort it?" I asked.

"And risk triggering another manic attack? No way." She swept the powdery Ritalin into the sink. "There's something I have to tell you."

"What?"

Artemis paused. I could see her swallow hard. She looked scared.

It made me nervous—I was used to Artemis always being confident and self-assured, no matter what. "What is it?"

"When I was in Shoal Creek, I started going to AA. Roxy, I'm an alcoholic."

"Oh, honey," I said. Her lip trembled. I've never seen her look so vulnerable. "I love you no matter what you are."

"Really?" she asked. She was tearing up.

"Of course, I've never met anyone like you. I'm glad you're sober and getting things sorted."

She threw her arms around me. "That means so much to me. Sometimes I worry people only like me when I'm off my rocker."

"If it's okay for me to be honest, a toned-down version of you would be a little bit of a relief."

"Don't worry. I'm not that toned-down. AA is full of hot guys. Addiction is like a whack-a-mole. And once they bash down their alcoholism, it's sex addiction that pops right up." She gave me a lascivious wink. "Now I know why I drew The Devil card, if you know what I mean."

"Because it's a card about being trapped by addiction?" I asked.

"Because it's a card about being naked and chained up with a hot guy!"

When we stopped laughing, I told her I was sorry for bringing a tarot deck to the mental hospital. "That was idiotic."

"Don't worry about it. I was just grouchy because I was in alcohol withdrawal. I love your inappropriate ways. I wouldn't stand for a girlfriend who brought me flowers or chocolates or something else really nice."

"Shut uuuup!" I laughed.

When we walked out of the bathroom, Annie's jaw dropped. "Wow!" she said. "I'd hire you." She bought me another latte for the road.

When we pulled into the Whole Foods parking lot, I said, "I need a minute to pray to Venus."

They said okay and climbed out of the car, leaving me to sit there alone for a moment. I pondered what I wanted to say to my favorite planetary deity. "Venus," I said. "I feel like I've been making bad choices every which way. Please just help me to go in there and do my very best. Help me and I will do everything I can to bring more beauty and love and friendship into this world."

When I climbed out I felt ready. The caffeine had cut through the worst of the opioid stupor. And besides, Artemis and Annie had busted me out of PharmaTrial before I received my afternoon dose. Artemis said she'd go in the store and buy a magazine and drink tea and wait for us. Annie and I took the elevators to the fifth floor.

Annie introduced me to Teal, the new receptionist they'd hired while I was in PharmaTrial. Teal's chunky hipster glasses and bangs made her look like she could be a nerdy librarian or the lead singer of an indie post-punk band. She welcomed us and walked us to a large room with a huge blackboard against one wall and a tray full of every color chalk imaginable. When I was a kid, drawing with chalk on the sidewalk was my jam. At the sight of those hundreds of chalk colors, I felt my inner artist child jump up and down yelling, "Can I draw with those? Can I?"

Teal spoke with the utmost seriousness. "For the first phase of your interview: You have one hour to complete the challenge."

"What?" I asked.

"Topher Doyle is currently obsessed with 'The Great British Baking Show,'" Annie explained.

"Your challenge," Teal continued as if she hadn't been interrupted, "is to draw a field of enticing eggplants with the words: 'Sale! Eggplants $4.99 per pound.'"

"Do I write out 'pound' or just 'lb'?" I asked.

"That's up to you," Teal said. She picked up a remote control and pointed it at a giant digital clock on the wall. "On your mark, get set, draw!" she shouted. As she punched a button on the remote, the clock began to count down from sixty minutes.

I felt gripped with the suspicion that I was still in PharmaTrial, that the opioid had driven me out of my mind and this was all a giant hallucination. I looked to Annie. "Is this real?"

"Real as factory farming," she said. "You got this, girl."

She and Teal left the room, pulling the door closed behind them. It was then I realized one whole wall of the room was glass and Topher Doyle sat in a chair watching, as if I was a zoo exhibit. Panic descended. How could I possibly draw in front of the CEO Lite of Whole Foods? But I took a deep breath and forced myself to imagine I was back in my living room, drawing signs. I turned my back to Topher Doyle and searched through the chalk, pulling out every shade of purple and green I could find. There was an abundance of each color—after I sorted them I had about fifteen different purples and just as many greens.

The feel of chalk on my fingers made me excited to get to work—it woke up that inner artist child who loved to draw with sidewalk chalk and who had no concern with recognition, or money, or paying jobs, or gallery shows, or prestigious art contests, or even with making art that would last past the next rain shower or blast of the sprinklers. When I was a kid, it had been all about drawing for the sake of drawing, not about getting anything more out of it. The ephemeral nature of the sidewalk chalk drawings had been part of the fun. It hadn't been about making art that endured or got me anything. It had just been about the beautiful, sometimes frustrating, but always glorious process of creation.

I lifted up a piece of chalk that was a perfect deep eggplant shade, stepped over to the blackboard, and started to draw. For the first moment or two I was still nervous, but then I settled into a trancelike state. It was as if Venus and my inner artist child had joined forces and I was just channeling them as they tried to sketch the most gorgeous eggplants in the universe. I drew and drew, pausing only to swap out one piece of chalk for another or consider shading or perspective.

"Ten minutes! You have ten minutes left of your challenge." I looked over to see that Teal had cracked the door and stuck her head in the room.

Shit! Where had the time gone? I stepped back and looked at my eggplants as a whole. I'd designed them around the "Sale! Eggplants

$4.99 per lb" lettering. There were a few shading gaps that needed to be filled. I stepped up to the blackboard and worked double time.

When the buzzer went off, Teal cried, "That's it! Step away from the blackboard! Put your chalk down!" I stepped back, holding my hands up instinctively as if she was a robber and I a store clerk. I turned to look at the blackboard, entirely covered in swollen eggplants shaded a dozen colors of deep purple, with glistening green tops. If Topher Doyle didn't like them, and if I didn't get the job, I might get thrown back in jail for failing to pay my court fines. I might lose my house. But whatever happened, I told myself, I had shown up and done my best with the guidance of Venus. Whatever happened, so be it.

"Have a seat," Teal said, gesturing to the table that held the tray of chalk. I sat down with my back to the glass wall, as it would be entirely too disconcerting to sit staring at Topher Doyle as he stared at me. Teal disappeared and a moment later, Topher Doyle and Annie entered. Topher Doyle sat down facing the chalkboard. He took in the eggplants in silence for a long time as I waited with bated breath. Then he spoke abruptly. "I've been thinking about it."

"Thinking about what, sir?" I asked.

"Please don't call me 'sir.'"

How should one address the CEO Lite of a health-food empire? I wondered.

"Topher. Call me Topher."

I nodded. There was another long, uncomfortable silence. I wondered if I should repeat the question. Annie made the slightest gesture with her hand, which I took to mean that I should wait it out.

Finally Topher Doyle spoke. "I've been really thinking about what you said at your protest regarding the intersection of Sixth Street and Lamar Boulevard."

"Oh?" It was astounding, really, to imagine Topher Doyle had been mulling over the very thing I'd been obsessed about all these months.

"Can you tell me a bit more about your philosophy of the intersection?"

"Of course," I said. "The intersection has historically been a hub of both local business and tourism. Whole Foods, BookPeople—such an amazing independent bookstore!—Waterloo Records, Waterloo Video, Amy's Ice Creams. People come to this intersection because it's bursting with what makes Austin unique and original. Keeping the intersection full of local businesses is what will keep people coming here. And the more people that come to the intersection as a local tourist destination and hub of cool, the more people you will have shopping at your flagship Whole Foods."

Topher Doyle nodded. "You've convinced me. I'm going to make a personal call to my friends at Lululemon and offer them relocation fees to an alternate location, as well as several months rent."

Everett, you can't imagine how I felt in that moment! After my certainty that my protest had been a failure, it was like a dream. I clapped my hands over my mouth in astonishment. For a moment, I was literally speechless. "Oh my Goddess! Really? Would they go for it?"

"People don't want to get on my bad side," Topher Doyle said with a devilish grin. "But I can only do it if I have a convincing argument for an unstoppable new venture in that location. Ideas?"

I stared at him, dumbfounded. "Are you suggesting I propose an idea for a small business?" I asked.

"I want you to pitch what would replace the Lululemon. But it has to be something even the Lulu execus couldn't argue against." Topher Doyle paused dramatically. "Ideally, your idea would be for a venture that transcends capitalism, a venture even a true villain could not oppose without risking annihilation in the mind of the collective conscious (i.e., the shopping public). We want Lululemon to know implicitly that it's in their best interest to comply."

"I like your style, Topher," I said. "Do you work with the planetary deity Mars by any chance?"

"I've been making offerings to Mars every Tuesday for the past seventeen years."

"Nice," I said. I made a gesture that I hoped encompassed the fifth floor, the flagship Whole Foods store, the entire health-food empire Topher Doyle helped to build from the ground up. "Clearly he appreciates your dedication. Venus is my girl."

He pointed at the chalkboard. "Hence your ability to create beauty with nothing more than a tray full of chalk."

Annie stared at us as if:

1. Unable to believe Topher Doyle and I were getting on at this level; and

2. Wondering how she had such goofballs for both a boss and a BFF.

"So," Topher Doyle said, "what's your idea?"

Silence blanketed the room. Topher Doyle and Annie both stared at me. I froze, everything a blank.

Nothing.

I had nothing. Not a single idea.

I had come this far, and would fail here on the edge of achieving my Great Work.

The three of us sat in a long, incredibly awkward silence. The lack of sound rang in my ears like the clanging of my own foundering.

And then, like Venus rising from the sea on a half shell, the idea rose up fully formed from the ocean of my unconscious mind.

"An adoption center for puppies rescued from puppy mills."

Topher Doyle's eyes widened. "Tell me more."

So I told him about the recent puppy mill bust and about how there were forty rescued adult female dachshunds—many of them pregnant—and about a bazillion puppies, which exceeded the capacity of the local no-kill pet shelter, Austin Pets Alive! The adoption center at Sixth and Lamar would be a showcase (and home) for puppies rescued from puppy mills. Adoption fees would be much lower than the price of a pure-bred dog. They could do fund-raisers, too, to increase awareness and raise money.

"I love it!" Topher Doyle said. "It could be a 501(c)(3) under the umbrella of Whole Foods."

"And could create a substantial tax write-off," Annie chimed in.

"Exactly," Topher Doyle said. "I'll call my people at Lululemon today." He glanced at his watch. "Now I need to get back to figuring out how to reduce this company's carbon emissions to a negative number. We want to be like a giant corporate ghost, leaving absolutely no carbon footprint."

"Okay," I said. I glanced at Annie. She nodded slightly. "And the job." I gestured at my army of beautiful gleaming purple phalluses. "When will I hear back about the job?"

"You can start sometime next week," Topher Doyle said. "Direct all salary negotiations to Annie. I'll be in touch about the Puppy Adoption Center." Before I could thank him, he stood up, took an unexpected little bow, and sashayed from the room. For a moment, Annie and I stared at each other. "Keep cool!" she said. "Keep cool just until we get out of here."

As we walked through the fifth floor, I was in a daze. We thanked Teal, who gave us a funny wink and said, "Nice eggplants." We rode down the elevator and when we stepped outside, Artemis was standing there waiting for us.

"Well?" she asked.

"We did it! We did it!" I said, jumping up and down and hugging

Annie and Artemis as tightly as I could until we were all sort of jumping up and down together. "I love you! I love my girls!" Normally we would have gone to Deep Eddy Cabaret for a few beers to celebrate. But since Artemis is newly sober, we went into Whole Foods for kombucha. A cashier named Rex—who I know for certain did the do with Artemis in the parking lot a few months ago—waved at her hopefully. But she made a shooing gesture at him and he looked away, clearly crushed.

We settled in at a table, and as I sipped a lavender-pear-flavored booch I said, "You know that without you two, I'd be in PharmaTrial right now, all doped up and trying not to fall asleep."

"True," Annie said. "But you're the one who did the footwork. You just momentarily gave up before the miracles could happen."

Despite the happy occasion, I couldn't help but notice Artemis looked a little morose. "What's up, Artemis?" I asked.

"I'm thrilled for you. Ecstatic! But for me I feel a little sad. I'm unemployed. Mostly sober, not manic. Haven't even felt like fucking a stranger in days. What am I going to do with myself?"

"I don't know," I said. "But I'm pretty sure it will come clear. Venus works in mysterious ways."

"That she does," Annie said.

"What are you doing in here, Poxy Roxy?" a voice boomed. Dirty Steve loomed over me. He looked larger than I remembered him and really intimidating. Had our constant jousting been sort of friendly? With the opioid's effects lingering in my brain, it was hard to remember. "Nelson told me you were playing dummy for Big Pharma."

"Not anymore," I said. "I just got hired to work on the fifth floor." I was gloating a little bit, I couldn't help it.

Dirty Steve's face fell. "You gotta be fucking kidding me. Annie's smart. Annie, I get. But you? Poxy? On the fifth floor? Fuck me. I've been working for this company for eighteen years and I'm still in the cocksucking deli."

I shrugged in a way that I hoped seemed casual, benevolent, and a little grand.

"What can she say? Topher Doyle knows talent when he sees it," Artemis said. We all stood up and headed out, giggling and triumphant, as Dirty Steve glared after us.

And now I'm home with my sweet furballs and about to climb into my own bed. While I'm thrilled to be home, I feel lonely—and maybe it's ungrateful to be lonesome with such good friends and a new job and Lululemon perhaps on the way out of Sixth and Lamar. But after PharmaTrial, I am now used to having a roommate and people around at every second of the day and night. I can't help but remember I live all alone and have absolutely zero boyfriend prospects. It would be so great if there was a nice, sexy guy here padding around the house in his bare feet.

But I don't want to spoil a wild and perfect day thinking about the one thing I don't have. I'm tired. And as Barbara Kingsolver so sagely wrote, "Even a spotted pig looks black at night."

Gratefully,
Roxy

October 22, 2012

Dear Everett,

This morning I called Mitch to tell him I'm not going to make the PharmaTrial $7,000 after all, but that I got a well-paying job as store artist at the mothership Whole Foods. I know he's my public defender and NOT my parole officer (who I will meet soon enough), but I wanted him to know.

"That's amazing!" he said. "Um, this may sound weird, but can I tell Sam?"

"Texas?"

"The very one."

"Why?" I asked suspiciously.

"He asks about you," he said.

"He bailed on being my lawyer. What does he want to know about me?"

"Doh!" Mitch said.

"Doh, what?"

"Doh. Don't you get it? Public defenders aren't supposed to DATE their clients. I mean, state statute allows for it—after all this is Texas—but we have a firm office rule against it. It would be an exploitation of power."

"Are you saying you want to date me?"

"Certainly not. No offense. My wife is number one in my My Girls: Period Tracker app."

A lightbulb clicked on, casting a glow over the confused murk of my brain, which hadn't totally bounced back from my week in an opioid haze.

"Are you saying Texas refused to be my public defender because he wants to DATE me?"

"I'm not saying it. But I'm not NOT saying it, either," Mitch said.

"Oh."

"I've revealed too much. What I should say is congratulations on your job."

As soon as I got off the phone I texted you and Nadia to see if I could buy y'all lunch as a thank-you for pet sitting (and as a way to distract myself from obsessing about Texas). You seemed pretty overjoyed to see me, which gave my self-esteem a little boost, I must say. Y'all both seemed really happy about my new job, too. You gushed that the kombucha I'd made was delicious. I feel hopeful that the spell I cast on that kombucha, ensuring that whoever imbibes it will be happy, powerful, and love their work, will come true for you. It's clearly working for me, as I was guzzling it before I went into PharmaTrial and I'm now—against all odds—gainfully employed! I know you are totally sick of working at Kerbey Lane Cafe, and I would love for you to have a well-paying dream job too.

When I hugged y'all goodbye, I found myself sorry to be parting from Nadia, your OM Queen girlfriend I once assumed would be some sort of emotionally damaged hussy. That's what I get for my contempt prior to investigation. She really is delightful!

So all in all, it has been an interesting (and unlikely) morning.

Mystified,
Roxy

P.S. I've now been staring at my phone, waiting for Texas to call and ask me on a date. Or at least send me a text saying hi? But so far, nothing.

CHAPTER TWELVE

October 28, 2012

Dear Everett,

I spent all week thinking Mitch would tell Texas about my new job and then Texas would be so impressed he would call and ask me out, but of course he hasn't. I told myself it's greedy to hope for great friends, great pets, a new job, AND a date. But at least obsessing about whether or not Texas would call kept me from worrying too much about starting my new job.

My mom and dad are finally back from Peru, so I went to visit them in Sun City yesterday. My mother bragged about my brother, who seems to have bullied the other Peace Corps volunteers into letting him take some sort of supervisory position. I did not tell them about my arrest, or my time in PharmaTrial, but I did tell them about my new job. My mother is annoyingly thrilled, as if I was previously homeless and now have finally agreed to come in off the streets.

"You look great, Dad," I finally said to change the subject. "The vacation did you good." It's true. He had a tan, but it was more than that.

"It wasn't the vacation," my mother said. "He moped through the whole thing. It's that pro-bono patient he's taken on."

"Captain Tweaker?" I asked.

"Roxy!" my dad said. "His name is Franklin."

"How's it going with him?" I asked.

"I'm almost done with his teeth," my dad said. "He looks like a new man. It was such a challenge. I haven't had one of those in so long." So my father has been cheered up by doing a good turn for Captain Tweaker! Venus truly does work in mysterious ways.

"I'm worried as soon as your father's done working on Franklin, he'll go right back to dragging around here like a biscuit that's been under the gravy too long," my mother said. I hope he doesn't. It perks me up to see my dad so happy again.

On Wednesday, my first day of work, I didn't have an electronic card for the elevator to the fifth floor yet, so Annie came down to ride up with me. "Thank you so much," I said for about the millionth time.

"Fugedabout it," she said. "It was all you. Guess what?"

"What?"

"Lululemon accepted Topher Doyle's very persuasive offer and has agreed to move the Lululemon to Ninth and Lamar!"

"Oh my Goddess! Oh my Goddess! Oh my Goddess!" I felt my eyes well up. I couldn't help it. I had never really thought I could accomplish my Great Work, had never truly believed the Waterloo Video location could be wrested back from the forces of corporate greed.

Teal showed me to my studio—a big open office with windows overlooking the intersection of Sixth and Lamar Boulevard. The Lululemon sign still hangs over the store like a dark cloud shading the intersection. But not for long. I know I haven't stopped national stores like Lululemon from taking over downtown. And I certainly can't keep Austin from growing and changing and becoming a city I hardly recognize. But all my obsessing and hard work has helped to bring a worthy venture to the former location of Waterloo Video (RIP), a store I loved so well. In its place will be a Puppy Adoption Center backed by Whole Foods, which may have transformed from a single little hippy grocery store to a global titan, but at least it's a global titan from Austin, Texas, and will never be the pawn of some evil corporate giant like Amazon or Google.

On my worktable, Teal pointed to a large blackboard easel and my job for the day, which she'd printed up for me as if I was in "The Great British Baking Show."

"Someone could just email it to me," I said.

"I'm a receptionist. Let me have some fun."

"Fair enough," I said.

At the doorway she paused and turned. "You have three hours for this challenge. Ready, set, draw."

She disappeared and I got to work on my assignment. But two hours in I heard a knock on the doorframe of my studio/office. I looked up to see Topher Doyle standing there. He came over to examine the drawing I was doing of a leg of lamb—which felt a little antithetical to my moral code, but I was giving it my best.

"I heard the good news," I said.

"Initially the execs at Lululemon were reluctant to move the store on such short notice, but when I pointed out the benefit for them of being on the right side of saving puppies' lives, they buckled quickly." Topher Doyle paused to stare out the window, as if he was remembering days long gone, when he was not the CEO Lite of a massive corporation, but a founding member of a scrappy little local health-food store. "I want the grand opening of the Puppy Adoption Center to coincide with Whole Foods' thirty-two-year anniversary," he said.

"Great," I said. "When is that?"

"In just over two months."

"Two months? That seems really fast."

"I've found if you pay a premium, you can get a construction crew to do in two months what would normally take six. And Annie of course has spoken with the people running the current emergency puppy mill rescue shelter they've thrown together for the dachshunds in a warehouse on the south side. They are all in. The adoption center will need a manager."

I swear I could hear a Zen gong ringing in my ears. "I know someone who would be perfect for the job," I said. "He's incredible with animals and would be totally dedicated."

Topher Doyle certainly seemed open to hearing about my candidate for the position.

I felt a little bad about having to leave work early on my first day for my meeting with my probation officer, but Annie whispered to me not to worry about it. "Are you kidding?" she said. "Topher Doyle loves that you are in trouble with the law. It makes him feel like he's in touch with the vegan gangster movement."

"Is there a vegan gangster movement?"

"I think we should just let him have his fantasies. Especially since they benefit you."

As I got off the elevator and was walking to my car, I saw Dirty Steve get out of his Mustang. He pointed at me with his first two fingers, then back at his own eyes and back at me again, as if to indicate he was watching me. It was really creepy. Clearly my ascendancy to the fifth floor has messed with his sense of a just world order. I've always thought of Dirty Steve as a very annoying, pigheaded, but ultimately harmless blowhard clown. But suddenly I sort of wished he didn't know where I work.

The waiting room at the probation center made me a little sad. No one looked like they had extra money to spend on court fees, except for one woman who rolled up into the parking lot in a Mercedes. She entered the waiting room carrying a Louis Vuitton handbag big enough to hide a body, and swinging a waist-length blonde weave. She winked at me in a way that could have been anything from lascivious to friendly to threatening. I was glad Artemis wasn't there, because she would surely adopt this woman as a role model or alter ego.

The meeting with my probation officer was surprisingly great. She's actually not a brooding middle-aged man drinking rot-gut coffee out of a Styrofoam cup, but rather a relatable woman named Teresa who sips green tea sagely out of a hand-thrown mug. She asked me lots of questions about myself and listened attentively in the manner of a well-paid therapist. It was really quite enjoyable and gratifying. As I left she congratulated me on all my hard work and progress, but I really felt like I should be slipping her a three-figure check for her time and attention.

"Next week, same time?" I asked. She looked at me a little strangely and said I didn't need to come back for a month, which was disappointing.

Then I had to go to the bathroom, where a mean-looking woman in a shiny cheap suit watched me as I peed into a cup, which I didn't love, but I'll take peeing in a cup in front of a stranger over eating a high-fat breakfast sandwich any day.

If there's anything all the craziness of the last few weeks has given me, it's perspective.

#blessed,
Roxy

October 31, 2012

Dear Everett,

Oh strange world! I just came home from Halloween at my parents' house. (At a supple twenty-eight years old, shouldn't I be out at the club shaking it in a sexy she-devil costume, you ask? My answer is no. I will not give in to the holiday as an opportunity to objectify women—I mean, if MEN were to dress up as scantily clad warlocks and warriors I'd be ALL IN. But I'm not participating in the sexualization of women on what was meant to be a children's holiday. And I know Halloween at a senior living community sounds lame, but it was actually really fun. Lots of people's grandkids came to trick or treat, and so my mom and dad and I gave out tons of candy. I was pleased to see about a hundred little girls all dressed up like Merida from the Pixar movie "Brave." I exhorted each of them to maintain their dedication to empowering, feminist Halloween costumes even when they reach adolescence and beyond!) My dad was more chipper than I have seen him in years! Even in his best humor he is quiet and stoic, so it took a while to get the reason for his good mood out of him. It turns out his spirits were so buoyed by fixing Captain Tweaker's meth mouth that he has decided to start a nonprofit dental clinic where he will fix the teeth of former meth addicts who have over a year of sobriety. This news makes me feel extremely mature—the old me hit my mom and dad up for money more often than I'd like to admit, but now I am a grown, independent woman who has helped my father find his path out of the dark aimlessness of Sun City to the light of productive community service.

I will likely be mush this entire weekend. Having a full-time, nine-to-five job is exhausting. I seriously do not know how people do it. At the deli I told myself I worked full-time, but it was really more like four shifts a week and at random times. At my new job, I do about four hours or so of work a day for the store—in that amount of time I can draw a sign start-to-finish if I'm cranking. The rest of the time I spend on an invigorating and surreal acrylic series of wiener dogs painted on flattened cardboard boxes leftover from shipments to the store. I have to say I'm really happy with how they are coming along, AND they will show at the Puppy Adoption Center for the grand opening!!!

After making all that art, I'm so tired by the time I leave in the afternoons that I can hardly see straight. I've been getting an IT guy named Lorne to walk me to my car. I keep thinking about Dirty Steve and his "I'm watching you" hand gesture. And once or twice I could have sworn I saw him kind of skulking around the parking lot. I've thought about reporting him to HR but worry about coming across as (a) paranoid or (b) vindictive. Also, in our own way, Dirty Steve and I walked a lot of miles together as dickhead boss/underappreciated employee.

I don't miss my deli days, I promise, especially not since my first paycheck will hit my bank account in another week. Despite this daily grind, I wake up early enough to walk Roscoe before work AND make a small offering to Venus. That powerful (and sometimes fickle) goddess seems to be getting me through my days. Making signs for the Lululemon protest really primed the pump—I haven't been "blocked" for a moment since I started this job. It's funny to think back to all the teeth gnashing I did when I wasn't making art about how badly I wanted to make art. It feels like I was swimming upstream with all my might and now I'm just floating along on my back, letting the creative energy of the Universe carry me.

Last week when I first started my job, I thought for a moment about trying to get Topher Doyle to chuck Duckie & Lambie out of Whole Foods, but then realized I have no reason to do harm to Brant Bitterbrush. Being over someone means really letting them go, not trying to stay emotionally snarled up with them by seeking revenge. I'm so glad Venus has helped me get clarity on that situation!

With days of vacation stretching ahead of me, I have to admit I am lonely. Annie is mostly too busy to hang out outside of work. She is still dating Jeff Castro. (Though their relationship has been made rocky by the fact that Annie kept hugging his identical twin Joe and claiming to have mistaken him for Jeff. But last week Jeff got a small neck tattoo of an empty birdcage with its door open. While he claims he's always wanted a neck tattoo and that it has no relation to Annie, she now worries she has no excuse for not being able to tell him and Joe apart. When I asked Jeff about the meaning and significance of the open-door birdcage, he said, "Don't cage the bird, man.") Anyway, he and Annie— despite or because of their ups and downs—are hot and heavy, and so her free time is limited.

Artemis is unemployed, so ostensibly should be available to hang, but she's still mostly MIA. Ever since she got sober, she's been going to AA meetings every night. Apparently, she has a different alter ego for every meeting she goes to, which is keeping her spirits up. When I complain about how she's never around, she says I should come to a meeting with her. HA!

And you, dear Everett, are busy with Nadia and whatever goes on at the OM house (which I can't even make fun of anymore since all the inhabitants pulled together to help me make bail!). I understand that you have moved on, and I am happy for you, but more than I'd like to admit, I miss the days when you were constantly available to watch movies and eat vegan junk food with me.

I've given up on thinking Texas will ever call. But I have an idea for how I could see him one more time—I'm going to insist we hire FAIL BETTER! to play the grand opening of the Puppy Adoption Center. If nothing jumps off from that, I'll swear off him forever. I'm going to make Annie do all the arrangements, though, so it doesn't seem like it was my idea.

Matchmaking (for myself),
Roxy

November 6, 2012

Dear Everett,

Last night was bizarre and ultimately deeply disheartening.

So here goes: Artemis has been bugging me and bugging me to go to an Alcoholics Anonymous meeting with her. "I like to drink, but I don't think it's come to that," I said.

"No, I just want you to come so you can see what I'm up to. That way when I tell you about it, you can picture it, right?"

"I've seen AA meetings in about a million movies," I said.

Artemis rolled her eyes. "Movies. Phff! How about we live real life? The stories are incredible. Heart wrenching. Hilarious. Last night a guy with fifteen years sober said back in his drinking days he woke up one time in a morgue—with a tag on his toe! People laughed so hard they cried."

"I guess you had to be there?" I said.

"Exactly. Please come with me. Puh-lease?"

Just then my phone dinged. It was Captain Tweaker, who was sending me photos of the new dental implants my dad put in. It was crazy how different he looked with his rotten meth teeth replaced with pearly whites. I showed the photo to Artemis.

"That guy goes to my favorite meeting!" she yelled.

"Shut the fuck up."

"He does. Text him. Tell him."

I texted Captain Tweaker, asking him if he goes to the 6 p.m. meeting at Our Lady of Sorrows off South Congress. He texted back that he goes every Monday through Friday!

"That is crazy synchronicity," Artemis said. "You have to come."

"It's not synchronicity. It's just a central Austin special. This town is a hotbed of run-ins and coincidence."

"It's not coincidence! It's a sign from a Higher Power."

"I can't believe you are using your newfound spirituality to manipulate me, but fine," I said. "I'll go."

Artemis cheered.

"But at the meeting, what do I say instead of 'I'm an alcoholic'?"

"Just say, 'I'm Roxy. I'm an Al-Anon.'"

"What's that mean exactly?"

"To alcoholics it means you're a worried, neurotic lame-o."

"Thanks!"

"No. Seriously, it just means you are friends or family of an alcoholic. Which you are!"

"Okay, fine," I said, just to get her to stop bugging me.

"Be sure and dress cute. There's alcoholic man candy galore."

So I dug around in my closet and for once found a sundress that isn't the flowered one I usually wear. This one is a maxi dress with a low back that's sexy in an I-just-threw-this-on-and-am-not-really-trying way. I should do a deep dive in my closet more often. Goddess only knows what other forgotten treasures it might hold.

Artemis drove. There was plenty of parking at Our Lady of Sorrows—we were walking distance to all the food trucks and fancy new South Congress restaurants, but didn't have to circle around forever looking for a parking spot. Who knew being a drunk would come with such perks? We went down the stairs to the basement. Someone was making a bad pot of coffee. Artemis started kissing everyone on the cheek and giving hugs. There were tons of hot musician-looking guys standing around, and everyone had tattoos and was uber hip. I could totally see why Artemis likes it. She was right—I hadn't been imagining it right. In my mind all the people were grim and sad, but really it was like all the cool people in town had found this secret haven together that happened to be in a church basement. I felt a tap on my shoulder and turned around to see Captain Tweaker giving me a huge smile to show off his new pearly whites. "I'm three months sober and I have new teeth!" he said. "All thanks to a Higher Power I never believed in and a cunt neighbor I never liked!"

I laughed. "Did you just call me a 'cunt'?"

"In the old days, that's what I thought," he said. "But I was as wrong about you as I was about God!"

Luckily, right then people started heading toward the folding chairs. Artemis and I settled in as the meeting started. The leader of the meeting—a man with sleeve tattoos of rain forests—read for a long time from a laminated sheet. "No cross talk during the meeting please. Cross talk consists of interrupting a fellow member or commenting on his or her share. We are self-supporting through our own contributions." Blah blah blah.

As he blathered on, I looked around the room, checking out all the people. Then the basement door swung open and in walked Texas! My eyes nearly bugged out of my head. He slid into an open chair. A fierce blush slid right up my neck and took over my entire face just as his eyes met mine. He looked surprised, and then gave me a big, glowing, happy smile. I smiled back and then looked away, embarrassed. I elbowed Artemis and she gave me a wicked grin—so she knew! She knew Texas went to that meeting, damnit, and she hadn't said anything to me about it. Just dragged me there with no warning. At least she'd encouraged me not to come looking like a ragamuffin. I tried to distract myself by listening to what the meeting leader was going on about. "The great thing about AA," he said, "is that we can come up with our own idea of a Higher Power. Your Higher Power could be Mickey Rourke, or the ceiling over your bed. Hell, your Higher Power could even be a stuffed raccoon, right, Sam?"

Everyone laughed and Texas groaned.

"One of the joys of having a sponsee," the meeting leader said, and everyone laughed again at this incomprehensible inside joke. They were speaking Greek to me, but I liked the easy sense of camaraderie be-tween the people and the fact that no one was pretending like they had everything together.

After the leader was done rambling on about how learning to "sur-render to win" had saved him from a life of vodka-seeking hell, he said, "So I guess the topic of the meeting is surrender." Then he opened the meeting for sharing.

Artemis jumped in first. "I'm Cupid Vanuncio and I'm an alco-holic," she said. It seems like even sobriety and regular meds consump-tion haven't dampened Artemis's enthusiasm for a great handle. "I've been having a hard time staying sober this week," she continued, "but my dear and loyal friend Roxy agreed to come with me tonight—even though she's mostly a normie." For some reason this elicited chuckles all around. "She's here to offer me support on my sobriety journey. I'm so grateful for her."

Everyone in the room applauded and smiled at me as if I'd single-handedly rescued a baby from the bottom of a well. I beamed, Artemis forgiven. Next, a lady shared that her landlord was selling her house so she had to move and she hoped her Higher Power could help her find a new place. Then a guy shared that he'd finally surrendered to the idea that his second ex-wife is as big of a bitch as his first ex-wife. This caused some of the women in the room to shift in their seats and roll their eyes. After he shut up, there was a pause, and finally Texas said, "Hi, I'm Sam, I'm an alcoholic."

"Hi, Sam," I said along with everyone else. There was something comforting about the call-and-response style of the meeting.

"As you all know, I've been single for what seems like forever. And a while back I met this new woman I really like. She's not like anyone I've ever met before." Everyone around the room smiled and nodded as I died inside. He'd met someone! I was such an ass. He probably thought I was stalking him by coming to his meeting, and this was his way of letting me know I should leave him alone. I could barely stand to listen to another word. I felt like I might explode out of my skin. Even my teeth itched. "But I wasn't able to ask her out because she was a client at my work and my boss has really strict rules about that kind of thing. But her case is closed—it's been closed for a little while now. And now I feel stupid, like I missed my window. I mean, I have no idea if she'd even want to go out with me." Now Texas was looking straight at me and even I could tell he wasn't talking about some other girl.

I wanted to let cross talk be damned, leap to my feet, and yell, "She does want to go out with you," at which point Texas would stand, grab me up in his arms, and kiss me in front of this circle of alcoholics, who would burst into applause. But of course I sat frozen in my seat.

"But I'm trying to surrender to the idea that I'm not in control of this situation. That's all I got," Texas said.

The rest of the meeting went by in a blur, with me too nervous and excited to do more than sneak an occasional glance in Texas's direction. When it was time for the meeting to end, the leader asked us to close with the Third Step prayer. Everyone stood in a circle, held hands, and closed their eyes. This gave me the chance to watch Texas as he said the prayer. He looked really cute with his head earnestly bowed and his eyes closed. As soon as the prayer was over, the circle broke up into little clumps of people.

"Go talk to him," Artemis said.

"Don't boss me, Cupid Vanuncio," I said. But I headed toward Texas.

"Hey," I said.

"Hey, Roxy," he said.

"Thanks for sharing." Could there be anything more awkward?

"I hope it was okay."

I nodded in a way I meant to be encouraging.

Just then three guys swarmed Texas, all hugging him and patting him on the back as if he'd just hit some kind of spiritual home run. They had a variety of piercings, rockabilly outfits, and neck tattoos. "These are my sponsees," he explained. "Hey, guys, this is Roxy."

"Nice to meet you," I said, even though it wasn't.

"I'm so glad we are going over our third step tonight," one of Texas's sponsees said. They all looked at Texas sort of reverentially.

"We go to Joe's Coffee every week for our after-the-meeting meeting," Texas explained.

"We need to get on with it if we're gonna get a good table," one of the sponsees said. The other two nodded in agreement.

"Yeah," another said. "I only have a babysitter until nine."

"Well, I better—" Texas gestured toward the stairwell, the world beyond this cozy church basement, and even I could tell he'd rather be leaving with me than going for coffee with a bunch of dudes.

"Yeah," I said. "Good to see you."

"Good to see you, too," Texas said, and then his three sponsees sort of swept him out of the building.

A moment later Artemis grabbed my arm. "Tell me you got his number."

I shook my head.

"Oh my God! I'm the world's best wingman and you are impossible."

We were headed toward the stairs when I heard Captain Tweaker yell, "Thanks again for the teeth!" I turned to see him waving goodbye at me and grinning his giant proud grin. I've never seen something so endearing from a man who had recently called me a cunt.

Artemis and I emerged into the dark night of the parking lot. "I can't believe you didn't get his number after he confessed his like for you in front of the entire meeting."

"I couldn't!" I said. "Not in front of Team Bro Sponsees. It was like he was a cult leader."

"He's just a good sponsor. Wait! I got it!" Artemis said. "You could leave a note on his car." She pointed to a black Prius.

"Absolutely not," I said.

"Come on! I'm sober and not the slightest bit manic. You've got to help me bring some fun into my life. This will cheer me up for a week!"

"Fine," I said. Truthfully, I didn't need much convincing. "Pen? Paper?"

She dug around in her purse and handed me a pen and a receipt. I started to write on it. Then I flipped it over and saw what it was. "Artemis! This is a receipt for a twelve-pack of condoms! I can't leave a note on this!"

"Might be good to let him know you come prepared," she said, but she looked in her purse again and found me a tattered blank envelope.

I carefully wrote:

Sam,

   Great to see you! Call me if you ever want to grab a cup of coffee.

            —*Roxy* 512-555-8792 *(My actual phone number)*

Artemis studied the note. "Basic and lacking in romance, but it will do."

We approached the car. As I was sliding the note under the wiper blades, I spotted the glistening eyes and sharp teeth of a snarling animal staring at me. I jumped back in alarm and then looked closer. A taxidermied raccoon sat in the passenger seat of Texas's car. "What the fuck!" I yelled. What a freak! I pressed my eyes against the glass. On the floorboards sat a wadded up Burger King bag. And Texas had claimed to be a vegetarian!

"Don't worry! That raccoon and those burger wrappers belong to Texas's sponsee Stuart. The raccoon is named Boris. He's Stuart's Higher Power."

"Jesus," I said. "That's fucked up."

"Stuart's a contrarian. He likes to push the limits of the AA philosophy that a person can pick any Higher Power they want." Suddenly Artemis screamed and pointed at Texas's car with a trembling hand.

"What?" I asked. "What is it?" I mean, what could be worse than a taxidermied raccoon?

Then I saw it there in the backseat of Texas's car.

A child's car seat.

"Oh, shit," I said. My heart sank. "Any chance that belongs to Stuart, too?"

"Doesn't seem likely," Artemis said mournfully.

In that moment I wished Artemis wasn't sober, so we could walk across the street to Güero's and get hammered together on margaritas. "Want to come over for a cup of tea?" I asked.

"I most certainly do," Artemis said.

In the end, I didn't leave the note on Texas's car. Artemis and I went to my house and watched my bootleg copy of "Pitch Perfect." It turns out she knows the complete choreography of the final dance sequence, and she taught me a couple parts of it. Roscoe joined in, dancing at our feet. So at least the night wasn't a total bust. But I am devastated that Texas likely has a kid. Will my desire to live a child-free life forever ruin my chances at love? I can't be any kid's stepmom or even stepmom-type person. I don't know how to deal with children, and kids come with a mom somewhere, and that's just a whole lot of baggage I don't need in my life. I'm barely not a kid myself.

I now feel I am certain to live the rest of my life alone and, like other oppressed groups before me, I plan to reclaim the name given to me by my oppressors—Spinster.

Woefully,
Roxy

November 7, 2012

Dear Everett,

I woke up this morning thinking maybe, just maybe I could deal with dating someone who has a kid. I mean, the kid still needs a car seat. Maybe it doesn't even talk yet. I could teach it how to dip french fries into ketchup. That would be pretty cute, a tiny little Texas person daintily dipping a french fry. It's something I could handle, maybe. But then Texas has all these sponsees. And I know they are needy, since they obviously worship him and he gets called in any time one of them has a crisis or whatever. When would he have time to pay attention to me?

I was pondering all this when my phone rang with a local number I didn't know. Against my usual inclinations, I answered it.

"Vet Girl?"

"Texas?"

"I got your number from Mitch. I hope that's okay."

"Yes! I was going to give it to you last night but then—"

"The sponsee storm hit."

"Exactly." And then I blurted out: "I thought you didn't want to be my attorney because you hated me."

"Hate you? Ever since I saw you teetering on that chair in the vet's office I've been totally intrigued by you. So I couldn't have you be my client. Dating a client—or former client—isn't illegal. But it's seriously frowned upon at my work. So I just had this lightning-bolt realization that if I took your case I could never date you without it potentially being disastrous for my career, and just kind of . . . not right. Like a shrink dating a past client or something."

"But then you weren't my attorney and you didn't ask me out."

"I wanted to wait until your case was totally closed. And then Mitch told me you went into PharmaTrial."

I groaned. "And then you really didn't want to date me!"

"I wasn't judging you! It's just that after a while I felt like I'd missed my chance or something. And then I worried I'd be too straight and vanilla and boring for you."

"Vanilla? Boring? You're a tattooed drummer."

"I mean, I saw you at that convention."

"Oh my Goddess, I told you, that was such a mistake. It was the first and last time I ever tried orgasmic meditation."

"Can I ask you something that's kind of forward?"

"Okay."

"Why would a man go to a convention to rub a woman's clitoris when he could do it at home all the time with a woman he's really into?"

Oh my. "It doesn't make sense to me," I said.

"I'm sorry about the sponsee swarm after the meeting."

"Your friend that tried to commit suicide?"

"He was a sponsee."

"So does that kind of stuff happen all the time?"

"No. Not serious stuff like that. But my sponsees, they do call me a lot."

"Texas."

"Yes."

"I saw the car seat in your car."

"That's what I was trying to tell you, that night we were at Dolce Vita." There was a pause. "I have two kids." TWO???? "Madelyn and Titus. They are three and seven."

"Three and SEVEN!" I said. "My Venus, how old are you?"

"I'm thirty-three," he said.

"Oh." The new horror that he had not one, but two children was trying to sink in. "Do they have the same mom?"

"Yes, of course. I mean, I was married to their mother. We share custody."

"So three and seven—they can both, like, talk?"

"Of course they can talk." Texas sounded confused and maybe frustrated.

"Oh my God," I said. Everett, you know I'm flummoxed when I mutter oaths at a patriarchal deity. "So you have two kids and they have a mom—who is your ex-wife?"

"Yeah. That's how it often works."

"And you have a gaggle of bro sponsees calling you every time they have drama or whatever."

He made a noise of exasperation. "I'm starting to think this conversation isn't going well. Look, I'm an adult with responsibilities, and I work hard to be of service to other people so I can stay sober, and I work hard to be a good dad. And I like you and would like to go out with you."

I felt sick, and a giant lump formed in my throat. "I want to go out with you, too," I said. "But you have so much going on. And kids . . . well, that's a lot." I hoped he couldn't hear the quaver in my voice.

But he could. "I don't think this is the right thing right now," Texas said. And I just stammered out some stupid things in agreement, and when we finally hung up I sat there for a long time, overwhelmed by sadness and conflicting emotions. Oh Venus, Goddess of Love! When it comes to my romantic life, why, oh why, is the timing always so damn off!

Self-pityingly,
Roxy

P.S. But at least I am a professional artist with a paying job and health insurance! I am going to see this glass as half-full no matter that it's empty of men! For today, I am resigned to a life of celibacy and solo sex.

P.P.S. I just asked Annie if we could cancel FAIL BETTER! as the band to play the Puppy Adoption Center opening. Annie said their band name

is already on all the promotional materials we've sent out, so unfortunately I have to suck it up. When I see Texas I will be aloof, gorgeous
and chilly, leaving him to regret his earlier choice to procreate and find
sobriety. (Okay, I'm not sure that makes sense. But hopefully I'll be cool
and detached and will not mope or even publicly leak tears of wistful
longing for what could have been.)

CHAPTER THIRTEEN

January 6, 2013

Dear Everett,

Between working full-time, getting through the holidays, taking care of the furballs, making sure I still meet up with my girlfriends on the regular, being a bridesmaid in Yolanda's New Year's Eve wedding, and prepping for the grand opening of the Puppy Adoption Center, I've been too busy to write—but last night was so perfect and magical I have to get it down.

Knowing Texas would be at the Puppy Adoption Center grand opening party playing with FAIL BETTER!, I splurged on a hot new black cocktail dress flecked with gold sparkles. I was a little nervous about seeing him. I didn't want my confusion and turmoil about him to spoil the night.

But I forgot about all of that as soon as I arrived. I parked and walked over to the site that had once been Waterloo Video, then the accursed Lululemon. I stared up at the sign that now reads: PUPPIES! PUPPIES! PUPPIES! The thought that every time a puppy mill crackdown occurs, the pregnant moms and their puppies will be whisked here to be adored and adopted out to loving homes overwhelmed me. The adoption center will take any breed of puppy, of course, but how fitting that, since I am likely a reincarnated wiener dog (more on that later), the first batch of residents is almost entirely made up of dachshunds.

Everett, there you stood at the door, proudly wearing a pin that said, "Everett Cantu, Adoption Coordinator, Puppies! Puppies! Puppies!" I hugged you. "You look great!" I said. I've never told you this, but I had floated you to Topher Doyle and Annie as manager of the whole operation, but they decided on a more experienced candidate. However, Annie was happy to hire you as an adoption coordinator. Your role vetting adopting families and training them on how to care for their new puppies is perfect for you! I am guessing it pays three times more than your Kerbey Lane Cafe gig AND comes with full health insurance and bennies. The best part is that now you and Nadia can afford to move out of the OM house and into your own place together! I feel relieved for both of you.

When you told me you were so nervous you had pit stains, I was surprised. You seemed calm as a PharmaTrial inmate after the morning opioid dosing. As the party was not just to celebrate the opening of the PUPPIES! PUPPIES! PUPPIES! but was also a fund-raiser, the place was already swirling with tech giants, trophy wives, and the old Austin aristocracy. How ironic that while I once hated seeing such types in Whole Foods, I was thrilled they (and their deep pockets) were in attendance to support PUPPIES! PUPPIES! PUPPIES! Their money would be cajoled from them and used for good!

Annie came up to give us both hugs. Her name tag said: Annie Rhimes, Vice President of Animal Rights, Whole Foods Headquarters.

"Oh my Venus," I said. "Is this for real?"

Annie's glow was all the answer I needed.

"I'm so freaking proud of both of you!" I yelled, pulling you and Annie in for a group hug.

The parquet floors of Lululemon had been replaced with hip concrete washed a lovely purple. Every available surface had been covered in candles and the walls were hung with my dachshund series—dachshund astronauts floating through space; dachshund bakers making cakes; dachshund scientists working in a lab. I'm critical of my own work, but even I was pleased. While there are many dog runs in the back, the big main front room was full of open puppy playpens where adorable dachshunds frolicked in shredded newspaper.

My mother sailed up to me with my father in tow. "Roxy! Your paintings are so delightful. They remind me so much of Wimpy." I hadn't thought of Wimpy in years! When my mother was nine months pregnant with me, her miniature dachshund Wimpy was run over by a car and killed. She buried him in the rain (I guess my father was at work, or napping on the couch). Anyway, the shock of Wimpy's death sent her into labor. I was born, which rocked my then four-year-old brother's world in a very negative way. To get back at me for stealing my parents' attention away, he always claimed I was Wimpy the Wiener Dog reincarnated. Throughout our childhood, and well into our teens, he would often pin me down and chant, "Wimpy! Wimpy! Wimpy!" right into my face. It wasn't until adulthood I realized he was probably right—I have the exuberance, childish joy, and easily hurt feelings of a dachshund. And of course, it's why Roscoe and I are such interspecies soul mates.

"Mom, are you crying?"

My mother wiped at her eyes. "I did love that little dog," she said. "But the day I lost him was the day I got you." She smiled at me kindly. It was a puzzling sort of non-compliment, but I'll take it.

My mom and dad ran off to talk to Captain Tweaker, and I circulated through the crowd. When I spotted Tim and Mario we all jumped up and down for joy while yelling "Vaya con Dios" and giggling hysterically. They told me the rest of their PharmaTrial stay was more boring without me, but when they were released and the $7,000 hit their bank accounts, they felt it had all been worth it. We went outside together briefly to admire the new underglow on Mario's Dodge Charger. It was kind of weird to see them out in "the free." It felt like when you are a kid and you have a best friend at camp and then you see them in your regular life and it's kind of awkward and strange, even though you still love them. But overall it was great.

Nelson and Jason arrived. Jason had his girlfriend in tow. Their newborn baby was in a sling on her chest and was quite adorable. And Patrick showed up with his burlesque girlfriend Sal. I was a tiny bit frosty toward him at first, but gave Sal a huge hug. I did bring myself to ask Patrick about his skating, and he said—modestly—that he's been making it to the skate park almost every day. "I wouldn't expect anything less of you," I said, and I meant it. I admire him for maintaining the slacker ethos we all grew up valuing so highly. I'm just also really glad he isn't my boyfriend. I said goodbye and made my way through the crowd.

I stopped and chatted with people I know as I went, like Teal, and a bunch of the burlesque girls, and my old college pals who I've gotten really close with again since we all went to about a million wedding events in the run-up to Yo's fabulous nuptials (where my reading of a passage from "Love in the Time of Cholera" was a big hit, I must say). Annie appeared at my side with the hotness squared Castro twins in tow. (She told me that now that Jeff has a neck tattoo, she's decided he's by far the sexier of the two and has thus laid off her risqué flirtation with Joe.) The three of them sailed off together to check over the microphones for the fund-raising games.

I was standing alone for a moment, taking in the happy crowd, when Artemis came up and grabbed my elbow. "How are you doing?" she asked. I had been a little nervous about Artemis being at a party with booze, but she looked perfectly content to be sipping a LaCroix. I couldn't help but follow her gaze toward FAIL BETTER! The entire time I was flitting around like a (very popular) social butterfly, I'd been trying to ignore the fact that the band was in the far corner playing a quiet acoustic set. Texas (a.k.a. Sam) was slapping the bongos, which I tried to tell myself looked stupid, but was actually pretty hot. Artemis and FAIL BETTER! lead singer Arsen Alton made steamy eye contact.

"I'm fine," I said. "I think I acted like a giant immature idiot to Texas, but I'm fine." I turned so my back was to FAIL BETTER! Seeing Texas was just too distracting. "How's work anyway?" I asked. A couple of weeks ago Artemis landed a job as the Girl on the Swing at the Old San Francisco Steak House. In her new role she wears an 1880s–style (family friendly) prostitute getup and belts out old jazz standards while curled up on a piano. She then performs a rather seductive and death-defying round on the swing. Apparently when she was in her early twenties, Artemis did a stint as a trapeze artist, and so the swing comes naturally to her.

"My manager says I learn faster than any Girl on the Swing they've ever had before. I could kick the bell on the ceiling and do a back flip off the swing after a week of practicing."

Right then Captain Tweaker joined us, grinning widely to show off his pearly whites. "How are my favorites doing?" he asked. We told him we were fine. "Hey," he said. "I don't mean to be nosey, but Sam told me he called you to ask you out and you said no because of his kids."

"I kind of did," I said miserably.

"You don't look happy about it."

"I'm not. I mean, I always kind of think of myself as a kid. But I don't even like kids. Or like, I've never wanted them."

"Did he ask you to be the mother of his children?" Captain Tweaker asked, inexplicably deploying his fake Irish accent.

"No. He just said he wanted to ask me out. But—"

"Did he even ask you to meet his kids?"

"No, but—"

"Would you want to go out with him?"

"Yes!" I wailed. "But—"

"Then why don't you just try one date? When I used to think ahead into the future I would get so stressed out I had to smoke meth just to deal. But now I take things one day at a time and my life seems to be working out fine." It was surprisingly good advice.

Just then Dirty Steve came through the front doors, flanked by two women flaunting alarmingly taut fake breasts who were most certainly strippers at Dirty Steve's favorite strip club The Yellow Rose—"where all the dancers wear is a smile." He was talking loudly and I saw his coked-up eyes scanning the room before alighting on me. His face took on an angry glower and he made a beeline in my direction, leaving the entertainers behind. "Oh, there she is," he shouted as he approached me. "Woman of the hour! Poxy Roxy turned too-big-for-her-britches."

"Whatever," I said, trying not to sound intimidated.

He reached out and grabbed me by both arms. I tried to pull away, but he'd really clamped down. It hurt! "You think you're so great, up there on the fifth floor, but you're nothing but a chickenpox-covered skank!" He shook me back and forth as he yelled, "I fired you! I fucking fired you!" My head jerked back and forth on my neck. Artemis tried to shove him away from me, but he wouldn't let go. Captain Tweaker gave a shove as well, but his skinny frame was no match for Dirty Steve's fat potential.

Suddenly there was a crashing sound and Dirty Steve's head was replaced by a bongo drum. I glanced around in confusion. Texas tackled Dirty Steve, taking him down to the ground and in the process knocking over part of the puppy pen holding fifteen frolicking wiener puppies, who ambushed the downed Dirty Steve—head still inside the bongo drum—crawling all over him, licking and leaking pee and barking with excitement. Texas staggered to his feet as Dirty Steve flailed around, trying and failing to get up.

Annie ran over. "Dirty Steve, you're fired!" she yelled at the bongo drum. "And if you EVER come near her again, I'll bring down the wrath of the entire Whole Foods legal team on your ass." She froze, perhaps mortified she'd overstepped her bounds. She looked toward Topher Doyle.

He gave her a slight nod, then spoke to the bongo. "You heard her," he said.

The police arrived in no time, and after talking briefly outside with me, Topher Doyle, Annie, Artemis, Texas, and Captain Tweaker, they took Dirty Steve away in handcuffs. The strippers stayed at the party—I later heard they each adopted a puppy! As the cops left, everyone else went back inside, leaving me and Texas alone on the sidewalk.

"I'm sorry about your bongo drum," I said.

Texas waved his hand as if it was nothing. "I always feel like that 'Portlandia' sketch 'Dream of the Nineties' when I play that thing anyway," he said. "It's ridiculous."

"Thanks for saving me from Dirty Steve."

"You don't need saving," he said.

"I was just talking to Captain Tweaker about you."

"Who?"

I struggled to remember Captain Tweaker's real name. "Franklin, from AA," I said. "He's my neighbor. Well, he was."

"I know. He talks about how great you are all the time. He's told me about everything you did to get his teeth fixed. He said it was like seventy thousand dollars' worth of implants."

Now I waved my hand as if it was nothing. "He said if I like you and want to go out with you, I should just focus on that. One date. Not, like, all the big picture stuff and the future."

"He did?"

"I'm sorry I was such an asshole about you having kids. I've never been very grown-up, and usually the guys I date aren't Real Adults either, so it was like a big shock that you are, and that you're caring for so many different people already."

"Just because I have kids and help other people doesn't mean I don't have room in my life for a . . ." He paused, like he didn't want to say "girlfriend" so soon. "For a woman who is special to me."

That's when I kissed him. And it was a kiss like the world's best ice cream after you've eaten strictly vegan for a year.

"So would you want to go on a date with me at some point?" I finally said.

"Depends."

"On what."

"When and where that date would be."

"How about after this party? My house?"

Texas looked as if he was considering it. "Okay," he said.

"Okay," I said.

We held hands as we stepped back into the PUPPIES! PUPPIES! PUPPIES! grand opening party. The room was abuzz, all the guests talking loudly about Dirty Steve's arrest. While Texas and I had been outside, someone had set up the wiener dog racecourse. Topher Doyle sailed up to us. "I appreciate Steve providing some much-needed excitement for our biggest donors," he said. "Studies have shown that adrenaline spikes result in higher donations at fund-raising events. We've already just had some unexpectedly large contributions!"

Everett, your voice boomed out of the speakers. I spotted you holding a microphone. At your elbow, I could see beautiful Nadia, beaming at you proudly as you announced the biggest fund-raising event of the night: the Wiener Dog Races. She looked adoringly at you, Everett, her kind, gainfully employed, rent-paying boyfriend. And normally such a thing would have given me a pang of jealousy. The old me would have thought: "Why couldn't you have been that boyfriend for me?" But instead, I just felt really glad for you both.

You've come so far, Everett.

I mean, last summer solstice you were unemployed, with only my roof overhead, and so lonely you'd use any excuse to bust into my room and talk for way too long. And now here you are! But pondering the ways your life has changed for the better made me realize that mine has changed too! I mean, by the time you moved in with me I'd already let myself sink into such a slump that I was totally unable to access my art, my activism, even my friendships. All praise to Venus that I found a glorious grrrl gang to help power me out of my underemployed, artistically stymied state.

As you introduced the Wiener Dog Races, I looked around and saw myself surrounded by people I love and who love me, my art hanging from the walls, puppies who (thanks in some part to my efforts) would soon find happy homes frolicking in shredded newspaper, and Texas standing by my side. It was all wonderfully overwhelming. But luckily I had the Wiener Dog Races to keep me grounded in the beauty of the moment so that I was not entirely carried away by my bout of navel-gazing.

Six wiener dogs had been put in starting blocks. They weren't dogs up for adoption, but rather were adult wiener dogs whose owners had trained them for the race. "Go ahead and put in your final 'bets' on your favorite pup," you said into the mic.

Everett, you'd explained to me how this "betting" system would end up in massive donation dollars, but I still didn't understand the details. The wiener dogs' owners stood at the end of the straightaway racecourse with bits of hot dog and other dog treats as encouragement. Holding Texas's hand tightly, I pulled him through the crowd of familiar friends and fancy donors until we were standing at the finish line of the racecourse, too.

"On your mark!" you called, clearly enjoying the limelight. I heard a girl next to me telling her friend you are "totally cute." Annie and Topher Doyle each took ahold of one side of the starting gate. "Get set! Go!" Annie and Topher lifted the gate. The wiener dogs took off running toward their owners, little legs flying and ears flapping. They moved with such joy that it made everyone in the room laugh with delight, because there is nothing in this world so beautiful as a happy creature running with all its heart and soul toward someone it loves.

After the party, Texas followed me home. As soon as we walked through my front door, he sat right down on the floor so he could really pet Roscoe, which made my heart just about burst. "Roscoe, wait until you meet my mastiff," he said. "You and Major Payne are going to be such good friends." And then I dragged Texas into my bedroom. He took my clothes off slowly. And then it soon became very clear that he doesn't need some OM group to teach him how to enthusiastically (but gently) pay attention to my clit. As a result, I had a mind-blowing, merman-free orgasm, right off the bat.

Texas spent the night. (He told me he'd texted one of his sponsees earlier asking him if he could feed Major Payne and take him for his evening walk. So maybe his sponsees are like a gang of Everetts—seemingly needy but actually totally awesome.) We slept like spoons—a perfect fit—and this morning we went at it all over again, only it was even better. When we finally dragged ourselves out of bed, I made him my famous bulletproof coffee. As we drank it he said, "I always hoped that someday I would meet someone and I'd like them and they'd like me and it would just be as easy as that. Do you believe that could happen?"

"I do," I said. "I mean, I think we've already gotten the comedy of manners–type complications out of the way."

"Doesn't a comedy of manners satirize the customs of fashionable society? In what fashionable society are that many men touching that many vaginas in one room?"

That made me laugh really hard, and he laughed, too. "Oh my Goddess, it was so horrible," I said.

"Can I ask you a question?" he asked.

"I guess."

"Those panties that were hanging off your shoe—what were they made of exactly?"

"Shuuutttt uuuuupppp," I said. Then we kissed again and headed back to the bedroom. Sexiness, a sense of humor, and an in-bed work ethic like his I'm not putting to waste. Later he ran home to pick up Major Payne—who is as mellow as I remembered him from our encounter at the vet's office. Then Texas and I walked Major Payne and Roscoe around the sun-dappled Hike and Bike Trail, where sunlight glittered on the water. Roscoe—who clearly adores Texas and Major Payne already—seemed jaunty and proud, and I did indeed feel reborn in so many ways. Afterward, Texas dropped Roscoe and me back at my house. He said he had to go pick up his kids from their mom's, but that he'd text me a little later.

And I believe him.

Feeling well loved (and rather emotionally mature),
Roxy

ACKNOWLEDGMENTS

I could not have written this novel without the loving support of my husband, George, my silent drummer. George, this book belongs to you. Thank you for listening to me read these letters as they unfurled each day (and then listening again and again as I edited them). The joy and happiness you've brought to my life made them possible. I love you more than Texas!

The day my agent, Allison Hunter at Janklow & Nesbit, took me on as a client is the day I became the luckiest grrrl on earth! Without her dedication and vision, this book would not exist in the larger world. Overwhelming thanks to my dream editors at Simon & Schuster: Christine Pride, whose delightful edits took this book up about a thousand levels, and Carina Guiterman, whose unstoppable magical mojo makes her the best in the business. I will be forever grateful to Marysue Rucci for her enthusiasm, support, and editorial guidance; and to my incredible publicity and marketing divas, Amanda Lang and Elizabeth Breeden, for their creativity, hard work, and expertise. What a dream team! And many thanks to the other literary superheroes at Simon & Schuster who worked to make this book all it could be including (but certainly not limited to): Marie Florio, Samantha Hoback, Lashanda Anakwah, Richard Rhorer, Jon Karp, Wendy Sheanin, and Cary Goldstein. I'd like to send special thanks to Clare Mao at Janklow & Nesbit. Thanks also to my most excellent copyeditor, Stacey Sakal.

To my father, Pete Lowry, who always encouraged my love for writing even when the way was dark and seemed impossible. To my mother, Candy Becker, who once said, "Mary Pauline, you are so funny. Why don't you <u>write</u> something funny?" and has shown me that making art joyfully is the way through the delights and challenges that life brings. To my incredible bonus parents, Eric Baker Becker III (RIP) and Mary Lowry—who can make David Sedaris laugh. To all my siblings, nieces, and nephews. To my magic cousin Fred Burke, for showing me from a young age that it's okay to follow cultural curiosities, wherever they may lead me. And to my amazing bonus family (aka my in-laws) who are so kind and supportive.

Thanks to my mentor, Brady Udall, for reading so many drafts and helping me to see the arc of the novel. And thanks to the rest of my Boise State University MFA family who supported and guided me as I wrote this book, especially Jackie Polzin (neighbors forever!), Ariel Delgado Dixon (first years forever!), Natalie Disney, Becca Anderson, Jackie Reiko Teruya, Di Bei, Rory Mehlman, Mitch Wieland, and Emily Ruskovich.

Thank you to Joy Williams, who was the first to believe in my writing and has been my Giving Tree for so many years. I hope that unlike the little boy, I have given a little something back, if only in adoration and gratitude. To Denis Johnson (RIP) and Cindy Lee Johnson, for showing me how to live a life devoted to writing and love. To Stephen Harrigan, without your years of support, I don't think I'd still be writing! And many thanks to the University of Texas MA in English (concentration in Creative Writing)—now The New Writers Project—for generous support and for introducing me to such incredible, life-changing mentors.

All praise and infinite gratitude to Rufi Thorpe (gateway to all of this!), Kimberly Cole, Julia Claiborne Johnson, Christa Parravani, Francesca Lia

Block, and Amanda Yates Garcia, who each supported this work in her own special way. Thanks to my bestie, Dawn Erin (the real-life Girl on a Swing at the Old San Francisco Steakhouse!), and Hilary Clausing (so many thanks, Hilary, for always recounting your adventures!). Thanks to David Moorman; and to my doppelganger, Jennifer Olsen. To Sarah Bird, for being an amazing role model and for writing the first book I ever read set in Austin that made me laugh really freaking hard. For being fun, hilarious, supportive friends and for also hiring me to do work that supported the writing of this book: Gillian Hayes, Steve Hosaflook, and Melissa Mazmanian. (On a slightly less related but irresistible note, thanks also to Melissa for arranging my marriage! I am forever indebted— seriously!) To Rachel Fershleiser, for generously sharing your expertise about literary agents. I've long idealized you from afar for being a true literary godmother, and you didn't disappoint. To Jennifer and Bryan Jack, for propping me up and making me laugh. To Charlize Theron, for rising above and lifting us all up with you. You are one cool cat!

And finally, last but certainly not least, to my sister, Margaret Lowry, who is there for me through every up and down, literary and otherwise. I couldn't have made it this far without you, dear sister!

And one final little author's note: I first started walking to the original Whole Foods store on Lamar Boulevard for ice cream with my mom and sister when I was four years old. I literally grew up at Whole Foods, which was always my "Cheers"—the place I'd go to run into friends and receive all sorts of sustenance. Whole Foods always felt like home to me. However, in this novel, any references to the store, its employees, and their practices are used fictitiously. All Whole Foods employees in the book are works of fiction. All characters are products of my imagination, and any resemblance to actual events or places or persons, living or dead, is entirely coincidental.

ABOUT THE AUTHOR

Mary Pauline Lowry is a proud native of Austin, Texas. When she's not writing for O: *The Oprah Magazine*, the *New York Times*, *The Millions*, and other publications, she's often hammering out thank-you notes on the typewriter she inherited from her grandmother because she believes that gratitude is powerful magic.